THE DISCOVERY

THE DISCOVERY

James Parry

THOMAS Y. CROWELL, PUBLISHERS

Established 1834   New York

For my father,

for his example, encouragement and assistance

To the extent that this book is medically accurate, I'd like to thank Dr. Stuart McCalley of Greenwich, Connecticut. Any medical errors or fabrications are my own.

J.P.

THE DISCOVERY. Copyright © 1978 by James Parry. All rights reserved. Printed in the United States of America. No part of this book may be used or reproduced in any manner whatsoever without written permission except in the case of brief quotations embodied in critical articles and reviews. For information address Thomas Y. Crowell, Publishers, 10 East 53rd Street, New York, N.Y. 10022. Published simultaneously in Canada by Fitzhenry & Whiteside Limited, Toronto.

FIRST EDITION

Designed by C. Linda Dingler

Library of Congress Cataloging in Publication Data

Parry, James, 1943-
  The discovery.
  I. Title.
PZ4.P265Di   [PS3566.A76]   813'.5'4   77-1904
ISBN 0-690-01166-0

78 79 80 81 82 10 9 8 7 6 5 4 3 2 1

THURSDAY

New York City

Passing a pet shop one day, Dr. Paul Justin's children had begged him to buy them a hamster. The children particularly liked the cute way the soft, furry animals ate. Instead of immediately swallowing their lettuce and carrot bits, the hamsters stuffed the food in their cheek pouches. The pouches puffed up. "Like he's holding his breath, Daddy," Steve Justin had said. "Oh, let's get him."

Paul Justin had bought his children a kitten instead. Justin didn't kill kittens for a living.

He did kill hamsters—and before today was over he planned to kill three more. For the cute cheek pouches of hamsters make them nature's perfect cancer victims.

It's all a matter of immunity. In most disease research, researchers inject lab animals with the disease-causing virus. But as of the late 1970s, no cancer virus had been isolated. So cancer researchers like Dr. Justin had to implant whole cancer cells. Unfortunately, an animal's natural immunity tends to reject foreign cells, even when that natural immunity is reduced by massive doses of cortisone. Thus cancer—so very difficult or impossible to stop—is very difficult to deliberately start.

But hamster cheek pouches have low natural immunity. And the pouches of Syrian hamsters have even lower immunity. So research institutes like Oakes-Metcalf stocked many Syrian hamsters. So, because they were handy, Justin was using some now.

With two important differences.

First, Justin had managed to induce cancer in these hamsters without implanting cells in their cheek pouches.

Secondly, these hamsters were not close to dying from cancer. In fact, they were now getting better.

Paul Justin thought he knew why the hamsters were getting better but he couldn't quite believe the reason. Today, to find out for sure, he would kill them.

The rising sun streamed through the windows of the eighth-floor animal room of the Oakes-Metcalf Institute. The three hamsters curled up in their cages and, like any nocturnal creatures, contentedly went to sleep. For the last time.

Dobbs Ferry, New York

"Hey, Dad," said Steve Justin, age twelve, between mouthfuls of cornflakes, "is Mom worrying about something?"

"What?" asked Paul Justin, distracted. He had been thinking about his hamsters. As usual, when he thought hard, he pulled his chin, making his long face even longer. It was the habit of a restless man approaching middle age.

"I said is Mom worrying about something?"

"I don't think so," said Justin. "Why?"

" 'Cause one day last week," put in Melissa Justin, age nine, "I walked into the bathroom without knocking and she had mascara running down her face and I bet she was crying."

Steve turned to his sister. "She was? Gosh, I was just going to say she's been staring off into space a lot."

"Yeah," agreed Laurie Justin, age seven, "I've seen her staring like that."

"Well," said Melissa, "people born in Libra do that a lot. Worry a lot."

Dr. Paul Justin thumped his coffee cup down. He looked around the table. "What is this?" he demanded. "It sounds like a conspiracy against your mother." He let his eyes rest on Melissa. "And what's with this astrology nonsense?" he joked. "Do you believe that stuff?"

"Well," said Melissa, "I'm a Sagittarius. And Timmy Polk says Sagittarians always talk like they're very sure of things—and he says that's what I do."

"Hmm," said Justin. "Well, you do, indeed."

"And Mom *is* worried," persisted Steve. "She even went to visit Grandma this week."

"Implying she does so only when she's sad or worried?" demanded Justin. He got up and started quickly putting dishes in the sink. "My God—my kids are astrologers and amateur Freudians. Now let's go. Steve, I've got to get to work. And if I'm going to drop you off first, we have to move."

Making shooing motions, Justin got his children out of the kitchen. The two girls bicycled off to the summer play program at school. Justin and his son got in the family station wagon and headed across town, to the Bedloes'.

Although Justin was in a hurry, he made himself stick to a legal thirty miles per hour and he came to a full stop at stop signs. Paul Justin fought a constant battle with his impatience. A good researcher is dispassionate but Justin had become a researcher because there was something he passionately wanted to discover. He hadn't discovered it yet. He hadn't made his mark. But the lab had made its mark on him. Years inside had made his pale skin even paler. Years bent over a microscope had bent his back a little and increased his nearsightedness. He now had to wear horn-rims all the time. And his sandy brown hair was thinning—he had run his fingers through it too many times in exasperation.

Yet the lab had also taught him to pay attention to data and analyze it. So, he thought wryly, have the kids observed something about Barbara that I've missed?

Paul Justin drove through the quiet suburban streets in the July sunlight and thought about his wife.

Before leaving for Boston three days ago, Barbara had seemed a little distant. In fact, the two of them had not slept together the whole week before. Justin had approached her, but there had always been something—"I'm tired" or "It's my period"—in the way. Still, it hadn't surprised Justin. His wife was a very sensual woman who waged battles with her Boston blue-blood upbringing. He'd just assumed that the blue blood was temporarily winning.

But perhaps there was more to it. With the progress he'd been making on the "D" series serum, Justin knew his mind had been more in the Institute than at home. Perhaps Barbara had some trouble she wanted to talk to him about, but sensed he wasn't really there to listen. Perhaps that's why she'd gone to visit her mother.

Justin wished that Barbara, who tended to run from her troubles, could borrow some strength from her indomitable mother, Mother Yates. If she's still down when she returns, Justin told himself, I'll make a real effort to help her. Make up for things. Paul Justin idly wondered how Barbara would cope if she ever had to face *real* adversity.

They reached the Bedloe house and Justin let Steve off. Steve and his friend, Kenny Bedloe, and Kenny's mother started getting into the Bedloes' car. The three of them were going to put posters all around Dobbs Ferry announcing that Governor Reed, Democrat from Michigan and probable candidate for presidential nomination, would be speaking in nearby White Plains tonight. Justin had mixed feelings about this. Like most people he was annoyed that presidential politics started so early these days—the election wasn't for another sixteen months. On the other hand, he was pleased Steve was interested—Reed seemed halfway decent. But it certainly complicated things.

"Remember," Justin called to his son, "the girls will be back at 4:30 again. So you'll have to be back, too."

Steve made a face. None of the three Justin children liked to have Steve baby-sit, but in the summer other baby sitters were scarce.

"Okay," said Steve. "But can *you* be back by 6:30 and take over? I really want to go to see Reed tonight."

Paul Justin sighed. If only his wife were home.

"Sure," said Justin. "I'll be back in time."

He waved good-bye and headed for the train station. He looked at his watch. He'd make the 8:12 with time to spare. Justin returned his mind to the hamsters.

Dobbs Ferry, New York

The 8:12 pulled into the station on schedule and Justin and the other commuters stepped aboard. As they did, a motorcyclist roared into the station parking lot. He screeched his Harley to a halt, spraying gravel on the neighboring Buick. He whipped off his helmet and sprinted for the platform.

"Hold it, Mike!" he yelled to the conductor. The conductor was about to signal to the engineer to start. "Hold the damn thing!"

The running man was Frank Lattimer. He was late because he had mowed his lawn this morning and caught a stick in the blades of the old hand mower. To Lattimer's friends in Manhattan, it was crazy. Why would a gregarious thirty-two-year-old bachelor give up the convenience of, say, an East Side apartment to wrestle with commuting and a lawn?

But to Lattimer it made sense. He worked in Manhattan because, for a reporter, that's where the action was. And he lived in Dobbs Ferry because, having grown up in the noise and soot of a Pennsylvania mining town, he liked coming home to a quiet house on a green lawn. This spring, he had even started a small vegetable garden. Being something of a gourmet, he liked the idea of growing the ingredients for, say, a salad Niçoise. Of course, he often didn't get home from the city at all—grabbing a hamburger at P. J. Clarke's and then spending the night on a drinking buddy's couch or in a young woman's bed. But when Lattimer did get home, he liked doing his own chores. And this morning, when he could least afford it, it was making him late. Lattimer was working on a story that connected a deputy mayor of New York with a Mafia-run wholesale meat company. And Lattimer had an informant at the company who had promised to meet him at a bar this morning at 9:30 with new information.

So Frank Lattimer had to catch this train. He was tall and strong, his long legs ate up ground fast. Two other commuters, just getting out of their cars, were walking slowly toward the platform, willing to wait for the 8:31. Lattimer dashed between them and up the steps. "Come on, you drunken Irishman," he yelled at the conductor. Below Lattimer's thick black hair, on either side of the once-broken nose that saved his face from Hollywood handsomeness, his dark eyes ordered the conductor to hold.

With one more long stride, as McNally was signaling the engineer and the doors were closing, Lattimer made it through the doorway. The train started moving away. "Thanks a lot, Mike," deadpanned Lattimer. McNally grinned and went off to collect tickets.

Lattimer looked around. He was in a smoking car—and he didn't smoke. But he doubted it was worth walking either up or back to the next car. By Dobbs Ferry, most of the 8:12 was filled up. A seat in non-smoking was unlikely. Lattimer considered hunting out McNally to ride standing next to him after McNally was through with the tickets. Properly prompted, the conductor was happy to tell horror stories about the Penn Central. And Lattimer, who could make friends with almost anyone and get almost anything out of them, was collecting McNally's stories for the story *he* planned to write. When he had the time.

But Lattimer decided that this morning he'd rather rest and read. So he walked down the car. He was about to sit next to a florid businessman in a circa 1955 Brooks Brothers suit, when the businessman opened his *New York Times* in a wide I-own-both-seats gesture. Lattimer didn't want to fight *that* battle all the way to Grand Central. So he walked further on—and sat down next to a scholarly-looking man in slacks and a seersucker sports jacket.

The two men nodded at each other. A doctor of some kind, Lattimer knew. Judd? Judson? The doctor lived down the block and the two had met each other once at a party and again at a softball game and generally around the neighborhood. But Lattimer didn't remember names very well unless he figured there was a story somewhere.

In fact, like the meat company employee and the railroad conductor, Justin had a story, too. And not just any story, but the biggest story of the decade.

Except, at the moment, neither Lattimer nor Justin knew this.

Lattimer dragged a battered paperback out of his pocket—*A Green Thumb*—and started rereading about why his lettuce wasn't growing.

Lander, Colorado

Dr. Christopher Ives was poring over Justin's file when he heard the truck skid off the road. First was a long squeal of brakes and tires and then a sudden crash of metal against rocks. Then silence. And then cries, not human but animal.

The monkeys! thought Ives. He lurched up from his chair and looked out the window, down the mountainside. The view was spectacular. The mountain stood in the middle of the Gore Range of the Colorado Rockies. The surrounding mountains rose in green-carpeted flanks to awesome summits where, on the north faces, snow still clung. The snow reflected bright sunlight, distant calm and beauty. Ives didn't share that calm. He craned his neck to spot the crash. But viewed from the sanitarium, the hairpin turn was hidden by giant rocks. All Ives could see was one white-suited attendant, and then another, running down the lawn toward the road. Ives dashed out of his office, out the door and after them, puffing.

Christopher Ives was out of shape. He was fifty-two years old and paunchy, used to sitting back behind a desk, sucking on his pipe and stroking his beard. In the last ten years, he hadn't even run far enough to hail a taxi. And as chief of research for Dacey Pharmaceutical and a fairly wealthy man, he hadn't had to: A Dacey company limousine had ferried him between his home and the company headquarters outside Kansas City. But in this last year, as his wealth had suddenly been threatened, Christopher Ives had learned to run for his life.

It began when Dacey supplied a polio vaccine to the Minneapolis public school system. In some of the vaccine, the virus was too active—and two thousand children were stricken with polio.

And, inexorably, Dacey was crippled also.

First, Dacey had lost the class action suit. It would have to pay $1.2 billion to the families of the stricken children. (Dacey's insurance company had found a loophole to get itself off the hook.)

Secondly, the directors of Dacey had lost the shareholders' suit. The fourteen directors—and Ives was one—would have to personally reimburse the company for as much of the $1.2 billion as possible. The directors wouldn't be millionaires anymore.

And thirdly, the SEC had set this November 18 as the date for a shareholders' vote. The vote was expected to throw the directors out on their ears.

So Christopher Ives ran after his rhesus monkeys. Along with Justin's file, they were a vital part of the only possible plan that could save him. And not just *save* him: If the plan worked, he wouldn't be a mere millionaire. He'd be a billionaire.

The attendants were now out of sight, behind the rocks. The monkeys' cries were louder. Gasping in the thin, cold mountain air, Ives rounded the rocks. He came onto the road and the scene of the crash.

If the scene weren't so serious, it would have been comic.

The serious part was that the panel truck lay crumpled on its side. Its driver was leaning, dazed and bleeding, against a wheel. And Ives was certain that, inside the truck, many monkeys were also injured, if not killed.

But the rear door of the truck had burst open, smashing several cages on the road. And, like a comic circus act, two dozen escaped monkeys now cavorted drunkenly on the mountainside while the two men in white suits made clownlike attempts to corral them.

The monkeys acted drunk because they had been shot with tranquilizers for shipment. But there were still too many of them to handle. The attendants would capture a handful of the squirming creatures and put them in the truck only to have them crawl out again. "Here," cried Ives. "I'll stay at the truck. You bring them to me."

This way, they gathered all the monkeys. "All except one," said an attendant. "I saw him going up the road."

"Yeah, there," said Ed Murdoch, appearing behind them. "There goes the bugger." And the three men turned to look where Murdoch was pointing with his pistol.

Fifty yards away, a little monkey was clambering over rocks. Instead of taking the easy route—down the mountain—he was perversely moving up toward the sanitarium. Murdoch started to squeeze the trigger. Ives grabbed his arm. The shot went wild, pinging off a rock. The monkey put on an extra burst of speed and disappeared.

"What the —?" Murdoch started to object to Ives.

"What the hell is going on here?" demanded the truck driver. "What are those monkeys for? And what's with the gun?"

When Ives and Murdoch bought the sanitarium two months ago, they told the locals they were going to convert it into a fat farm for the rich. So all the driver knew was that he had picked up a shipment labeled "Exercise Machines."

"For experiments with a new diet," Ives quickly explained to the driver. "We don't want to try it on people yet. Hey, that's a bad cut. Let's get you down to Lander, to the hospital." Ives gestured to one of the attendants. The attendant led the driver away, before he could ask more about Murdoch's gun. And before, reflected Ives, Murdoch could turn the gun on the driver, to silence the man for what he had seen. Ed Murdoch was chief of security for Dacey Pharmaceutical. He had taken the job after being eased out of his FBI post—head of the Miami office—for leading his agents on too many trigger-happy raids.

After sticking a piece of wood across the smashed truck doors to keep them closed, the other attendant went to get help for the monkeys. Inside, the monkeys continued their crying. "Goddamn it," growled Murdoch in his low, gravelly voice. "Why didn't you let me shoot the thing?"

"Why bother shooting?" asked Ives. "Up there, tonight"—Ives gestured at the mountaintop—"he'll die of exposure."

"Easier my way," grumbled Murdoch.

Dr. Christopher Ives sighed to himself. In the last year, he had been moving ever closer to violating the law, morality and his Hippocratic Oath. He knew that soon he would even be an accomplice to murder. His increasing cold-bloodedness made him uneasy. So it pleased him that he could give life—if only for a day—to one small rhesus monkey. Ives imagined the monkey moving up past the sanitarium, up to 12,000 feet, to the very summit, and then down the other side toward freedom. And freezing to death.

"Okay, Ed," said Ives with attempted casualness, trying to change the tone of things. "What do you have for us?" Ives took his pipe out of the pocket of his fancy suede shirt-jacket, stuck it in his mouth and started laboring his way uphill. Murdoch fell in with him.

Ed Murdoch was Ives's age. But while Ives had a butterball sleekness, Murdoch's clothes—and even his skin—hung gray and rumpled on him, as if he had recently lost a lot of weight. Ives supposed that the folds of skin got caught in Murdoch's razor, for the man's face was a patchwork of shaven spots and bristles, with cuts everywhere. And Murdoch's eyes, ringed with more drooping skin, appeared half-asleep. But this was deceptive. Ives knew that Murdoch's mind was as alive as his trigger finger. And Murdoch's mind had established a worldwide system that truly deserved the name "intelligence network."

"I've got a death in Johannesburg," said Murdoch. "Martin Kruger."

"The diamond man?" asked Ives. "Too bad."

"Yeah. But two new ones. We got hold of DeCathe's biopsy and it confirms the rumor. Colonic cancer. That's eleven million there—disposable."

"Francs?" asked Ives.

"Dollars," said Murdoch. "Plus another possible—Wan Ho in Singapore."

"Who's he?"

"Shipping. Banking. And probably heroin. My man says brain tumor. He's checking it out. It would mean close to 150 million—dollars."

"Whoo." Ives let out his breath, as much from the effort of the climb as to show he was impressed.

"And one more thing," said Murdoch. "It's good and bad: I learned Ash is going under the knife—right now—and, in medical lingo, prognosis is poor. So, on the one hand, Ash's number two man may be more receptive. And on the other hand . . . "

"Ash may die too soon," said Ives.

"Damn right," said Murdoch, his voice rumbling like boulders going down the mountain. "I tell you, Chris, we ought to do this *now*. Go to implementation. We've got our hundred pigeons. And the longer we wait, the more curious any people are going to be about *why* I want the pigeons."

"And I've told you," said Christopher Ives, breathing heavily, " . . . we've got to get our own confirmation . . . on hamsters, monkeys . . . man."

"But—" began Murdoch.

In the last three days, they had had this argument thirty times. Because, since Monday, it suddenly looked as if all their work of the past year might bear fruit. On Monday, they learned they were about to add the crowning piece of data to their file on Paul Justin. On Tuesday, they actually had the data. Yesterday—Wednesday—Ives had turned the data into an experiment on a half-dozen leukemic hamsters. He had explained the experiment to Murdoch and today Murdoch was arguing the experiment was already producing results: The hamsters' skins looked better, their abdomens were shrinking. And, most convincingly, their white cell counts were dropping rapidly.

But Ives didn't want to be rushed. "Seven weeks," he said. "I've been telling you: One week for this experiment. Six weeks for the others. Total of seven."

"We can't *wait*," repeated Murdoch. "Hurry it *up*."

Murdoch's itchy trigger finger versus Ives's caution. Or is it my fear? Ives asked himself. Or what's left of my scruples? Ives wished his psychiatrist, Dr. Lindenmeyer, were here to help him now.

"All right, a month," Ives heard himself conceding. "Results in a month."

Murdoch's eyebrows went up in pleased surprise. "But," he said, his face falling again in folds of flesh, an unhappy hound, "Justin is still running around loose. I tell you, Chris, we ought to—"

They had reached the sanitarium entrance. Several attendants were coming out. Murdoch shut up—none of the attendants knew of the plan.

"Today," said Ives. "I think we can do Justin today. Now relax."

Murdoch gave Ives a disgruntled look and walked away, his gray, wrinkled coat seemingly weighing him down. This was resort country and Ives dressed nattily; Murdoch dressed like a tired businessman from Kansas City.

Ives climbed the flight of steps to his office and gratefully sank into his desk chair. He put away Justin's file and took out the master list. The list named the hundred richest people in the world who were dying of cancer. The people, or their families, had combined assets of roughly $6 billion. With the information Murdoch had just given him, Ives updated the list. Then, stroking his beard, he rechecked it, alphabetically.

"Ash, Mathew," he read.

Houston, Texas

Mathew Ash had once given $100,000 to Loring Memorial Hospital. He had not given out of the goodness of his heart because, as everyone in Houston knew, Matt Ash had no heart. But when his wife, Virginia, was in Loring for a hysterectomy, a hospital administrator had pleaded poverty to her. Virginia, who was softhearted, then pleaded with one of Ash's aides. The aide discovered how, by the tax laws, a $100,000 gift would cost Ash only $15,000. So the aide authorized the gift—to what was already the wealthiest hospital in the Southwest.

When Ash found out, he fired the aide. He hurled a string of vicious obscenities at fat, pleasant Virginia. And the same day, in a minor pipeline deal, he made back the $100,000—and then some.

To replace the aide, Ash hired Ray Ryker. Like Ash, Ryker was a self-made man, instructed by the slums of North Philadelphia and Harvard Business School. Like Ash, Ryker was bright and cold, tough and greedy. He stood only five-foot-five and weighed 135 pounds. But that was 135 pounds of concentrated energy. And it took him far. Today, in his early forties, Ryker was the Executive Vice President of Texahoma Pipeline, a multimillionaire and Ash's right-hand man. He was in Ash's mold, the son that Virginia had never produced.

And, in Ash's mold, Ryker kept track of every dollar. So he was pleased to note that today Matt Ash was finally getting something back from that $100,000 gift. The money helped pay for the thread that sewed up Ash's belly and the cart that wheeled him out of the OR into the recovery room and the intravenous line that was stuck in his frail, old body to keep him alive.

The six doctors now walked out of the OR to tell Virginia Ash and Ray Ryker how long Mathew Ash would stay alive.

"Is he—?" began Virginia, her triple chins trembling. "Is it—?"

"Yes," said Dr. Quinn, the surgeon. Ryker liked Quinn because he didn't waste time—with a scalpel or with words. "Yes, he's alive. Yes, it's malignant. And yes, as I told you before the operation—"

"He waited too long," said Ryker, finishing the sentence. Larrabee, the Ash family doctor, nodded. His old rheumy eyes watered. "Matt never told me. Never would see me. I should have insisted. I . . ." Larrabee trailed off.

"But how long will he . . . ?" Virginia also trailed off.

"Each case is different," said Dr. Yeager, the oncologist. "We can never predict."

Oncologists—cancer specialists—didn't like to predict. Surgeons were more willing. "A week," contradicted Quinn. "A month. At most, a few months."

"That's all?" asked Virginia, stricken.

"Mrs. Ash," said Quinn. "We removed your husband's stomach. But the cancer has spread to his lungs, liver and spleen. And probably more places. We just can't get it all."

"Metastasized," said Ryker.

"Well, when can I . . . take him home?" asked Virginia.

"I'm afraid you can't," said Yeager, softly. "Without his stomach, he has to be fed intravenously."

"You mean," sniffed Virginia, "he has to stay until . . . until . . . ?" She broke off and then wailed, "There's *no* cure? None at all? No hope?" Virginia loved Matt Ash so blindly she didn't realize he detested her.

"Well, there's always hope," said Dr. Castle, the hospital's chief of surgery, who had witnessed the operation. "But realistically—"

"Yes, there must be hope," insisted Virginia, who didn't want to be realistic. "There's God," she pointed out brightly.

"Yes," said Larrabee, touching her. "God will help him, Virginia. And at least Matt isn't feeling any pain anymore."

Ray Ryker couldn't stand this sloppy sentiment. He knew that when Ash awoke, the pain in his gut would be intense. And soon the pain of breathing also. As for divine intervention, Ryker placed as little faith in Virginia's religiosity as Matt Ash did. Ash had built a half-billion-dollar empire on anything but Christian virtues. The near-illiterate tycoon had always had his contracts written to give him the edge. And the way he printed his name on those contracts— "M. ASH"—gave the word a meaning in Texas long before it meant a movie and TV series. It meant being mashed by an expert.

Matt Ash had mashed many a man without pity and, now that Ash was being mashed by cancer, Ryker doubted he'd want any sympathy in return.

"Gentlemen," said Ryker briskly to all the doctors, "I thank you for your efforts." He then singled out Quinn, Yeager and Friedman (the anesthesiologist): "And gentlemen, if you'll check your bank accounts you'll find your bills have already been paid—in full and by me personally. And now I know you have other commitments . . . "

Quinn, Yeager and Friedman, who were the top in the nation in their specialties, nodded and headed off, to catch their flights to Cleveland, Baltimore and Seattle. To get them all to Houston today, Ryker had doubled their normal huge fees. They left richer—and free. Virginia and the other three doctors remained.

Ryker next dismissed her: "Now, Virginia, if you'll excuse us . . . " And he started shepherding Doctors Castle, Larrabee and Goodhue (Houston's own top oncologist) down the corridor.

Goodhue, who was a sensitive man, even a timid man, glanced back to see Virginia standing alone and forlorn, uncertain where to turn her large bulk. Goodhue thought to go back to her—but he felt the power of Ray Ryker driving him along. Control, thought Goodhue. This slight millionaire is obsessed with controlling every situation. Goodhue was both fascinated and frightened by Ryker. He saw Ryker holding himself in a viselike grip. Why? wondered Goodhue. What is Ryker afraid will happen? And what, wondered Goodhue, if that grip ever slips?

As the four men waited for an elevator, the grip almost slipped. The elevator door opened and a burly male nurse backed out, wheeling a patient on a gurney. The nurse nearly ran into Ryker. Ryker automatically clenched his fists and rocked on the balls of his feet. For a moment, Goodhue actually thought Ryker would throw a punch. And Goodhue was not far off the mark. Little Ray Ryker hadn't survived the toughest part of North Philly without using his fists. And he still worked out every day. Goodhue saw on Ryker's face the message to the nurse: Watch it, fella. I can break any man. Like that.

The male nurse mumbled an apology and left. Goodhue, too, looked forward to getting away from Ryker. He had been consulting on this case for three weeks and now that the verdict of surgery was in, now that the case was over, he . . . wanted to collect the balance of his fee from Ryker and leave. Goodhue couldn't imagine what last word Ryker had for the three of them but he was pleased it would be the last word.

Smiling, Ray Ryker ushered the three doctors toward Castle's office. He knew it wasn't going to be the last word at all.

Dobbs Ferry, New York, to New York City

The tracks of the Penn Central's Hudson Division provide passengers with two contrasting views. To the west, only a stone's throw away, is the broad river—on this morning, deep blue, dappled with sunlight and the white sails of a few small boats. To the east is the smear of factories, junkyards and rundown houses on the Railroad Streets of all the river towns. Paul Justin sat next to a window with a view of the Hudson and he stared at it. But its beauty didn't register on him. He was wondering why he hadn't told his wife about the hamsters. And why she wouldn't tell him what was on her mind.

It wasn't just during the past week or month that he and Barbara hadn't spoken much about things that mattered. Thinking about it now, Justin realized that this selective silence stretched back perhaps a year. Perhaps longer. When *had* it begun? And why was he contributing to it?

Paul Justin had long ago accepted his wife's reluctance to talk. Barbara had grown up in a secure home on Beacon Hill where problems were not supposed to exist and where her vigorous mother constantly held forth, to the exclusion of everyone else. And Barbara had gotten the idea that if she did talk about a problem, it might mushroom. Better simply to deal with it. Or, better still, ignore it and hope it would disappear.

Because Paul and Barbara loved each other deeply, and because they talked and laughed about small things, their marriage "worked." But Paul Justin wondered if some larger sharing was missing. And if he, too, had been pulling away. If he had—and if he had to put a date on when he'd started—it would have been, damn it, two summers ago. That was when his "C" particle research was getting him in trouble.

Until then Paul Justin had been open and enthusiastic about his work. He'd talked with his colleagues about it, he'd come home every day and told Barbara. In the early 1970s, when he joined the hunt for the elusive particle, he'd talked all the more. In the first years of his hunt, as he felt he was actually closing in on it, he became a torrent of words. Often, after sex with Barbara—when, he knew, she had wanted soft words and tenderness—he would instead tell her about what he hoped to discover in the morning, about what the electron microscope might reveal.

And the next year, when it became clear that he *wasn't* closing in, when reputable researchers abandoned the hunt for the "C" particle, calling it a will-o'-the wisp . . . Paul Justin felt like a fool. Not for pursuing the hunt but for boasting of progress he hadn't really quite made.

Because Justin still believed in "C" particle research, he continued it. Because he had to protect himself, he kept quiet about it at work. Because he was angry with how he'd let it dominate and distort his marriage, he kept quiet about it at home.

Perhaps, he felt now—looking unseeing across the Hudson to the Jersey palisades—*too* quiet. He had prevented himself from sharing an important part of himself with his wife. And had this led him to withhold other important parts of himself as well? For, as his research had progressed last year and this year, he had told Barbara only that "Things look promising." He hadn't allowed himself— allowed *both* of them—the joy of saying, "Hey. I've got three hamsters that I may have *cured* of cancer!"

Tonight, Paul Justin promised himself. Tonight, after I've done the hamsters, I'll call her in Boston and tell her.

It was in this open, talkative mood that Paul Justin rode through the Bronx and into Harlem and into the tunnel under Park Avenue. He was in this mood when the train stopped in the tunnel.

At first, none of the commuters paid much attention. Penn Central trains often stopped here for no apparent reason and then moved on. Minutes passed. The train didn't move.

And then the air-conditioning shut down.

The smoking car became even denser with cigarette and cigar smoke. And the heat—the sticky July heat trapped and amplified deep under the streets—was building up. Those men who hadn't already done so took off their suit jackets. Others loosened their ties. A low mumble of complaint began.

Paul Justin was annoyed. He was eager to get to the lab to kill and autopsy the hamsters.

Next to him, Frank Lattimer was annoyed. He had to get to Beazle's Pub in Greenwich Village to meet his informant—a man named Tommy Vernon—on the story about the deputy mayor.

The lights in the car flickered.

The whole scene was beginning to remind Lattimer of the time when, as a child back in Cardiff, Pennsylvania, his uncle had taken him for a forbidden ride in a mine car: The air filled with coal dust. His own coughing. The darkness. Lattimer wished that McNally were around so they could bitch to each other. But the conductor had disappeared somewhere forward.

Lattimer felt like talking to someone. He turned to Paul Justin. Since Dobbs Ferry, neither man had spoken. Justin had been deep into his thoughts, Lattimer deep into his book.

"Lousy, isn't it," said Lattimer, "to be stuck in the smoking car when there's a breakdown."

"Well," Justin smiled, "it's not much better up there." He pointed up to the street. "You know the cliché: Living in New York is the equivalent of two packs a day."

"Creating lots of cancer cases for you," said Lattimer.

"Oh, I rarely see cases. I do research, you know. Hamsters."

"Mm," said Lattimer. "And what does research have to say about how smoke causes cancer?"

"Not my bailiwick," said Justin. "But several of my colleagues ... " Justin launched into a description of some research in lung cancer being conducted on another floor at Oakes-Metcalf. Lattimer became bored.

" ... and Halleck thinks there's a virus in the smoke ... " Justin was saying.

Lattimer's ears pricked up. Justin had emphasized "in the smoke" a bit disdainfully, as if he, Justin, knew better.

"So where is it, then?" interrupted Lattimer.

"What?"

"The virus."

"Oh, I don't know," laughed Justin. "No one knows if there's a cancer virus anywhere at all."

"Oh," said Lattimer. But he wasn't satisfied. Justin's laugh had sounded—what?—forced? "But you're looking for it?" Lattimer persisted.

"It's my department," said Justin airily.

Lattimer could sense when someone knew more than he was telling. He also knew how to get information out of a reluctant expert: present some confused knowledge which the expert can correct.

"Well," said Lattimer, "I mean with all the work being done on DNA and RNA ... isn't a virus simply a bit of DNA or RNA wrapped in ... uh ... carbohydrate?"

"Protein," corrected Justin. His opinion of Lattimer went up a notch. Seeing him around Dobbs Ferry, Justin had gotten the impression that his neighbor was a sort of roughhewn, hard-drinking reporter in the tradition of *The Front Page*. But now it appeared Lattimer knew and was interested in biology more than the average layman.

"So that must give you an idea of where to look," said Lattimer. "I mean, would a cancer virus be like the DNA in our bodies?"

"Not just *like* it," Justin found himself saying. "The virus is already in your body."

"It is?"

"I mean," said Justin swiftly, "that's one theory."

"Tell me about it."

"Well, the idea is—it's Heubner's of NCI—"

"NCI?"

"National Cancer Institute. His idea is that cancer is caused by the 'C' particle. And the 'C' particle is in the DNA that's in all of us. Normally, it's inactive. But when it gets hit by something—oh, a hormonal imbalance or a chemical agent like cigarette smoke—it gets turned on. And produces rapid cell growth—cancer."

"Fascinating."

"Yes," said Justin, warming to his subject. He had been forced to keep quiet about his work for so long, it was a joy to talk. "And then Temin—"

"Temin?"

"Howard Temin of the University of Wisconsin. He showed how Heubner's theory could be true. You see, the trouble with the 'C' particle idea is that the only cancer viruses ever found are RNA viruses—not DNA ones."

"So?"

"So there was a logical dilemma. It was thought that RNA couldn't make DNA. So how did the 'C' particle ever get inside us? And worse: How could it ever be turned off?"

"Right," said Lattimer. He tried to concentrate on what Justin was saying, but the car was getting noisier. The train was still motionless and the commuters were now coughing. The smoke was too dense to be just from cigarettes and cigars. People asked each other what they thought was happening. A few went up to the forward car, to try to find out.

"... in the cancerous chicken cells," Justin was saying, "proving that RNA *could* make DNA, which in turn meant that RNA programming was feasible."

"Programming?" asked Lattimer. He was having trouble following Justin, but that wasn't too important because Justin's real message was his excitement. It told Lattimer that Justin thought he was on to something.

"To turn off the 'C' particle," answered Justin. He laughed again. "But first, of course, I had to try to isolate it."

"What is it?" one of the commuters called out to a friend who had just returned to the car. The friend shrugged.

"Ah, I bet we burned a brakeshoe," answered another man. "It happened last week."

"Where's a conductor?"

McNally and the other Penn Central conductors seemed to have vanished in the smoke.

"... and that's hard," Justin continued, "because ... "

A conductor—not McNally—appeared. He walked down the aisle making his announcement.

"All right," he said officiously. "There's fire on the tracks. But it's way down around 60th Street and they've got it under control. Just be patient."

"For how long?" asked someone.

"Just be patient," said the conductor and he walked into the next car.

He left grumbling behind him.

"... way to run a railroad."

"... aren't being told the whole truth."

"You were saying," said Lattimer to Justin.

"What?" Justin was thinking about the conductor's words.

"Isolating the 'C' particle," reminded Lattimer.

Justin, angry at the railroad, didn't watch what he was saying. "Yes," he said, "it was very difficult. It—" Justin stopped. "I mean," said Justin more carefully. "It is difficult. Hard to imagine it'll ever be done. It's all just theory, you know. What are you reading there?"

Lattimer turned the cover of his book to Justin. "Ah, gardening," said Justin. "My wife tried her hand at it but ... " He blandly accepted the loan of the book from Lattimer.

Lattimer put on an equally bland expression, as if he'd heard nothing. So Dr. Justin *has* isolated the "C" particle, he thought. And that's incredible news. It would hit the front page of every newspaper in the world. It would—but wait, is that all? The way Justin talks ... has he also managed to program RNA—whatever that means— against the particle? To—*cure* ... ?

Lattimer had gotten Justin to make one slip of the tongue— maybe he could force another. And maybe, thought Lattimer suddenly, there's nothing here but a scientist and a reporter who are both letting their imaginations run away with them.

So Lattimer turned his thought to the meeting in Beazle's. He had planned to go there to listen to Tommy Vernon, not to drink. But after this ride, a cool gin-and-tonic ... ? He hoped Vernon would wait for him.

Ten, fifteen minutes passed. Paul Justin read how to spread blood meal to keep rabbits out of a garden. Rabbits made him think of hamsters. I've *got* to tell Barbara, he told himself. I can't go around like this, almost blabbing it to strangers.

The conductor returned.

"All right," he announced. "It's been decided to evacuate the train. If you'll slowly walk to the back of the—"

"Wonderful," said someone, sarcastically. "The back, naturally."

"—of the train," continued the conductor, "the firemen will assist you to the surface."

"Come on," said the sarcastic man. "I can see a catwalk right here. Why didn't you let us out of *this* car?"

"Just form a single line," said the conductor.

The commuters all stood and formed a line. There was more smoke and a great deal of coughing. They were drenched in sweat. They waited another ten minutes.

Then the lights went out.

"Oh, Christ," said someone.

In the dark, Lattimer got an insight. Or at least, he told himself, a strong hunch. And now was the time to play it.

Lattimer, who was at home in this coal-mine setting, turned to Justin, who was not.

"A leap in the dark, eh, Paul?" he said. "You know just so much and then you make a leap. So how did you leap to the right programming?"

"Well . . . " Justin's voice was small. Around them was a babble of other voices—a few frightened, all annoyed.

"Yes," prompted Lattimer.

"Well, when the hamsters didn't die, I—"

The lights came back on. Justin blinked.

"What?" asked Lattimer.

"What?" asked Justin.

"You were saying."

"What?" asked Justin. "Did I say something?"

Justin was oriented again. Damn, thought Lattimer. If only the dark had lasted.

"No," said Frank Lattimer, "you didn't say anything."

The line started moving. Lattimer followed Justin. So the hamsters didn't die, thought Lattimer. Does that mean the good doctor *has* found the right programming? And does that mean . . . ?

A hand gripped Lattimer's shoulder. "It was the IRA what set the fire, me boy," said a fake Irish brogue.

"Hi, McNally," said Lattimer. He laughed with the conductor and then let the line propel him on. Twenty minutes more and they reached the last car of the train. Firemen had a ladder up against the rear door. They helped the commuters down the ladder, along the catwalk and up another ladder to the street. Lattimer and Justin emerged into a knot of policemen, firemen, reporters and photographers. They breathed in the cooler, cleaner air of Park Avenue. They winced in the bright sunlight. Next to them, a fellow passenger was giving a TV camera crew an angry interview.

And I've got a story to get out of Justin, thought Lattimer. But it'll have to wait. He swiftly shook Justin's hand, said, "Let's talk again," and headed for a phone booth to call Beazle's. It was 10:30, an hour late.

Justin looked around. He was on 77th Street, not far from the Institute. Now if only the Penn Central stopped here *regularly* ...

Houston, Texas

"All right," said Dr. Castle, when they were all in his office, "what do you want, Mr. Ryker?"

Castle, Larrabee and Goodhue were seated. Ryker leaned over them.

"It's not what I want," said Ryker. "It's what I've already arranged. I just thought you should know."

That *control*, thought Goodhue.

"What?" asked Castle.

"I've arranged protection for Matt Ash," said Ryker. "I want to make sure nobody pulls the plug."

Castle was flustered. His face reddened. He tried not to show a mounting sense of insult. "That's ... that's quite unnecessary," he managed to say.

"It's damn necessary," said Ryker. "Because, otherwise, this week or next week or damn soon, Mrs. Virginia Ash would persuade the three of you to let him die."

"But she loves him," exploded Castle. "She can't even *accept* his dying, much less want to hasten it."

"And even so," put in old Larrabee, "would that be so bad? I mean, it's not uncommon that when a patient has no hope of recovery and is only being kept alive by artificial means ... that even a doctor ... out of mercy ... "

Castle shot Larrabee a withering look. Larrabee was making Ryker's argument.

Ryker ignored it. What he said was, "Mercy, shit. She'll want to *kill* him."

"Why?" demanded an incredulous Dr. Castle.

"Because the old man hasn't written a will yet," explained Ryker. "Because he couldn't admit that he might die. And if he does die without a will, his beloved wife gets the estate. Even after the taxes and lawyers, that's 200 million dollars."

"But why kill—?" began Castle again.

"Because beloved Virginia will figure that maybe when beloved Matt wakes up he's going to finally realize that he *could* die. And decide to make a will. And cut her out. Flat. Without a penny."

"But why?" Despite himself, Goodhue couldn't help but ask.

"Because he hates her," said Ryker.

"And he loves you," said Castle, attempting sarcasm. "So you want him to live so he'll make out his will to you."

"Oh, no," said Ryker with a barking laugh. "No, the old man hates everybody. Me he just tolerates a little more. If he does make a will, he'll probably leave the 200 million to . . . " Ryker shrugged. " . . . oh, make a solid gold statue of himself."

"So then why do you want to keep him alive?" asked Castle. "If he's so . . . inhuman."

"Because he *is* human, Doctor," retorted Ryker. Ryker placed his hands on Castle's desk and leaned forward. From the side, Goodhue saw Ryker's overly bright eyes protrude. His lips pulled back to reveal larger than normal teeth. The teeth clicked together. Goodhue thought the man looked like an attack dog—an attack dog in a five-hundred-dollar suit barely restraining itself from lunging.

Goodhue was glad he wasn't in Castle's chair. He shrank even further into his own.

"Human," repeated Ryker. "Matt Ash is as crude as the oil he pumps, but he's a human being. He's fought hard all his life and I know he wants to go out fighting—not murdered."

"Nobody's going to be murdered in Loring Memorial," said Castle, but with less conviction.

Not in the Presidential Suite anyway, thought Goodhue, wryly. That *would* be sacrilege. The suite was the one to which Ash would soon be returned. It had two bedrooms, a living room-dining room, a kitchen and two and a half baths—overdecorated and overpriced. To have a patient murdered there would do the hospital out of five hundred dollars a day.

"Of course no one's going to be murdered," agreed Ryker. "And to make sure, I've provided three private nurses who'll be with Ash in shifts around the clock. They report solely to me. If anyone makes any attempt to radically change Ash's medication—or radically change *any*thing—the nurses have orders to—"

"Orders?" sputtered Castle. "Your orders? Why, it's ridiculous. You can't take over this hospital like this. Why, you have no—"

"Now, Ronald," drawled Larrabee, holding up a shaky hand to stop his colleague, "let's not get all in an uproar. Certainly, patients have had private nurses here before."

"But they report to the doctor," insisted Castle. "A doctor that the hospital has granted privileges to."

"Well," said Larrabee, "suppose—for the sake of form—they report to one of us." He turned to Ryker. "For form's sake, Mr. Ryker," he said, reassuringly.

Ryker allowed himself a slight grin. He nodded his head an inch. "Which one of you?" he asked.

Yes, thought Goodhue. Which one will be your cat's-paw?

"Not me, damn it," said Castle. "I won't be used."

"All right," said Ryker. "But not you, either, Dr. Larrabee. Your friendship with Virginia . . . " he said smoothly. "No offense."

"Of course not," said Larrabee.

You bastard, Larrabee, thought Goodhue. Arthur Goodhue had a sudden insight that Larrabee—who wasn't as foolish as he seemed— had seen this coming. Larrabee had seen that somebody's professional reputation was going to be jeopardized. And he was going to let the "somebody" be Goodhue.

"So that leaves you, Dr. Goodhue," said Ryker.

Arthur Goodhue had a round face with apple cheeks and a twitching, rabbit nose. He close-shaved his face to a healthy pink. He used a fair amount of cologne. It was as if Goodhue were always trying to please his patients by how clean and nice-smelling he was. But that was not how he would please the other men in the room. Ryker needed a doctor he could boss. Castle, for all his protests, needed to provide that doctor. It seemed they had elected Goodhue.

Goodhue was confused. What had started as a simple cancer case was moving onto unrecognizable terrain. Goodhue could not understand why Ryker so fiercely wanted Ash to live. He could not figure out if Ryker's fears of Ash being murdered were real or paranoid. He could not guess to what extent Ryker would go to keep Ash alive. *Were* there any limits? Or was Ryker's desire for control infinite?

Goodhue felt Ryker's bright, steady gaze on him. "Okay," Arthur Goodhue heard himself saying. His voice was thick. "Okay," he said more clearly, a rabbit pretending he wasn't transfixed by a hound.

And what have I agreed to? Goodhue wondered. He had another sudden insight (insights being what Goodhue had instead of strength). Goodhue sensed that, if he was right about Ryker, he may have, in some implicit way, committed himself to do more for Ryker than just guard a dying old tyrant.

But before Goodhue could object to that, clarify that, Ryker had smiled, turned and lightly walked out of the office, out of the hospital.

Boston, Massachusetts

Barbara Justin's fears had brought her back to her hometown and to her mother. For several days she had been building up her courage to talk about them. This morning she had awakened intending to finally do it. But there had been no opportunity. In the morning, her mother had run Barbara's legs off in Filene's Basement.

Upstairs, Filene's is one of Boston's top two department stores, as expensive as any in New York City. The Basement, however, is a bargain basement, a madhouse where women fight tooth and nail over bins of every imaginable marked-down item. Barbara had again been impressed by how her mother took to the place.

"Here," she cried to Barbara, "this dress will fit Melissa fine."

"Madam," she snapped at a South Boston Irish housewife in curlers. "I saw those pants first. Let go."

"Barbara," she said. "Take this shirt for Steven. You'll never find it for $2.59 in New York."

Chipper, birdlike, sixty-six-year-old Elizabeth Everett Yates was of the original Everetts of Salem. Her heritage included three hundred years of Yankee aristocracy, a handsome house on Beacon Hill and a giant stock portfolio carefully nurtured by First Boston. So she could just stay in her home and clip coupons. But Elizabeth Everett Yates was all tough sinews over fleshless bones. She loved the combat of saving a dollar at Filene's. It was, Barbara reflected, how the Everetts and the Yateses had built their fortunes.

Barbara wished that, along with her mother's broad Boston a, she had inherited half of her mother's drive and self-confidence. But somehow Barbara had always felt unworthy of the accident of birth that had heaped a fortune on her. And after growing up gawky, she had never adjusted to her transformation into what men saw she was—a tall, lush, beautiful woman. As she had in adolescence, she continued to try to look inconspicuous. Her unconscious efforts to disguise her five-foot-nine-inch height still provoked many a "Don't slouch, dear" from her mother. And her habit of biting her lip gave her lovely face a certain vulnerability, as if she anticipated being hit.

For Barbara was always a little afraid. She half expected the world to recognize its error and take it all—her wealth (the wealth she would inherit), her body, her husband, her children—all away. And now maybe the world was about to.

Now, over lunch in Filene's restaurant, Barbara tried to tell her problem to her mother. She felt she could, because Elizabeth Everett Yates was talking about her friends' operations.

"... had her gall bladder removed but frankly I think that's just because it's fashionable today—like removing children's tonsils used to be. Of course, Louise Chatworth did fall and fracture her hip and that's real enough but she's mainly used it as an excuse to get a chauffeured limousine which is, if you ask me, ostentatious. And Margaret Hadley's liver acted up again, but if she'd only stop sneaking snorts of Drambuie . . . now was there something you wanted to say, Barbara?"

Oh dear, thought Barbara Justin. I'd forgotten what perfect health Mother always has and how she views people who don't have it.

"Uh . . . well . . ." said Barbara.

No, I won't get a sympathetic ear from her today, thought Barbara. She'll just chew me out for waiting so long and not telling Paul—and I've chewed myself out already. And she'll tell me to see Dr. Picard—and that's what I'm doing tomorrow anyway. And then she'll tell me not to be worried about a silly old operation—and I'm terrified.

"Uh, no, Mother. Nothing." Barbara pushed back her chair. "Are we finished? I'd like to go home."

"Yes," said Elizabeth Everett Yates, setting down her teacup and the remains of her cucumber sandwich. "But we're not going home yet. There's one more thing downstairs." And she marched off on her thin, birdlike legs.

Barbara mutely followed her mother back down to the Basement. Her mother led her to a pile of blankets.

"But we don't need any more blankets," protested Barbara.

"It's not a blanket," said Elizabeth Everett Yates as she reached into the bottom of the pile and pulled out a golden cashmere sweater. "It's just your size. I found it two weeks ago and hid it. So you can buy it now."

She pointed to the price tag. The tag said the sweater was $30 on the first week of the sale, $25 on the second, $20 on the third . . . and now only $15.

"It's beautiful," said Barbara.

"Try it on," said her mother.

The sweater was made to be worn next to the skin, but Filene's Basement isn't fancy enough to have dressing rooms. That doesn't stop some people. Several times Barbara had seen women undress right in an aisle to try on clothing. That was hardly appropriate for an Everett or a Yates, so Barbara started to pull the sweater down over her blouse.

As she did, she froze. She could feel the elastic wool—tighter than her blouse—start to press against her breasts, making her more aware of them.

Barbara Justin had, she had been told, nice breasts. It wasn't supposed to matter in these liberated days, but they *were* larger than average and, after three children, still firm and upright. Men still looked at her on the street. All of which was still disconcerting to the gawky adolescent girl within the adult woman, the sixteen-year-old girl who had stuffed handkerchiefs into her bra in front of the mirror in her bedroom and despaired of ever filling out.

The girl within her was unsure of the breasts. In college, when she had finally filled out, Barbara had felt the breasts were foreign to her. In her marriage, it had taken several years before she really enjoyed having Paul suck on them. It was not until her third baby that she could even *try* what some of her friends did so casually: breast-feed in front of others. And still today, she was unsure of them. Should she tell Paul when his nibbling and biting produced mild pain? (Or was she resisting the pleasure of the pain?) Should she, when they made love, tell him not to compare her erect nipples to his erect penis? (Or should she be turned on by this talk?) And should she wear clothes that did nothing for her breasts—or that made the most of them?

In the last twelve days, the answer to her last question was simple: Barbara had worn only loose clothing and nothing low cut. This tight sweater was exactly what she didn't want. Because in the last twelve days she had become only too aware of her breasts. Too fearful of what might be happening to them, too fearful of what Picard might confirm was happening to them.

It was cruel. It was unfair. It was as if the despair of her sixteen-year-old self over not having breasts was finally being justified. And the sweater was an unwelcome reminder.

Barbara saw her mother looking at her with an expectant smile. "Thanks, Mother," she said, "but it's too small. Even without the blouse, it'll be too small." And she started taking it off.

"But it says 12 right on the label," said Mother Yates.

"Well," said Barbara, handing the sweater to her, "the label is wrong."

"I'm disappointed," said Elizabeth Everett Yates. "Gold is just your color." She left the sweater on top of the pile, so somebody else could find it.

Somebody, thought Barbara, who hasn't found a lump recently. Somebody who doesn't have what is probably breast cancer. Oh, Paul! Barbara Justin cried to herself. I want so much—and feel too ugly—for you to make love to me. To suck and bite and talk sexy to me. To reassure me I still have the sex I'm afraid of losing. Oh, Paul, my own beloved cancer researcher. What a lousy, lousy irony!

Houston, Texas

For one hour every morning, Virginia Ash attended the prayer meeting at the Unity Church of Christ Reborn. The rest of the day she sat in the living room-dining room of the Presidential Suite, ate constantly and watched the 23-inch color TV. She watched news shows, hoping they would report the cure for cancer. She watched game shows to learn how—as the contestants did—she, too, could outwit fate. She watched soap operas, to see how other people coped with suffering. And especially, at ten o'clock every morning, she watched "Saving Grace."

It was almost ten o'clock now. Virginia walked alongside her husband as he was wheeled, still unconscious, from the recovery room to his suite. She left him to the nurses. She raided the kitchen for a quart of butterscotch ice cream. She went to the TV, switched to the right channel and sat down, just in time, as the Saving Grace chorus came on, singing the hymn. Then came the announcer, Hal Kinney. Then the Cancer Healer himself, the Reverend Richard Watson Trumbull.

Trumbull was a youngish man, but his handsome face was lined, as with great experience. And he spoke today's sermon with a depth of sorrow, hope and vision beyond his years. His resounding baritone would have made him a success even if television had never been invented. Virginia ate her ice cream faster. Yes, she said to herself. Yes. But get on to the healing.

"And from right here in Hutchinson, Kansas," said Hal Kinney, "Mrs. Josephine Gerdes."

The studio audience applauded. A middle-aged woman was escorted on stage. She tried to tell her story, but it was difficult. Her story was that she had cancer of the larynx. Hal Kinney helped her tell it. Then Reverend Trumbull interrupted, soothingly, to say that the details didn't matter. All that mattered was, did she believe in Jesus Christ the Son of God? Did she believe His grace could save her?

"Yes," whispered Mrs. Gerdes. "Oh, yes."

Virginia Ash moved to the edge of her seat.

With his strong hands, Reverend Trumbull softly touched the woman's throat.

"Then through me," he intoned, "as His unworthy instrument, let this be done. Let ... "

Trumbull's golden voice continued but Virginia suddenly wasn't listening. An idea had seized her. I'll get him here, Virginia Ash decided. I'll bring the Cancer Healer here!

She sprang to her feet, spilling ice cream on the Bokhara rug. Her large body quivered.

If you really are near death, Matt, if you really can't be moved, then I'll bring *him* to you! If Ray Ryker can spend thousands of dollars for worthless doctors, I can spend whatever it takes to bring you this one great man of God! For you, Matt! Trumbull will touch you and you'll be saved!

Virginia rushed for the door to Matt's bedroom. She ignored the fact that Matt Ash was a confirmed atheist who believed only in himself. If he could, he'd throw Trumbull out on his ear. Virginia flung the door open.

When Matt had been wheeled on the gurney back to the suite, he had had only an intravenous line into his arm. That Virginia could accept. But while Virginia had watched TV, the nurses had attached tubes into his belly, tubes leading to a machine. And a nurse was now bent over the machine, turning dials, making the tubes gurgle. This repulsed Virginia. This was obscene.

"Matt!" she cried, trying to rouse him. "I—"

But the nurse came at Virginia with a warning, shushing finger. Even more angered and determined, Virginia spun around. She headed for one of the living-room phones.

We'll pull those tubes out of you, Matt, swore Virginia to herself, and connect you instead with Christ!

New York City

"Is that a grain there?" asked Underwood.

"Where?" asked Justin.

Underwood touched a pencil point next to a nearly invisible dot on the photograph.

"There. In the nucleus."

"No," said Justin.

"How about this one?" asked Underwood. "In the cytoplasm."

"Possibly," said Justin. "Let's get an enlargement."

"Right," said Underwood. He laid down another photograph. "Now, Paul, in this one I think we have . . . "

Paul Justin's thoughts were on his hamsters across the hall in the animal room. But he could see it was going to be tough to get to them this morning.

He had made it to the institute about 10:45 and walked into his section—virology—just as his six colleagues were finishing the daily cell feeding. He had accepted his morning cup of coffee from Roberto Cruz, the Puerto Rican lab assistant who ran both the scientific "kitchen" and the human kitchen (the human one was less extensive—only a hot plate). Sipping it, Justin had told of his problems with the Penn Central. But he got only brief sympathy. His work was backed up. Stefan Wojik, the other associate in the section, had corralled Justin to take a look at their joint cell surface project. The two men stripped off part of the surface of cancerous cells with the VCN enzymes to see if this also stripped off a cancer-causing enzyme. Then Hugh Underwood, the section head, had asked Justin to look at just-developed photographs on their benzepyrene project. Justin begged off for a moment to call Barbara in Boston. There was no answer. With his mind on his wife and his hamsters, Justin allowed himself to be led back to benzepyrene.

He squinted to follow Underwood's pencil point. "And is *this* a grain?" Underwood asked.

Justin tried very hard to care. The project was an investigation of how normal cells take up DNA from cancerous cells and become cancerous themselves. In nature, this process is inefficient. Only some cells—not enough to study—become cancerous. So Underwood and Justin had spent three years learning how to hook benzepyrene, a component of smoke, onto DNA. So more cells could become cancerous. And this year they were tracing the effect of that benzepyrene. By making the benzepyrene radioactive, it would show up on a cell photograph as silver grains. This morning, Underwood had some particularly good photographs for the two of them to examine. Since Underwood *was* the section head, Justin could hardly say no.

"A grain?" Underwood asked. His southern voice was full of patience. Hugh Underwood was from Montgomery, Alabama, the son of a black maid and black garbageman. Via college and a Ph.D. and his career, he had accomplished the long, difficult feat of becoming a white-thinking, white-acting man. And since he had been born with a limp, he knew even more intimately how slowly things moved. So Underwood took the long view on everything. He was prepared to spend another decade—if need be—on benzepyrene. Until recently, Justin felt he had disciplined himself to be patient, too. But now he squirmed with eagerness to get in and kill his hamsters.

"Yes," said Justin. "A grain."

Around them, in the two crowded, equipment-filled rooms—further divided by a half-dozen specialized cubicles—the white-smocked members of the virology section continued their steady work. Dr. Wojik was now putting the VCN-treated cells through the centrifuge to separate out the molecules. Mr. Crawford and Miss Scully, the doctoral students, were running a dialysis experiment in the cold room. Holmes, a technician, was copying data off a spectrophotometer graph. Beauchamp, the other technician, was mounting and staining slides. Roberto Cruz was washing glassware in the "kitchen."

And Justin knew that down the hall the same scene was being played out in two more sections. And on more floors, in more sections.

And across the street, across the glassed-in bridge that joined the Oakes-Metcalf Institute with the Oakes-Metcalf Hospital, more men and women in white smocks labored. And so on, up and down the East River, from Bellevue at Twenty-seventh Street to the Metropolitan Hospital at Ninety-ninth. A hum of medical research and healing. Everyday. Ordinary. Familiar. Justin heard Roberto whistle a pop tune. He watched Scully put her half-eaten blueberry yogurt back in the refrigerator, next to bottles of chemicals. His other colleagues passed each other in the rooms, talked a bit about their work and then went on with it. But Justin could not casually go on with it. On the wall in front of him, between a chromosome chart and a list of exposure times, Scully had taped a funny birthday card she had just received. She was twenty-four. Next month, thought Paul Justin, I'll be forty. My life is half over. Either I'm right about the hamsters or ... or ... or I do this for the next quarter century? Impossible.

Paul Justin looked back at the cell photograph. He tried to decide if the speck that Underwood's pencil had now moved to was benzopyrene or simple dust. Forty years, he thought. Almost half of them dominated by cancer. He remembered how it all began.

Justin had been away from home in his second year at Boston University Medical School. As he heard the story later from his mother, his father had come back from a canoe trip with an ache in his left wrist. When the ache didn't go away, Walter Justin worried that it might be arthritis. The elder Justin was a skilled tool-and-die maker and a man who loved to use his hands. He could tie a fly, fix a TV set and whittle a corncob pipe better than anyone his son knew. In a month, with his wrist more painful and now swollen, Walter Justin saw his doctor. His doctor sent him to the Mayo Clinic for tests. Walter Justin had bone cancer.

Eleven hundred miles away in Boston, Walter Justin's son felt the pain almost as much as Walter Justin did. Paul had been thinking of becoming a pediatrician or heart specialist. But when he heard the news, he got hold of every book, article and monograph on bone cancer. He buttonholed senior faculty members. And as he learned the oldest and newest theories about the disease and the treatments for it, all of them were being tried on his father.

First drugs. Then radiology, with weekly sessions under a 250,000-kilowatt X-ray machine. But the cancer spread up the arm. After a year and a half, the doctors felt the only way to stop the wild cells was surgery. Walter Justin had his arm amputated just below the elbow. When Paul returned to Minnesota that Christmas vacation and saw his father, Paul wept openly.

But the cancer had traveled past the scalpel. So, eight months later, the rest of Walter Justin's arm and most of his shoulder was removed. A few weeks after this operation, they discovered a growth in his chest.

Walter Justin had been an active, brave man who had been willing to sacrifice anything to keep living. But he was tired of burying one part of his body at a time. And he wanted some money left for his wife and some money to see his son through medical school. He refused an operation on his chest. Paul Justin pleaded. Walter Justin refused. By the next Christmas he was dead.

Paul Justin finished medical school, but he never took his internship, never took his medical boards. For he had lost interest in practicing medicine on people. Instead, he started over again, working days and studying nights—studying for an M.A. and then a Ph.D. in microbiology. Paul Justin became a cancer researcher. He had spent the last dozen years searching for the cure for cancer.

Except, of course, there never would be such a thing as the cure for cancer.

As researchers tried to make clear to the popular press, this was a piecemeal business. There would be no single shot like the Salk vaccine to prevent cancer. No single shot like penicillin to cure it. Instead, what the world could look forward to over the next quarter century was the discovery, perhaps, of one drug that would retard the growth of some stomach cancers by a few months. And another drug that would increase leukemia remissions by five percent. And another drug... and so on. Until slowly, painfully, cancer might eventually be almost conquered.

Despite himself, Paul Justin had come to believe this, too. Not in any of his previous positions, not in his job at Oakes-Metcalf, had Justin made any major discovery. He had worked hard. He had had insights. But in all, as he admitted to himself, he had pushed back the frontiers of knowledge only an inch. In fact, two and a half years ago, when Oakes-Metcalf had budget problems, he had nearly been let go. At thirty-nine going on forty, Justin was old *not* to be section head. Underwood, who was Justin's own age, had many more scholarly articles to his credit. And Underwood had recently been given a plum—a grant from Senator Prentice's National Cancer Control Act.

But Paul Justin's passion was undiminished. The image of his father's mutilated body still burned in his brain. And so, for the last four years—in between all the other projects that came and went— Justin stubbornly ran his project on the "C" particle and RNA programming. Now, across the hall, was the fruit of his determination. A week ago, his three hamsters had been on the verge of death. Like the hundreds of hamsters before them, they should today *be* dead. But Justin had given them one more version of his serum. And today the hamsters lived. More than lived—they thrived. And today Justin would kill and autopsy them to see how and why. He could not really believe his serum had done it. It couldn't be this simple. There must be a dozen other explanations. Mustn't there?

But Justin couldn't think of what the dozen were.

"I said, 'This is a grain. Yes?' "

"What?" asked Justin, snapping out of his thoughts.

"I said," repeated Underwood, losing his famed patience, " 'This is a grain. Yes?' " He tapped his pencil on the photograph.

"Oh," said Justin, looking at what was definitely a speck of dust. "Yes. Right you are. A grain."

I've got to get out of here, thought Justin. I've got to get at those hamsters.

New York City

Frank Lattimer needn't have worried about the train making him late for his meeting with Tommy Vernon. When he called Beazle's Pub to see if Vernon was still waiting for him, the bartender said that nobody of that description had come in today. And when Lattimer called his city room to see if Vernon had left a message, the switchboard operator said no.

So now Lattimer had a *real* worry. Until today, Vernon had been very reliable. The few times they'd met, Vernon had been on time and had had the information he'd promised. Today Vernon had promised to bring proof that the company he worked for—B & B Meat Purveyors, downtown on Washington Street—had gotten lucrative city contracts without the required competitive bids. And proof that the deputy mayor—whose law partner was a silent partner in B & B—had arranged the contracts. Vernon's working day started at 6 A.M., so he'd said it'd be no problem to bring his proof on his break at 9:30. But obviously there was a problem. Lattimer stood in the phone booth at Park and 77th and debated what to do.

He could spend the day working on other people who had access to files on other angles of the story—people like the clerk he knew in the Municipal Building or the secretary at the deputy mayor's Wall Street law firm. Or he could do what Vernon and he had agreed he'd never do: contact Vernon at B & B.

Lattimer's judgment said one thing. His instinct said another. He hailed a cab and ordered it to Washington Street, in a hurry.

Files, thought Lattimer, as the cab made its way down Park Avenue in the Fifties. The world was run on files of paper. On both sides of Park rose forty-floor buildings housing the headquarters of America's major banks and corporations. And on each floor, tens of thousands of cubic feet of filing cabinets. Sales records, personnel records, tax records . . . detailing and hiding tens of thousands of maneuvers, jealousies, even crimes. If a man knew how to pierce the confident facade of steel and glass, if he knew where to look . . .

Lattimer's first newspaper job—ten years ago this September—had been on the sports desk of the Wilkes-Barre *Tribune*. It was the lowest job on the desk—covering high school football, which was supposed to mean reporting only the scores. But Lattimer got interested in a local high school star, Bob Domewicz, who had just entered the University of Pittsburgh and was being touted as an All-American. From one of Domewicz's former teammates, he learned that Domewicz had been a terrible student, that it had been a surprise that Domewicz graduated. At the time, Lattimer had been living with a girl and in love with her. But to get the story on Domewicz, he slept with the secretary to the high school principal. And from the files she let him go through, he made Xerox copies of proof that the school had raised the grades not only of Domewicz but also of a dozen top athletes over the last several years.

In the wake of Lattimer's exposé, the principal and three other school officials were fired. Domewicz lost his football scholarship and was forced to drop out of Pitt. But the school never discovered the secretary's role in the story (Lattimer protected his sources) and neither did Lattimer's girl friend (Lattimer protected himself). And Lattimer took a general reporter's job at double the salary on the Pittsburgh *Courier*.

Mary Ann, Lattimer's girl, came on with him to Pittsburgh and they got married. But as his career thrived, Lattimer's personal life fell apart. He was always out late and on weekends, working on a story. Payoffs to city health inspectors, the dubious campaign contributions of a major steel company, the surprising stock holdings of a local "environmentalist" . . . Lattimer was fascinated with finding out what went on behind the facades. But upon returning from an all-night vigil at the hospital bed of a state policeman shot under unexplained circumstances (Lattimer suspected a feud in the department), he found Mary Ann packing her bags.

"Facade!" she yelled at him. "Facade! Did you ever look at what's going on behind the facade of this so-called marriage! Fuck you and the Pulitzer you want. You'd *better* get it, Frank, and frame it. You can put it right next to your divorce papers!"

He had pleaded with her. He had even cried. But it was too late. She was out the door.

She went back to Wilkes-Barre. He went on to the big leagues, to New York. The divorce papers came through and he filed them away. Sometimes now, Lattimer wondered where she was and how she was (they had had no children—he was thankful for that). But sometimes he also wondered whether it was real feeling or just curiosity, like wondering what ever became of Domewicz. And so, with occasional bouts of loneliness and occasional might-have-beens, Lattimer zestfully pursued his career. He dug into other men's files for the true stories of what they did to each other in pursuit of money and power. His own file he kept as brief as possible.

Going west on Fourteenth Street, the cab got stuck in a traffic jam. An excavation was blocking one lane. Lattimer looked at his watch. "Goddamn Con Ed," swore the cab driver. "Someone ought to investigate those idiots." It's been done to death, thought Frank Lattimer. The cab turned onto Washington Street and entered the wholesale meat district and Tommy Vernon's newer story.

The district is a series of ramshackle buildings jammed between the western edge of Greenwich Village (with its hip bars, like Beazle's) and the West Side Highway. The narrow streets are choked with large parked trucks. Two blocks from his destination, Lattimer got out of the cab and walked.

Within twenty minutes, Lattimer was able to stop worrying about Tommy Vernon. And start worrying about himself, about whether he was about to become an item in a coroner's file.

Lattimer got in easily enough. "Hey," he said to the man on the B & B loading dock. "I'm from Tom Vernon's insurance company. If he doesn't sign these papers"—here Lattimer tapped his jacket pocket—"we don't collect from the other insurance company. And Vernon doesn't get his money on his car claim. Where is he?"

The man in the bloodstained white smock looked at Lattimer suspiciously. "In there," said the man, hefting a giant side of beef onto his shoulder and pointing with it. "I guess," he added. "I haven't seen Tommy for a coupla hours."

Lattimer went inside the old building from one room to another, around crates of squawking live chickens and stacks of hams and boxes marked "Portion-Control Halibut." There were few people and none of them had seen Vernon recently either. "So where'd you see him *last*?" asked Lattimer.

"Maybe the back room?" said a man going through invoices.

Lattimer checked. The back room was refrigerated. It had overhead tracks with hooks hanging from them. From the hooks hung the giant sides of beef. They hung like suits in a cleaner's. As Lattimer walked in, the man Lattimer had met on the loading dock was hooking up another carcass. He pushed it down the track to make room for more.

"You still?" asked the man.

"Yeah," said Lattimer.

"He's not here," said the man, and left.

But Vernon was there. Back up against the far wall, pushed along by all the sides of beef the man had brought in, hanging on his own hook, was Tommy Vernon. The hook entered his back and exited just under his chin. Blood dripped down his body onto the floor. And unlike the other carcasses, Vernon's had a head. And the head had a horrible, slack-jawed look of agony and surprise.

Lattimer looked at the source he had failed to protect. Somebody didn't just want to kill Vernon, thought Lattimer. They wanted to leave him as a warning to any other B & B employee who might consider crossing the company. Except the warning had gotten hidden behind the morning's deliveries. Filed away.

Lattimer took his tiny Minox out of his pocket. His own newspaper would never print the photo and, unlike some reporters, Lattimer had no interest in picking up fifty or a hundred dollars from the sex-and-gore papers that would print it. But the picture would be evidence of some kind. Lattimer had a friend, Detective Lieutenant Pete Whitcomb, in the city's Anti-Crime Strike Force. Maybe Whitcomb could use the picture. Lattimer started shooting.

He only got off one shot.

"Hey," said the voice behind him, heavy with menace. "Are you the guy that's been asking about Vernon?"

Lattimer spun around. Lattimer hadn't seen this man in the building, and would have remembered him if he had. The man was huge, easily six-foot-six and 275 pounds. His thick, wrestler's shoulders and neck, bulging out of a T-shirt, supported a massive, scarred, grinning head. Like some wrestlers, he had shaved his head smooth, so it had the visual impact of a cannonball. But Lattimer didn't concentrate on the head. He concentrated on the large butcher knife the man was swinging gracefully in his right hand.

Lattimer had gotten in easily enough. He now wondered how he was going to get out. It had been easier going up against high school principals back in Wilkes-Barre.

Bexar County, Texas

At the moment that the big man was coming at Lattimer with a knife, a rattlesnake was coming at Ray Ryker.

The snake came out of a hole that held a rotting fence post. The fence post was in the middle of a vast plain in West Texas. The only other people within ten miles were Harry Wissenbach, who was Ryker's only friend, and the pilot of the Cessna 172 who had flown Wissenbach and Ryker out to the middle of this nowhere. The pilot was a safe hundred yards away, next to the plane. But Wissenbach, bending over next to Ryker to snip a piece of fence wire, was also threatened by the rattler.

"Jesus Christ!" said Wissenbach, dropping his attaché case.

Both men wore shoes instead of boots. From ankle to calf, the rattler could strike right through their thin, city pants and hit flesh. What a hell of a way to go, thought Ryker. He was furious at Wissenbach for getting him out here. But when Wissenbach had suggested the barbed-wire hunt, Ryker couldn't refuse. For, in addition to running the third largest bank in Texas, Harry Wissenbach was a barbed-wire collector, a "barbarian." On his office walls were displayed his twin passions: Dozens of framed stock certificates, bonds and merger and acquisition agreements, representing deals he had made. And hundreds of different strands of barbed wire from all over the nation.

The two passions intertwined. Hunting barbed wire put Wissenbach in an expansive mood, made him more open to deals. And since Ryker needed Wissenbach dearly for the deal he had in mind, Ryker had come along today. But now Wissenbach wasn't being expansive at all. As the snake angled slightly away from Ryker and toward the banker, Wissenbach tightened up, tried to make himself smaller. He looked ready to bolt. ,

"Don't move, Harry," said Ryker sharply. Ryker held a piece of barbed wire which he had already snipped. (He told Wissenbach he shared his interest in collecting.) It was an 18-inch piece of Slocum Double-Plate Lock Link. Wissenbach said it was worth over $1,000. Wissenbach had looked for likely wire from the air, making the pilot fly at 500 feet, sweeping high-power binoculars over the dry, desolate land. When he had spotted these hundreds of yards of wire on the abandoned fence, he had ordered the pilot to land. And when he had discovered it was Slocum he had become ecstatic.

"Lookee at that," he had said. "Usually, if you find Lock Link, it's only a piece or two in a rubbish heap. And at that, you have to use a goddamn *metal* detector. But here's all *this*—under God's heaven. In-credible!"

And the discovery, as Ryker had hoped, had made Wissenbach expansive. "Yes, siree," he'd said, snipping off 18-inch segments, "I do believe we could corner the whole Lock Link market, if we wished. Get 'bout as much of it as yore boss has of Texahoma. Eighty-six percent, right?" he'd asked Ryker.

"Right," Ryker had said.

"And that's what you want to talk 'bout today, right?"

"Right."

Wissenbach knew the truth. And the truth was *not* what Ray Ryker had told to the doctors this morning. Ryker didn't want Matt Ash to live longer because he admired the old man's fighting spirit. He wanted Ash to live longer so he, Ryker, could put together a group to buy the pipeline company from him. And, for this, Ryker needed Wissenbach's help.

Wissenbach had stuffed the wire into his attaché case and started to cut even more. "So. So we'll talk. But 'bout what? Eighty-six percent? Hell. Las' ten years, you've been trying to get 'im to part with some of that. Offer some of it so you can attract better executives. Or better yet, go public, so you can *really* build the company. An' for ten years—for forever—he's said no. So what makes you think he'll sell now?"

"Because now," Ryker had said, "now that he realizes he's going to die, I can work on him. Convince him it's crazy to have sweated and slaved building up his company only to let his dumb wife inherit it. Tell him *we'll* do a better job running it."

"He's ornery," Wissenbach had said. "Mebee you won't convince 'im ever."

"If I have a definite offer I can," said Ryker. "I'll put up fifty million of my own money. With your bank plus the people you can bring in, we can give him a definite offer."

"Ah don't know, Ray."

"What do you mean, you don't know? We get a fantastic company. Then go public and make a goddamn fortune. What's the problem?"

"You," Wissenbach had said bluntly.

"Me?" Ryker had asked.

And at that moment the rattlesnake came out of his hole.

Ryker's bowels had started to tremble. He clenched his fists. Ray Ryker had a city boy's fear and ignorance of snakes. At age twelve, he had gone to a YMCA summer camp for a week with his new stepbrother who was four years older and half again as big as Ray. On the first day, the stepbrother's friends had easily pinned Ray to the ground while the stepbrother let a garter snake crawl up Ray's thin chest, telling him it was poisonous. Ray had crapped in his pants and they mocked him.

Not again, thought Ryker. He willed himself to stop trembling. He forced his hands to loop his piece of barbed wire into a noose. "Don't move, Harry," he said to Wissenbach. "And keep talking." He had to keep Harry talking or Harry would bolt. And then the snake would strike. "You were saying the problem is me. Why?"

Wissenbach eyed the approaching snake nervously. "Well." He licked his lips. "Well, you'd be president, right?"

"Right," said Ryker. "I'd own the largest block. And I'm the only one who can talk to Ash. And I've been running Texahoma already—I *know* it."

"Yeah. But people know *you*."

Ryker was slowly circling behind the snake. "What does that mean?" he asked. He knew very well what Wissenbach meant.

"Other people,"—Wissenbach swallowed—"think yo're too much like the Old Man. So they're not shore they want you president of their company." Two feet from Wissenbach, the snake stopped its forward motion. It started to slowly coil and uncoil. "They're afraid you maght try to Mash 'em a bit," said Wissenbach. The banker was showing his own fear. Beads of sweat stood out on his face. He started to jiggle one foot. This was Wissenbach's native ground, but years in corporate boardrooms had leeched any physical courage out of him.

But Ryker coolly closed in, dangling the noose. "Shit, Harry," he said, "the other investors would own a controlling interest. They could vote me out anytime they felt I crossed them."

"Less you divided 'n' conquered 'em," Wissenbach said, hoarsely. The snake raised its head, preliminary to striking. "Like normal," gulped Wissenbach.

For an instant, the snake's head was still. In that instant, as Wissenbach finally bolted—and tripped—Ryker struck.

He dropped the wire noose over the snake's head and yanked hard. The barbs of Slocum Double-Plate Lock Link pierced the snake. The snake flapped convulsively in midair, at the end of the wire. Ryker dropped the wire and stepped on the snake's head.

"Goddamn," said Wissenbach, picking himself up.

"Huh," grunted Ryker. He shook the remains of the snake free from the wire. With his wire cutters, Wissenbach snipped off the tail of rattles. Another display for his wall, Ryker knew. The two men walked wordlessly back to the plane.

Yeah, thought Ryker, Harry knows me well. But he also knows I won't settle for less than being president. After all these years of being Number Two Boy under Matt Ash ... Ryker gritted his teeth. There were other banks, investment companies, rich individuals. They'd put together the money all right, but they wouldn't give him the presidency. If he wanted that—the ultimate control—he needed Harry Wissenbach. Harry was the only person who, as Harry once put it, "could persuade somebody into lettin' Ray Ryker be chief fox in the hen house." Until now, Harry hadn't acted like he would try to persuade somebody. But now Harry owed Ryker something: his life.

Airborne again, flying back to Houston, Wissenbach did act as if he recognized the debt. And with fear behind him, his heartiness returned. "Give me time, Ray," he said. "Let me talk you up a bit. Say yore a really good ol' boy. Git some fellas up here to go huntin' with us. Let 'em see yore human."

"You're talking weeks, months," said Ryker. "By then Ash could be dead."

"Well," said Wissenbach, "Ah'll move on it." He clapped Ryker on the shoulder. "Tell you what. Ah've got a board meetin' tomorrow at Trans Con. Ah'll bring up the idea with Earl Benson. He'd be a natural for this. Him 'n' me 'n' Joe Pettigrew are flyin' down to Acapulco this weekend for some high gamblin'. Ah'll suggest you join us 'n' we'll all talk. Okay?"

"Yeah," said Ryker. "Okay."

"Ah'll call you tomorrow," Wissenbach promised Ryker, "after Ah talk to Earl. Meantime, don't let the Old Man die, huh?" He laughed.

"Yeah," said Ryker.

Ryker certainly knew he needed the Old Man to live. And he also certainly wanted to drop the barbed-wire noose around the Old Man's neck.

New York City

"And what the fuck is that you're holding?" demanded the big man, dancing closer to Lattimer, pointing with the butcher knife. Despite his size, the man had the nimbleness of a pro lineman slipping a block. He came at Lattimer between two rows of sides of beef that reached almost to the floor. Lattimer was literally up against the wall.

"Is that a fucking camera?" demanded the man, a light coming into his eyes. The man was now a foot away. He towered over Lattimer. His breath condensed in the cold air and blew down into Lattimer's face. Lattimer realized that this must be the man who'd had the strength to lift Tommy Vernon up and then slam him down through the meat hook. Lattimer imagined the strength that the man could put into one swing of the knife.

At this moment, when Lattimer should have been thinking about how to save himself, he thought about Bob Domewicz. Poor big dumb Domewicz, used by people bigger than him to further their own careers. Like the deputy mayor was indirectly using this giant with the butcher knife. It made Lattimer mad. When you came right down to it, the men behind the steel-and-glass facades were happy to rely on muscle. Someone else's muscle. Lattimer was briefly nostalgic for the last unfair fight he'd been in. At least then the opposition—five football players—had been out only for themselves.

It had been in Lattimer's senior year in Cardiff High School. He had decided that editing the school paper was more important than playing ball, although he could have easily reclaimed his job as first-string halfback. For a month, the other players cajoled him to stay on the team. Then the cajoling became threats. One night, the entire middle of the offensive line—five big miners' sons—surrounded Lattimer outside the town pizza parlor. "You're letting the team down, Frank," announced the center. "So you've got it coming." Lattimer saw they were serious and saw this could keep up all fall. So he made them a deal. He'd fight them tonight, one at a time, and if anyone beat him he'd play. But if he beat them all, they'd leave him the fuck alone. Okay? The players agreed. And in the alley behind the store Lattimer beat the first and the second and the third and—although his nose was broken and bleeding and his body was sore and each new boy was fresh—the fourth and the fifth.

Which had been tough enough. But at least none of the players had a knife in his hand.

But I, thought Lattimer suddenly, snapping back to the present, have a camera. He now hurled it at the big man's face.

Lattimer's attacker had expected his quarry to try to guard his precious pictures. So he was totally unprepared. The Minox caught him square in the mouth, splitting both lips and shattering teeth. The big man howled. In the split second he had, Lattimer ducked under one of the rows of beef and sprinted for the door. Behind him, he could hear the man screaming wildly and then running after him. The man swung the knife as he ran, slicing the air and the sides of beef. Lattimer was out the door and flying through the building.

"Stop that son of a bitch!" screamed his pursuer.

Lattimer slipped in a pool of water leaking from a crate of lobsters. He fell on the crate. He got up and ran again and burst out onto Washington Street. After the cold room, the sudden heat was overwhelming. And his right leg was aching now from where he'd fallen. But he kept going, around the buildings, around the trucks and finally out into the crowd of afternoon shoppers on Fourteenth Street. That was pretty fair broken-field running, Lattimer told himself, gasping for breath. Still a good halfback.

He seemed to have shaken the big man. Ignoring the stares of passers-by—his pants leg was ripped open and his shin was bleeding—Lattimer walked back south and east into Greenwich Village.

On Charles Street, he rang the doorbell of a brownstone. On the second floor lived a young actress with whom Lattimer had a sometime thing. Last he knew, she had a part in an off-Broadway play and so might be home in the middle of the afternoon. He rang the bell again. He waited. Damn it all, he thought. I don't even need sex. I'll accept a bandage and a fresh pair of pants (the actress usually had bits of men's clothing around). But still no answer. The play had probably closed, Lattimer reasoned, and she's out auditioning again. Lattimer jingled the keys in his pocket. One of them was to the apartment of a friend, Barney James, on the Upper West Side. Out of the corner of his eye, Lattimer saw a yellow car flash by.

"Taxi!" yelled Lattimer, dashing down the steps. "Taxi!" Ignoring the ache in his right leg, feeling good about his rediscovered running ability, he sprinted for the intersection fifty yards away, where the cab was now slowing to a halt at a red light. Get to Barney's place, thought Lattimer, clean up, change and then pursue the story—the clerk in the Municipal Building, the lawyer's secretary. Lattimer was halfway to the cab, confident the driver was about to notice him, when he felt a sudden yank in his left thigh.

He pulled up in acute pain, hobbling. The light turned green. The cab drove off.

I lost a source, thought Lattimer, limping to the curb. I lost a camera. I nearly lost my life. And now I've lost my senses thinking I can still move like I was eighteen years old. What a profitless day.

New York City

It was not until midafternoon that Paul Justin was able to get out of the virology section and cross the hall to the animal room. Around him, dozens of rats, chickens, rabbits and hamsters sat in their cages. Justin approached his own hamsters.

"Hiya, fellas," he said. "How you doing?"

His hamsters were doing fine. They were alive when, according to all medical knowledge, they should be long dead. At the moment, they were sleeping. They slept in a furry clump so it was hard to tell where one hamster ended and another began. Justin opened the cage, reached into the clump and brought out a hamster.

He held it firmly. If it woke up, it might try to jump out of his hand. If it did, the fall could kill it, for hamsters have fragile bones. And Justin had to kill it properly.

Justin carried the hamster to the animal room's miniature dissecting table. His fingers probed gently. He could feel no tumors. Only a week ago the hamster had been grossly deformed by them.

But of course he had to make sure. "Right, fella?" he asked.

He swung the little blade to chop off the hamster's head. He felt dozens of pairs of eyes on him.

As the blade fell, Justin wondered what Louis Pasteur had felt on the verge of his discoveries a century ago. Pasteur, the first modern researcher, who had been born into a world that still believed diseases were caused by maggots. Who instead proved that some diseases were caused by infection, by the transmittal of small things he found under his microscope, things he called bacteria.

Impressed by Pasteur, some of Pasteur's contemporaries took bacteria found in animal cancers and put them in healthy animals. But the healthy animals did not develop cancer. So what had caused the cancer in the first place, if not the bacteria?

This was the beginning of the hunt for a disease-causing organism too small to be seen even under a microscope. The hunt for what became known as a virus. And the beginning of Paul Justin's profession: virology.

At the same time, in 1877, Julius Conheim proposed his theory of embryonic rests. A theory that, for almost a century, was the beginning of nothing.

Conheim proposed that cancer originates from small, isolated clumps of embryonic cells which remain dormant in a body—until activated into sudden growth by chemical or physical irritation. But Conheim didn't know where to look for an embryonic rest. And certainly no one associated this idea with a virus. Conheim's theory soon fell into oblivion.

But the hunt for a virus went on.

And in 1892 Dimitri Iwanowski offered the first evidence of a virus. In studying the mosaic disease of the tobacco plant, he crushed juice from infected leaves and passed the juice through a porcelain filter. The pores of porcelain are too small to let bacteria through also. Yet *something* passed through with the juice. Because when Iwanowski injected the filtrate into healthy tobacco plants, they developed mosaic disease.

Other experiments followed. By 1900, it was agreed that viruses did exist. And it was predicted that someday these viruses would be isolated.

But no one could find evidence for a *cancer* virus. In fact, the virus theory of cancer was so discredited that when evidence came, it wasn't recognized.

In 1908 Ellerman and Bang transmitted chicken leukemia via a filtrate. This attracted little attention—it was not then known that leukemia is a form of cancer.

And in 1911, when American scientist Peyton Rous performed the experiment with cancer found in chicken muscle, he was violently attacked by other researchers. Some claimed Rous's experiment was faulty. Others claimed that, even if he had transmitted a chicken cancer by a virus, this had no application to mammals, no application to human beings.

So, for over two decades, no important work was done on cancer viruses.

But, in 1928, bacteriologist Frederick Griffith did work in another area that—like Conheim's idea of embryonic rests—appeared at first to be unrelated to viruses. Griffith took a pneumonia-causing bacteria, killed it with heat and injected it into mice. The mice promptly developed pneumonia. Griffith recovered live bacteria from the mice—and found these bacteria had several "fingerprint" characteristics of the dead bacteria. The dead bacteria had transferred their properties to the previously harmless bacteria. And these characteristics were then transmitted by heredity to succeeding generations of bacteria.

It was clear that something had caused a chromosomal change. But what?

The question remained unanswered for sixteen years. But in the meantime, in the 1930s, virus work continued. Wendell Stanley finally isolated the first virus—the virus that caused Iwanowski's tobacco mosaic disease. And researchers returned to cancer viruses. In 1932 Shope's work with rabbits proved viruses can cause cancer in mammals. Between 1936 and 1942, Bittner's work with mice reinforced this.

And in 1944, Avery, McLeod and McCarty found what had caused the chromosomal change in Griffith's bacteria. It was not, as most had suspected, protein. Instead, it was deoxyribonucleic acid: DNA.

So revolutionary was the finding that Avery himself did not accept it. Convincing evidence had to wait until 1952 when Hershey and Chase demonstrated that the DNA in a virus could nullify a cell's genetic instructions and replace it with its own.

Inspired by these experiments, James Watson and Francis Crick took a shot at unraveling the complex structure of DNA. And on a late winter day in 1953 they dashed out of their Cambridge laboratory and into the nearby Eagle Pub where Crick proclaimed, "We have discovered the secret of life!"

They had indeed. Their description of DNA's helical structure was to win them the 1962 Nobel Prize for Medicine. And it inspired other researchers to dig even deeper into DNA. And into RNA—the "messenger" which DNA makes in its own image, to carry out its orders in the body.

During this time, from the early 1950s through the early 1960s, cancer researchers also made a number of important discoveries. Although they remained unable to actually isolate a cancer virus, they did find proof of more animal cancer viruses. Then proof of human viruses that caused cancer in animals. Then animal viruses that caused cancer in cultivated human cells. And then viruses that caused cancer in living human beings.

The cumulative evidence was convincing. And in starting it all, for his pioneer work in cancer viruses, Peyton Rous was belatedly awarded the 1966 Nobel Prize in Medicine.

Finally, researchers had accepted that a virus could cause human cancer. But they also had to accept a dilemma. For while Hershey and Chase had shown that a virus could contain DNA, many of the cancer-causing viruses for which researchers had found proof were *RNA* viruses. And while RNA can carry a cancerous message to a cell, it takes DNA to make that message "stick." So for an RNA virus to cause cancer it would somehow have to reverse the normal birth process and make DNA in *its* image.

Clearly, that was impossible. So researchers concentrated on DNA. With some success.

For instance, using the so-called Hela cells—obtained decades ago from a woman who'd had uterine cancer, and subsequently cultivated for many generations—Aaron Bendich of Sloan-Kettering showed that DNA acted by adding new genetic material to the cell. He proved it actually penetrated the cell nucleus.

So, by the early 1970s, the next step was clear: Find whether and how DNA penetrated not just the nucleus but also as deep as the chromosomes. This was the work that many researchers across the country now pursued. Underwood's and Justin's benzepyrene project was one such effort.

But Paul Justin had become dissatisfied with the pace of the research. For even if they eventually discovered how damaged DNA altered chromosomes, how could they prevent it? In theory, a synthetic DNA molecule could be programmed to shut down the altered chromosome, to stop it from reproducing and spreading cancer. But how could this molecule ever get to the cancerous cell? As soon as it could be injected into the bloodstream, the body's enzymes would eat it up. Of course, RNA—the "messenger"—was designed to survive in the bloodstream. If only, thought Justin, RNA *could* make DNA.

But then in 1970 came a new idea and a new piece of evidence. Added together, they made Paul Justin believe a cure was possible.

In 1970, Robert Heubner of the National Cancer Institute harked back to Julius Conheim's 1877 theory of embryonic rests and proposed the idea of the "C" (for cancer) particle. Heubner theorized that, like the embryonic rest, its activation produced rapid cell growth—cancer. But whereas Conheim left the identity of his villain vague,

Heubner labeled the "C" particle: It is, he said, part of an RNA virus that at some time in human history made DNA, incorporated itself into someone's genes, and has been passed on to people ever since.

In other words, the cancer virus isn't like other viruses. It's not a damaged DNA that invades the body. Instead, it's already inside all of us—a time bomb, ticking away. And when a hormonal imbalance or a chemical agent like cigarette tar hits the "C" particle, it explodes.

An interesting idea. But it depended on RNA's being able to make DNA.

And in the same year, 1970, Howard Temin of the University of Wisconsin finally proved RNA *could*. Using a culture of malignant RNA-type virus—the same kind Peyton Rous had used—Temin caused cancer in chicken cells. And in the cancerous cells, Temin found DNA that resembled the RNA. The only way the DNA could have gotten there was if the RNA *had* made it.

So cancer could start the way Heubner theorized. And that pointed to how cancer could be ended: Look inside the DNA molecule, find and analyze the "C" particle and then program a synthetic RNA molecule to shut it down.

So, in 1970, many researchers started looking for the "C" particle. While continuing his other work, Paul Justin joined them.

He ran many experiments. At one point, he published his findings and ideas in an article in *Virology Monthly*. But then he and other researchers began having problems. The further they got into the DNA problem, the more complex they realized it was. The "C" particle might be in there somewhere among all the other particles, but where? It was like trying to examine one million nearly identical snowflakes—while the snowflakes were melting. And by the mid-1970s, virologists were also feeling pressured by their rivals, the immunologists. Immunology was now promising faster results than *any* virus research. So the virologists gave up the tedious hunt for the "C" particle and rationalized their decision by saying the particle didn't exist anyway.

But Paul Justin did not give up. He knew that, in the century since Pasteur, many ideas had been laughed at only to be eventually proven correct. So he persevered. But the few other virologists who knew of his work criticized it. So then Justin persevered more quietly. He spoke to no one about the "C" particle. He wrote his notes in a personal shorthand and kept them locked in his file cabinet. The most that anyone knew—Underwood, Wojik and perhaps Joan Scully— was that Justin still ran his pet project. And Underwood only barely tolerated it. He viewed it as the waste of a fairly good scientist. Some days Justin viewed it the same way.

But beginning one day in June of last year, Justin knew it was not a waste. Working with DNA from a man dying from lung cancer, Justin used several enzymes to break down a DNA molecule into smaller pieces, into rows of nucleotides. And using the electron microscope to go within the nucleotides, he spotted a particular pair of acid bases that seemed unusual.

Through the summer he compared this pair with the corresponding pair in healthy people and in people with a wide variety of cancers. A pattern emerged. In all healthy people the pair of acid bases had one configuration; in all cancer victims it had another.

Could these two configurations be the active and inactive modes of the "C" particle? The only way to test the idea was to build up an artificial RNA molecule which would include the suspicious acid base and then inject this RNA into a healthy person and see if cancer developed. But ethics forbade this. So Justin turned to hamsters. And found the same pattern!

At this point, self-restraint became a Herculean task. Normally, Justin would have rushed to publish his findings and establish priority. Only because of the unfavorable professional climate and because he knew no one else was pursuing the "C" particle was he able to stay silent.

Unlike humans, hamsters were fair game for experimentation. So in early December Justin synthesized artificial hamster RNA and included the suspected "C" particle from a cancerous hamster. He then injected it into a healthy hamster. The hamster quickly developed cancer. And Justin knew he had completed the century-old quest—he had definitely isolated the cancer virus! Paul Justin celebrated Christmas by treating Barbara and himself to a one-hundred-dollar dinner at La Caravelle in Manhattan. He told her he'd won the football pool at Oakes-Metcalf.

Then, in the new year, Justin synthesized artificial hamster RNA and included the suspected "C" particle from a *human* cancer victim. He injected it into another healthy hamster. This hamster developed cancer also. Justin's hopes soared. If active "C" particles from both humans and hamsters had the same effect, then perhaps the "programming" that would shut off one particle would shut off the other. A serum to cure cancer in hamsters would also cure cancer in humans.

Now, Justin told Barbara, he was on to something.

But how to actually construct the serum? Building the chemical programming device was at least 90 percent guesswork. Through the spring and early summer of this year, Justin's serum series A, B and C proved failures. Dozens of hamsters, racked with cancer which he could induce but not cure, died before his eyes.

Paul Justin kept pushing. And last Tuesday—nine days ago—

when he mixed the synthesized RNA protein and other chemicals to make serum D4, he felt he was getting closer. How close he did not know. Last Wednesday—eight days ago—Justin took three hamsters, into which, back in May, he had injected carcinogenic RNA, and gave them D4.

The hamsters had been cancer-ridden, torpid, on the verge of death. So on Thursday Justin was shocked to see they were eating a little. By Friday he could see their hair was growing back. My God, thought Justin, what's going on? He had never expected such a dramatic reversal.

Over the weekend, Paul Justin lost six straight sets of tennis. That wasn't like him. But he simply couldn't keep his mind off what might be happening back in the animal room.

On Monday, when his wife left for Boston, Justin barely noticed her departure. What counted was that he could see and feel that the hamsters' tumors had shrunk dramatically. By Tuesday, he couldn't detect them at all. Spontaneous remission? he wondered. For three animals that was an impossible coincidence. Still, Justin kept the news to himself. He wasn't going to be laughed out of the section.

Yesterday, Wednesday—exactly one week after the injection of serum—the hamsters seemed fine, recovered. Justin trembled at the sight. He was eager to kill them, cut them up and prove himself right or wrong. And he *could* prove it: As with all hamsters, he'd taken tissue samples when the animals were cancerous and from these samples he'd taken electron microscope photographs of their "C" particles in the active mode. Now, if the new photographs showed the particle in the inactive mode, his theory was proved.

But the goddamned cell surface project and liver project took up all of yesterday. Justin had to wait.

Until today. Now.

The blade chopped off the hamster's head. Paul Justin slit the hamster from neck to groin. The hamster's organs looked healthy. Justin removed the organs and started making tissue samples.

"Okay, fella," he said, pulling his chin. "Now what's really going on here?" He removed his eyeglasses and peered closer.

New York City

"And stay off it for a week," the internist said.
"Yeah," Lattimer said, grumpily.
"The hamstring has to have a chance to heal."
"Yeah."
"After all, you're not eighteen years old anymore."

"How did you know?" Lattimer asked.

The internist smiled smugly, closed the file folder he had opened on Lattimer, stood up and shook hands. Lattimer limped out of the internist's office and stared suspiciously at the hot, leaden sky that pressed down on the city. His right shin ached from the gash, his left thigh ached from the muscle pull, he had just wasted time and cab fare (thirty seconds after the hamstring pulled, another cab came by) to have a doctor tell him what he already knew, and now he suspected he was going to be caught in a downpour. And his pants were still in shreds.

What should he do? From the doctor's waiting room, Lattimer had called Lieutenant Whitcomb and told him about Vernon's murder (getting a wide-eyed look from the doctor's secretary—Lattimer could only imagine her look if he'd also reported his own near-murder). But that was as much as he felt like doing on the story today. The story required leg work and he didn't have two legs. Follow the doctor's advice, Lattimer advised himself, and go home to bed.

Except . . .

Except the conversation on the train this morning with Paul Justin nibbled at the edge of Lattimer's mind. Of course, there was probably nothing to it. But at least a few phone calls—to disprove it—would get it off his mind. And at least it would give him something he could *do* with the rest of the day. Now that there was nothing else to do.

Lattimer took a cab to Barney James's place. There he changed into a pair of Barney's pants—much too big for him—and poured himself a small J & B neat. He lay on his back on Barney's bed and shoved a pillow under his left thigh per doctor's orders. He pulled out his black book and turned to his list of doctors—not doctors like the smug internist (damn him), who were handy mainly for repairs, but doctors who had helped him with stories, doctors who had connections. (One was the county medical examiner whom Lattimer had gotten to know after a rape-murder-suicide story. Lattimer was tempted to tell the examiner that he'd nearly had a chance today to autopsy Lattimer.)

But what he said to the doctor was: Whom do you know who's big in cancer research who'll also give me some quick answers?

Supplied with a half-dozen names of cancer researchers, Frank Lattimer sipped scotch and started dialing. It was hard getting the researchers to the phone and hard getting them to talk. But Lattimer led them to believe that he was preparing a story for a major news-magazine and that he might even be sending out a photographer. Then, without mentioning Justin's name, Lattimer described the re-search which Justin had described to him. Is such research feasible?

he asked. Could it be getting close to a cure for cancer?

The researchers were eager to rebut such a ridiculous idea.

"The 'C' particle is the lazy man's shortcut," shouted Dr. Lewis Emory of Montefiore Hospital in the Bronx. "If, as we are certain, cancer is caused by *adding* genetic material to the cell—by a sick DNA molecule—then detecting that molecule is very hard. There are anywhere from a half million to more than one million DNA molecules per cell. How can we find one molecule among one million? That's a needle in a haystack. So of course, it's easier to believe that *every* DNA and RNA molecule contains a mysterious 'C' particle. But that makes as much sense as believing that the entire haystack is made of needles."

"And it can't be?" asked Lattimer.

"Of course not."

Lattimer called Dr. Wong Chu of Washington University in St. Louis. Chu gave the same objections that Emory had given but Lattimer persisted. "But just for argument's sake," he said, "let's assume that the 'C' particle did exist. If it did, how could it be found?"

"Well, it would be impossible," objected Chu. "A DNA molecule is incredibly complex. It contains several million different sequences— pairs of acid bases. To analyze each pair, to find out which *one* pair can cause cancer, is like looking for a needle in a haystack ... "

That cliché again, thought Lattimer.

" ... and that analysis is impossible today. We need advances in molecular biology, in electronics—advances we won't have for ten to twenty years."

"Thank you," said Lattimer. He called Dr. William DeVoe of Sloan-Kettering. DeVoe was equally negative.

"But assume," Lattimer persisted, "that someone *has* found the 'C' particle. What then?"

"What then?" DeVoe sputtered. "You mean how do we fight it, how do we turn it off? You talk blithely of RNA programming. You mean, I assume, getting RNA to the cancerous cell. But RNA is only the messenger molecule. *DNA* must be present to fight cancer."

"But I was told," said Lattimer, "that RNA could reverse the birth process and make DNA in its own image."

"That was Temin's theory," said DeVoe. "Disproved this spring."

"Oh," said Lattimer. He started to ask how it had been disproved but DeVoe had hung up. Lattimer shifted his leg.

New York City

In the personnel records of the Oakes-Metcalf Hospital and Institute, Roberto Cruz's previous employment was listed as Hermino's

Coffee Shop, Miami, Florida. This was not true. Nor was "Roberto Cruz" true. But the man who went by that name had been assured that, if anyone checked, his past and his identity would stand up. In fact, Roberto—which was how, since most people called him that, he mostly regarded himself—had a more interesting past. His actual previous employment was washing dishes in the State Penitentiary in Raiford. Before that he had been a numbers runner, small-time heroin dealer and finally, at age twenty, shakedown specialist. Then one liquor store owner didn't like being shaken down. Roberto was slashing the owner as the off-duty FBI man walked in. Roberto was arrested.

The FBI man, Ed Murdoch, knew Roberto. He knew that the slashing wasn't spontaneous. Roberto was, as always, simply following his employer's orders. Murdoch also knew Roberto was patient, could keep his mouth shut, had fair intelligence and almost no imagination. By the time Roberto got out of Gainesville, Murdoch was out of the FBI. And Murdoch now needed a man like Roberto. Roberto thought Murdoch's offer was crazy, but he accepted. In early May of last year Murdoch sent Roberto to New York, to take an apartment in east Harlem and apply for a lab assistant's job at Oakes-Metcalf, a job traditionally taken by poor Puerto Ricans.

Roberto mostly followed Murdoch's orders. He went to his job interview looking clean-cut. And he did have experience washing dishes, which wasn't much different from washing pipettes and cover slips. He was hired.

Roberto did well on the job and was well liked by the people in the virology section. But Roberto's real job was watching Dr. Justin's progress on his "C" particle project. Using the duplicate key he'd made, Roberto regularly opened Justin's file cabinet, Xeroxed copies of Justin's notes and mailed them to Murdoch at a post office box in Kansas City. And almost immediately, his effort paid off. One day in June, Roberto saw Dr. Justin look puzzled and fascinated over a photograph of a cell. After Roberto sent a copy of the photo to Kansas City, Murdoch wrote to Roberto's post office box in New York, to congratulate him. (Roberto and Murdoch agreed there should be no mail to Roberto's home address. The mailboxes there were often robbed.)

Through last summer and fall, Roberto sent more Xeroxed copies to Kansas City. Paul Justin noticed that Roberto was taking an interest—he thought it was only a casual interest—in Justin's work. This impressed Justin. He once suggested Roberto go to night school and become a lab technician. Roberto grinned. He sort of liked this scientist he was snooping on.

At Christmastime, Roberto saw Justin get excited again. And after he sent Justin's Xeroxed notes off to Murdoch, he got a special delivery letter demanding he call Murdoch at a number in Kansas City. When Roberto called, Murdoch said they'd have to stay in closer touch from now on and would Roberto, for Christ's sake, finally get a phone at home. (Roberto had said he didn't need one.) And Murdoch then put a "Mr. Smith" on the line. "Smith" described some of the things in Justin's experiments which Roberto should watch for. If he saw any, he should phone them at once.

Winter and spring passed and Roberto saw nothing. The people in Virology marveled at Roberto's dedication to the job, for the usual turnover in lab assistants was high. Roberto even stayed long enough to qualify for a vacation. He took one week of it last week. It was the wrong week to be away. When he returned this Monday, he called Murdoch and Smith about the sick hamsters that were starting to get well. Smith screamed at Roberto to send him all of Justin's notes from last week *now*! Then Roberto caught a few seconds of Murdoch and Smith screaming at each other—before they put him on hold. They kept him on hold for fifteen minutes, then told him to call back in an hour. When Roberto did call back, Smith said that he was sending Roberto photographs of hamster cells. He told Roberto that, when Justin killed and autopsied the hamsters, Roberto must compare these photos with the slides and photos Justin would make. And, Murdoch added, we're also sending you a small packet of pills and two small bottles of liquid medicine, one with an eyedropper dispenser. Bring them all to work and keep them handy but hidden. Murdoch also said that he and Smith were flying immediately to Colorado and Roberto must phone them there every day. Make that *twice* a day, said Murdoch.

By this time, Roberto had a fair idea of what was going on and he knew it wasn't crazy at all. The next day, Tuesday, he received the photos and the medicines. And he called Murdoch and Smith in Colorado to report the hamsters were still getting better. Wednesday he reported they seemed completely cured. This morning, Thursday, the same. And now, at 5:30, after everyone else on the eighth floor of the Institute had left for the day, Roberto Cruz again entered the animal room. Two of Dr. Justin's three hamsters lay dissected on the small table. Next to them was a neat stack of tissue slides. The third hamster still slept.

Roberto looked at the slides under the light microscope. They looked like Smith's photographs of normal hamster cells. Roberto left Oakes-Metcalf, walked to the phone booth down the block and called the number in Colorado. He told Murdoch and Smith what he had seen. Smith was even more excited than on Monday.

"But what about the photo from the electron microscope?" asked Smith.

"He hasn't looked yet," said Roberto. "Dunbar—from down the hall—was using the microscope from about four o'clock on."

"So Justin will get it first thing in the morning?" asked Murdoch.

"Yeah. After cell feeding time," said Roberto.

"All right," said Smith. "Tomorrow, during feeding time, you get hold of that medicine we sent you. And when Justin goes to the electron microscope . . ."

"Mr. Smith" explained the final responsibilities of "Roberto Cruz's" fourteen-month-long job.

Houston, Texas

All day, Matt Ash had been dreaming he was in an oil well. Deep underground in the warm, thick, black liquid, blind to everything, he was soothed and comforted. But the oil slowly buoyed him up toward the surface, toward pain. He realized this in his dream and he fought to stay down. It was in vain. In the early evening, Matt Ash broke through the surface and regained consciousness hurting like hell.

He saw a bunch of tubes stuck into him. He saw a young woman in white—a nurse, he realized—hovering over him. Ash thought she wore a shit-eating, fake-reassuring grin. So the operation was a failure. A strange thought entered his mind: Maybe I *am* gonna die. Ash yelled and thrashed around for her to get him out—"Out of this expensive mausoleum!" he yelled. To punctuate his remarks he farted. But the yelling gave him even more pain. Gasping for breath, he calmed down. The nurse hovered over him. Miss Jambois, she said her name was. She was young, plain and eager to please.

"Honey," Ash whispered, "fetch Goodhue."

Jambois did.

"Okay, Doc," said Ash, forcing a levity he didn't feel, "like they say on Marcus Welby, am I gonna die of this terminal dandruff or not?"

"What?"

"Gallows humor, Doc. I want to know—am I gonna die?"

Goodhue hesitated. "Yes," said Goodhue.

Huh! thought Ash. "How long?" he asked.

"Maybe—"

"No maybes, damn it."

"A month at the most," said Goodhue.

Umph, thought Ash. "And these scorpions crawlin' around in my belly?"

"The pain?" asked Goodhue.

"Yeah, the pain," said Ash. "Will it go on like this?"

Before the operation, Matt Ash had been willing to bear the pain, believing the operation would relieve it. But now, if he was going to die, he wasn't sure.

"I can give you more morphine," said Goodhue. "More demerol. But there's a limit to how often: only once every four hours. And there's a limit to what they'll do for you."

"Yeah," sighed Ash. "Okay," he sighed. "You can leave."

Goodhue did, gladly, leaving behind a whiff of cologne.

Ash regarded his surroundings again. Five hundred dollars per fucking day. And I might as well be in a ward at City Hospital. He looked at the sludge pumping through the transparent tube into his vein. The microwave oven in the suite's kitchen could turn out a steak in two minutes. But what could he do with it? Ash thought of the spreads he'd had on his ranch back in Big Springs, the ribs and chicken turning over on the massive barbecue, the—

Aaah. A wave of even greater pain swept up from his stomach and lungs, passed through the barrier of drugs and twisted his whole body. His throat constricted, gasped for air. His spine arched. Aaah . . .

Miss Jambois was hovering over him again.

"Is there anything—?" she began.

"Get the fuck out of here," he gasped. "Stick your . . . paid sympathy up your—" Aaaaah . . .

"I . . . " Jambois drew back, sat down in a Louis XV chair, still looking at her patient.

Jambois had been warned about Mathew Ash. But when she had first seen him in the recovery room, she had been impressed. Ash had a rugged face—all planes and angles. His high cheekbones hinted of Indian blood. Years in the sun had wrinkled his skin like old leather and had given his eyes a perpetual squint. He was topped by a crown of well-tended, pure white hair. He looked like a patriarch. And seeing his rough humor, Jambois had almost liked him. Well, that's a mistake, she thought. I guess I've just had a taste of being Mashed.

Shit, thought Mathew Ash, staring at the ceiling. The feast at Big Springs was a wisp, fading now with everything else he had ever enjoyed, fading with the smell of dust from the plains and the sweet smells of oil and crisp greenbacks and leather chairs at the Cattlemen's Club and sweet women's flesh . . .

This is worth shit, thought the seventy-eight-year-old man. Hurtin's worth shit.

Mathew Ash thought of his gun cabinets at home—smooth Winchesters and Purdys behind glass. He had put several horses and cattle out of their misery. He wished somebody would put him out.

"Virginia!" he yelled. "Get the hell in here! And you"—he pointed a shaking finger at Jambois—"Ah said get out."

The two women passed each other going through the door.

"Virginia, Ah—"

"Oh, Matt, I was down the hall. How long have you been awake? I'm so happy, so happy. How do you feel? I'm trying to get Reverend Trumbull to come here and I'm talking to one of his assistants and—" The words tumbled eagerly, excitedly, out of her soft, fleshy mouth. Her hands trembled rolls of fat.

Her husband cut her off.

"Shut up, goddamn it, and listen."

"Yes, Matt, yes. Anything."

"Ah want," Matt Ash started to explain, "to die—"

"No—"

"—and since Ah can't do it by myself—"

"—you must have hope—"

"Ah'd just mess up these tubes—"

"—and Trumbull—"

"—and Jambois sure ain't gonna help—"

"—will help—"

"—so that leaves you."

Virginia sat open-mouthed, stricken, as the man's words finally sank in.

"But Trumbull—" she said. "But God—*they'll* help!"

Ash roared at her. "There *isn't* any God!" he proclaimed. His eyes bored into her. "There isn't any—*any*thing!" As he had throughout their whole married life, so now, on the edge of death, Matt Ash imposed himself on her. His nostrils flared around the tubes stuck into them. "There is only me," he announced, "and you. And you," he commanded, "are gonna do this for me."

Virginia Ash's mind, never very orderly, was in a wild confusion. She knew she couldn't do what Matt wanted. She knew she had always done what Matt wanted.

Virginia Ash bolted from the room.

New York City

Joan Scully and David Crawford, the two doctoral students in the virology section of the Oakes-Metcalf Institute, were standing in line outside a movie theater on Manhattan's Upper East Side. Crawford had recently split from the girl he'd been going with for the last year. So he'd noticed that working next to him every day was a very pretty, vivacious, young, single woman. This was their first date. Crawford was trying to impress Joan Scully with his knowledge of cancer politics.

"Hell, you don't think I've been working on polyoma SV40 for a year because it's scientifically *valuable*, do you?"

"It isn't?" asked Joan.

"Well, sure—it is, a little," admitted Crawford. "But mainly it's because Hazeltine loves it. He's directing my Ph.D. at Cornell. And he's on the Board of Scientific Advisors."

"I didn't know that," said Joan. She did know that every three months, the Board came in from the outside and rated the Institute's work. Their ratings helped determine how much money different sections got.

"Sure," said Crawford. "Why, I'm doing us all a favor. God— Justin and that 'C' particle work he used to do nearly sank us a couple of times. Somebody's got to compensate."

"But couldn't you do other work—work you believed in—and still get your Ph.D.?" asked Joan. "I mean—that's what I'm doing."

"Oh, sure," said Crawford. "But this way, Hazeltine really notices me. I'm already helping him write his statement for the World Health Organization meeting in London next month. I may even fly over with him."

"Is that important?" asked Joan. She was playing dumb. If I were really honest, she thought, I'd let my anger show.

"You bet," said Crawford. "Hell, I'm not going to keep my nose in a test tube all my life, like poor Justin or Underwood. The *real* power in cancer is with the people who control the money. People like Hazeltine. People at NCI. People on Senator Prentice's staff."

Joan Scully felt that the National Cancer Institute was a bunch of thick-headed bureaucrats. She felt that Prentice's National Cancer Control Act was a political grandstand play. She was about to tell Crawford so—but why bother, she decided. Why argue with such an opportunist as he turned out to be?

The line moved and Joan Scully went into the movie slightly depressed. She'd known too many men like Crawford. Men she'd known in college—who were going on to med school for the money that doctors made. And other men she'd dated in New York—who scorned the ads they wrote or the TV shows they produced but loved the status. Even her own brother, an up-and-coming major in the air force. "Goddamn it, Joanie," he had yelled at her once. "I'm not a professional killer. I'm a systems analyst. I may not do any good but I certainly don't do any harm. And if I play my cards right, I'm set for life—right up to the Joint Chiefs."

As a cute, sexy little redhead, Joan Scully attracted many men who saw her as an ornament to complement their rising careers. As a bright woman who wanted a career of her own and usually spoke her own mind, she soon discouraged them. The only kind of man she really liked and respected was a man like Paul Justin. Now there, she thought, as the movie started, is someone who cares what he does, who does it for the value of the thing itself. Joan Scully knew a little bit of Justin's "C" particle work. And sometimes the sheer physical intensity of his body bent for hours and hours over that work even turned Joan on. That's the kind of man I want, she thought.

The movie, starring Warren Beatty, had some good, subtly and not-so-subtly erotic scenes. Joan Scully left it hungry for sex. But at the door of her apartment, she turned Crawford down. Nicely, because they had to keep on working together. But firmly.

Joan Scully went into her bedroom and took out her vibrator.

Dobbs Ferry, New York, and New York City

Paul Justin's naked-eye examination of his hamsters' organs had told him they were cured of cancer. His examination with the light microscope confirmed this. And after Dunbar left and the electron microscope was free, he could have gotten final confirmation. His slides—treated with enzymes to break the DNA down into nucleotides—were ready. But it had been late. Justin had phoned his son and asked if he could *please* find a baby sitter for the girls. Steve called back and said there weren't any available and he really wanted to go to see Governor Reed tonight. So shortly after five o'clock, with great reluctance, Paul Justin had left the Institute and caught a train to Dobbs Ferry. Watching the Hudson go by, he wondered if Louis Pasteur had had to interrupt discovering bacteria so he could get home and baby-sit.

This time, the train made the trip without incident. Justin took over from his son, fixed dinner for his daughters and then called the Yates home in Boston. But his mother-in-law told him Barbara had just left, to visit some friends. "Would you ask her to call me when she gets in?" he said. "And how *is* Barbara?" he asked. "I don't know, Paul," answered Elizabeth Everett Yates, "but something is bothering her." Something was bothering Melissa Justin, too. She was concerned about people who had Cancer as their zodiac sign. "Like my friend Sarah Klassen," she said. "I mean, Cancer. Yuk. That's awful." So, as it got dark, Justin took his elder daughter out on the front lawn, pointed at the newly appearing stars and tried to explain. "Cancer's just a constellation," he said. "A bunch of stars far away. They can't hurt you or help you." Still Melissa persisted. "But cancer's also a disease, isn't it? And it's really bad if you get it. And it's really hard to cure because even *you* can't do it. That's right, right?" "Yes," said Justin, "but it has nothing to do with the stars."

But Melissa still worried about her friend Sarah. And Laurie Justin was also upset—she missed her Mommy. And finally, by nine o'clock, after much comforting, Justin was able to tuck both girls in bed. At ten, Steve came home brimming with political enthusiasm. By eleven, Steve was also asleep. The cat was out for the night and Paul Justin was watching the TV news, bored, wishing his wife would call. She didn't. Missed connections and family blues, he thought. He finally went to sleep himself, marveling that such problems coexisted with the possible cure for cancer.

Down the block, Frank Lattimer cautiously pulled in on his motorcycle. He supposed his hamstring still ached but, with a half-dozen beers and an equal number of whiskeys in him, he could barely feel it. Barney James had returned to his apartment with two tickets for the fights at Madison Square Garden that night. And after the fights Barney demanded Lattimer match him drink for drink to celebrate all the bets he had won. God, thought Lattimer, groping for the front door, I didn't know Barney liked boilermakers. He found his bed and sprawled across it, fully clothed. "Cure for cancer. Cure for schmancer," he muttered to himself. "Tomorrow I'm gonna need a cure for a hangover." Tomorrow he'd also give Justin's story the burial it deserved and get back to something real.

Twenty-five miles away, in the eighth-floor animal room of the Oakes-Metcalf Institute, the one hamster that had been spared deaths by both cancer and the guillotine woke for the night.

FRIDAY

New York City

Every morning, the virology section of the Oakes-Metcalf Institute spent the first hour checking and feeding its supply of cells in the sterile room.

All the cells were on petri dishes, but different bacteria were in different stages. Today, Holmes and Beauchamp fed some cells with amino acids and serum from calf fetuses. Then they put these cells in the incubator. Meanwhile, Crawford and Scully took cells that had been fed days before. They removed the nutrient from these cells and then, using glass pipettes which Roberto Cruz supplied, they passaged the cells into bottles. These cells were now ready to be used in experiments. And some cells were already involved in experiments. Underwood, Wojik and Justin speculated on their progress.

"What do you think, Paul?" asked Underwood. "Are my liver cells doing best here—or not?"

"Where?" asked Justin.

Underwood pointed at one of three dozen petri dishes containing liver cells from rats with "Gunn rat" disease. In Gunn rat disease, the liver fails to produce glucuronyl transferase, a needed enzyme. So Underwood had added the enzyme and was now trying to make cells grow. He hoped eventually they would make their own glucuronyl transferase.

"Yes, Hugh," said Paul Justin. "We can transfer them now."

Joan Scully heard the disguised boredom in Justin's voice. She felt for Justin. She knew he itched to be on his "C" particle work. But she also knew that Justin—and she, herself—were lucky to have Underwood as a boss. True, the man was dull and plodding. But he was fair. Unlike Hazeltine, Underwood let his subordinates pursue work that honestly interested them and never took credit for their work. He was probably the only kind of boss that Joan Scully could work for. She knew she had a hard time playing second fiddle to any man. It wasn't that she was combative. It was—damn it—that she knew she was just as good.

Joan Scully watched Justin purse his thin lips as he listened to Underwood. With a sudden shock, she remembered the dream she had last night after giving herself an orgasm: Justin's mouth was pressing down on hers and she was yielding. Yielding willingly.

Joan Scully let out her breath—whoo—and blew a single note across the mouth of the glass pipette. She grinned at her dream. She shook her thick red hair. Well, she thought, well.

"So we're growing some liver," said Wojik, looking at the rat cells.

"If you manage to grow enough," put in Lou Beauchamp, "give me some. I destroyed my own last night."

"We were out drinking," explained Holmes. "A friend's bachelor party."

"Cooney in Immunology," said Beauchamp. "His fiancée's really his second choice," Beauchamp said to Joan. "He confided to me that it's you he really lusts for."

"You mean *you* do," said Holmes.

"Ah, my secret is out," laughed Beauchamp.

Joan Scully was glad it was just light banter. With Crawford wanting her and her own subconscious apparently wanting Justin, she couldn't take any more involvement with colleagues.

But Crawford didn't let it pass. "Ah, Lou," he said, "don't ask her out. She's unapproachable."

"Right," said Joan. "I'm dedicating my summer to my thesis. Try me in September, when I can relax as *Dr.* Scully."

"Speaking as a Ph.D.," said Dr. Wojik, "I know you will then be *totally* unapproachable." He exaggerated his Czech accent for effect and got a laugh.

"Yes," said Underwood, lost in thought, still looking at the cells. "They're almost covering the cover slip. Let's grow them out, Paul."

"Fine," said Justin. Underwood limped out of the sterile room and Justin followed.

In the kitchen, Roberto Cruz looked up. But no one was noticing him. He had already unwrapped the packet of pills which Murdoch and "Mr. Smith" had sent him. Now he unwrapped the two bottles of liquid.

Boston, Massachusetts

Barbara Justin had put off seeing a doctor for almost two weeks. By letting herself oversleep this morning, she put it off another hour. Now, at 10:30, as she turned onto the block of Commonwealth Avenue where Dr. Picard's house stood, she realized there was no turning back. So, to comfort herself, Barbara imagined that something else was bringing her here. She imagined herself a child again, coming here with her mother, for some typical childhood complaint—a strep throat perhaps. With a child's eyes she saw the trees arch high above the broad avenue. Her mother held her hand. Now be good for Dr. Picard, her mother had said, and he'll give you a lollipop. Barbara had always liked and trusted funny Dr. Picard.

Barbara Justin climbed the steps to Dr. Picard's door. She turned the antique, ornate door chime and walked in.

The hallway was as she remembered it. The rich, dark paneling. The old umbrella stand. The faded oil painting of the Rhone near Avignon. The painting brought back the romantic stories Dr. Picard had told her of this land of his birth—of the Roman amphitheaters, the antipopes and knights of the Middle Ages, Van Gogh painting in the burning fields of Arles . . .

Barbara's father had died when she was four. She had adopted Dr. Picard as the man in her life. In a way, he still was. If she had cancer, she wanted to hear it from him.

Barbara walked into the waiting room, gave her name to the nurse, whom she did not recognize, and took a seat with the other patients. The nurse went into the doctor's inner office and returned a moment later.

"Mrs. Justin, would you like to go in now?"

"Say," objected another woman. "I've been waiting half an hour. Why do you—?"

"It's all right," said Barbara to the nurse. "I am late. I'll wait."

"Well . . . " said the nurse.

Don't offer again, thought Barbara. Don't. I'll wait.

She picked up a magazine and buried her head in it. Fifteen minutes passed. A half hour. Forty-five minutes. The grandfather clock in the corner ticked away. The waiting room gradually emptied.

"Mrs. Justin," said the nurse.

Barbara had almost forgotten what she was doing here. She looked up. She was the only one left in the waiting room.

"Yes," said Barbara.

She walked into the inner office. Dr. Picard was there to meet her, a smile breaking his creased face. Barbara was momentarily taken aback. Picard looked so much older. But then, it had been— what?—ten years since she'd seen him last. Picard took her hands.

"Barbara. So nice. It's fine to see you again."

They stood looking at each other. Picard's face had aged and his dapper mustache had turned pure white. But he still held his slight body erect. And his blue eyes were still bright and lively. They seemed to miss nothing. His hands held hers firmly.

"And how is Paul? And the children? And . . . "

They chatted for a minute in the comfortable, familiar office. Barbara was pleased to discover that, through her mother, Picard had kept up with her life.

"Well," he said finally. "What brings you back here? Is this a social call on an old roué? Or perhaps, with the scanty medical knowledge I remember from the University of Lyons . . . ?"

Barbara smiled. She knew Picard read all the journals and attended all the medical conferences. He was fiercely proud that, as a G.P., he was as up-to-date as any specialist.

"It's your medical knowledge I want," said Barbara. "You see, I have"—she bit her lip—"this lump." She stopped.

"Where?" asked Picard.

"On my breast." She touched her left breast.

"When did you notice it?"

"About a week ago," she lied. She looked at Picard. "No. Twelve days ago." She couldn't lie to this man. She wanted to tell him all. How she had been in the shower, feeling warm and clean and alive—even allowing herself the pleasure of caressing her own body—and then how her soapy hand passed under her breast and felt a lump, a tiny little thing really, hardly there at all, but—there. And how she pretended not to have felt it and then how she wished it away but it didn't go away. And how she began to have dreams of it growing as large as a golf ball, then a tennis ball, then a softball, and how she woke sweating, needing another shower, but no shower could wash it away.

But how could she tell Picard this? "I'm a little worried," was all that Barbara Justin said.

"Well," said Picard, "let's see about that. First, let me check my records." He went to a big, old, wooden filing cabinet. "Now, I know I have your mother's file here and—ah, yes, you, too." He brought both back to his desk and opened them. "Yes," he said, studying them. "Fine. Now, since I saw you last, have you . . . ?" And Picard took a brief medical history of Barbara's last ten years. And then how had she been feeling recently? Any loss of weight or appetite? Any pains? No? "Good," he concluded. He consulted the files again. "Now. I don't see it here, but is there in your family any history of cancer?"

The word, thought Barbara. For the first time the word had been spoken aloud in reference to herself. Picard said it calmly but, to Barbara, it hung in the air of this handsome office like an obscene remark, a four-letter word. Despite the fact that it was Paul's line of work—and thus a casual word at their dinner table—it was like hearing it now, *really* hearing it, for the first time. Cancer. Can-cer. It had a soft, sweet, high sound. The body feasting on itself, slowly eating its sweet meat alive. Can-cer. Can-nibalism.

Barbara shuddered. Where did this morbidity come from? she wondered. It was so unlike her. "No, no history of cancer," said Barbara, briskly. Not in my family. I think—she thought. But she remembered the first and last time she saw Paul's father, before he died.

"All right," said Picard. He stood up and escorted her to the examining room. The room gleamed with modern instruments. We're getting closer, thought Barbara. Closer to medicine, to disease. "If you'll undress," said Picard, "and put on this gown and then lie on this table, on your back, I'll be right in." He left. Barbara did as she was told. She stared at the ceiling. She tried to keep her mind a blank.

Picard returned. He smiled down at her. He looked like a thin, spry god, cheerful but serious. If I do die, thought Barbara, and if there is a God, I hope He has the grace to resemble Dr. Picard.

"Now, if you'll untie the gown," he said.

In Dobbs Ferry, Barbara's doctor was a woman gynecologist. It had been many, many years since Barbara had been naked in front of any man except Paul.

She untied the white gown.

"Now, if you'll put your hands behind your head . . . "

She did.

Once Picard started touching her, Barbara relaxed. And, after having delayed it so long, she found the examination went very fast and matter-of-factly.

"You know," said Picard, casually, as he probed and moved her left breast, "there are lumps and there are lumps. In women under thirty, a lump is usually a simple cyst. Now you are thirty-seven . . . ?"

"Yes," said Barbara.

" . . . so there is some chance of cancer," said Picard. "But you are still having regular periods, correct?" he asked.

"Yes."

"And that's good. Because only *after* menopause would a lump almost certainly be cancer."

Barbara nodded.

"Nor is the skin over the lump shriveled. And the lump itself does not seem attached to the muscle. Fine."

Picard was now probing under Barbara's left arm.

"And I don't find anything in the nodes," he said, "and that is good, too."

This was another reason why Barbara had always liked André Picard. Unlike most doctors, he talked to you. He told you what you might have and how he would treat it—in uncomplicated, unpatronizing language. This made his manipulation of her breast a lot less uncomfortable.

Picard now examined her right breast.

"But I don't have—" she began.

"If it *is* cancer, it's probably here, too," he said.

"But," he said after another minute, "I feel nothing here. So we must contend with this one lump. Let's get an X-ray." Picard summoned his nurse.

"Helen," he said, "we need a mammogram of Mrs. Justin." He gestured to Barbara to go with the nurse.

In the X-ray room, the X-ray plates felt cold and hard against her. The nurse only spoke to ask her to turn left, turn right, hold up the breast, let it go, hold up the other.

"I thought X-rays just showed broken bones," she said to the nurse.

"You never heard of a mammo—?" the nurse stopped herself.

"No, I guess I haven't," said Barbara, catching the amazement in the nurse's voice. I guess I *am* naive, she thought. And I guess I'd better get over it.

"Well," said the nurse, "it can tell Dr. Picard the shape and density of a lump. Plus if there are any hidden lumps anywhere."

"Oh," said Barbara. Hidden lumps, she thought fearfully. She wasn't sure if she appreciated the nurse's being as frank as Dr. Picard.

They finished. The nurse told Barbara she could return to the examination room and put her clothes back on. Barbara did, with great relief. She took her time, adjusting her blouse and skirt just so, carefully rebuilding her public self. She felt she had been stripped bare in several ways.

She emerged into Picard's office as the doctor was examining the developed X-rays. She joined him.

"What do you see?" Barbara forced herself to ask. Faced with the X-rays, she felt vulnerable again. She was now not stripped to the flesh—the X-rays stripped her even deeper.

"No other lumps," said Picard. "Just this one. And"—he turned to her and shrugged an expressive French shrug—"I don't know. I'm not a specialist. I take it you're returning to New York?"

"Yes. Tomorrow."

"Well, ask Paul who his favorite doctor is at Oakes-Metcalf and I'll send the X-rays there. But do it immediately, Barbara. Call him today."

"All right," said Barbara. She understood she was being chided for waiting almost two weeks before having this examination. If it is cancer, she knew, it would spread fast.

Picard must have read her mind. "And don't worry, Barbara. It's not about to spread all over. Within the week, your surgeon will have it out. And its location is good, too. If it *is* benign the fact that it's under the breast means a scar won't show. And it may very well be benign. If it were cancer, it'd more likely be on the outside of the breast and higher up."

"But if... anyway... it is..." Barbara couldn't finish the sentence. She visualized, vaguely, her eventual death. And more concretely, she saw her disfigurement, the surgeon's knife descending to lop off her breast.

"If it is cancer," said Picard, again reading her mind, "you do not necessarily have to lose the breast. Depending on what your man in New York finds, he could recommend a partial or subcutaneous mastectomy. And since the lump is far from the nipple, the nipple could be saved. And there's a high cure rate for breast cancer. Almost two-thirds, I believe." Picard took her hands again. "But I'm getting far ahead of myself, Barbara. We don't know it even *is* cancer."

She looked up at Picard. Barbara was only a few inches shorter than the doctor, but she still looked up to him as she had when she was a child. She saw her reflection in his quizzical, smiling eyes.

"Thank you, Dr. Picard," she said, as she had said years ago.

"Thank you for coming, Barbara," he said. "I'm very touched. And tell me what happens, please."

"Yes," she said. She squeezed his hands once and turned to leave.

"And next time, bring the children," said Picard. "I'd love to see them. And they might like a lollipop."

She turned back to him and smiled. "Of course," she said. And I could use one, too, she thought.

This time Picard did not read her mind. He waved briefly and Barbara found herself going out the door, through the waiting room and down the front steps, alone again. She felt a confusion of hope, fear and gratitude. What have I really learned? she wondered, walking unseeing down the avenue. I don't know if I *have* cancer. I don't know if I *don't* have cancer. After two weeks of waiting all I've learned is I'm going to have to wait a little longer. And the final verdict would come not from warm Dr. Picard but from some unknown specialist in New York.

Correction, thought Barbara. I've also learned that cancer or not, they're going to cut into my breast. The thought chilled her, a cool stainless steel blade cutting through the warm, leafy sunshine. She slumped in despair. It was not unexpected—she had somehow always known that something like this was going to happen. But having known it didn't make it any easier.

I've got to tell Paul, thought Barbara. She hurried home from Dr. Picard's to call the other man in her life.

New York City

Shortly before eleven o'clock, Paul Justin was able to get away from Underwood. He went to the file cabinet and removed the folder with his coded notes. He looked at the photographs of the "C" particle to make sure he'd recognize it. Then, taking a cup of coffee from Roberto Cruz, he crossed the hall to the animal room.

His slaughtered hamsters and his slides were where he'd left them. He took the enzyme-treated slides into the electron microscope room. He sat down and turned on the machine. He loaded film into the machine's camera. Sipping his coffee, he increased the microscope's magnification to the millionth power. He focused on a nucleotide and increased magnification to the limit, two million times normal size. The picture of the particular pair of acid bases—the "C" particle—appeared on the attached TV screen.

The pair were in their normal, inactive mode.

He had cured the hamsters of cancer.

Paul Justin took a deep drink of coffee. He set the cup down on the console. He pressed a button to take a photograph. I've done it, he thought, trembling a bit, I've done it, haven't I? A dozen years of hard labor had led to this moment and now that it was here he couldn't quite believe it. It was easier to believe that the TV screen showed something different, that the hamsters' recovery was some horrible coincidence, that he'd have to scrap all his work and put in another dozen years. But no—I've done it, I've really done it, Justin told himself.

A series of images flashed through his mind: Watching his father bang out "Joy to the World" on the family piano with one hand the Christmas after the left arm was amputated. Struggling with a microbiology text at 4 A.M. while trying to feed his baby son Steven a bottle. Pounding his fist on the lab table when his cell respiration work was failing five years ago—his fist accidentally smashing a test tube, driving glass slivers into his hand.

Justin looked at his hand now. It shook a little. He imagined what was to come: showing his findings to Underwood and then to Brown, the head of the Institute. Getting permission to try his serum D4 on human volunteers. The day—when?—weeks, a few months from now?—when the first dying person was cured of cancer. And then another and another in a spreading flood. And then modifying the serum to be a vaccine—an innoculation against cancer. And thus the final death of the disease, the end of King Cancer. My God—the impact of that! Justin knew the statistics well. One out of every four Americans gets cancer. One out of every six Americans dies of cancer. So his vaccine would save thirty-five million of his countrymen alive today. And how many more lives around the world? And the lives of how many people yet unborn who would otherwise get the disease? And how much physical and emotional suffering that went with it?

Until now, Paul Justin's world had been his daily routine. Up in the morning, breakfast with his family, kiss Barbara good-bye, take the train and settle into his lab work. Now his world exploded to encompass the whole world. For what would the world do for the person who was about to save hundreds of millions of lives, deliver it from the horror of cancer? Paul Justin had not sought fame. But he realized that, by comparison, Fleming's discovery of penicillin and Salk's polio vaccine were like inventing Band-Aids. Why, the world would give him, Paul Justin, all that it had. Money. Power. The Nobel Prize. The adulation that would utterly transform his small, private life.

His mind was exhilarated but his body was suddenly, strangely, being overcome by a vast lassitude. Justin imagined it was allowing itself to relax after years of constant effort. He started to rise from the electron microscope. He was too tired to speak any momentous words to announce his discovery: he had no "giant leap for mankind." He simply wanted, before their lives were changed utterly, to drag himself to the phone, call Boston and say, "Hello, Barbara. How're you doing? I've missed you. And I've got some good news."

Justin rose and started to turn. He couldn't. He felt heavy, groggy. He put out a hand to steady himself. He slumped back into his chair. Wow, thought a tiny, alert part of his mind, what a powerful psychological reaction. But that part was being overwhelmed by waves of sleep. Justin let his head drop onto the console, narrowly missing the coffee cup. He was dimly aware of somebody walking toward him. Then he was unconscious.

Roberto Cruz had told the people in the virology section that he was going to get more flasks from the supply room. But for the last thirty seconds Roberto had been silently watching Justin and the TV screen. Roberto had not been able to tell whether the picture on the screen was what "Smith" had hoped for. But Justin's excitement was enough. Now, with Justin unconscious from the pills Roberto had put in his coffee, Roberto could act.

Swiftly he put the syringe through the top of one of the bottles and drew 2 cc's of the colorless liquid. He took Justin's right arm, rolled up the sleeve of the lab coat and, with rubber tubing, tied a tourniquet above the elbow. A vein bulged out, throbbing. He pricked it with the syringe and drew the syringe back a little, drawing a little blood to make sure he was actually in the vein. He wiped away the blood. Then he released the tourniquet and drove the plunger down all the way. Justin's unconscious body jerked and stirred.

As Cruz watched, fascinated and horrified, all the muscles in Justin's arm started to twitch and ripple. Like a bunch of worms, Cruz thought. He looked at Justin's face. The rippling had spread there, too. And suddenly Justin's breathing was very shallow.

Cruz continued to do as he had been told. He drew 8 more cc's into the syringe. He lifted Justin's body and unbuckled his belt. He pulled down Justin's pants. Trying to ignore the rippling that convulsed the scientist's buttocks—Jeez, his whole body is going crazy, thought Cruz—Cruz drove the syringe into the right buttock.

He redressed Justin and sat him in the chair. He stuffed the syringe, bottle, tubing and a bloody Kleenex into his pocket. He also pocketed Justin's slides. He switched off the electron microscope. Then he waited.

The seconds ticked away. "Smith" had said it would take only a minute. Cruz hoped so—he couldn't stand watching Justin's face. And suppose somebody walked in?

The rippling slowed down, then stopped. Justin was completely rigid. He was barely breathing. Cruz quickly emptied the cup of coffee onto the floor next to Justin. Then he pushed Justin—it was like pushing a stiff corpse—off the chair.

Paul Justin hit the floor on the right side of his head, breaking the frame of his eyeglasses. Cruz took out the second bottle, squeezed its eyedropper, pushed up Justin's eyelid and let a drop fall into his right eye. Then Cruz stood up. He was scared. He was almost as paralyzed as Justin. He liked the scientist enough not to want to kill him. He hoped "Smith" was right: that if he got help fast, Justin *wouldn't* die.

Roberto Cruz snapped out of his paralysis. He ran from the room. "Dr. Underwood! Dr. Underwood!" he yelled as he dashed down the hall to the virology section. "Help! Help!"

Dobbs Ferry, New York

Frank Lattimer had awakened earlier with his predicted hangover, but had been unable to get out of bed. Then, figuring that nothing would be as sobering as news of a plane crash or earthquake, he made it downstairs and picked *The New York Times* off his doorstep. There was no such news on the front page. But his lawn was sobering enough.

"Oh, hell," swore Lattimer. He stared at the lawn. It had been high when he cut it yesterday and, in his rush to finish it and catch the train, he hadn't raked off the cut grass. And though he had sensed rain, rain hadn't come. Instead, all day yesterday, the hot sun had burned the clumps of cut grass and burned the fresh grass underneath. His lawn was yellow patches.

"Hell, hell, hell." Lattimer looked at the ruined grass. He couldn't face it. He went back inside and opened the refrigerator, thinking of something nice and cheerful, like orange juice. But he couldn't face the food either. His stomach turned. He sat down at the kitchen table and opened the *Times* to the sports section. He looked forward to losing himself in mindless hits, runs and errors.

The phone rang.

"Hello?" Lattimer managed.

"Good morning," said the man's voice, doing a sarcastic version of a cheerful wake-up service, "and how is everything at B & B Meat Purveyors?"

What? thought Lattimer, not entirely with it. A threat? Had Tommy Vernon's employers traced him?

"I said—" began the man again.

"Ah, hell, Knappy," said Lattimer, recognizing the voice. "What is it?"

"What is it?" asked Oliver Knapp, who was the assistant city editor and Lattimer's boss. "What is it?" The irony in the voice was now losing out to indignation. "I only thought that you might contact us once in a while. Come in and type up a story perhaps? Or, if you've forgotten how to type, perhaps phone it in? Or are we only your answering service? In that case, perhaps instead of *us* paying you—"

"Aw, Knappy—"

"Aw, yourself, Ace. Look, have you also forgotten how to read? No? Well, do you, by any chance, up there in your bucolic fiefdom, happen to have this morning's *Times*?"

"Um," said Lattimer. Among his running battles with Knapp was Knapp's insistence that anyone who covered the city ought to damn well *live* there.

"Turn to page twenty-six," ordered Knapp.

Lattimer did so.

"You see it?" demanded Knapp.

"Um," said Lattimer. At the bottom of the column headed "Metropolitan Briefs" was a small story about Tommy Vernon. It wasn't much of a story. Just body found, police investigating. Just somebody copying the facts from the police blotter.

"Well?" demanded Knapp.

"Well what?"

"Jesus Christ, do I have to spell it out for you? You tell me for the past month you're onto this story about Spaeth and this major meat company." (Spaeth was the deputy mayor.) "It's so big, it's taking up most of your time. So while you develop it, you hardly file anything."

"That's not true," said Lattimer. He hated to defend himself against Knapp, but it was necessary. "I filed—"

"So yesterday," continued Knapp, running over him, "there's a *murder* for Christ's sake at your meat company and how do I find out about it? Not from you. Oh, no. From Kincaid at police headquarters."

"Kincaid's a great police reporter," said Lattimer. "Keep him on."

"Keep him longer than you, I think. So we're going this afternoon with what Kincaid's got, which is the same as what the *Times* has got, which is the same as what the *News* and the *Post* have got. Which is zilch. Unless, of course, you'd like to add a word or two—seeing's how"—the sarcasm was thick—"you're on the story."

"Thanks for the offer, Knappy," said Lattimer, "but nothing to add."

"Why?"

"Prejudice the rest of the story."

"There *is* a story?" demanded the assistant city editor.

"Yep."

"Then have it typed on my desk Monday morning. *I'd* like to feel as confident as you are. And you could include in there how Vernon was your informant and how you found his body."

"What?"

"Come on, Frank," said Knapp. "It stands to reason. Kincaid says the murder was reported to Whitcomb. Not 911. Not the local precinct. To *your* friend. And Donna at the switchboard says you called yesterday asking if Vernon had called. About the time the M.E. says Vernon was very dead."

"A coincidence," said Lattimer. "Two coincidences."

"Gimme the story so far," said Knapp. "By 9 A.M. Monday."

"Or?"

"Or go to work for the Dobbs Ferry *Gazette*."

"Ha, ha," said Lattimer.

"Ha, ha," said Knapp, tonelessly. He hung up.

Frank Lattimer made a face at *The New York Times*. He knew Knappy's request was a fair one. But this morning, the sarcasm and the threats (even though the threats weren't serious) were too much to take. Lattimer felt he had to get out of here. He stalked off to the garage and grabbed a rake. With aching legs and aching head, he attacked the ruined grass, pretending it was Knapp and all editors.

As he raked, Lattimer looked at the Justin home down the street. It was a neat colonial, quiet under the maples and elms. There was no activity there. Justin must be down in the city by now, Lattimer thought, back in his lab. What's he really doing there?

Frank Lattimer finished raking and went back inside. If it hadn't been for Knapp's call, he might have typed up what he had so far on the B & B story—if only to help keep it straight in his head. But after Knapp's call, he'd be *damned* if he'd do it today. Instead, Lattimer pulled out his list of cancer researchers.

New York City

Roberto Cruz rushed down the corridor. As he passed the elevator, Dr. Hatch of Immunology stepped out with a sheaf of papers in his hand. Roberto banged into Hatch and sent the papers flying. "Electron microscope room," blurted Roberto, pointing over his shoulder as he kept on running. "Justin!" Hatch started to retrieve his papers, thought better of it and ran toward the electron microscope room. As Roberto reached the door to Virology, it burst open and Crawford and Wojik, attracted by Roberto's cries, came rushing out. Roberto dodged and barely missed banging into Wojik. "What is it, man?" demanded Crawford. "Dr. Justin," said Roberto. "He's hurt. On the floor. Electron microscope room." The two researchers dashed off.

By now all the doors on the eighth floor were flying open and staff members were rushing out. They crowded to the door of the electron microscope room. Roberto walked back to the room and watched, fascinated, over their shoulders.

Hatch had been the first to reach Paul Justin. He knelt at his side, though he didn't know what to do. Like almost all the researchers at the Institute, Hatch was a Ph.D., not a medical doctor.

"Get help from the hospital," he called as Crawford and Wojik burst in.

"Damn it," yelled Joan Scully, coming in swiftly behind them, "he's not breathing. Get some air into him."

"What?" asked Hatch.

"I'll get help," said Underwood, who had also come to the door.

Joan Scully had been around doctors and infirmaries all her life. She remembered fifteen years ago—a hockey player ramming himself unconscious on the boards and barely breathing. So she did now what her father had done then.

She stuck her left hand into Justin's mouth to get his tongue out of the way. Justin's teeth snapped down hard on her. Joan Scully ignored it. With her other hand, she started taking Justin's pulse. "Don't wait for the hospital," she said. "Get a cart."

"What kind of cart?" asked Crawford.

But Joan didn't answer. She had her mouth full on Justin's and was steadily, firmly forcing air into the man. Last night's dream came back to her. She dismissed it.

Crawford stared at Joan. He was angry. He almost envied Justin. More people were now crowding into the room.

"Get out," cried Stefan Wojik. "Out. Don't get in the way."

"Cart?... What?" Crawford asked Hatch.

Hatch started to shrug his shoulders.

"Lab cart, goddamn it," said Joan, tearing her mouth away. "In the closet. Next to the john." She went back to her resuscitation.

Hatch pushed through the crowd and disappeared. Wojik held the crowd back.

"Let me in," demanded a section head, up from another floor. "What's going on?" asked another technician. But Wojik, who instinctively felt Joan Scully knew what she was doing, stood as firm as if he were barring the Russians from entering his native Prague.

"Okay, David," announced Joan. "Your turn."

"I—" he stammered.

"It's not the Continental Baths, for Christ's sake," she said. "It's a dying man."

Crawford tried to ignore the homosexual reference. He dropped to his knees and started pumping his mouth on Justin's.

As he did, Joan started taking off Justin's shoe. "It could be a heart attack," she said to no one in particular, "but he's got a good pulse. And since he seems to be... paralyzed... maybe a stroke?" She stroked the bottom of Justin's foot. "But no Babinski reflex," she said, noting that the toes failed to fan out, "so maybe not. So"—she peeled back Justin's eyelids—"yeah, dilated. Possible head injury. Right side. Why? Did he just fall?" She felt something wet and then saw the cup. "Coffee. Spilled coffee. So he slipped? But paralyzed like this... have to be a stroke?" She turned to Wojik. "And where in the hell is the cart?" she cried. "We've got to get him over there. Where's Hatch?"

"Your turn," gasped Crawford. He looked at Joan. He was torn between being angry at her and being impressed by her. He desired her even more than last night.

Joan didn't notice. She put her mouth back on Justin's—as Hatch came pushing the cart through the crowd.

Joan Scully frowned at the papers clutched in Hatch's hand. The man had taken the time to retrieve them from the floor outside.

"You..." she started to say, angrily. She bit her lip. "Okay," she said instead. "Up he goes." Hatch, Crawford and Joan Scully lifted Justin onto the cart. "Okay," she yelled, "let's go!"

"Out of the way," cried Wojik, as they spun the cart through the doorway.

Crawford pushed, Hatch ran ahead to get the elevator, Joan Scully ran alongside. She looked down at Justin's crumpled, rigid body, at his long, blood-drained face contorted by the silent struggle going on in his brain. Justin's eyelashes—so pale they were almost invisible—were the only part of him that moved, barely fluttering, like a wounded butterfly. "Come on," Joan quietly urged Justin. All around them, people were milling and jabbering. The elevator doors were opening. They had to get Justin down to the sixth floor and across the bridge to the hospital. There was very little time. Joan Scully put her mouth back on Justin's and kept on keeping him alive.

The elevator doors closed behind them, leaving in their wake Roberto Cruz, staring at the whole wild scene.

Roberto, of course, was not supposed to be witnessing the confusion. "Smith" had told him to *use* the confusion. After getting help, Roberto was supposed to go back to the virology section and, for the last time, unlock Justin's file cabinet and remove the entire folder on RNA programming and serum D4. Remove it this time not for Xeroxing but to send to Colorado.

But Roberto, swept up in the chaos he had caused, momentarily forgot his mission.

New York City

In his haste to get to the electron microscope, Paul Justin had failed to return his file folder to his file cabinet. The cabinet drawer was open. The folder lay on his desk, open to photographs of a "C" particle. While Justin was out using the microscope, many of his colleagues had passed his desk, but none paid it any attention. Then, when he had his stroke, all his colleagues rushed out. But Hugh Underwood limped back to call the hospital emergency room. And Underwood, who knew he couldn't do anything more for Justin, stayed in the section.

Underwood was alone. Ignoring the noise outside, he intended to resume his liver study. Moving toward his liver cells, he passed Justin's desk. His sharp, trained eyes fell on the folder.

What, Underwood asked himself, stopping and fingering the photographs, do we have here?

A pair of DNA acid bases, he answered. The same pair over and over in photo after photo. But not quite the same pair—two different configurations of the same pair. What causes that? Underwood wondered. He'd love to find out. But he hesitated. He and Paul Justin had an unspoken agreement: As long as Justin didn't let his "C" particle work eat up too much time, Underwood wouldn't pry into it. And anyway, Underwood didn't like going through another man's papers. But would Justin ever recover now to reclaim these papers?

Hugh Underwood's fingers itched to flip past the photographs and read Justin's notes. They were unusually well-behaved fingers. At work, they knew how to rest in his lap listening to someone describe a theory or a problem. At home, they knew enough not to touch his wife when—as usual—she wasn't in the mood. They knew how to be patient.

His itchy fingers flipped past the photographs. His eyes quickly scanned the notes. Underwood was simultaneously impressed and frustrated. The notes were voluminous and meticulous, apparently detailing step after step, experiment after experiment. Underwood had no idea Justin had gone into DNA nucleotides this deeply. But, frustratingly, Underwood couldn't figure out what Justin had found. The notes were in some sort of shorthand, a code that was almost baffling.

Almost but not quite. Underwood knew, in general, how one might go about looking for the "C" particle. So from some of Justin's strange abbreviations, he could start to guess at some of Justin's findings. And his first guesses were tantalizing. Why, thought Underwood, if *this* symbol means *this* and if these figures on this page mean *that*, then . . .

My God, thought Underwood, I think the man has actually found the "C" particle! *That's* what the photographs are. And more than that, Underwood realized. What Justin had begun working on— maybe he's already found—a way to shut the particle off!

Dr. Hugh Underwood shut the folder swiftly. Instinctively, he knew it was a Pandora's box which he should never have looked into. But he had. And out of it had sprung knowledge that he could not now lock up. What could he do with the file—put it back? No. It could be misplaced and that would be a tragedy. I'll keep it safe for Paul, Underwood quickly decided. If he recovers, it'll be waiting for him. And if he doesn't . . .

Hugh Underwood refused to think about what he would do in that case. And he refused to analyze why, along with excitement, the file also filled him with fear and depression. Black depression. Blacker than his skin.

The door to Virology opened. Underwood shoved the file under his lab coat. He closed the open drawer of the file cabinet and it automatically locked. As swiftly as he could, he limped away from Justin's desk. As Roberto Cruz came in, Underwood made it back to his liver cells. He stood there as if, for the past twenty minutes, he'd been completely engrossed in Gunn rat disease.

Roberto Cruz remembered he had to get Justin's file and he dashed back into Virology. The section looked empty—he didn't see Underwood—and he went for Justin's file cabinet. With a quick twist of his duplicate key, he opened it. But to Roberto's horror, the file was gone. Roberto rifled the cabinet again. Everything else was there, but not the one file which Smith and Murdoch wanted so badly. Roberto's knees went weak with fear. He looked frantically around him. Could it be in the desk? Or jammed under those books? He started to look. But then someone came in behind him.

It was Beauchamp, and Holmes and Wojik were on his heels.

"Lou," said Cruz, straightening up fast, "will he be okay?"

"I don't know," said Beauchamp. "I guess we wait."

"It's a good thing you were walking past and saw him," said Wojik to Roberto, "or I don't think there'd be a chance."

"Yeah," said Roberto.

"What happened, Roberto?" asked Underwood, coming from around one of the room dividers—and Roberto had a sudden stab of panic. So Underwood had been here all the time. Had he seen or heard him open the cabinet? Apparently not—Underwood gave no indication of it. "Did you see what happened to him?" continued Underwood, "why he fell? Or was he already on the floor? Or what?"

Roberto told the four men his version of what had happened to Justin. Then everybody praised Wojik for guarding the door. And they said what a great job Joan Scully and David Crawford had done helping Paul. They tried not to speculate on what the verdict might be across the street right now, where Joan and David were delivering their colleague. It was sinking in on them that Paul Justin might have suffered brain damage or might even die.

"And he's a nice guy, too," said Roberto.

"Yeah," said Holmes.

There was little more to say. Paul Justin had been a pleasant man, but also an intense and reserved man who for some time had been marching to a different drummer. His colleagues really hadn't known him very well. An awkward silence descended.

"Well," said Underwood, clearing his throat and reaching for a phone. "I guess I'd better call . . . his wife." But there was no answer in Dobbs Ferry. And that, for now, was that. The researchers drifted back to work and then down to the cafeteria for lunch. Scully and Crawford hadn't returned yet. Roberto Cruz remained behind briefly. Into a wastebasket in the kitchen he dropped the syringe, tubing, vial and eyedropper. He crumpled some paper and dropped it over the evidence, hiding it. He thought some more about the missing file. Justin must have taken it, he nervously decided. Fighting back his fear, Roberto went outside to call Colorado.

New York City

When Joan Scully and David Crawford got across the bridge to the hospital, they were met by a crash team coming the other way. The crash team, led by a surgical resident, snatched Justin and rushed him to the nearest treatment room. Joan followed. She stood by, watching anxiously, her colleague's fate now out of her hands. The resident stuck a tube down Justin's throat, attached a black bag to the tube and started squeezing the bag to force Justin to breathe. He asked Joan, "Who is this? What happened?" and Joan tried to explain. One of the nurses started an intravenous line and another nurse started taking Justin's blood pressure and then the resident yelled, "Get him down to ICU and call a neurosurgeon," and the nurses wheeled Justin out fast. Joan, alone with the resident for a moment, asked what was wrong with Paul. "I don't know," said the resident, "but whatever it is, I think you saved his life. At least for now. And you'd better get your fingers bandaged. They're bleeding."

Joan slumped wearily into the nearest chair.

Dobbs Ferry, New York

Frank Lattimer called Dr. Barry Zimmerman of Johns Hopkins in Baltimore. Lattimer described Justin's theory and listened to Zimmerman's objections, which were very familiar by now.

"But assume," said Lattimer, "that the particle does exist, has been found and that RNA programming—based on Temin's theory—is feasible."

"Feasible?" laughed Zimmerman. "Do you know what chemical programming really is? Do you think it's something that can be learned in night school, like IBM programming? Listen, my friend, RNA programming would mean manipulating individual pairs of bases—individual *atoms*, for God's sakes. Does anyone know how to do that today? No!" Zimmerman calmed down a bit and said, "Now, about my research, I think your readers might be interested to know ... "

After listening for a decent minute or two, Lattimer managed to hang up. He called Dr. Beatrice Sachs of New York Hospital. She also doubted the theory and doubted anything could be done without more sophisticated scientific tools.

"But assume they existed," said Lattimer.

"Well then," said Sachs, "the research you describe would take an entire *team* of people several *decades*. And you say this was done by one man—in only five years?"

"Yes."

"Science fiction," snapped Sachs.

Lattimer's last call was to Dr. Henry Neuwirth of Peter Bent Brigham in Boston. As Lattimer outlined the research for the half-dozenth time, Neuwirth interrupted.

"Is this Justin you're talking about? You mean he's nutty enough to *still* pursue this harebrained thing?"

Lattimer denied that the research was Paul Justin's. He hung up, crossed Neuwirth's name off the list and was very happy there were no more names.

Lattimer got up and stretched. His hangover seemed to be fading, but now his neck was stiff from where he'd been cradling the phone for the past half hour. And his fingers were stiff from taking notes—although with each phone call he had written less and less. There was simply less and less evidence that Justin was doing anything in that lab. In fact, that should be it. It was time to get back on B & B and the deputy mayor.

Still . . . Frank Lattimer half remembered a quote from somewhere. Something about "when a distinguished scientist tells you an invention is impossible, someone else is almost certain to invent it . . ." something like that. Yeah, Lattimer thought. I can't bury this quite yet.

He walked to the window and looked at the house down the street.

New York City

Dr. Michael Dewing, the neurology resident, got to the intensive care unit just as Justin was being wheeled in. Dewing was surprised. When he was paged, he assumed it was for one of the patients already in the unit. He'd guessed either Mrs. Nowlis, who was recovering after removal of her brain tumor, or Mr. Ziebarth, who had gone into shock after being given a new drug for his stomach tumor. But hey! thought Dewing, seeing the intern and nurses pushing the unconscious man on the cart, what's this? The man was in street clothes and a lab coat. As she trotted alongside, one nurse was adjusting an intravenous line, another was squeezing the Ambu bag. "From over in the Institute," explained a third nurse. "They say he simply collapsed."

Dewing stepped aside to let them through, then followed into intensive care. They were joined by Joseph Falcone, an assistant resident. "Get him on a respirator," ordered Dewing, "and get a chest doctor." Dewing looked at the man. "Why the hell isn't he breathing?" he demanded. "What happened?"

"The people who brought him over said maybe he fell," ventured the youngest nurse.

"Huh," said Dewing, dubiously. The nurses took the man off the cart and put him on the empty bed between Nowlis and another patient. They closed the curtains around the bed and hooked the man up to the respirator. Dewing took out his ophthalmoscope. He looked in the man's eyes. "Right eye dilated. So maybe a fall. Still, could be a lot of things. Who is this guy?"

"Dr. Paul Justin," said a nurse. "From Virology."

"Well, Justin," said Dewing, "I'm going to hurt you." And he pressed his hand hard right above Justin's eyebrow. There was no reaction. Dewing then ground his knuckles into Justin's chest. Again, nothing. Dewing was surprised again. In most unconscious people, this should produce *some* reaction.

"This guy's in really deep," said Dewing. "Maybe stroke or a subdural. We'd better do an arteriogram." That would test for a blood clot. "Plus a spinal tap. And let's get a blood barbiturate level."

"Overdose?" asked Falcone.

"I don't know. Ask the people over there—would this guy do it to himself? Was he depressed?"

"*You're* sure not depressed, Dr. Dewing," pointed out one of the nurses, an older woman. She had been a nurse for thirty-four years, which was longer than Dewing had even been alive, so she spoke how she pleased. "You look as happy as a child with a new toy."

Dewing gave her a crooked grin. She was right, of course. After five years at Oakes-Metcalf, Dewing was getting a little tired of cancer patients. He relished those few emergencies like this one that came in from the immediate neighborhood. Especially this one. Because, medically, it might be interesting, a challenge. And because, since it was the Oakes-Metcalf "family," it might have some added importance.

"Ah, family," said Dewing, snapping his fingers. "Call the guy's wife. And see if Kitteridge can be here when she comes in." Dr. Jonathan Kitteridge, the chief of neurosurgery, had to be notified in a special case like this one. But Dewing hoped to solve it alone. It would be a feather in his cap.

Lander, Colorado

It had been two months ago that Dr. Christopher Ives had broken the code in which Dr. Paul Justin wrote his notes. And since Roberto Cruz had been sending copies of the notes to Ives just as soon as Justin wrote them down, for the last two months Ives had been able to stay only a day or two behind Justin—duplicating his serums and experiments. Unfortunately, last week Cruz had gone on vacation. So although Justin had made the D4 serum last Tuesday, it wasn't until this Monday that Cruz had been back in the virology section. Cruz had immediately seen that Justin's hamsters were starting to get well and had phoned Murdoch and Ives with the incredible news.

That had prompted a stormy session between Murdoch and Ives. Murdoch, fearing that Justin was about to publicize what he'd achieved, wanted to kill the virologist at once. But Ives felt that Justin would say nothing until he'd autopsied the hamsters and examined their tissues under the electron microscope. So Ives had persuaded Murdoch that, once Justin did this, they'd have Cruz paralyze him with anectine. "But how long do we keep him unconscious?" Murdoch had demanded. "Until I can thoroughly test *my* hamster," Ives had replied. "And then test the serum on monkeys. And then on a human. If they're all cured, *then* we kill Justin. If they're not cured—if Justin's hamsters turn out to be freaks, some kind of natural remission—we let Justin recover and return to his research. And he won't suspect a goddamn thing. He'll be out cold when Cruz gives him the anectine." Murdoch still hadn't liked it. "I'll have to find a replacement for Cruz," he'd complained. "I'm sure you have a list," Ives had replied primly.

So the next day, Tuesday, the copy of Justin's notes spelling out serum D4 had arrived from Cruz. And on Wednesday—two days ago—Ives had duplicated the serum and had injected it into his own leukemic hamsters.

The hamsters had started with white cell counts averaging 50,000—about seven times normal. Yesterday, with the serum in them, those counts had fallen to 27,000. Now, as Ives again ran the hamster blood through his Coulter counter, he saw the digital readouts averaged 14,000. My God! he thought. Cut by almost half again. At this rate, they'd be normal by tomorrow. Justin's hamsters were no freaks.

With a shaky hand, Ives turned off the counter. He remembered how confident he had sounded on Monday, talking about "replacing" Cruz and then, if the cure tested out, killing Justin. Then it had been a theory. Now it was becoming a possibility. Dr. Christopher Ives was becoming very upset—upset he was about to succeed at being rich, upset he was about to succeed at killing people. And he was especially upset that, in order to run these tests, he had been forced to leave Kansas City on Monday and come here to the sanitarium. Because, by leaving, he had missed both of this week's sessions with Dr. Lindenmeyer. Dr. Lindenmeyer was the psychiatrist at the Menninger Clinic in nearby Topeka who was helping Ives resolve his fears of success.

Unfortunately, seeing a psychiatrist created two new fears for Ives: One, that Murdoch would discover he was going to a shrink. (He figured that Murdoch would want to kill him, suspecting he was about to blab all about their project.) And two, that he *would* blab to Lindenmeyer. So far, Ives had avoided it. He'd told the psychiatrist about how he had been raised by puritanical parents. About how he was terrified of enjoying himself, terrified of committing sin. About how the impending collapse of Dacey Pharmaceutical seemed fitting retribution. Of course, Lindenmeyer answered that Ives had a right to pleasure, had a right to success. That Ives was a good person.

Ives wondered how Lindenmeyer would react if he knew he was making Ives feel a little better about killing a few people en route to blackmailing a lot more people for $6 billion.

Ives felt a little better, but not good enough. He ran a nervous hand through his beard. He was a physician, wasn't he? He had spent his life *serving* people, hadn't he? Ives angrily knocked his pipe on the hamster cage. The hamsters flinched. Ives walked out of the animal room.

His trouble was, he told himself—popping a 5-milligram tablet of Valium to try to calm down—the trouble was that he wasn't just a good person. He was also a damn smart person. Smart enough to realize how smart Paul Justin was.

It began two years ago when Ives had been impressed by Justin's *Virology Monthly* article on "C" particle research. Later, at a medical conference in San Francisco, Ives heard that Justin's work was running into skepticism at Oakes-Metcalf. He also heard that Oakes-Metcalf was trimming its budget. Several associates would be fired and Justin might be one.

Ives thought more highly of Justin's line of research than anyone else did. So he had his own staff at Dacey Pharmaceutical explore it. But they lacked the skills to get anywhere.

Ives then had an employment feeler put out to Justin. The answer was no. Justin wanted to stay with a nonprofit institution of Oakes-Metcalf's caliber. But Ives didn't want Justin fired from Oakes-Metcalf and going elsewhere; Justin would have even less freedom for "C" particle research than Underwood permitted.

So, through the Endicott Foundation, which Dacey controlled, Ives had a $75,000 grant made to Oakes-Metcalf with the stipulation it go to the virology section. And Justin kept his job.

The Endicott Foundation had made many such quiet grants for the advancement of science. At the time, Dr. Christopher Ives felt he was simply making one more. But then, last April, the polio disaster struck Dacey Pharmaceutical.

From the start, Ives knew the disaster doomed the company. He suspected it also doomed his own personal fortune. He would be ruined. How could he face his wife and daughter? But a cancer drug would certainly be a valuable piece of insurance. So while everyone else at Dacey was running around trying to put out day-to-day fires, Dr. Christopher Ives looked ahead.

He knew that, in the face of criticism, Justin had stopped writing and talking about his research. But Justin still *did* his research— with Dacey money. So what was more logical than for Dacey to install the only information pipeline to Justin?

But how to install that pipeline? Ives thought of Murdoch, his own chief of security. He suspected that Ed Murdoch was, at heart, a crook. He sounded him out. And the two agreed to make a long-shot investment. For a long-range plan.

To their astonishment, it started paying off immediately—when Cruz sent the photograph of the possible "C" particle. And this year, as Justin worked on serum series A, B and C, Ives and Murdoch felt they might soon hit the jackpot. So Ives secretly siphoned off company money to buy the sanitarium and pay the staff to run it. And then he sent Cruz the three drugs he would need for the big day: the chloral hydrate to put Justin to sleep, the anectine to paralyze him and the atropine to make the doctors think the paralysis was caused by a head injury.

Yes, smart, thought Ives. And today, possibly right now—as he stood in the sanitarium courtyard and gazed at the snowcapped Rockies—right now, in a lab in New York City, it could all be happening. The mountaintops glistened pure white in the sun. They spoke of perfection, that everything would go well. Christopher Ives wished he were up in those mountains. Despite his girth, he was a fair skier, and he imagined himself soaring down those slopes—free but controlled, on his way to his goal. But then Ives thought of the truck smashed on the road yesterday and the monkeys running wild. Was it an omen? Were the monkeys the gibbering, greedy beast within him? He wished he could ask Dr. Lindenmeyer. He wished—

Ed Murdoch's gravelly voice rumbled across the courtyard. "Cruz is on the phone."

For the second time in two days, Ives forced his plump body into a trot. Taking the phone in Murdoch's office, he caught the grin that split his partner's droopy, patchwork face. But Cruz hadn't yet gotten to the bad news. Yes, said Cruz, Justin saw something on the TV screen that made him excited. Yes, I knocked him out okay. Yes, I'm sending you the slides. But Justin's file . . .

Ives exploded. "You stupid son of a bitch! Did you look in the *other* file drawers? Did you look on the desk? Did you—"

"Mr. Smith," came the scared voice. "I looked. I looked."

"Well, look again, you dumb spic. If you don't find it, I'll come out personally and—"

"Mr. Smith, please."

"Mr. Smith, fuck," snapped Ives. He was fed up with the charade of Mr. Smith. He wanted to tell Cruz that he, Dr. Christopher Ives, director of research and member of the board of directors of the Dacey Pharmaceutical Company and originator of the largest, most imaginative business coup of history wasn't going to let any goddamn *lab* assistant fuck it up. But Murdoch, on the other phone in the room, cut in.

"Forget it," said Murdoch calmly, to Cruz and to Ives. "Roberto's a good man. If the file's gone, it's not his fault. Justin must simply have taken it home, right, Roberto?"

"Right," agreed Cruz, gratefully.

Ives stared at Murdoch in disbelief. "But—"

Murdoch waved at him to shut up. "So, Roberto—"

"Yes?" Eagerly.

"Roberto, you've done fine. There'll even be a bonus for you. My man will have it for you today. Monday, go to work, act like everything's normal. Stay with it. I'll contact you in a couple of weeks. Okay?"

"Okay." Relieved.

"Good-bye."

"Good-bye."

Murdoch hung up. Ives turned on him. "Taken it home? Do you honestly believe—"

"No," said the Dacey chief of security. His gray, drooping eyes stared balefully at Ives. "No, we have to act on the assumption that somebody else stole it."

"Who?"

"And we have to assume that that somebody can quickly break Justin's code."

"Why?" demanded Ives. "It took *me* over a year. Who could possibly—"

"Another cancer researcher," suggested Murdoch.

"But why assume the worst? And . . . and . . . " Ives was stammering, "and if you think it is the worst, why were you so easy on Cruz?"

Ed Murdoch rubbed a thoughtful hand over the left side of his chest, where Ives knew he had his gun holster.

"I was easy on Cruz because I don't want him nervous. I want him relaxed and off guard when my man comes to kill him today."

"Oh." Ives swallowed hard. The first death was actually coming.

"And I'm going to assume the worst because that's my job. That's security. That's why we're going into implementation today. I'm calling up our hundred pigeons."

"No!" cried Ives. "We don't know we have the cure. I need my month to find out for certain."

"Your hamsters are getting better, aren't they?"

"Yes . . . "

"What's the blood count?"

"14,000 white," admitted Ives.

"Down again," noted Murdoch. "And Cruz says Justin's hamsters looked totally cured, right?"

"Yes . . . but—"

"And when Justin looked at their cells on the microscope's TV screen, Cruz says—"

"But we've got to test on monkeys! On man!"

"No time. In one week, Justin's serum could be front-page news."

"But if I could have just a few more days," Ives was begging, "to see at least if my hamsters are really cured."

"You've got them. We call the pigeons tonight, but they won't have their representatives here till Sunday. By then, your hamsters should be fit as a fiddle, right?"

"Well, if they follow Justin's . . . "

"They will. And then Justin's a dead man. And we're rich." Again, the hound-dog face grinned.

Dr. Christopher Ives was shaking. He pointed a finger at his partner. "Damn it, Ed, you're *happy* this has happened. You always wanted to move too fast, and now you've got your excuse. You never cared about the research. You—"

Murdoch cleared his throat and spat a wad of phlegm into a rumpled handkerchief. He laughed a gravelly laugh. No amount of spitting would ever get out the gravel. "Research. Ha. Doc, you've got to face it. As of today, you're not a researcher anymore. You're an accomplice to one assault and battery plus one murder. I think that makes you a criminal. Maybe, like they used to say, an arch-criminal. How do you like the sound of that?"

Dr. Lindenmeyer, thought Ives desperately, *tell* me.

Boston, Massachusetts

Barbara Justin walked quickly through the Public Garden. There were children laughing in the swan boats, but she was too wrapped up in her worries to take pleasure from them. Perspiring now in the noon heat, she climbed Pinckney Street to the crest of Beacon Hill. By the time she turned in at the solid brick house with the white pillars she was slightly out of breath. Her blouse clung stickily to her. She mopped her brow. She opened the door and was heading for the phone on the little Chippendale table in the hall when her mother came out of the living room.

"Barbara," said Elizabeth Everett Yates, "they just called from New York and—"

"I have to call Paul," said Barbara. "It's very—"

"—said Paul's had an accident."

"—important." Barbara had the receiver off the hook, ready to dial. She stopped and looked at her mother. "What did you say?"

Elizabeth Everett Yates stood with her hands clasped calmly, firmly behind her. The cords of her neck stood out like strong rope as she spoke.

"The hospital called. Somehow they tracked down this number. It was a nurse. She tried to be vague but I made her tell me what she knows. Paul apparently fell and hit his head in his lab. Or possibly a stroke. Or a —"

"A stroke?" gasped Barbara.

"—or a cerebral hemorrhage. Anyway, they needed permission to do a spinal tap or X-ray or something—"

"What?"

"So I said all right. And he's in sort of a coma but they think he'll live."

"Live? Oh, my God," said Barbara. It was like a two-by-four hitting her in the face. The receiver fell out of her hand. It pulled the phone down with it to the floor.

Her mother strode over and picked up the phone. "Now we can't have that," she said. "I'm expecting another call. The emergency room promised that Dr. Dewing—he's the attending physician—will call back and tell us the extent of the paralysis."

"Paralysis," said Barbara, dully. Her tall body went slack. She felt her mother help her into the living room.

Elizabeth Everett Yates sat her daughter down on the sofa. She kept her strong, bony arms around Barbara for a moment. Then she pulled back. "Would you like some tea, dear?" she asked.

Hot tea on a hot day, thought Barbara. Drenched in sweat from heat and fear, she burst out crying and laughing.

"Oh, Mother. Mother—tea!" Great, racking sobs tore her body. Oh, it was so funny and so terrible. Her mother, so Boston, so proper. "Paul's paralyzed for life—" she blurted, hysterical.

"Nobody said life, dear."

"—and you offer me Earl Grey. Or is it S. S. Pierce's Special? Which mixture? One lump or two?"

"Barbara," said her mother firmly.

"Oh, tea will cure it all. No illness too serious that tea can't cure. Cure a stroke. Cure cancer—"

"Who said anything about—"

"Cure anything!" Barbara flung her arms wide.

"—cancer?"

Barbara's hand hit a china figurine on the side table and sent it smashing to the floor.

That sobered her. "Oh, Mother." She bent over, looking at the pieces. "I'm sorry," she said softly. "I'm knocking everything . . . around. Aunt Matilda's good delft shepherd—"

"Barbara," said Elizabeth Everett Yates. "Never mind it. Now, what's this about cancer?"

Barbara dried her eyes. "Well, I saw Dr. Picard and—"

The phone rang. Elizabeth Everett Yates got up to answer. Barbara continued to dry her eyes. Her cheeks still hurt from laughing. Her stomach hurt as if someone had just kicked her. A stroke? she wondered. A hemorrhage? A stroke at age thirty-nine? But he's so healthy, she protested. And I was so healthy. She had a sudden image of the two of them, a month ago, vigorously playing badminton in the backyard. And now, so quickly, out of nowhere, both of us hit—like this. I wanted him to comfort *me* and now he needs— oh, oh, oh.

And Barbara started crying again. She dug her knuckles into her eyes. Gone. All gone. I knew it couldn't last. My life was too good. Me. Paul. What about the children?

"The children!" She half rose from the sofa. "Do the children know . . . ?" she called, but her mother was talking in hushed tones into the phone.

"What? What does he say, Mother?" asked Barbara. "Is Paul . . . ?"

She collapsed back into the sofa. She burrowed her head into the fabric. It had an interesting pattern. With her tear-filled eyes she traced the stem of a rose up past a leaf into the flower and over to another rose and down past a leaf . . . and over . . . and over . . .

She felt a hand on her shoulder. Her mother was sitting next to her again.

"Margaret Hadley," snorted Elizabeth Everett Yates, "and her liver. Had to call me with another bulletin."

"Oh," said Barbara, still concentrating on the roses. "I thought it was ... "

"Don't worry. The doctor will call. Just wait."

"No," said Barbara dully. "I don't want to wait. I should go home, I guess. The children ... the children need me." She turned away from the roses, back to her mother. "Do they know ... did you call?"

"Yes. But nobody's home. I don't know where they are."

"At the summer school. The play program."

"Oh."

"So I'd better go home," said Barbara more decisively. "Would you help me pack, Mother? I'll ... try to catch the two o'clock shuttle."

"Fine," said Elizabeth Everett Yates briskly. She believed in wiping away one's tears and getting on with things. "But first," she said, her sharp aristocratic nose pointing at Barbara like a kingfisher's beak, "did you say something about cancer?"

Barbara Justin took a deep breath. Courage, she thought. Don't slouch. You can't be a frightened little girl anymore. People need you. Paul. And the children. So even if you can't really be as strong as Mother, try to act it. And if you act it, maybe a little bit of it will come true.

As calmly as she could, Barbara told her mother what Picard had told her. When Barbara said that, one way or the other, they'd have to cut into her, Elizabeth Everett Yates recoiled. Her head jerked as sharply as a bird hearing a cat. Then she hugged Barbara again. She offered to come to New York with Barbara, but Barbara said thanks, but not yet anyway. Elizabeth Everett Yates phoned for a cab, then went upstairs to pack Barbara's clothes. Then, still holding herself together by sheer willpower, Barbara Justin called the play program at Dobbs Ferry. She asked one of the counselors, Mrs. Freesmith, if someone could take care of Melissa and Laurie and Steve in case she had to stay with Paul at the hospital. Mrs. Freesmith volunteered to do it herself. "But what's happened to Paul?" she asked. "A stroke," Barbara said—and then regretted it. "But don't tell the children," she added. Mrs. Freesmith said, "Of course not."

Barbara's mother came back downstairs with the luggage. The two women waited in the hallway for the cab.

"Would you like that tea now?" asked Elizabeth Everett Yates. "Hot liquids cool you off, you know."

Barbara Justin shook her head and smiled at her mother with weary admiration. "All right, Mother," she answered.

Houston, Texas

Outside the Texahoma Building, in the mid-distance, the city was disappearing in a hot, humid haze. Ray Ryker's eyes often strayed to look out at it because he was bored by the problem one of his assistant vice presidents was presenting to him. Texahoma wanted to expand one of its pipeline branches in Arkansas and the executive, Terrell, was in charge of preparing the environmental impact statement that Arkansas required. The problem was that the Little Rock bureaucrats were giving Terrell a rough time.

"They said it'd have to be completely rewritten," he complained to Ryker. "But we don't have time."

Having exhausted the view out the corner windows, Ryker looked around his huge office. On the walls were cold, hard-edged purple paintings by a contemporary artist—paintings worth, Ryker had been told, $50,000 each. Ryker would have preferred some Western scenes, maybe some Remingtons, but the abstract art served its purpose. It made Ryker's visitors feel slightly put off, slightly at a disadvantage. The desk Ryker sat behind—an enormous slab of Carrara marble set on one massive steel pedestal—served the same purpose. Across it, Terrell looked small, and looked as if he felt small.

"They were even criticizing the writing *style*," protested Terrell, clutching his thick report.

Ryker was not only bored; he was annoyed with Terrell. The man was letting his feelings show, and had probably let his feelings show in Little Rock. The bureaucrats must have been gleeful to see an oil company executive hurt. It must have made them stick Terrell all the more.

Now even the neighboring Conoco Tower was disappearing in the haze. "The fog comes in on little cat feet," remembered Ryker, "and covers the city." When Ray Ryker entered his teens, he had read and written poetry. Into his poetry he had poured all the fears of a small, Protestant boy in tough Irish Catholic Kensington, all the loneliness of an only child growing up without a father. But then Ray's mother remarried and Ray acquired not only a stepfather but also a big, bullying stepbrother. So Ray wrote more poetry, enough to fill a whole loose-leaf notebook. And one day when he was fifteen his stepbrother discovered the notebook.

That night on the windy slum playground, standing mock-dramatically under the lone lamp, the stepbrother gleefully read from the notebook to a group of his buddies. Ray came upon them and raged at his stepbrother to stop. But the older boy laughed and continued. "And get *this* one, guys," he kept saying. "Get *this* poem from Shorty." And as he finished reading each poem, he carefully tore it out of the notebook and let the wind take it. Ray Ryker remembered desperately scrambling for the pages as the wind blew them into the darkness—scrambling, screaming, tripping over junk and teeter-totters, crying, bleeding. And all the while his stepbrother called after him, mock-solicitously, "What's wrong, Shorty? What's wrong, Shorty?" . . . that hateful nickname.

Ray Ryker never wrote poetry again. He was beginning to learn the lesson the world was throwing at him: To show your feelings is to be mocked. To even *feel* your feelings is to lose control of your body and your whole self.

Little Ray Ryker began to learn to close himself like a fist. And he learned to use his fists.

Now Ryker closed his fist, crushing the empty can of Dr Pepper. The sound startled Terrell. Ryker took another vicious bite of his ham sandwich. He was making it clear Terrell was intruding on his lunch, making Terrell wish he'd never asked for this time.

"So I guess we'll rewrite it," said Terrell, lamely. He stood up and pushed the report across the desk to Ryker. Ryker barely noticed it. "I mean," said Terrell, "if we work evenings, weekends . . . "

"Do that," said Ryker.

Terrell, Ryker saw clearly, was not going any higher at Texahoma. Mainly because Terrell didn't understand what going higher meant. It didn't just mean more money—now that Ryker had several million dollars, he didn't care about more money, except maybe to play with. Mainly, going higher meant more control—and now Ryker was only one step away from the topmost control. Soon he might actually be there. He'd move into the opposite corner office where that son-of-a-bitch old man still held sway. Held sway although in a normal corporation he would have retired ten years ago. Held sway although he was across town in a hospital bed. How long could the old man keep hanging tough over there? Goodhue and the nurses reported Ash had had a bad night. And how long before Virginia thought of pulling the plug? Ash had liked to boast about his Indian great-great-grandfather—a chief who, in his late seventies, led a small band against the U.S. Cavalry and wouldn't let any young buck replace him. But Ryker had looked up the chief's story and discovered he had died of syphilis at age fifty-five.

On the cover of Terrell's environmental impact statement, Ryker drew a piece of barbed wire. Stay alive, goddamn you, ordered Ryker.

Ryker's intercom buzzed.

"Yes," he said.

"Mr. Wissenbach," said his secretary.

Ryker waved a curt dismissal at Terrell, who was only too glad to leave. Wissenbach, thought Ryker, as Terrell went out the door. Since talking to Wissenbach yesterday, Ryker had sounded out a few other men—in the state and out—who had as much money and clout as Wissenbach. They had been interested in combining with Ryker to buy Texahoma, but not, they subtly made clear, with you as president. Given enough time, he might change their minds. Given as little time as he really had, he needed Wissenbach to change people's minds for him. Ryker felt like a tightly coiled spring. He stood and rocked on the balls of his feet.

"Put him on," Ryker told his secretary. Ryker switched on his speaker-phone.

"Hello, Ray," Wissenbach's voice boomed out of the speaker. "How you doin'?"

"Fine, Harry," Ryker said to his desk microphone.

"Ah'm callin' from Dallas like Ah promised," said Wissenbach. "Jes' finished mah meetin' on Trans Con. Fascinatin'. We're gettin' inta mod-u-lar housin'. Made of plastic, paper, even—how's this grab you—compacted garbage."

"The sweet smell of success," said Ryker.

"Haw, yeah. We ran through a lotta jokes on it. But seriously, Ray ... " Wissenbach paused.

The speaker-phone let Ryker pace behind his desk with his hands free. He turned and said, "Uh-huh."

"Ah talked to Earl Benson afterwards. 'Bout you joinin' us to Acapulco this weekend. Gettin' to know you better 'n' all. 'N', well ... " Wissenbach's big voice hesitated again.

Ryker wanted to pretend only mild interest. Already, Wissenbach knew too well how much he cared.

"Yeah?" Ryker prompted.

"Ol' Earl said no," said Wissenbach. "Leastways not right now. 'Course Ah coulda pushed it on 'im. But Ah figure better not. We'll all get together next week at the mayor's dinner. You do plan on bein' there?"

"If it'll help," said Ryker. To try to keep his voice calm, he did an isometric exercise, one hand fighting the other.

"It'll help. Lotsa good fellas be there. Ah'll put together a group afterwards. Have a few drinks. Maybe bring in a few girls."

"Great," said Ryker.

"See," said Wissenbach, "Ah'm tryin' fer you. But it's gonna take time."

"Okay," said Ryker.

"So keep that ol' coot alive."

"You bet."

"See you, Ray."

"Bye."

Ryker snapped off the phone. He reached down and, on the cover of the report, drew the barbed wire points even longer and sharper. From one of the points, he drew blood dripping. It looked like even Harry Wissenbach wasn't going to be able to change people's minds in time.

The Conoco Tower was now completely lost in the haze. Ray Ryker felt totally alone. He was used to it. Usually he liked it. Today it worried him. He drummed his fingers on the Carrara marble desk. What the hell could he do? He couldn't control everything.

He did an isometric exercise against the desk, so hard he felt either his fingers or the marble would break. It still didn't calm him.

Dobbs Ferry, New York

A lone man among suburban housewives, Frank Lattimer shopped at the A & P. In the produce section he got a look of interest from a fortyish but trim and handsome woman in tennis dress. Lattimer, however, was too busy selecting the mushrooms for the coq au vin he planned to make for himself sometime this weekend. He left. The trip back took him past the Justin house again. On impulse he stopped his motorcycle and walked up to the porch. Not long, he promised himself. There was also ice cream in the saddlebags and the sun was hot.

He rang the bell, hoping to get Mrs. Justin. Normally at this point in investigating somebody, when a man was clamming up, Lattimer would start quizzing the man's colleagues at work. Of course that would get back to the man and he'd be even less likely to talk. But in this case, since they were neighbors, Lattimer realized he could get at Justin through his wife. Invite the two of them over for coq au vin. I'll have to buy more chicken, Lattimer told himself, and hope to get—what was her name, Barbara?—talking.

He rang the bell again. Lattimer had a vague image of Justin's wife. Tall, blond hair, pretty, a bit vulnerable looking. Mainly, he knew her from her voice, calling, "Steve, Melissa, Laurie. Dinner!" from down the block. The voice carried far enough, but it always struck Lattimer as a bit hesitant, as if it didn't quite expect to be obeyed. Yes, Justin's wife should be fairly easy. Thinking that, Lattimer suddenly heard, from five years ago, the voice of his own wife, Mary Ann: "You're a phony, Frank. You don't care about people. You only care about your stories and you just *use* people to get them. Like you use me. Like you—" Lattimer shut the voice off. He didn't think the accusation was true. But it still bothered him.

He rang the bell again. Well, if nobody was home, he could go through the Justin mailbox. He had done that before on stories—and even opened mail. But this time the memory of his wife—ex-wife—stopped him.

Frank Lattimer was turning to go when a car drove up and a boy got out. As the boy walked toward him, Lattimer recognized him as Justin's son. But the driver wasn't Mrs. Justin.

"Hi," said Lattimer, "I'm Frank Lattimer. From down the street. Where's your Mom?"

"In Boston," said the boy. "But she's coming back today."

"Oh, that's nice."

"Yeah, I guess so."

The boy walked past Lattimer, opened the door and went in. Lattimer thought he was a handsome kid, although he had his father's long face and right now it looked long and serious.

"Why just 'I guess so'?" asked Lattimer. "You didn't want her back?"

"Yes." The boy's head turned sharply. "Naw ... I mean ... " He was looking around the living room. "Gee, I thought my chem set was here."

"You mean ... " Lattimer let it dangle for the boy to complete. This was like working on the father on the train yesterday morning. He was glad Mary Ann wasn't hearing it.

"I mean," said the boy, "she's coming back 'cause she has to. 'Cause my Dad got a stroke."

"A stroke?" asked Lattimer. He tried to stay matter-of-fact but failed. He was shocked.

"Yeah," said the boy, rummaging in the stereo cabinet. "He's totally paralyzed. Anyway that's what they said. So my Mom's coming home and I gotta go with that dumb Mrs. Freesmith out there. I don't know why we couldn't wait for Mom here at our home."

"Well, I'm sure Mrs. Freesmith—" began Lattimer.

"Yeah. Sure, sure," said the boy, picking up the patronizing voice of the adult.

Damn, thought Lattimer, I've lost him.

"Yeah, here it is," said the boy and walked out past Lattimer, holding a battered chemistry set. He got in the car—Lattimer now noticed two girls in the back seat: Justin's daughters?—and the car drove off.

"Well," said Frank Lattimer after a moment. "What?"

Sure, the boy could have gotten it wrong. But it *sounded* pretty definite. Stroke. Totally paralyzed. Lattimer himself was slightly paralyzed on the porch. He made himself walk back to his motorcycle. A stroke at Justin's age? Well, the man *had* seemed tense yesterday morning. He could have high blood pressure. Whatever caused it, it was really rotten—Justin seemed like a nice guy. So, strokes happen.

But Lattimer was still troubled. Something wasn't right.

Lattimer kicked his Harley into action, then throttled it down and sat on it a moment. Serendipity, he thought. It helped reporters more often than they admitted. He'd gone looking for the mother and instead got a thunderbolt from the son. A stroke of luck, he thought grimly. Lattimer looked at the peaceful home, thinking of the lives of those inside so quickly changed. Lattimer was a logical man. But instinct also helped reporters more than they admitted. Yesterday morning, his instincts told him to go to B & B. Now his instincts said there was a connection between Justin's claim of a cancer cure yesterday and his stroke today.

Frank Lattimer headed home, to put the groceries in the refrigerator and catch a train down to New York. But first, he opened one saddlebag. He nodded glumly. The ice cream was soup.

Houston, Texas

For twenty-four hours, Virginia Ash had been trying to get hold of the Reverend Richard Watson Trumbull. She had first called his Saving Center in Atlanta. That had been easy to find because its address was flashed on the screen several times during each "Saving Grace" program. It was the address to send contributions to. And Virginia expected the Center would tell her where Trumbull was in Hutchinson, Kansas—because that's where the program was coming from this week. But a secretary at Trumbull's headquarters told her he wasn't really there. The programs had been taped *last* week. "So where is he?" Virginia had asked. The secretary had said she didn't know. "So who *does* know?" Virginia had asked. Virginia was not ordinarily this forceful. But now she felt her husband's life was at stake.

The secretary had transferred Virginia to some assistant. The assistant took Virginia's name and promised that when Trumbull came to Houston in November, her husband could come on stage and be healed. "But you don't understand," Virginia had insisted. "There isn't time. Reverend Trumbull must come *here now*. To this hospital."

The assistant said the Reverend couldn't do that. Virginia said—proudly, but embarrassed to throw her husband's name around—"Don't you know who this is? Do you think Matt Ash can't afford to pay the Reverend's way out here?"

When the assistant understood he was talking to the wife of one of the richest men in America, he promised he'd see what he could do. An hour later, a man who said he was Peter Seabring, Reverend

Trumbull's "executive assistant," called back and asked how would next week be?

Virginia had wavered and started to agree. Then she had thought how Matt would react. "No," she insisted. "*Now*. Tomorrow. At the latest. Why *can't* he come? Isn't"—she picked a figure out of the air—"ten thousand dollars enough?"

Seabring had mumbled something.

"Fifty thousand?" asked Virginia. The numbers meant nothing to her. But she assumed they did to other people.

"We *appreciate* your offer," said the executive assistant. "But I don't know if it's physically possible. The Reverend has schedules, commitments . . . "

Virginia was about to say "a hundred thousand" but then figured maybe they were playing with her, trying to get her to go higher. She remembered how angry Matt had been when she gave $100,000 to Loring. And, come to think of it, who would authorize the payment of even the $50,000?

"Fifty thousand," she insisted. "Tomorrow." She felt she was striking a hard bargain. Matt would be proud of her.

"I'll call back," Seabring had said.

That was yesterday. Today the man hadn't yet called back. Virginia wasn't sure what to do. Many times, early this morning, her fingers had trembled on the receiver. But she had stopped herself from picking it up. To call again would be a sign of weakness. So she had shuttled back and forth in the Presidential Suite. She nervously ate in the living room and kitchen. She went into Matt's bedroom and watched him as he slept—and watched him wake in pain and again demand that she let him die. "God . . . " she started to say to him. And "Reverend Trumbull . . . " But Matt's curses of God drove her out. At ten o'clock, she watched "Saving Grace" again. And again it thrilled her. When it ended, she couldn't help herself. Again, she phoned for the executive assistant. But she couldn't get him. She figured they were trying to up the price. She hung up upset. She wondered if Reverend Trumbull knew what mercenary people were working for him.

What Virginia Ash didn't realize was that the delay had nothing to do with Trumbull's schedules and commitments nor with Seabring's desire for more money (although he wouldn't have scorned it). The executive assistant was delaying calling her back because the Reverend Trumbull was an alcoholic. And two days ago, Seabring had checked his boss, very drunk, into an exclusive drying-out farm. And he was now trying to determine if the farm could dry out Trumbull faster than usual. So he could go to Houston, if not today, then at least tomorrow.

At 2:15 Atlanta time, 1:15 Houston time, the executive assistant got the word. And the phone rang in the Presidential Suite of Loring Memorial.

It was lunchtime for Virginia Ash. "Hello?" she said, getting the word out through a mouth full of fried chicken.

"Yes, hello. This is Peter Seabring of 'Saving Grace.' God's will be done, Mrs. Ash—I have good news for you!"

"*Praise* God!" she cried.

It didn't matter all that much that Trumbull couldn't come today or even tomorrow (Seabring said he had appointments). What mattered was he *was* coming. And coming, appropriately enough, on the Lord's day, Sunday. Virginia Ash hung up full of heartfelt thanks and excitement. Matt would be saved. The Healer was coming, Matt would be saved.

She dashed into the bedroom to tell him. A cry of pain greeted her at the door. Matt was writhing in agony. "Fuck! Shit! Goddamn it! What the fuck! What—?" he was screaming.

She backed away silently. Matt was in no shape to learn of Trumbull's coming. Virginia decided it would have to remain her wonderful surprise for him.

New York City

A little after three o'clock, Frank Lattimer found his way to the virology section of the Oakes-Metcalf Institute. Below the official "Virology" sign on the door was another sign: "This is the chemists' shop where we dispense with accuracy."

Lattimer smiled and went in. "I'm looking for Paul Justin," he said.

"He's not here," said Dr. Stefan Wojik. "He's in the hospital. And who are you?"

"A friend of his," said Lattimer. "I heard he had a stroke and I'd like to visit him. What hospital?"

"Right over there," said Wojik, waving his hand. "Intensive care. Now if you'll excuse me, I have some work to do." He walked away through the lab.

"About the work Paul was doing . . . " said Lattimer, following Wojik.

"What?"

"His research. What kind was it?"

"Different kinds," said Wojik. "I don't keep track."

"Who does?"

"Dr. Underwood."

"Who's he?"

"Our boss," said Wojik wearily, "and he's out right now." Wojik was adjusting a dial on the centrifuge. He looked up and folded his arms across his chest. "Now really, Mr.—"

"Lattimer," said Lattimer. "Did Paul have the stroke here?" he asked.

"No," said Joan Scully, who had been watching what was going on and had decided to come to Wojik's rescue. "He had it down the hall, in the electron microscope room."

"Oh," said Lattimer. His eyes took in the attractive little redhead in the lab coat.

"And I suggest you go down the hall, too, Mr. Lattimer," said Joan. "Out of here. For a friend of Paul's, you're certainly making a prying nuisance of yourself."

"Well," said Lattimer, smiling disarmingly, "I have a confession to make."

"What?" asked Joan. She also had folded her arms across her chest. Lattimer wished she wouldn't do that. It flattened her nice breasts. He also noticed several fingers of her left hand were bandaged.

"I'm not just here as a friend of Paul's," said Lattimer, leaving Wojik and addressing himself to the woman. "I'm also here as a reporter."

"Reporting what?" asked Joan Scully.

"I'm not sure," Lattimer confessed. He shrugged. "Paul and I rode the train together yesterday. We talked about his research. He said he was on to something. Today I heard he had this stroke. I thought I'd try to find out what that research was."

"On to something?" asked Joan, puzzled. "On to what?" She stopped. "And look," she objected. "Who *are* you? Do you have a press card or something?"

Lattimer dug into his wallet.

"And why ask us about it, anyway?" continued Joan. "Ask Paul when he recovers."

"What if he doesn't?" said Lattimer, producing the card.

Joan examined it dubiously. "Some friend," she said. "You sound like a ghoul."

"Well, Paul said his research—his 'C' particle stuff—was important." Lattimer paused. "Was it?"

Joan Scully looked at Lattimer. His manner had really annoyed her. He thought he could jut his firm, handsome jaw into anything. But behind the manner, maybe there was a decent man. His eyes—

charcoal gray, almost black—were intense, but kind.

"It would have been," she said finally. "If he could ever have found the particle."

"How was he going about looking for it?"

"Well," sighed Joan. "That's complex. I doubt that a layman—"

"Try me," said Lattimer. "I've been boning up."

"I don't have time now."

"Then some other time," said Lattimer. "Tonight?"

"God, you move fast," said Joan.

David Crawford called from across the room. "Joan, you want to come and take a look at this graph?"

Joan looked at Lattimer. "I too have work to do. Good-bye, Mr. Lattimer."

"It's Frank," said Lattimer. "And wait. Did Paul keep notes on his work?"

"Of course," said Joan.

"Where are—?"

"I think his 'C' particle notes are in his file cabinet. Locked. And you're not really going to jimmy it open, are you?"

"Not unless I have to," grinned Lattimer. "A key would be easier. Who has one—besides Paul?"

"Paul," said Joan.

"Swell."

"And you couldn't get any of us to open it even if we did have a duplicate," said Joan.

She started moving away. As she did, Lattimer noticed the sign on the piece of equipment she'd been standing in front of: "Unless you are nude, please do not lean on this machine. Buttons and belt buckles scratch."

Lattimer smiled again. It was nice to discover that cancer researchers were human and had a sense of humor. As Joan tried to go, he grabbed her arm. "Wait," he said, "one more thing."

Joan Scully considered shaking off Lattimer's hand. She didn't. "What?" she asked.

Lattimer let his hand drop. "The stroke," he said. "Isn't it a little unusual, Paul having it so young? Too much of a coincidence?"

"I'm not a doctor," said Joan. "And coincident with what?"

"I don't know," admitted Lattimer.

"Some reporter," she said.

"But I'm bothered," he said. "So I'm fishing. Had he ever had any little strokes—anything like that—before?"

"No."

"Had he ever—"

"Look," said Joan, "we found Paul on the floor. I put my hand in his mouth to keep him from choking. He bit me. We got him over to the hospital. They think he had a stroke. That's all I know."

"Wait," said Lattimer. "Let me get the sequence straight. He went right from here to the electron—?"

"Hey, Joan," interrupted Crawford. "Do I have to rip off the graph and bring it to you? Or will you come over?" He started stalking toward them.

"Can I find out more tonight?" asked Lattimer.

"There is nothing more," said Joan.

"Joan," said Crawford, insistently.

"Well, let me buy you dinner anyway," said Lattimer. "Make up for barging in on you like this."

"Well . . . " said Joan.

"I promise I won't mention the 'C' particle. Or the 'A' particle or 'B' particle."

David Crawford was now standing next to Joan, looking increasingly angry at Lattimer and possessive at her. Joan would normally have said no to Lattimer, except she felt Crawford had no right to look possessive.

"Okay," said Joan.

"I'll pick you up at—" began Lattimer.

"No, I'll meet you there."

"Fine," said Lattimer. " 'There' will be the Spanish Table at eight o'clock. And do you have a name, Madame Curie?"

"Joan Scully," said Joan Scully. And she walked off with Crawford to read the graph on the spectrophotometer.

Catching a last frown from Stefan Wojik and a puzzled look from a young Puerto Rican washing glassware, Frank Lattimer left the virology section, deep in thought. "We found Paul on the floor," Lattimer remembered Joan saying. But who's "we"? I'd like to talk to that person, too, thought Lattimer. Well, it can wait.

He went down the elevator and over the connecting bridge to the Oakes-Metcalf Hospital.

New York City

" . . . but those damn Washington bureaucrats won't listen," said Dr. Warren Brown. "Just won't listen."

"Um," said Hugh Underwood.

"And even some of our private funds are being cut. Damon Runyon is cutting. And the budget simply won't stretch. Why, do you know what the price of oil is doing to the price of half the chemicals you use?"

"Um," said Underwood. "Up."

"Up," echoed Brown. *"Everything* is up. I hope," said Brown, holding up the report that Underwood had handed him, "that you make a good case for virology, because the Board is going to be really tough on us next week. We're going to have to cut somewhere."

"Probably," agreed Underwood, looking into space.

Usually when he sat in the top-floor, corner office of the Director of the Institute, Hugh Underwood was alert. He liked and respected Brown. He leaned on Brown. He would explain his section's problems and trust Brown to solve them. And when the Board of Scientific Advisors was due in, he would strongly defend his section's budget and personnel—and trust Brown would agree. But this afternoon, Hugh Underwood's mind was not on the Washington bureaucrats. If Justin's notes were what he thought they were, this whole conversation was beside the point.

The particular Washington bureaucrats were in the Department of Health, Education and Welfare. And they were giving Warren Brown sleepless nights.

HEW had been under attack recently for not enforcing the laws that required that all private institutions receiving federal aid have a "positive minority hiring program at all levels." So HEW, to prove it really *was* tough, had decided to go after not just any institutions but the most prestigious. And since—Puerto Rican lab assistants and black typists didn't count—Oakes-Metcalf had only *one* high-level minority member ... Brown shuddered. HEW had a list of Institute jobs that had to be filled by minority members on a regular schedule starting in September—or else. Or else drastic cuts in aid. Cuts in NCI money. Cuts in Cancer Control Act money. Cuts. Cuts. Of course, Brown and his aides had been beating the bushes, talking to all their influential friends in Washington, trying to get somebody to get the HEW ruling modified. But to no avail. Warren Brown was getting desperate. He peered over his eyeglasses, regarded his one high-level minority member and wished Hugh Underwood were twins.

"I don't suppose," he said to Underwood, "that, before the September deadline, you can figure out a way to get another grant out of the Cancer Control Act?"

"Uh," said Hugh Underwood noncommittally.

Last year, Senator Prentice had pushed for a program to cure cancer by, he said, 1988. That would be, he pointed out, the tenth anniversary of the death of Hubert Humphrey and hence a fitting memorial. But it would require, he said, a *crash* program like the one that built the first atomic bomb or the one that beat the Russians to the moon. So Prentice's bill called for a single, multibillion dollar project. His fellow senators had forced Prentice to scale down his bill to a number of individual grants. And Underwood had gotten one. But it was a mixed blessing. The grant was only for certain kinds of research and Underwood had to fill out a dozen forms to prove he was complying. He'd often told Brown he didn't want another such grant. Even with the Institute's funding threatened, he wasn't sure he wanted to apply. But Underwood was too lost in thought to argue now. If Justin's notes contained the cure for cancer . . .

Hugh Underwood now understood why he'd felt fear and depression this morning. Justin's cure for cancer would be a great thing for Justin and for the world in general. But for the tens of thousands of cancer researchers, administrators and public relations people around the world—my God, just think of all the local chapters of the American Cancer Society!—it would be a disaster. Warren Brown would be out of a job. So would Hugh Underwood. Underwood could already hear his wife berating him for the loss. And not just the loss of a job. It would also make a mockery—as his wife would immediately sense and taunt him with—of his whole life, of all his years of patient effort.

For, from the beginning, Hugh Underwood had bought the established way of doing things. Sure, the established way had been unfair—growing up poor and black in Montgomery he'd had to try twice as hard as any white, and try quietly as well, to "know his place," even as he was trying to rise above it—but that was the only way there was. And there *were* payoffs. Hadn't Booker T. Washington made it? And many more black scientists since? Yes, if he stuck to the rules, there would be a place for him in white society.

And so how horrified Hugh had been, as a college student, when young Dr. King threw out the rules and started the Montgomery bus boycott. Hugh wouldn't participate. He rode to his classes in the back of the bus, thank you. And later, at graduate school, when some of his fellows sat in at white lunch counters . . . "Count me out," he'd said. Of course, Hugh had been pleased that their actions had succeeded. But, by calling into question so much of what he believed, the success also temporarily upset Hugh Underwood's world. But only temporarily. Underwood had been able to suppress the upset and adapt happily to the change. But how could he adapt now to the upset—the end—of his entire career? Why had he dreamt of Booker T. Washington or ridden the bus—in front or back—to class at all?

Underwood could see the reporters cramming into the section to interview him and Wojik and Scully and Crawford and Holmes and Beauchamp and even Cruz: "What do *you* think of Paul Justin? What kind of person is he? What are his hobbies? His favorite foods? Any funny anecdotes?" Of course, if Justin recovered from his coma, Justin would graciously credit Underwood with letting him pursue the research. Or, if Justin didn't recover, Underwood could gain more credit by deciphering the notes. But either way, it was a bitter role. He, Hugh Underwood, must play loyal black servant to the wise white doctor, limping, shuffling along behind him. And how nice, how *democratic* that he was black. See? Even a black could help the man who cured cancer. Hugh Underwood, who had worked long and hard to think and act like a white, right now felt very black indeed.

Shit, thought Underwood. We all dedicated our lives to curing cancer, but which one of us thought it would ever actually be accomplished? And what happens to our lives now? And can I really let this happen to *me*? He thought of Justin's notes, now safely nestled in his own desk.

"And I don't suppose," asked Dr. Warren Brown with a sigh and a smile, "that you have friends in the NAACP who could tell HEW what nice guys we are?"

"I'm afraid not," said Underwood. Friends in the NAACP!—not for him. But he was pleased that Dr. Brown joked with him. It made him feel closer to the director.

"Well, ask your staff whom they know," said Brown. "Sure, it's a longshot, but frankly—" Brown paused. "By the way," he said, "speaking of your staff—is Justin any better?"

"He's still unconscious," said Underwood. "They're running tests."

"It's a shame," said Brown, and he went back to discussing Virology's budget.

Both men left unspoken the fact that, if Justin died soon, the strain on the budget would be partly relieved.

New York City

A sharp stab in the side of the neck brought Paul Justin out of the blackness. A burning sensation rushed up his neck into his head. His head was full of fire. His eyes were staring at a black bag and a hand rhythmically squeezing it. The bag connected to a tube that went down his throat. What? his mind demanded in panic. The tube made him want to choke. He tried to choke, tried to close his eyes against the burning pain in his head and the macabre sight of the tube and the bag, tried to twist his head away. His vision was strangely clouded on the right-hand side and for a moment he wished it was *totally* clouded. But he couldn't even shut his eyes! He was stunned to find his whole body—including even his open eyelids—was locked as if in a vise. He could feel only the tube pushing air into his chest and his chest being forced to rise and fall in rhythm with the squeezing bag—*whoosh, whoosh,* it went—as if he weren't a person anymore but merely a pair of bellows. What? his mind screamed. His mind tottered on the edge of a blackness larger than that it had awakened from—the blackness of terror.

And then a man's voice next to him was saying, "Shoot," and there was a loud, metallic *bang*! and *bang*! and machinery whirred above and below his head and *bang*! and he strained to move his eyes but they wouldn't and *bang*! and the hand kept squeezing the bag and his head was exploding like the inside of a fiery sun and *bang! bang! bang! bang!*

And more bangs and then suddenly they stopped. "Okay," said the man's voice, "let's get him back." And hands were under him—he realized now he was lying on his back—lifting him onto something. And he was aware of other things now: tubes going into his arms and a tube into his penis—God! that felt strange and awful. And now he was rolling out of the little room and down a corridor and he caught parts of white uniforms to the side and above him. A hospital? He forced his mind to think, to pull itself back from the edge. Am I in a hospital? Why? How? He remembered—or did he dream it?—seeing the "C" particle on the electron microscope screen and then—falling asleep? Why, he wondered, would I do that? And why can't I move? And he could do nothing but stare at the hand squeezing the black bag and, above it, the white acoustical panels and bright lights of the ceiling sliding past. Did I go insane? he wondered. Did I have a fit? Did the shock of seeing the "C" particle knock me out, paralyze me somehow? Or did I only *imagine* I saw the particle, drive myself into seeing it, go psychotic? Jesus! Justin tried to think, to analyze. But the fear and the sticking, choking pain of the tube down his throat and the fire in his head—although that was now subsiding a bit, like a fever—clutched him, made logic impossible.

And then they were stopped and waiting and then they moved again into another small room. And then the room dropped away under him and although he realized—his mind grasping— that, of course, this was only an elevator, it felt like a descent into hell. And he yearned for a return to unconsciousness, but it wouldn't come and he knew that hell wasn't down anywhere—it was where he was now.

New York City

Barbara Justin had never been inside the Oakes-Metcalf Hospital before and she didn't like being here now. Partly it was because of what Paul had told her about it. Like other hospitals, he'd explained, it ran an outpatient service. Here people who had cancer came for their regular treatments with drugs or radiology or whatever. But unlike other hospitals—where a person might stay for a week to recover from an illness—once you were in *bed* at Oakes-Metcalf for more than a few days, it meant you weren't getting out of bed. It meant you were there to die.

And now Barbara, who was afraid she had cancer herself, had come to visit Paul in bed.

She knew her associations were foolish. She knew Paul didn't have cancer. She also knew—because Dr. Dewing had told her—that she shouldn't be afraid of the phrase "intensive care unit." "Actually," he'd said, "most of the people here have just come out of an operation. We've fixed them up and now we'll watch them closely." And he added the sometimes-truth, "And then we'll send them home."

But Dewing's words didn't comfort her. "So will Paul be coming home soon?" she asked.

"I don't know," admitted Dewing, annoyed that he had left himself open for that.

"And where is Paul?" she asked, peering into the two rooms that faced the nurses' station.

Dewing looked in also and saw the empty space. "Up in X-ray," explained Falcone, the assistant resident, who had joined them.

"You're X-raying for broken bones?" asked Barbara. She was confused. She thought Paul had had some kind of stroke.

"No," said Dewing, "not that." Dewing didn't like talking to patients' relatives. And—one nice thing about cancer—most relatives didn't *want* to know anything. But Mrs. Justin still had a questioning look on her face. And since she was the wife of a staff member, he figured he'd better answer.

"We X-ray to see if there's a blood clot," he explained.

"I thought X-rays only showed bones."

"We inject a dye"—he didn't mention the risks involved, that would just scare her—"and the dye shows his arteries."

"Oh," she said. "But—"

"And here he is now," pointed out Dewing, glad to be able to interrupt this dialogue.

A doctor and a nurse came down the corridor, wheeling a bed. Barbara walked quickly up to it and, looking down, saw Paul.

"Oh." She recoiled slightly, one hand tentatively touching the bedrail, the other flying to her mouth, where she bit on a knuckle. "Paul," she said.

He looked so pale and—she groped for the thought—waxen. Like a store mannikin. And above the obscene tube down his throat, his pale brown eyes stared at her unblinking, unnatural. Like a mannikin's. Like a blind man's. Or worse—as in a horror movie she had seen as a child and always remembered in fear—like a man whose soul has been possessed.

"His eyes . . . " she said.

Dewing and Falcone joined her, following the bed into the room.

"Eyes?" asked Dewing. He looked. Damn, he thought, some idiot has failed to close them.

"Can he see—?" began Barbara Justin.

"No. I'm afraid not," said Dewing, reaching over and closing Justin's eyelids. "He can't hear us either. He's completely unconscious."

"Oh," said Barbara. Having Paul's eyes closed made her feel only a bit better. She was reminded of putting pennies on the eyes of the dead.

"And now if you'll excuse us for a moment," said Dewing, drawing the curtain around Justin and leaving Mrs. Justin outside. He needed to ask her some questions. But once these were over, he hoped she'd leave and not come back too often. The intensive care unit allowed relatives to visit for only five minutes every hour on the hour—and Dewing figured that was sufficiently discouraging. Dewing and Falcone watched as Justin was reconnected to the respirator and as the electrodes were reattached to his chest to monitor his pulse and record an electrocardiogram. The monitor resumed its steady beep-beep. The nurse checked the I.V. and the catheter. A cuff had been left wrapped around Justin's left arm and the nurse now used it to take his blood pressure: 120/70. Normal. The nurse nodded. Dewing pulled the curtain back and, like a diffident magician or impresario, again presented Paul Justin to Barbara Justin.

She looked at Paul silently. Then, finally: "How is he? What is wrong?"

"We don't know yet," admitted Dewing. The barbiturate level was normal. So it wasn't an overdose. The spinal fluid was normal. So it wasn't any usual encephalitis nor—because there was no blood in the spinal fluid—was it a hemorrhage. So that left the probability of a hematoma, or a stroke caused by a blood clot. But naturally, Dewing wasn't going to discuss this with a layman.

"We don't know yet," he repeated. "But maybe you can help us."

"How?"

"Had your husband had any blackouts lately? Any fainting spells."

"No." Barbara was puzzled.

"Even any headaches?"

"Well . . . he was working hard. But no—no particular headaches, I don't think."

"Was he ill at all?"

"No. He was very healthy. Very—"

"On any medication?"

"I don't think so. You could check our family doctor. He'll—"

"We did. Could you check your own medicine cabinet?"

"All ... all right."

"And one more thing," said Dewing, matter-of-factly. "Was he depressed?"

"Depressed? Paul? Why?"

"Depressed enough to mention suicide?" he asked bluntly.

Barbara Justin was enraged. "Do you think," she stormed at Dewing, "that my husband—" Her hands clutched in mid-air; she was unable to continue. "How dare you—" she began.

She turned to Falcone for help. Falcone looked uncomfortable.

The three of them stood over Paul Justin. Barbara felt her knees weaken. She suddenly wanted to fall. Fall on Paul. Or fall on Dewing—for support or to throttle him. As she was about to act—do something, she wasn't sure what—another doctor appeared. "Mrs. Justin?" he said smoothly. Barbara looked at him. He was an older man, with an air of authority.

"Yes?" she said.

"I'm Dr. Jonathan Kitteridge, professor of neurosurgery. I heard about your husband." He held out his hand and shook Barbara's. "I'm very sorry. And I'll do—we'll all do—everything we can. Dr. Dewing is particularly expert at this kind of thing."

Dewing nodded, satisfied. Falcone wasn't quite as satisfied. He knew—the whole hospital knew—that Dewing was brilliant and quick. But also brusque. There were softer ways to ask a wife those standard questions about depression and suicide. And Dewing's brusqueness had another, more serious consequence: If his brilliance couldn't cure a patient quickly, he tended to write the patient off. Falcone worried that this case wasn't going to have a quick cure.

"Well," said Barbara Justin, to Kitteridge, "can you tell me"— she turned to include Dewing—"can *you* tell me—is he—is Paul"— she had trouble with the word—"paralyzed?" she said finally.

Dewing was angry to hear the word. What idiot nurse, he wondered, had mentioned the possibility to Mrs. Justin? But Kitteridge handled it calmly. "We won't know until he wakes up," he said.

"When ... ?"

"Within the week," said Dewing. Usually consciousness was regained in a day or two, but Dewing wanted to leave plenty of room.

The woman was still distraught. "Don't worry, Mrs. Justin," said Dewing. "These first few hours and days are crucial. So far your husband is doing fine."

"But it probably is a stroke, isn't it?" she demanded. "So he will be paralyzed? At least a little?" Her voice was pleading to be told that she was wrong.

"We really don't know, Mrs. Justin." Personally, Dewing was coming to believe this was a massive stroke. He wouldn't be surprised if Justin was—and would remain—paralyzed completely.

Barbara saw she was going to get little concrete out of the doctors. She moved closer to Paul. For a moment she had the fantasy that Paul was just napping. She saw him wake from this little nap, yawn and get up, trailing the silly, superfluous tubes and wires. She touched his cheek to wake him.

He didn't react at all and the fantasy passed.

"Oh, Paul," she said.

She could see now that his long, serious face seemed abnormally set, with deep lines etched in his forehead. It was as if he were wrestling with some hard problem. I hope you solve it, she thought. I know I can't. Barbara Justin weakened again and wanted to lean on Dr. Kitteridge. But she sensed his body stiffen like Paul's. Unlike Dr. Picard's, Dr. Kitteridge's sympathy didn't include an offer to be leaned on. Barbara tried to pull herself together.

"We'll call you when we know more," said Kitteridge. "Why don't you go home now and get some rest."

"All right, Doctor," she said. "Thank you."

She turned and walked out. Out of the room, past the nurses' desk and down the hall. She wasn't sure where to go from here. The last five hours had taken their toll. On the plane, Barbara had gazed down at the rolling green farmlands of Massachusetts and Connecticut. She tried to take strength from the idea that down there life went on. But several times, when the plane's engines changed pitch, Barbara thought of the plane crashing and realized she would not be unhappy to die. If Paul dies, she thought, walking down the hospital corridor, I would like to die, too.

And then she thought of her children—and knew that, no, not yet, she had to go home and go on.

New York City

Frank Lattimer took the elevator to the fifth floor, to the intensive care unit. The elevator door opened and he was confronted with an unhappy-looking woman. He started to walk out, she started to walk in. "Going down?" she asked. "Up," he corrected her. "Oh," she said, and stood in the doorway, a bit confused.

A nurse tried to go around the woman and walk into the elevator, but the woman backed up into the nurse. The nurse side-stepped her and made it inside, muttering. The woman started to apologize. Frank Lattimer stepped out.

"I'm sorry," said the woman to no one in particular. "My husband—" She gestured vaguely, trying to explain.

"Yes," said Lattimer. He took a guess—he had nothing to lose: "Excuse me, but are you Mrs. Justin?"

"Yes," said the woman, warily. She looked at Lattimer as if he might have more bad news for her.

"Yes, well, I'm Frank Lattimer. I live down the street from you—in Dobbs Ferry—and—"

"Yes?" Puzzled.

"—and I rode in on the train yesterday morning with your husband. When I heard what happened I naturally came—"

"Lattimer? Are you a friend of Paul's? He never mentioned—"

"Well, yes, a friend," lied Lattimer. "To ride the train with, you know."

"Oh."

"And we had an interesting talk. Paul said that—"

"Yesterday?" she asked, trying to get it straight. "You mean, just before—?"

"Yes. And—"

She gripped Lattimer's arm. "How was he yesterday?" she asked. "Was he feeling all right? What did he say?"

Lattimer regarded the tall, beautiful—and distraught—woman. He noted his good luck. If she knew anything of her husband's research, now was the time when she'd be most likely to blurt it out.

So Lattimer played on her trust a bit. "Well, gee," he said, "Paul seemed fine to me. We talked . . . you know, nothing in particular— about the garden I'm working on—he said you had tried gardening, too . . . "

Barbara Justin smiled, encouraging him to go on. "Ah . . . what else?" said Lattimer. He pretended to try to remember. "Well, we talked like we always did, about his work on the 'C' particle. He said he'd thought he'd found it." Lattimer paused. "Is that right, Mrs. Justin?"

But Lattimer didn't get an answer. At that moment, the other elevator opened and Stefan Wojik appeared.

Wojik shot a dark look at Lattimer and cut in. "I'm Stefan Wojik," he said to Barbara, his manner full of middle-European charm.

"Oh, yes," she brightened. "You work with Paul."

"Yes," said Wojik. "Well, we—in the section—heard you were here so I came over to see—and to say how sorry we are. The whole section is. Can we do anything for you?" Wojik put a protective arm around Barbara. He glared at Lattimer as if to say: You again? Don't hound this woman.

Wojik started telling Barbara what had happened this morning. Since Wojik had seen Justin *after* Lattimer had, Barbara turned her attention to the kindly Czech.

Frank Lattimer withdrew gracefully. Talking his way past the nurse, he went into the room where Justin lay. He looked at the man he had talked to yesterday morning. Damn, thought Lattimer, is the cure for cancer locked up in your head? If it is, you deserve to be up and about doing something with it. And to be with your goodlooking wife who obviously loves you. Lattimer sighed. Yeah, coincident with what? he thought. It sure didn't look as if Paul Justin was being held captive by Soviet Intelligence or by Little Green Men from Mars. It looked as if he'd simply had a stroke. Had a stroke, and was annoyed by it: Justin's lips were pressed together in a tight, thin line. He looked stubborn and determined. But he was powerless. Well, okay, thought Frank Lattimer, I'll be stubborn for you.

This was a new idea. Yesterday, on the train, Lattimer had been Justin's friendly adversary. Today, he felt himself becoming the man's ally. For you and for me, thought Lattimer. I'll try again to get something out of your wife. Out of your colleagues across the street. Out of the doctors over here. Out of—

"Who are you?" demanded a man behind him. "And who let you in?"

Lattimer turned around. "Frank Lattimer," he said to the young man in white. "And I just sort of . . . came in. I'm a friend of his. And who are you?"

"Dr. Falcone. But—"

"Are you treating my friend?"

"Yes, but you shouldn't—"

"Well, let me ask you, Doctor . . . " Frank Lattimer began his ingratiating grilling.

New York City

Roberto Cruz was reading a poster on the wall of the subway station—the uptown side of the 77th Street/Lexington Avenue station—when the man came over to him. The poster said: "How to get a college graduate's job without 4 years of college." Well, thought Cruz, why not? Dr. Justin had said he'd be a good lab technician. And after knocking the doctor unconscious today, Cruz felt a change. As if one life—the shakedown, the slashings, prison—was over, and a new life was about to begin. As if—to borrow the beliefs of a crazy friend of his from Haiti—by striking at Justin he had acquired some of Justin's strength, his knowledge. He would henceforth be like Justin—clean, white, a man of *science*. Cruz searched his pockets for a pencil to write down the address on the poster. Around him, the subway platform kept filling up with more of the rush-hour crowd.

"Hey, excuse me," the man said softly.

Roberto Cruz was startled. The man was so slight and nondescript, it was surprising he was there at all. Cruz looked at him. He had a small mouth and dark, sad eyes. He wore an old black suit, white shirt and no tie. A clerk, a nobody.

"Murdoch sent me," the man said softly. He had a slight accent that Cruz could not place. "Murdoch liked how you handled it."

"Oh," said Cruz. He was happy. "Thanks. He told me."

A single drop of sweat dangled from the end of the man's long, turned-down nose. It made the man look a little silly. Jeez, it's hot, thought Cruz. There was a rumbling coming up the tunnel. Okay, he thought. So get on with it, mister.

"Yeah," said the man. He pulled a roll of bills halfway out of his pants pocket. "And this is the bonus." He pushed the roll back in. "Ride one stop with me and I'll count out your thousand."

For two years now, Roberto Cruz had been off the streets. His street-wise suspicions were dulled. Besides, he was almost a *scientist* now.

"Great," said Cruz. One stop was what he'd intended to ride anyway, to see a movie on 86th Street.

"Come on," said the very thin man, moving toward the edge of the platform.

The train rumbled toward the station. Cruz followed the man, who went through the crowd as easily as if he were invisible. Other people moved forward, too. The rumbling was louder. Behind the growing light in the tunnel grew the dark bulk of the first subway car. The crowd jockeyed for position. Bodies pressed against Cruz. I won't ride this way much more, Cruz promised himself. He was sure Justin took only cabs. And a thousand dollars will sure help. Hey, Murdoch must really be pleased.

The train was roaring into the station and the crowd was instinctively pulling back. At that instant, with the first car closing at them from twenty feet away, the man Murdoch had sent put one bony, expert elbow into a certain point in Cruz's spine and Cruz went off the platform.

Roberto Cruz screamed in mid-air. There was a gasp from those in the crowd who saw him go flying. Grasping for his promised future, Cruz tried desperately to remember the address on the poster. He flew into the train. And then down onto the track and under the wheels.

The train screeched to a halt. Under the train, where no one—thankfully—could see, were the remains of one of the few people who knew about the cure for cancer. And the only person, besides Murdoch and Ives, who knew the link to Dacey Pharmaceutical.

The very thin—but very strong—man certainly didn't know. He'd killed Cruz as he always killed, for cash and no explanations. This was how Janko Velic, born in Croatia forty-five years ago, living in America since the end of World War II, routinely made his living. His only stray thought in this job was that he wished he'd been permitted to use a knife. He was even more expert with a thin, quiet knife.

Velic calmly made his way out through the hysterical, surging crowd. No one had noticed him commit the murder. No one noticed him leave.

New York City

All through the dinner of paella and wine, Frank Lattimer had kept his promise to Joan Scully. He hadn't asked her about Paul Justin. Instead, he'd asked her about herself.

Her answers were fairly standard for a first date. He learned how long she'd lived in Manhattan (two years) and where she went to graduate school (Columbia) and college (Grinnell) and where she grew up (a small city in Nebraska). He learned her work was very important to her and that for relaxation she went to movies ("I'm a nut") and played, she claimed, "a mean game of backgammon." And that once she'd gone white-water canoeing (not a safe, organized, group trip but "me and a guy and a canoe and we nearly killed ourselves") and might be tempted to do it again.

"So what are you doing staying in the city on a broiling weekend?" he asked her. "Why aren't you at least on a train for the Hamptons?"

"For the same reason I don't go to singles bars in Manhattan. I don't like that scene."

"Then what *will* you do tomorrow?"

"Turn on the air conditioner and read."

"Ah. So now you're a stay-at-home."

"Or go to the Mets game. They're playing the Reds and Johnny Bench is back in the line-up."

"I didn't know he was out."

"Foul tip on the finger."

"Oh," Lattimer had said.

"My father was the doctor for the athletic department at the college back home," Joan had explained. "I went to all the games with him."

"So that's why you—"

"—went into medicine? Or at least medical research? I guess so. Dad could heal a broken bone just by looking at it. I don't have that talent, but ... "

Lattimer had had an insight. "So you're Daddy's girl."

"Sort of."

"Haven't found any man to replace him?"

"I keep looking, Mr. Lattimer," Joan Scully had said.

After dinner, they walked aimlessly for several blocks and then, because they were near the East River, they crossed the Drive and walked along the water's edge. A faint breeze came up from the river. Across it, in the dark, the factories of Queens were strangely handsome outlines with sparkling lights. Somewhere behind them on the path, someone had a transistor radio playing Simon and Garfunkel. It was a soft, warm night.

"So tell me about Paul Justin," said Lattimer.

Joan Scully shook her head in dismay.

"It *is* after dinner," he pointed out.

Joan sighed. Then, in ten minutes, she very precisely described the theory behind "C" particle research and how Paul had probably tackled it and the obstacles he had probably run up against. Lattimer was disappointed. It was no more than what he had learned from Justin on the train and from his calls to the experts yesterday and today.

"That's all?" asked Lattimer. "Are you *sure* Justin hasn't discovered something?"

"Frank," said Joan, "I think more of Paul's work than anybody in the Institute. If he'd come up with the slightest thing, I'd be the first to tell you he was about to cure cancer."

"So the Institute's down on his work?"

"I hear two years ago it nearly got him fired."

"Why wasn't he?"

"Oh," said Joan vaguely, "I think Virology got a grant from outside. It saved the budget."

"Is that usual? A grant to a particular section?"

"No," Joan said. "But so what? We take the money where we can."

"Who gave the grant?"

"Before my time. I don't know."

"Who would?"

Joan Scully laughed. "Frank, you're really going to pursue this?"

"You bet I am. Who'd know?"

"Underwood, I guess."

Lattimer nodded. They crossed back over the Drive. "Well," he said, stopping on the corner of First Avenue, "thank you very much. Can I walk you home or shall I leave you where I found you—on some neutral ground?"

Joan Scully didn't know whether to laugh or be angry. "Damn it all," she said. "You make it sound like a bribe. Buy me dinner so you can play Twenty Questions. Don't I get to ask who *you* are?"

Lattimer smiled at her, a slightly lopsided, unforced smile that she liked very much. Come to think of it, she had very much liked the tall, good-looking man's presence all evening.

"Just a simple ace reporter, ma'am. Trying to make a deadline."

"The hell you are," she said. "You're a dog with a bone between your teeth. Look at you: You've been limping around the city for the past half hour, trying to soften me up on a casual little stroll so I'll tell you about Paul Justin—when any *sane* man would be home in bed resting that leg."

Lattimer smiled again. "Touché," he said. "But how do you know I wasn't born with this leg? How do you know you're not making fun of a cripple?"

"The pain shows," she said. "What did you do to it, anyway?"

They were on First Avenue in the Sixties, in the heart of the uptown Friday night scene. There was a constant stream of people going past them, in and out of the chic bars and restaurants. Couples were laughing, having a good time, and singles were determinedly looking for it. In the midst of the whirl, Lattimer was suddenly tired. He allowed himself to feel the throbbing in his thigh.

"Touch football," he said to Joan Scully. "Thought I was still eighteen. Thought I could run forever."

"And you're not?" she asked, teasing. "Not an iron man?"

At the old nickname, which Scully had stumbled on totally unawares, Lattimer winced. He nodded ruefully. "No, sometimes even us simple ace reporters push too hard. Just like my uncle hitting a vein of coal. It's a rare good vein so you drill and drill and you get so carried away you don't put up enough timber supports and so the whole damn roof falls on you."

"What?" asked Joan Scully. Lattimer had barely talked about himself, so she didn't know what he was referring to.

They resumed walking—more slowly, Lattimer not forcing the leg—and he told her. He told her about his childhood in Cardiff. About his father's relatives and friends—miners all—pushing themselves. Pushing themselves in a worked-out mine for low pay, because the big coal company had given up on the mine and the new owner was trying to run it on a shoestring. And his father pushing himself into bankruptcy in his grocery store because his relatives and friends ran up bills they couldn't pay. And so Frank Lattimer pushing himself to get *out* of Cardiff and then pushing himself in his job, because it was all he knew how to do. And so pushed himself into better jobs and out of his marriage.

While he talked, Lattimer had been following Joan Scully up the avenue. She now stopped in front of a brownstone in the Seventies, between First and Second. Lattimer's revelations had surprised and pleased her. She was glad to see what she had guessed was there— inside the reporter, a person. Lattimer was also surprised. Hell, he laughed at himself, I'm as bad as Paul Justin letting stuff slip on the train yesterday.

"Speaking of Paul Justin . . . " said Joan Scully.

Lattimer was taken aback. "Which we weren't," he said. Because I'm speaking my mind, he thought, does that mean she can *read* my mind?

"But speaking of him," she persisted, "I still don't see why you're pushing yourself on *this* job, on what you think is *his* story. I mean, it's really not Paul, is it? You're not a lifelong friend of his."

Joan Scully had unlocked the front door of the brownstone and they were walking up the stairs. "Nope," admitted Lattimer. "Just ran into him on the train. Had a long talk while a fire stalled us in the tunnel."

"So what's this to you, then?" asked Joan. "No 'simple ace reporter' would waste his time trying to build a story out of an ordinary meeting on a train and an ordinary stroke and an ordinary grant of money."

"Well," said Lattimer, as Joan unlocked the door to her second-floor apartment. "Let me tell you another story. One of the first I covered in Pittsburgh."

They were inside her apartment now and both were conscious that perhaps there was more of mutual interest than just Frank Lattimer's stories.

Houston, Texas

In the antebellum-type mansion in River Oaks that Ray Ryker shared with his third wife, only son and domestic staff of three, one whole wing was off limits to everyone but Ryker.

Here he had a small gym, which included Nautilus exercise equipment, a swimming pool and a sauna. Here was also his office-library, which included a computer terminal and a billiard table. Ryker was now running racks on the table. It was how, back in Philly, he had hustled money to go to college and then to business school. This evening it was how he was trying to work off tension.

He lined up his next shot—cue ball into the ten, low and slightly off to the left. The ten ball to hit one back cushion, then one side cushion, then the other side cushion and into the corner pocket.

It was similar to the shot that had finally broken Ray Ryker's stepbrother.

It happened the day after New Year's 1958, when they were both back in the old neighborhood. They ran into each other in the Shamrock Bar. The Shamrock had a pool table where Ray had spent the week taking on some of the best people in the city and beating them one by one. Around noon, his stepbrother came in, drunk and careless. He started making digs about Ray being too short to see the balls, much less hit them. Ray stayed calm. A couple of high-rollers who had been betting on Ray suggested his stepbrother put his money where his mouth was. His stepbrother said sure. He said he could afford it—he owned part of a printing business. As the afternoon wore on, he lost $2,000 and then $5,000. He tried to recoup and got $8,000 in the hole. Then, in the early evening, Ray found himself facing a difficult three-cushion shot. "This sure is a tough one," said Ray. "Ten thousand dollars says you don't make it," said his stepbrother. "I'll take some of that," said several of the gamblers. "And I'll take some, too," said Ray. "I've got four grand." he added. Then he looked at his stepbrother. "But do you really have ten left?" he asked.

"Sure," said his stepbrother.

With perfect control, Ray made the shot. His stepbrother, it turned out, had only enough to cover half of the $18,000 he now owed. He paid that and tried to raise the other $9,000. He couldn't raise enough fast enough. The gamblers called some friends and one morning Ray's stepbrother was found in an alley with multiple fractures of both legs. They never did heal right. Ray Ryker supposed the man still limped around the printing plant, somewhere back in Philly.

Remembering now, more than twenty years later, Ray Ryker tapped the cue ball and watched the ten ball follow its predetermined pattern to the pocket. Now the five ball, side pocket . . . Ryker chalked his cue and frowned. The satisfaction of memory was crowded out by his present problem: How was he going to keep the Old Man alive while he put together a group to buy the company?

Goodhue had called Ryker this afternoon with the news that Ash was making out a will. Even though Ryker had told the doctors yesterday that Ash might do this, the fact of it disturbed Ryker. It meant that Ash might not fight as hard to stay alive. Plus now Virginia—getting nervous about being disinherited—

would start bugging the doctors to pull the plug. So how much longer *would* Ash live? Ryker felt the time pressure. Should he settle for less? Put together a group now to buy Texahoma—*without* him as president?

That idea destroyed Ryker's concentration. He hit the cue ball too hard. The five ball rammed the lip of the pocket, spun fast in it and spun out. Ryker's string was broken.

"Damn," he said.

He lined up his next shot.

The phone—his unlisted one—rang.

"Damn," he said again. He crossed to the desk and pressed a button on his phone console.

"Ryker," he said.

"Mr. Ryker," said a man's low, gravelly voice, "we're calling about Mathew Ash."

"Who is this?" demanded Ryker.

The man went on. "We know Mr. Ash will be dead in a month or less. And we have a way to save him."

Ryker reached for the button to disconnect the call. But something in the man's voice stopped him. The voice was very businesslike, very sure of itself.

"All right," barked Ryker, "talk. You've got thirty seconds."

He pressed another button on the console. It started a tape recorder.

"Very simply," said the man, "we have discovered a cure for—"

Beep. Beep. An electronic tone cut in. Then a recorded voice cut in: "Attention. The recipient of this call is using a mechanical recording device. Attention. The recipient of this call is—"

"Shut it off, Mr. Ryker," said the man.

Ray Ryker was impressed. It's not a nut, he thought, it's an elaborate swindle. Ryker was amused. He shut the tape recorder off.

"That's better," said the man dryly. "And don't try to trace this call either. You'll be wasting your time. Now, to the point. We have discovered a cure for cancer. The cure takes effect immediately and is absolute and permanent. One week after the serum is administered to Mr. Ash, there will be no cancer cells in his body. Thus his lungs, liver and spleen will be able to function normally. And although his stomach has been surgically removed, you'll discover that the doctors will be able to devise a substitute. Thus—"

"Absolute and permanent?" said Ryker. He was still chuckling over the basic claim.

"—thus, according to the actuarial tables and Mr. Ash's medical records, he can be expected to live another seven point two years." The man's voice became gently ironic. "Plenty of time for you to convince him to sell you Texahoma."

Ryker kept playing along. "And the price?" he asked.

"One-third of your assets. Shall we say $18 million? Of course," added the man smoothly, "you could tap company funds."

Ryker computed. Yes, his stocks, bonds, real estate—all the things he had worked so hard to accumulate—were worth between 50 and 60 million. And his caller knew it.

"Payable when?" asked Ryker.

"Half when you receive proof of the cure. The other half when we administer the cure."

"Uh-huh," said Ryker. "And what proof *will* I receive?"

"We suggest you secure the services of a cancer specialist whom you trust to remain discreet. Maybe Dr. Goodhue? In two days— Sunday—we will call to set up an appointment for your specialist. He should have his bags packed and ready to go. Once he arrives here, he will be permitted to phone you to verify the legitimacy of our operation. At that point, I would suggest you start raising your money. Then in two more days—Tuesday—we anticipate calling again. On *that* phone call, we anticipate that your specialist will verify the cure itself. We will then instruct you as to the method of making the first half payment—nine million—and set up an appointment for Mr. Ash." The man paused. "I apologize," he said in the same calm, ironic, infuriating voice, "for talking more than thirty seconds."

And he hung up.

Ray Ryker picked a billiard ball off the table and rolled it between his palms.

Well, he thought. Well, well.

In twenty years of Texas oil business, he'd gotten a lot of crazy, worthless propositions. But *this* one . . . ?

Could some scientist really have found the cure for cancer? Ryker wondered. Could that scientist now be trying to profit from it? Not measly Nobel Prize money—but real profit?

Think of it: Compile a list of what?—one hundred? two hundred?—multimillionaires dying of cancer. And then hold up each dying man—or his relatives or his partners—for a third of their fortune. Money they'd gladly pay to stay alive. What would you net? A billion dollars? Five billion? More?

Think of it: A discovery of such benefit to the whole human race turned into salvation for only the few who could pay the price. And into profit for even a fewer few!

But wait, thought Ryker, why the hurry-up? Why everything to be wrapped up in less than a week? Was it simply to make it hard for him to track down his caller? Or was it because someone else was about to *publish* the cure? Imagine spending eighteen million dollars for something that, in a month, would be free!

And of course, nine chances out of ten, the whole thing was probably just a swindle anyway.

Well, he had to pursue that one remaining chance.

Ryker made a mental list of some people to call: His accountants—to trace who'd been snooping into his finances. And a telephone electronics expert—to trace Sunday's call when it came. And then, because Ryker felt these two would fail, he put his broker on the list—to prepare to start selling his stocks. And Dr. Goodhue— to be ready to check out the claim.

Ryker wondered what other multimillionaires around the world were making similar lists tonight. In Manhattan penthouses, Acapulco villas, German castles, Arab palaces. All of them doubting the voice on the phone—but none able to disregard it.

Ray Ryker rolled the billiard ball across the table into the far corner pocket. After the frustration of having to wait for Wissenbach, it felt good that he, Ryker, could take action. He grinned, showing a lot of teeth.

New York City

Joan Scully's place was a standard half-floor, one-bedroom apartment facing the street. And it was furnished on a graduate student's income—secondhand couch and chairs, grass rug, pine bookcases. But the room was bright and alive. There were plants and hand-covered pillows on the couch, and modern prints (not the standard ones from museum gift shops, noted Lattimer, but ones that were a lot more . . . challenging was the right word) on the walls. I like it here, he concluded.

Joan Scully waved him to the couch while she fiddled with the air conditioner. "Go on," she said, "yes? One of your first stories in Pittsburgh?"

"Well," said Lattimer. He sat back and relaxed. "The *Courier* started me as a cub reporter all over again. Gave me a week covering night court. Family knife fights. Whores rolling johns. Big news, right? Well, then there was this bum the cops brought in, drunk in the gutter, and they were going to throw him in jail. Sort of a favor, because it was a cold January—like that O. Henry story, you know?"

"I know," Joan said, frowning at the air conditioner.

"Well, he sure looked like a bum, like another of the hundreds of ordinary cases I'd seen that week and I was nearly asleep. It was 2

A.M. and I was bored. But something—I don't know what—something woke me up and I paid attention."

"Yes?" Joan was standing in the middle of the room, her own attention wandering. "How about some music?" she asked. "Record player's broken. The radio?"

Lattimer waved an okay at her. She turned on a soft rock station, on low. "Go on," she said, "just background. I'm listening." I'm only part-listening, she thought, because I'm part-wondering what—now that I've invited him in—what happens next? It was very disconcerting because she realized that she very much wanted to go to bed with Frank Lattimer, very much wanted to do it *now*, tonight. But she'd never slept with a man on a first date and so where were her supposed standards, huh? Where? she asked herself.

"So I went over to the bum," said Lattimer, "and looked closer. He was awful. Unshaven. Clothes in rags. And he reeked of cheap wine and no baths. But his jacket was unbuttoned and I thought I saw something on his shirt."

"Speaking of cheap wine," said Joan. "Would you like a drink? Wine? Something stronger?" She felt the need to distract herself by keeping busy.

"What are you having?"

"Scotch."

"Fine," said Lattimer. Joan went to the liquor cabinet. " . . . Anyway," said Lattimer, "sure enough, there was a monogram on the shirt. J.J.M."

"Soda? Water? Straight? On the rocks?"

"Jesus!" said Lattimer. "This is an earth-shattering story. Do you want to hear it?"

"I want to hear it."

"On the rocks then," said Lattimer. Joan went to get glasses. " . . . Anyway," said Lattimer, "that rang a bell. John Jordan Meredith."

"Meredith," said Joan, from the small kitchenette. "Damn," she said, "the air conditioner's stuck on low again."

"Are you listening?" asked Lattimer.

"I'm listening and sweating. Meredith. The crazy millionaire. He was missing for a month or something."

"He was missing till I found him. It made page one. And to this day I can't tell you why I knew he wasn't an ordinary bum wearing somebody else's thrown-out shirt. It was just instinct."

"Nonsense," said Joan Scully, putting ice in the glasses.

"The same instinct that I've got about Paul Justin. That something else is going on."

"Nonsense," said Joan. "It was something else you saw about Meredith. Like he wore a Harvard class ring."

"He'd pawned his rings."

"Or you heard him talk. You know—upper-class Long Island lockjaw." Joan poured the scotch.

"Meredith was from Cleveland. He sounded like you and me."

"Or . . . well . . . " Joan Scully came in with the drinks. On the radio, the music was over. The announcer was reading the eleven o'clock news.

" . . . the IRT Lexington Avenue uptown local was delayed at rush hour this evening when a man fell in front of an oncoming train at the Seventy-seventh Street station."

"Yesterday, fires on the tracks," said Lattimer, accepting his glass from Joan. "Tonight, bodies."

The announcer went on. "The man, tentatively identified as Roberto Cruz of 236 East 106th Street, was—"

Joan Scully dropped her glass of scotch. It missed the rug and smashed on the floor.

"—killed instantly. In other news, the City Council today voted to—"

Joan had one hand over her mouth. "Oh," she said. "Oh." She bent to pick up the shards of glass.

"Joan," said Lattimer. "What's wrong?"

Joan, still in a daze, cut several fingers of her right hand on the glass. Blood flowed.

"Joan!" demanded Lattimer. He bent down with her and gripped her shoulder.

"Um, clumsy," she said, sucking her finger. "I—I know"—she waved her hand at the radio—"that boy, Roberto. He worked with us. In Virology. A really nice boy. Funny—he was the one that found Paul this noon, ran to get help. Now he's—"

"He—" began Lattimer.

"—dead."

"—discovered Justin?" finished Lattimer.

"Yes. Um, that smarts."

Why didn't I talk to him when I had the chance? demanded Lattimer of himself. And why is he dead now? "So why is he dead?" he asked aloud.

"Huh?"

"Why?" stormed Lattimer. He waved a fist. "Why did Justin have a stroke and why did Roberto whatever—"

"Cruz."

"—Cruz get killed?"

"Frank," said Joan Scully, "is this your damn instinct? You think there's a connection . . . " Her eyes widened. " . . . that somebody *deliberately* . . . ?" She stopped. "You can't mean that." Forgetful of her finger, she was now letting it drip on her dress. "But who? Why? How?"

"Tell me about Roberto Cruz," said Frank Lattimer evenly.

"Oh, God," sighed Joan. "He was just a nice boy. A lab assistant. A Puerto Rican. I gathered he was pretty much alone in New York, trying to make his way up. Sometimes I practiced my Spanish with him. That's—that's all. I can't think of anything else."

"There must be more. When did he—"

"Look, Frank," said Joan Scully, "I'm dripping. Let me bandage myself first. I can see this is going to be a long evening."

While she was gone, Lattimer wiped up the puddle of liquor and glass. He fiddled with the air conditioner—but it remained stuck. The apartment was hot and muggy. On the radio, the announcer was saying that the current humidity was 86 percent and the chance of rain tomorrow was 60 percent. Lattimer wished the percentages were reversed; they needed some rain to break this heat. He turned around to see Joan leaning against the door frame. In addition to the Band-Aids on her left hand, there were now Band-Aids on her right. But that was the least interesting part of her. Joan had gotten out of her dress and into jeans and a T-shirt. Unlike the dress, the jeans and T-shirt clung to her body. Shocked by Roberto's death and what Lattimer was implying about it, she was only partly aware of changing into some of her tightest casual clothes. But Lattimer was completely aware. He thought Joan Scully looked fantastic.

"Still smarts," she said, waving her finger. "Like a paper cut."

Lattimer took her fingers. "Let me kiss it better," he said, pressing them to his lips.

"Oh," she objected. Their eyes met, questioning. Standards? wondered Joan. Does she want to? wondered Lattimer.

"And then I'll kiss the rest of you better," he said, moving to her lips. At six-foot-two he was exactly a foot taller than Joan Scully, but their bodies fit together perfectly—her flat stomach against his narrow waist, her smooth cheek against his broad chest.

"Frank," she started to object between kisses, "I—"

Embracing her, he watched the tips of her red hair brush back and forth on her long, creamy-white neck. A vein on her neck throbbed. He bent down and kissed it.

"Oh—" she moaned, throwing her head back.

Her arms had been wrapped around him. Now she raised her hands to caress his face. She stopped. "The bandages," she said, "I feel clumsy. Another night—"

"Your mouth isn't clumsy at all," he said.

Kissing her, he walked her toward where he sensed the bedroom must be. But they never made it. Earlier, on the street, something had broken within Frank Lattimer and he had talked about his past. Now something broke within Joan Scully. She was all over him and he all over her and he took her on her back on the hard wood floor of the hallway. He's right, she thought, I didn't need my hands. And her mouth and his mouth sucked pleasure from all over each other's bodies.

Much later, lying in bed in each other's arms, Lattimer asked drowsily how Daddy's little girl was doing. So she squeezed his testicles very hard. "Oof," he said.

"For that," she said, "you can take me to the Mets game tomorrow."

"Rain check," he said, rolling over, aching. "I've got to look into Justin's work plus talk to Underwood plus talk to whoever knew Roberto Cruz. For a start."

Well, Joan Scully told herself, you always did want a man who cared about what he did and then stuck to it.

"I'll go with you," she said.

"Unless you are nude," he murmured, stroking her nude body as he started to fall off to sleep again, "please do not lean against this machine."

"What?" she asked.

"Something I learned today in Virology." And he slept.

Dobbs Ferry, New York, and New York City

Steve and Laurie went to sleep all right but Melissa kept waking up. First she wanted Barbara to get her a drink of water. Then she wanted help finding her favorite doll to sleep with. Then she wanted the light on in her closet to keep the ghosts away. Finally Barbara Justin sat down on Melissa's bed and talked to her again. Was she afraid because of what had happened to Daddy? Yes. Did she understand that Mommy was right down the hall and would be nearby all night? "Yes," answered Melissa, "but why were you sad and crying before you went away to Boston? Was it 'cause you knew Daddy was going to get stroked?" Barbara didn't know how to answer that. She hugged Melissa and tucked her in once more. Melissa curled up sucking her thumb, something she hadn't done for almost two years. Barbara Justin went into the master bedroom and prepared to sleep yet another night without Paul. Then dutifully, as Dewing had instructed her to, she got up to check Paul's medicine cabinet. The only thing that didn't belong there was a cufflink he'd apparently misplaced long ago. Barbara slipped it in the pocket of her robe. She telephoned Boston to get some mothering for herself.

Thirty miles away and in another world, Paul Justin was drifting into and out of foggy dreams. He was fishing with his father on Stone Lake. His father was asking him something. "Mr. Justin," said his father, "Mr. Justin." "Mr. Justin," said the nurse, "squeeze my finger, Mr. Justin." She put her finger in the palm of his hand—as she had every hour since this afternoon—and, as before, there was no response. The nurse continued her other hourly tasks. She checked her patient's pulse with her fingers and compared it against the result on the monitor. Normal. She wrapped the cuff tight around his arm (Justin's father was now squeezing his arm demanding an answer) and took his blood pressure. It was also still normal. She shone a pen light in his eyes (the sun was hot over Stone Lake; it burned Paul Justin's eyes) and noted the right pupil was still dilated. Then, as she did every two hours, she briefly took him off the respirator (Paul Justin gasped for breath; he had fallen out of the boat, gone underwater). The nurse suctioned out the mucus that had accumulated in her patient's bronchial tubes (he was gagging underwater, wanting to cough but unable to) and reconnected him to the respirator. Then, as she did every four hours, she rolled him on his side (the lake currents buffeted him) so he wouldn't develop bed sores. She moved on to the next bed. (Paul Justin, deep underwater, still heard his father calling his name. His father was demanding to know the cure for cancer. Paul struggled to speak but his mouth filled with water. He was drowning. Drowning and trying to scream but unable to scream . . .)

SATURDAY

New York City

The morning began, unromantically, with the grinding sound of the garbage truck below her window. Resentfully, Joan Scully stirred. Half-awake, feeling warm toward him, she stretched out a hand to touch Frank Lattimer.

Frank wasn't there. Joan woke up completely. She threw back the sheet and sat up against the headboard. The grinding continued. If it weren't for the fact that the garbage would stink on the sidewalks, she wished the garbagemen would stage one of their periodic strikes.

The grinding stopped and she could hear water running in the bathroom sink. Joan threw on a robe and went into the bathroom. She pressed herself up against Frank Lattimer's back as he shaved.

"Hi," she said.

"Hi," he said, shaving with one hand, the other hand moving down to fondle her thigh. He gestured with the razor. "Hope you don't mind," he said, "but I found this man's razor in here—figured I could use it."

"It's an ex-boy friend's. I keep it for just such occasions," said Joan dryly. "But usually on those occasions, the man doesn't rush right out of bed to try it out—while he absent-mindedly touches me."

Frank Lattimer stopped shaving.

"Sorry," he said, "but it wasn't absent-minded. It was quite deliberate. And it felt nice."

"Well," she said, "you could have waited. You don't have to shave right now, you know." She paused. "Or do you have to make some deadline?" she asked, as dryly as before.

"But shaving helps," said Lattimer, as he started shaving again. "It's a nice mechanical thing to do while my mind sorts things out—in the cold light of day."

The last phrase bothered Joan Scully. She pulled away, leaned against the bathroom wall and watched his eyes in the mirror. "So how do things sort?" she asked carefully.

"I think," said Lattimer, as he rinsed out his razor, added more lather and attacked under his chin, "that maybe I got carried away last night. Justin and Cruz. I mean, what's the connection—*really*? Did somebody kill Cruz because he knew too much? But what could he know? Did Justin," he asked rhetorically, "ever discuss his work with Cruz?" He turned matter-of-fact: "*Did* he?"

"No," said Joan. "I never heard him."

"Could Cruz have seen something on the TV screen or the electron microscope—and understood it?"

"No."

"Well, then—what's the connection? Okay, let's say Justin was getting close to the cure. Let's say somebody doesn't want him to find it. So they pay Cruz to kill Justin—and then kill Cruz so he doesn't talk." Lattimer grinned through his lather. "Sounds like a thriller—doesn't it?"

Joan nodded, getting more and more bothered.

"But—still possible. But—unlikely. First of all, there are easier ways to make a death look like an accident. I mean, why not push *Justin* in front of the train? Secondly, Justin isn't dead. I mean, if somebody wanted to kill him, they'd kill him. Thirdly—"

"Frank," said Joan, "what does this add up to? That you aren't going to pursue it any further?"

"Well, I didn't say ... "

"Because if you don't," she said, getting angry, "if you never intended to, if all this talk about Paul and Roberto was just a cheap way to get my time, get me interested, get me into bed ... " She turned and walked into the kitchen. "You son of a bitch," she said, softly.

"Hey, wait a minute," said Lattimer. He tossed water on his face, grabbed a towel and followed her. "Hey, wait. Last night you were bugged because you thought I was more interested in a story than in you. Now you're bugged because you think I'm more interested in you than in a story." Joan was in the corner formed by the stove and the sink. He blocked her way. "Now you can't have it *both* ways. What *do* you want?"

Joan felt a little confused. She tried to get hold of what she meant. "Well, it would be nice," she said, "if you were interested in *both*. Me and your story. But it looks more like love 'em and leave 'em. I mean, why didn't you stay in bed this morning—what are you afraid of?"

"Afraid of?"

"We could have," she said, spelling it out, "made love."

"So we will," said Lattimer, softening. "We will again. But do we have to make love on your schedule?" He got a little harsh. "Did I flunk the 8 A.M. test?"

"No ... " She was more confused. He did have a point, she felt, about her getting bugged either way. And about judging him.

"It's just ... " she trailed off. Then she got firm. "Frank, it's just that I ... that's the first time I've ever gone to bed with anybody on the first night."

"I'm flattered," he said, meaning it.

"And ... I guess I'm afraid of what I've committed myself to. I mean—"

Joan Scully stopped herself. Words like "committed" were not words you used after sleeping with somebody on the first date, especially not when it was with a handsome, single young man on Manhattan's Upper East Side. What she wanted to say was that she wanted to be sure that he took her as seriously as she took herself— but she couldn't say that either.

And what Frank Lattimer wanted to say was that he also was afraid of what he was committing himself to. Because the last person he had liked this much was his wife—and he had destroyed that relationship. He was sensitive to the idea of flunking tests precisely because he had set up tests for Mary Ann. So naturally Mary Ann had flunked them and he had justified pulling away from his marriage and into his career, before things could get close.

Just as, he wondered, he'd pulled away to shaving this morning?

And Joan Scully wondered if maybe she *had* set up an 8 A.M. test for Lattimer, so he could flunk it, so she could justify pulling away from him now, before things could get close.

"I mean," Joan Scully finally continued, trying to keep it simple, "because I can see you really mattering to me."

"Same here," said Frank Lattimer, putting his arms around her.

They looked at each other for a few moments, silently, soberly.

"I think," said Joan, finally, "that we better get going before we waste the morning. You through in the bathroom?"

He felt his beard. "Well," he said, "before I was interrupted by a passionate young woman ... another few seconds under my nose."

"Okay," she said. "You do that. I'll put on coffee."

"Fine," he said, returning to the bathroom.

"You could let it grow, you know," she called. "I might like you in a mustache."

"You think," he asked lightly, "that we'll last that long?"

"We just might," she said, smiling.

The rich smell of coffee filled the apartment. From under the window came the whoop! of wild laughter of a teen-ager. Lattimer finished shaving and Joan started toward the bathroom. As they met in the hall, Lattimer said, "I'm calling my cop friend—Pete Whitcomb—about Cruz. And then we'll head over to your lab again, and look around. You could really help. Okay?"

"Okay," she said. "If you butter the toast."

"Fair enough," he said.

They passed each other in the narrow hall, their sides brushing. Joan Scully felt the brushing was sexier than many lovemakings she had known.

New York City

As part of his successful effort at making himself into a white man, Hugh Underwood owned a cottage in one of the more WASP communities on Fire Island. He had planned to go there last night with his wife and children. He had looked forward to the breezes off the Sound. But instead, he sent his family on ahead. And this morning, stooped under a sun that burned the Manhattan asphalt and stooped also under the weight of what he had discovered on Justin's desk, Underwood made his way, dragging his bad leg, to the Oakes-Metcalf Hospital.

He looked in on Justin. The man was still in a coma, breathing on a respirator, being fed intravenously. There didn't seem to be any doctors around, but the nurse who let Underwood into Justin's room was up on the news.

"Really got them stumped," she said. "It could be a massive brain hemorrhage or a massive stroke or a subdural hematoma. They just keep him alive and keep testing."

"*Will* he live?" asked Underwood.

"Who knows?" said the nurse. "For now, he's stable."

"But he will regain consciousness?" asked Underwood hopefully.

"Again: Who knows?"

Underwood crossed the bridge to the Institute and rode up an elevator. His possession of Justin's notes weighed him down even more. What if weeks go by and Justin is still unconscious? Do I have the right to determine when the existence of the notes should be revealed? Do I have the right to start deciphering them? (He had taken the notes home last night, had put them in his suitcase next to his bathing trunks, had closed the suitcase—and then, looking at the suitcase sitting there like a ticking bomb, knew he lacked the nerve to take it to Fire Island and start working on it.) But, on the other hand, Underwood asked himself, as he got off on the top floor of the Institute, do I have the right to simply keep it all in the closet?

Goddamn it, he swore. It was bad enough that somebody might be about to reveal the cure for cancer and thus destroy his, Underwood's, career. But that the somebody was *himself* . . . !

Hugh Underwood was a section head, but he was not a leader. He didn't want to be the sole possessor of this knowledge. And just as, years ago, he was happy to let other people decide what lunch counters he could eat at, so he now wanted other people to decide this one for him.

In this case, "other people" was Warren Brown. Underwood found the director of the Institute as he knew he would: in his office on Saturday morning, trying to prepare yet another report that might somehow mollify Health, Education and Welfare. And simultaneously prepare a report for the Board of Scientific Advisors. The director's desk was a sea of paper. As Underwood came in, Brown was standing over it, rifling through it, muttering, "Now where did I put that lousy . . . ? Oh, hello, Hugh. What are you doing here?"

At first Underwood wasn't sure what he should say. He was used to seeing Warren Brown, as the director, in suit and tie. It went with his big top-floor, corner office, with his plaques for scientific and civic accomplishments on the walls. But today Brown was wearing Bermuda shorts and an old T-shirt. And the T-shirt was plastered to his chest with sweat. Brown wiped his brow. "Damn building," he said, as if partially reading Underwood's mind. "They turn off the air-conditioning on weekends. Sweat drops on my reports, huh? Lousy. Now what can I do for you?"

Feeling a little better, Underwood told him. How, for several years, although few people were aware of it, he had let Justin continue his hunt for the "C" particle. ("*That* dead horse?" said Brown. "No, no," he waved reassuringly. "Go on.") And how, yesterday, he had found Justin's notes, how he had hoarded them, and what he was certain they meant. Finishing his tale, Underwood felt his burden lifted.

Warren Brown sat down.

"You *are* certain?" he asked.

"Yes."

"No doubt?"

"Not in my mind."

"What if other researchers looked at the notes—would they be certain also?"

"You mean, because I know Paul, am I really in—?"

"Yes."

"No," said Underwood. "It's there."

Brown looked at the ceiling.

"*I'd* like to see the notes," he said.

"Of course."

"Today?"

"Oh . . . yes." Underwood was suddenly relieved. "I'll bring them here. Leave them with you."

"Well," said Brown. "We'll make a couple of copies. You keep the original, of course."

"Of course," said Underwood automatically. He stopped. "Why?" he asked.

The director gathered together some of the mess of paper into a pile. He tapped the pile several times on his desk to line up the edges. He slowly moved his fingers around the edges to line them up even more. "Why?" he repeated, reflectively. "Because they're *your* notes, too, of course."

"Mine?" asked Underwood. But I didn't want anything to do with them, he thought. That was the whole point of my coming here and—

"Of course. You've been Paul's supervisor. You've guided him."

"I—? No. I only permitted him to—"

"You're modest, Hugh," said Warren Brown. "Perhaps you can't honestly recognize your achievement. Let me put it this way: You had the instinctive genius to recognize that a discredited idea was actually the right idea. And the determination to see that it was pursued."

"But—"

Brown waved a hand. "Of course, as section head, responsible for so much *mandated* research, for doing it and supervising it, you couldn't pursue the 'C' particle all by yourself. So, knowing Paul's interest, you had him—had him do the actual *tests*. While he consulted with you, and you advised him—*directed* him. Yes, directed him, Hugh. You are his chief, you know."

Hugh Underwood sat dumbfounded. He looked around the huge office, but there was no answer anywhere. He couldn't understand why the director was concocting this lie. Did he hate Justin? Did he honestly *believe* Underwood had directed the research? Well, it would be nice to believe it also. Better the instigator of the cure for cancer than the humble black servant. But he knew the truth. And Wojik, Scully, the whole section—they knew, too. Or could Brown make them, too, believe the lie? And could—? And why—?

Warren Brown saw Underwood's confusion and tried to handle it. "Relax, Hugh," he said. "Don't think about it now. Go get me the notes and then get out of this lousy city this weekend. You *were* going somewhere?"

"The Island."

"Sure, great. Play some ten—" Brown stopped, remembering the man's bad leg. "Drink, sail. Whatever." Brown stood up, extended his hand and shook Underwood's in a firm grip. To Underwood, he suddenly looked—sweaty T-shirt and all—very much like the director again. "And congratulations, Hugh," he said. "You've done a great service. For humanity. For the Institute. Don't think about it now, don't talk about it now—but you'll see later. It's true."

And with that, the director gave a half-wave, half-salute and Underwood found himself going out the door in a blaze—and in a haze.

New York City

"Frank," objected Joan, "it *is* burglary."

"Yeah," said Lattimer, twisting the paper clip in the lock. "Well, I sure would have preferred it if Justin had left the cure for cancer lying on his desk, but since, as you say, it's probably in this cabinet—"

"I said that's where his notes are. I didn't say you should pick the lock to get them."

"No? Well, what *do* you—damn." Lattimer removed the paper clip and bent it differently. He put his eye to the keyhole and talked to himself. "Come on. This one isn't so hard."

"You mean you've done this before?" asked Joan. She was bothered. "Where?"

Lattimer put a finger to his lips. "Professional integrity."

"Huh!" said Joan Scully.

They were alone in the virology section. Joan had signed them in downstairs and unlocked the door to the section. Now she stood across the small partitioned space from Frank Lattimer, trying to distance herself from what he was doing. Justin's terrain wasn't much—a battered desk heaped with papers and books, the wall above it pinned with photos and charts, the filing cabinet next to it topped by a dying ivy plant—but in her mind's eye she saw Justin lying on the floor unconscious, helpless to stop this violation.

Lattimer turned the paper clip in yet another direction. There was a soft click.

"Ah," he said. He slid the file drawer open. "Okay," he said to Joan Scully, "which one is it?"

"You want me . . . to pick out his file on the 'C' particle research?"

"Well, *I* wouldn't recognize it if it bit me."

"But . . . " Joan recognized her reluctance was silly. She was already a part of this.

She went through the files in the drawer. "Nothing . . . nothing . . . nothing . . . hey," she said jokingly, "here's something important. A copy of Paul's medical insurance claims." She went past them.

"Hey," said Lattimer, "wait. Let's have that file."

"You serious?"

"Sure."

"What for?" To Joan, this was even worse—prying into Paul's *personal* life.

"I want to see if he was ever treated for anything that could have contributed to his stroke—or whatever it is."

Joan shook her head—but handed it over. "I suppose," she said, "that if I find some love letters from a secret girl friend, you want those, too?"

"Sure."

"Hey—I'm joking."

"I'm not. If he had a girl friend, maybe he told her about his work."

"Frank," she said firmly. "Paul wasn't the type."

Lattimer shrugged his shoulders. Joan Scully kept looking.

"Nothing... nothing..." she said, "and nothing." She had looked through the whole drawer. "It's not here," she announced.

"But he kept it there?" asked Lattimer.

"Yes. This drawer."

"Well, maybe he didn't keep it there yesterday. Why don't you check the other drawers."

There were no locks on the other two drawers. With a sigh, Joan Scully went through them also. "Nothing," she said.

"And in the desk?"

She looked.

"And *on* the desk?"

She looked.

"Nothing." Joan Scully had been at this almost an hour. She was tired and bored. "Look, Frank, maybe he took it home."

"But you said you saw him take it out yesterday."

"Yes," she sighed. "I did."

"So somebody stole it," he concluded.

His statement hung in the air.

"Roberto?" Joan finally asked.

"Maybe." Lattimer sat on Justin's desk and thought. "It might explain," he said, "why he was killed."

"If he was killed."

"If, if," Lattimer granted the possibility and went on. "Suppose Cruz steals the file yesterday and gives it to somebody. Then somebody kills Cruz—because he *does* know too much."

"Okay," said Joan, dubiously. "But how did he steal it? Pick the lock like you did?"

"Sure," said Lattimer. He stopped himself. He got up and looked closely at the keyhole.

"No!" he said.

"How can you tell?"

"See those scratches?" He pointed.

Joan looked close. "Yeah. So?"

"So they weren't there—at least I don't think they were there—when I started. The lock was clean. If Roberto did it, he used a key."

"I repeat: 'So?' "

Lattimer stuck his thumbnail between his two front teeth.

"Hey," said Joan Scully, "do you bite your nails?"

"No," he said. "I'm thinking. I'm thinking a key could mean a lot of things."

"Okay. *Be* mysterious. Do we track down those 'things' now?"

"No. You show me where it happened."

"Where what happened?"

"Justin—his stroke—or whatever."

"What for?"

"I don't know," admitted Lattimer. "Get a feel for it, maybe."

Joan Scully shook her head at him and led the way down the hall to the electron microscope room.

They went in. Lattimer walked around. In contrast to the crowded, cluttered lab, it was just a plain room containing little more than a big machine and a chair in front of it. Lattimer pointed to the floor. "You found him here?"

"Yes."

"What was he doing?"

"On the floor?" Joan joked mildly.

Lattimer smiled. "With the microscope."

"I don't know."

"Well, he'd be looking at something, right? What would it be? A slide?"

"Sure. But I don't know what *of*."

Lattimer nosed around the microscope. "Where's the slide now?" he asked.

"Huh?"

"I mean, if he was looking at a slide when it happened—when he collapsed—wouldn't the slide still be in the microscope?"

"I doubt it," said Joan Scully. She looked. "No, it's not there. Whoever used the microscope next must have removed it. Or maybe Paul hadn't put it in yet."

Lattimer raised his index finger. "But if somebody removed it, wouldn't they have brought it down to your lab—I mean, they'd know it was Justin's, right?"

"Yeah, I guess," she said. "Well, so he hadn't put it in yet. Or he'd taken it out already."

"Then wouldn't it be around here?" asked Lattimer, nosing some more. The microscope and the surrounding counter tops were bare.

"It could be in his lab coat," said Joan Scully. "Sure. That's where it must be."

"Sure," said Lattimer, only half convinced. "Well, I'll check with the hospital. They'd have it now."

Joan Scully picked up his doubt. "Hey," she said, "where else would it be? Hey," she joked, "you don't think somebody stole it, too?"

"Maybe."

"But that's crazy," she objected.

"Is it? Wouldn't the slide tell whether the person or animal or whoever the slide came from had cancer or not? And if they did, what kind and how bad—all that?"

"Yes, but—"

"And if they *didn't* have cancer, if they were cured—"

"Frank," sighed Joan, "I tell you, it's so unlikely—no, *impossible*— that Paul found the cure, that you're completely ... " She broke off. It was no use arguing with him.

"Okay, okay," said Lattimer. He looked around some more. He tapped the TV monitor. "What's this?" he asked.

"It shows what's on the slide."

"But when you came in the room—" began Lattimer.

"—it was blank," Joan Scully completed the sentence. She contemplated the blank screen. "And it's too bad," she added, "because that would be even more valuable than the slide."

"Why?"

"Because it would have shown the enlargement—would tell us what part of the cell Paul was interested in."

"Mmm. Yeah. Too bad," said Lattimer.

"Of course," added Joan Scully, "if Paul *had* looked at a slide, maybe—before he collapsed—he could have taken a picture of it, of the enlargement."

"A picture?" asked Lattimer eagerly.

"Sure," she said.

Lattimer tapped the microscope. "Would it still be in here—the film?" He was excited.

Joan Scully checked the microscope's camera. "Yes, there's some advanced film. Of course," she pointed out, "we don't know whether it's Paul's." She paused. "Except," she said, "nobody else would leave it in here."

"Well, take it out, woman," urged Lattimer. "And let's get it developed."

Joan unloaded the camera. "I'm afraid it's going to have to wait till Monday," she said. "Till Reece—he's the technician—comes in."

Lattimer held out his hand for the film canister. "I don't want to wait."

"Well, I don't care who you know at what Rexall store," joked Joan Scully. "Nobody's equipped to handle this except somebody who—" She gestured at the towering microscope. "It's special film."

"Please," said Lattimer. He took the canister. "You'd be surprised whom I know."

Joan Scully regarded him and again shook her head. "No," she said slowly. "I don't think I would be surprised. Who else works weekends with an electron microscope besides the CIA?"

"You give me far too much credit," said Lattimer. "I have a friend at IBM up in Armonk. If I can reach him today, I think he'll do it." He juggled the canister thoughtfully. "Now, what can I tell my friend about this stuff? Do you have *any* idea where it came from?"

Joan Scully considered this a moment. "Well," she said. "Paul hadn't mentioned, recently, any work with people. So maybe," she suggested, "from the animal room?"

"Lead on," said Frank Lattimer.

Houston, Texas

"Is it nine o'clock yet?" Ash was screaming. "Is it nine o'clock?" He was sweating and tossing and he would have been tearing at the sheets and the tubes except that, an hour ago, when the pain had started getting intense, the nurse had strapped his arms to the sides of the bed. "Goddamn it! It's got to be nine o'clock by now!"

The nurse, Mrs. Crippen, was sitting on the far side of the room reading a paperback. She looked at her watch.

"I'm sorry, Mr. Ash. It's only quarter to."

"It can't be! It was twenty-to twenty minutes ago!"

"I'm sorry, Mr. Ash. Really." Crippen went back to her book. She was a stocky, matronly woman whose broad, flat face showed little sympathy. So Ash had easily turned her into a monster. He was wrong. Hardened as she was by thirty years of nursing, Crippen felt much pity for the old man. She had tried to distract Ash from his pain by suggesting television or music or even conversation. He had rejected them all. All he could do was scream for his nine o'clock shot of morphine. And it wasn't nine o'clock yet.

"Ah can't take it!" screamed Ash. "It's not fair!"

Crippen was getting a bit exasperated. "Mr. Ash," she said, "as John F. Kennedy said, life isn't fair."

"What?" he demanded.

"This book—about the Kennedys. It really shows how lucky we

all are, Mr. Ash. Yourself included. Why, did you know that after John F. Kennedy hurt his back in PT-109, he was in pain for the rest of his life? And that happened when he was a *young* man."

Ash was amazed at her. "Fuck Kennedy!" he screamed. "What? Ah don't care! Ah don't care!"

"Well, you should care. You've led a healthy, vigorous life for what?—seventy years? No major injuries, right?"

"Now!" screamed Ash. "Ah hurt *now!*"

"You haven't had three of your sons taken from you—violently. Two of them shot down in cold blood. You haven't felt the pain that Mother Rose Ken—"

"Fuck her!" screamed Ash. "Ah want to die!"

Crippen closed her book and slapped it down on the coffee table. She got up and advanced on her patient.

"Now, Mr. Ash, that's no way to be. Why, you have resources of strength you haven't even *started* to draw on. Now, you take Rose Kennedy. She says that by relying on God—"

"God*damn* God!" yelled Ash. "You really think that He exists? You really think He watches over us? Helps us? Hell—nobody— God—nobody—ever did anythin' for me. *Ah* did it for me. *Ah* did."

Nurse Crippen was shocked. She was not a churchgoer herself, but it was hard to imagine that a man like Matt Ash . . .

"You never . . . " she asked, "even as a little boy . . . you must have believed?"

"Oh, Ah believed!" screamed Ash. "Ah believed mah uncle when he said mah mamma would get well if we all prayed an' she *still* died of pneumonia an' the next year mah poppa ran away, jes' left, gone, an' Ah don't know where, an' mah fucking uncle, the fucking preacher, said don't worry, chillun, Ah'll raise you, an' Ah said, fuck you, fuck God, Ah'll raise mah*self*, an' Ah did—goddamn it."

Nurse Crippen touched Ash's arm just above the strap.

"Well, if not God, then," she said softly, "your family. Like Rose Kennedy says, *her* family has sustained *her*. And like you prayed for your mamma and poppa—"

"Prayed," spat Ash.

"Cared for them," said Crippen, "your family—your wife—cares for *you*."

Ash broke into a high laugh. "Family. Family. Fat, fat cow. Fat cow of a wife. Cares more about goddamn chocolate *cake* than she does me. Would give birth to goddamn Sara Lee *cake* before she'd give me a family, give me sons."

Crippen looked at the handsome, ravaged face, the feverish eyes, sweat glistening on the high cheekbones.

"Mr. Ryker . . . " she said softly, "*he's* cared for you like a son. Got all the top doctors for you. Pays for me, too. Out of his own money."

"*Mah* money!" screamed Ash. "Money Ah pay him! Pay him the only thing he understands. Not love. Not oil. Not the business. *He* never worked twelve hours straight twistin' casin' together with no power tongs—till his arms come out of their socket. Never pounded a hot steel bit an' got burnin' chips flyin' off at him like shrapnel. No! Harvard Business School. Flow charts. Decision trees. Bottom line. Fuckin' smart. Probably smarter 'n me. But never had his hands in *oil*—jus' money. No oil in his blood, not of *mah* blood, not *mah* son, not gonna give *him* mah business. No, *sir*! Gonna die first. Wanta *die!*"

"*Some*one," Crippen pleaded softly. "There must be someone, something . . . " She touched his forehead. "We all have—or remember—*some*thing. We can't all be Rose Kennedy but—"

"What time is it?" asked Ash evenly, teeth clenched.

Crippen looked at her watch. "Why, it's nine," she said, pleasantly surprised. She reached to the bedside cabinet for the hypodermic and the morphine.

"Probably later," spat Ash. "Probably later." He screamed, "YOU BITCH, YOU PROBABLY MADE ME WAIT!"

Nurse Crippen sighed and gave Matt Ash his shot.

New York City

Joan Scully unlocked the door to the animal room and turned on the light.

"Does the ASPCA know about this?" asked Lattimer.

"What?" asked Joan.

Lattimer surveyed the wall of cages, filled with hundreds and hundreds of sleeping, eating, burrowing, stretching or just plain dead-staring-ahead animals.

Joan caught on. "I assure you," she said, "that they're well cared for."

"Mmm," said Lattimer. "Looks like Leavenworth. Okay, Justin comes in here yesterday—what does he do?"

"I guess he makes a slide from one of his animals."

"You mean he kills it?"

"Uh-huh."

"Which one?"

"I'm not sure. Probably a hamster." Joan started looking closely at the cages. "Let's see—I think he had some over here—yes." She pointed at the label on a cage. Lattimer came over to read it.

"Justin AX532-06," read Lattimer. "What does that mean? And

what's that little fellow doing in there?"

"I don't know—that's Paul's own code, I guess. And that hamster—well, I think . . . earlier this week I remember seeing a few more in there."

"So Justin killed a few yesterday?"

"I guess."

"Why? To test the cure?"

"Oh, come on, Frank."

"Okay, okay. So where does he kill them?"

She showed him the dissecting table. "Here."

"Right," he said, taking it in. "And he makes slides?"

"Uh-huh."

"And what happens to the rest of the hamsters—the carcasses?"

She pointed to a bin. "They get thrown out, of course."

Lattimer looked inside the bin.

"My God, Frank!" She was startled. "The bin gets emptied every night. Or are we now going out to a garbage dump on Staten Island and look for hamster bodies?"

"No," he said. "I guess not."

"But you would," she said, amused, accusing.

"Well, I'd sure like to know if he cured those hamsters of cancer."

"But, Frank—you still wouldn't know. Even if you found cut-up pieces of a healthy hamster, you wouldn't know if he'd had cancer. It's not like finding healed TB lesions."

"Yeah," Lattimer said. He pointed at the lone remaining hamster in the cage. "So for all we know *that* guy could have had it and be cured—and you couldn't prove anything."

Joan turned to look. "No," she said, "I couldn't prove . . . " She lapsed into thought.

"But?" said Lattimer, eagerly. "But? You were going to say 'but'?"

Joan walked over to the cage. She ran a finger over the wire, tracing the pattern of the mesh. Behind it, the hamster slept, his furry body throbbing slightly with each breath.

"I was going to say . . . " she said, "that the last time I looked at this one—and his buddies—maybe early in the week?—that . . . " She stopped. "Well, I didn't really *look*—just a glance."

Lattimer waited her out.

"Well . . . anyway . . . from a glance, mind you—"

"Okay," he said, "from a glance."

"They looked pretty sick."

Their eyes met.

"So you think—" began Lattimer.

"I think nothing," said Joan, firmly. "I think we'd better get out of here before your imagination infects mine. Or pretty soon you'll have me placing collect calls to the White House and announcing—"

"Gee, not that," said Lattimer. "I was thinking of going to the *very* top."

Joan smiled. "You mean . . . " she said, breathlessly, "all the way to Howard Cosell?"

"Or the Gong Show, at least."

"You'd have to teach it to sing and dance," she pointed out.

"I think just sing would be enough," he said.

"Well, I get 50 percent," she said.

"Done," he said. In the air, he mimed filling out a marquee: "Joan Scully and Her Cured Hamster."

"Too impersonal," she said. "He needs a name."

Lattimer thought for a moment. "How about Wilbur?" he suggested.

"Why Wilbur?"

"Well, the hamster—formerly sick—is now all right. So Wilbur . . . All Right . . . "

Joan understood and groaned. "Wilbur Wright? That's awful!"

"Yep,"grinned Lattimer. "Sure is." He waved good-bye to the hamster. "See you, Wilbur," he said. He took Joan Scully's hand and led her out of the room to find, he hoped, some evidence that was more tangible. But he shot a last look at the cage. He wondered if Wilbur really was the cured hamster, if that little creature, unknown and unknowing, could indeed be the first living thing ever to be saved . . .

New York City

Paul Justin was drifting again when he felt the cool wetness on his feet. He paid attention. He felt hands on him—smooth hands, a woman's hands—and the cool wetness moving up his calves. The hands now turned him and continued up his legs. The sensation stirred a memory from his childhood, his infanthood, really. He realized he was being bathed. A sponge bath.

The gentle hands moved up his thighs, the outside of his thighs and now inside. Justin felt an erection grow. With the catheter inside, it stung terribly. The hands and the sponge moved to his genitals and he felt himself swell. The hands moved on up his body, turning him gently this way and that, washing his stomach and back. Justin was filled with powerful, conflicting feelings: Pain. Pleasure. Adult eroticism. Childish dependence and cared-for-ness. Humiliation and anger at this helplessness. He needed to see who was doing this to him. As yesterday he had tried to force his eyes shut against the burning pain of the dye in his head and the sight of the tube in his throat, Justin now tried to force his eyes open.

He tried. He tried harder. He was angry at that doctor—Dewing—for shutting his eyes yesterday, for allowing him only a brief glimpse of Barbara. Barbara! he thought suddenly, feeling a stab of need and love for her, pain for the pain he had seen on *her* face yesterday. And pain at the horrible, cold questions Dewing had flung at her. Depression, indeed! Suicide, indeed! He would live! He would open his eyes and be alive and, with this erection, take his wife to bed.

The woman finished washing his trunk and now moved to his arms. The sponge tickled his armpits. He needed to laugh but could not. And he could not, could not, open his eyes. He felt as if he was in a nightmare, as if he was struggling to wake from it, but blackness pushed down on his eyes. Justin had a sudden terrible thought: Had they *taped* them shut? Would they really open easily if only the tape weren't there?

The woman gently sponged his face. He tried to find the muscles that controlled his eyelids. How amazing, he thought, that our eyes normally open so effortlessly! How we take it for granted. Somehow, his eyes had come to symbolize his strength. If he could just open them—he was mentally sweating, mentally gritting his teeth now at the effort—that would be the first small step to becoming free again.

The woman's hands were gone. He saw—or imagined—a glimmer of light. He pushed it, forced it. His eyes came open. He saw his curtain-enclosed cubicle. But things were still blurry on his right side. The woman—she was a nurse—returned to him carrying a white gown. She was loving and beautiful. He felt his penis harden again and felt pain-pleasure again and embarrassment. Sitting him up in bed—the rest of his body, he realized, was as limp as a newly dead man's—she put the gown on him. He stared at her, sure she would notice his open eyes, sure that this would *tell* her something. See what I did! his mind shouted. But she was too bored and efficient. She laid him back down. She rolled him to one side of the bed, pulled the sheet out from under him, rolled him to the other and pulled the sheet out from that side. Repeating the process, she put a fresh sheet under him. She reattached the electrodes to his chest. The beep-beep of the monitor resumed. She pulled open the curtain and she left.

She left Justin staring at the ceiling, his arms at his sides. He listened to the monitor. He listened to the respirator—and tried not to gag on the tube. He listened to the low moans from one of the other beds. His eyes tried and failed to trace a pattern in the acoustical paneling on the ceiling. He gave up. He was bored, lulled. He started to drift back into his fog. Then he felt an ache in his right wrist.

The ache grew. It swelled. It was hot and getting hotter. He figured that the nurse had accidentally left his hand at a funny angle. It lay twisted in the bed—probably only slightly twisted, he realized, but it grew in his mind to an enormous deformity. It burned as badly as his head had yesterday and it was beginning to burn worse. He tried to move his hand but it wouldn't budge. Come on! he insisted. If you can get your eyes open, surely you can . . . but no go. Come on, he willed. A half inch, a quarter inch, anything. He felt his hand balloon. He mocked himself for having been so annoyed at the discomfort of an erection. He offered to trade with the fates: closed eyes for a painless hand. He tried to shut his eyes to effect his part of the bargain. But his eyelids wouldn't move either. He remembered his hand moving freely, touching Barbara's face. He remembered his father's hand, first swollen, then amputated.

Paul Justin lay in agony on the fresh sheets. His body was beginning to course with sweat, destroying the effects of the nice sponge bath.

New York City

"You're becoming a necrophiliac," Whitcomb had said to Lattimer when Lattimer had called earlier in the morning to ask Whitcomb for information on Roberto Cruz. "First Tommy Vernon, now this guy Cruz. You're surrounding yourself with dead people, Frank. Why?"

"Spare me," Lattimer had said. "Could you just check him out, huh? And vouch for me when the 19th precinct calls you?"

"Why are they going to call me?"

"Because Cruz died on their turf. And I'm going over there to see what they can tell me."

"Spare *me*," Whitcomb had said, with the smallest of laughs.

But the 19th precinct had little to tell Lattimer and Joan Scully. They sat at the desk of Detective Prosser, who showed them the report. Two transit cops had responded to the scene, called their supervisor and notified the radio patrol. While the transit cops supervised jacking up the train to recover the body, Patrolmen Doran and Humenuik interviewed the motorman, conductor and people on the platform. Net: nothing. Several people had seen Cruz fall, but nobody saw him *start* to fall.

"In the absence of anything else," said Prosser, "it's an accident."

"Swell," said Lattimer, unhappily.

"Frank," said Joan. "Do you *want* him murdered?"

Prosser grinned and shook his head. He didn't often have a pair like this—a reporter and a beautiful redhead—sitting in the station house on a Saturday morning.

Lattimer plunged on. "Body's at the M.E. now?" he asked Prosser.

"Yeah, no news yet." Prosser looked at Joan Scully. "You worked with him, huh? You knew him? You think the M.E. will find anything—drugs?"

Joan shrugged. Prosser consulted the report again. "Hey," he said, "body not identified yet by anybody. How'd *you* like to, Miss?"

Joan blanched. Prosser laughed, not unkindly. "That's what you get for coming in and being nosy. Hey, but seriously—you ought to go down and look at the body. Civic duty. Besides, maybe it *won't* be him. Always a chance." Prosser turned back to Lattimer. "Now what else can I do for you?"

"You can tell me what the results of the search of Cruz's apartment were."

"Jesus," said Prosser. "You want the world and you want it now." Prosser turned and yelled out through his open door, into the squad room. "Swan! Who'd we send up to this Cruz guy's place—the IRT thing?"

"I think Iacavelli," answered a sergeant.

"Well, tell him to file his report," said Prosser.

"No news there either?" asked Lattimer. "It's been over twelve hours."

"So Iacavelli has more important things to do than paperwork," said Prosser. "What else?" he asked the reporter.

"A list of what was on the body."

"That I got," said Prosser, passing it to Lattimer.

Lattimer read. "That's all? A wallet?"

"Here," said Prosser. "Hasn't even gone down to the property clerk yet." He reached in a bag and slapped a plain, black wallet on his desk.

Lattimer and Joan went through it. Sixteen dollars. A couple of pieces of paper stuck in with the dollars—some stamps, a movie ticket stub, a dry cleaning receipt. And, under the transparent plastic, a social security card and a New York State driver's license. The license said Roberto Cruz lived at 236 East 106th Street. That was Spanish Harlem. Again, no news.

"What were you expecting to find?" Joan asked.

It was Lattimer's turn to shrug.

Lattimer returned the wallet to Prosser. "It doesn't list any 'in case of accident, please notify.' So who did you notify?"

Prosser shifted uncomfortably. "Well... it appears... nobody yet....Unless Iacavelli found somebody else—a roommate or somebody—up there." Prosser brightened. "Anyhow, miss, you say he worked for you at Oakes-Metcalf?"

Joan nodded.

"Well," said Prosser, "if nothing else, then come Monday, we'll check with your personnel department. They'll have a relative's name on file." He looked at Lattimer again. "That is it, right? There *isn't* anything else?"

"No," said Lattimer, "there is. Something's missing."

Prosser sighed. "What? A dagger in his back? A threatening letter in his pocket? You see," said Prosser, smiling, "your friend Whitcomb called me and explained your suspicions."

"Nothing that dramatic," said Lattimer. "Just a set of keys."

"Keys?" asked Prosser.

"A man doesn't walk the streets of New York without at least a key to his apartment. Where is it?" He pointed. "Not on your list."

"Uh ... " said Prosser, even more uncomfortable. "Uh ... you've got a point. But so what?"

"So why didn't"—Lattimer turned the report to read it better—"Humenuik or Doran find it? Didn't they search Cruz's clothing? Didn't they search the tracks?"

"Well, they damn well *searched*," said Prosser. "They're good men. But it'd be easy to overlook a lousy little key, for Christ's sake. And—again—so what?"

"So I want to see the body. And see Doran and Humenuik."

"Help yourself," said Prosser, who was plainly pleased to be rid of them. "You know where the body is."

"And the patrolmen?"

"Swan!" yelled Prosser. "Where are Doran and Humenuik?"

"Off duty," came the response. "Doran's up in the Catskills, I think. Humenuik—I don't know where he is now. After lunch I think he's playing the Fortune guys."

"What does that mean?" asked Lattimer.

"It's a softball game," said Prosser. "Central Park."

"What diamond? What time?"

"Jesus, you're persistent." He yelled again: "Swan! Where and when is the game?"

"Sheep Meadow," called the sergeant. "Diamond three. One o'clock."

"Is *that* enough?" asked Prosser.

"For now," said Lattimer. "Thanks." He and Joan Scully left.

New York City

This being a Saturday, morning rounds were late. It wasn't until just before noon that Dewing, Falcone and Kitteridge arrived at intensive care. The nurses told the doctors the same thing Underwood had been told: There was no change with Paul Justin. "Except," said one of the nurses off-handedly, "he did get an erection when I gave him a bath."

Dewing smiled. "Probably just some primitive reflex response," he said. "You don't have to worry about turning him on," added Dewing. "I'm afraid his brain isn't 'on' to begin with."

Now, looking down at Justin, Dewing wondered whether the *nurse's* brain was on. "Damn it," he said, "who keeps leaving his eyes open?"

"Not me," said the nurse.

Dewing closed Justin's eyes. Damn it, but this case was beginning to bother him. The arteriogram had shown no clot, no sign of a stroke in the cortex. So that seemed to eliminate everything except a stroke in the brainstem. But it was only more negative evidence— Dewing wished he had something positive. He wished he had the clincher to offer to Kitteridge, to impress the chief of neurosurgery. Unfortunately, several of the tests that Dewing needed couldn't be done on the weekend.

"First thing Monday," he told Falcone, "I want an EEG." That would check for brain death, which Dewing now figured was likely.

"Right," said the assistant resident.

"And a full battery of toxicology—not just barbiturates."

"Right."

"And check his hemoglobin and electrolytes."

"They're already ordered."

"And let's get the inhalation therapist in here. I want to know if he's breathing right."

As far as Dewing could tell, the patient was breathing fine. But Dewing wanted to show Kitteridge he was checking everything. A nurse went off to find the therapist.

"Well, Dr. Kitteridge," said Dewing to Kitteridge, "what do you think?"

Kitteridge had been standing silently regarding Justin. The chief of neurosurgery had enormous black, bushy eyebrows that extended across his nose. The longer he looked, the more the eyebrows frowned into a deep V. "I think we'll know more on Monday," he said. "Right now, I call your attention to our patient's pulse rate." He pointed to the monitor, which was beeping faster.

Dewing cursed himself for not having noticed.

"Well," he fumbled, "what . . . ?"

"And if you'll look at our patient's wrist," pointed out Kitteridge, "you'll note it's red. So if we do this"—the chief of neurosurgery straightened Justin's wrist and let his hand lie normally—"things will get better."

Dewing shot an angry look at the nurse who had given Justin the sponge bath. Damn it, he thought—she really was mucking up his patient.

Kitteridge turned to leave. "I'll be home all weekend," he said. "If anything happens, keep me informed."

Both doctors knew nothing was going to happen. It was clear Justin was in deep—and was going to stay there. But Dewing couldn't let it go at that. He turned to Falcone. "I want him awake by Monday. Is that understood?"

"I'll try," said Falcone. Dewing was also going to depart for the weekend, leaving Falcone in charge. For the next forty-eight hours, Joseph Falcone would work and, when he could grab the time, eat and sleep at the hospital. Falcone didn't mind that. That was the lot of an assistant resident. But he did mind Dewing's impatience and imperiousness.

"Okay," grumbled Dewing to Falcone, "now let's check a live one." They moved on to Mrs. Nowlis.

Lander, Colorado

Humph, thought Dr. Christopher Ives. To my twin professions of medical researcher and arch-criminal I'm now adding the most demanding one of all: hotel manager.

When, in the wake of the missing notes, Murdoch had moved up the schedule yesterday, he had put an enormous burden on Ives. Since they hadn't been expecting guests in their sanitarium for several more months, they barely had beds in the rooms. Now they hoped for close to one hundred oncologists on Sunday and an equal number of multimillionaires on Tuesday. So while Murdoch had the pleasure of phoning around the world and presenting their terms to the last of the hundred multimillionaires—their "pigeons," as he kept referring to them—Ives was spending this morning on the phone performing more mundane chores. He was hunting up several hundred pillows, blankets and sets of bed linen, several hundred bath mats, shower curtains and bars of soap—and more—all to be delivered by tomorrow at the latest. "But tomorrow's Sunday," said Ives's bewildered would-be suppliers in Denver, who pointed out Ives was lucky to catch any of them even open on *Saturday*.

"And what," Ives demanded of Murdoch, walking in on him between Murdoch's calls to land and cattle baron Ernesto Vesquez of Argentina and Sheik Abu Ahmed Wadi of Pakistan, "are we supposed to do about *food*? We can feed the doctors on sandwiches. But don't you think, for multimillionaires, we ought to open the kitchen, get a chef? But then," he said, "how can we do that by Tuesday?"

"Sandwiches for the pigeons," replied Murdoch, looking up the sheik's phone number and their price for his life. "Any chef we can get will never match what they're used to eating. So we shouldn't even try—we'll just lose face. Ham sandwiches will be fine—chicken salad sandwiches for the sheik and Mordecai Slisky."

Grateful for small favors, Ives started to leave. "But," continued Murdoch's gravelly voice, "a chef for the doctors. We've got to wine them, dine them, impress the hell out of them."

"A chef by tomorrow?" cried Ives. "You're crazy! You're—"

"And food for him to work with," said Murdoch, slamming the door in Ives's face.

Just as swiftly, Murdoch opened the door. The hound-dog face stared out. "And how's the blood count?"

Ives's own blood froze. As busy as he had been today calling for hotel supplies, he had not neglected, an hour ago, to run today's count of his hamsters' blood. And he didn't want to tell Murdoch the results.

"Well?" demanded Murdoch.

"It's just one day's count," hedged Ives. "We have to see if it stabilizes."

"So it *is* normal!" said Murdoch triumphantly.

"Averaging 7,400 white cells," said Ives, unhappily. "Plus normal hemoglobin and a normal differential." Ives cursed himself for having explained to Murdoch, back on Wednesday, how a blood count worked. Now it was no use lying. Now Murdoch could check him on it.

"Normal," said Murdoch. "We've got a cure. We kill Justin today."

In his whole life, Christopher Ives could not remember having felt so awful. Where his stomach should be there was a huge hole, a huge emptiness.

"Please," begged Ives, "let me check it again tomorrow to see if it stabilizes. If it *keeps* dropping, it's just as bad. One day. Please."

Murdoch looked pityingly at Ives. "One day," he snapped. "And when you do the tests, I'll be there." He slammed the door again.

Ives stood there, looking at the closed door. Things were going bad between Murdoch and himself. There was a tension in the air, a sense of things going wrong. First, Cruz's report that Justin's notes were missing. Then the call last night from Murdoch's other man in

New York, reporting that Cruz hadn't lived where he'd claimed to. Bad omens, felt Ives. Bad.

He trudged back to his office. Out the window, the mountains were wreathed in gray clouds. The day felt heavy, as before rain. Ives thought of the monkey, dead on the mountain behind him. He lit his pipe, opened the Denver Yellow Pages and started calling cooking schools and restaurants. After a dozen calls, he still hadn't found a chef, but the restaurant ads were beginning to affect him. He thought of being back in Kansas City and dining on Steak Diane at La Bonne Auberge. Beneath Ives's big girth, his stomach felt as empty as a chasm. Dr. Lindenmeyer said he felt guilty about enjoying himself and therefore overate to punish himself, to prove he couldn't eat without suffering. Dr. Lindenmeyer had suggested that whenever Ives felt like gorging himself, he should call Dr. Lindenmeyer. "I'll give you some psychic nourishment," he had said. "Instead of calories." Thus far, Ives had felt unable to call. "That's because you're afraid of being close to me," Lindenmeyer had said.

Well, I'm not too close now, thought Ives. I'm a thousand miles away. Charging it to his home phone in Mission Hills (Ives didn't want Murdoch to know about it), Ives called Lindenmeyer's office in Topeka. He got the psychiatrist's answering service, which refused to give him Lindenmeyer's home number "unless," the woman said, "this is an emergency. Is this an emergency?"

"No," said Christopher Ives.

"Well, if you'll give me your number, I'll have the doctor—"

"No," said Ives swiftly. "No." He hung up.

Briefly, Ives considered calling his wife back in Kansas City. But she was not a strong woman. In his present situation, he felt there was not much nourishment she could give him. Instead, Ives popped another 5-milligram Valium. He was now up to three of them a day. He went back to calling restaurants.

New York City

The pitcher—a bank robber who had wounded a guard—wound up and threw the softball. The batter—a detective in the Safe & Loft Squad—swung and missed. The catcher—who had led a gang of car thieves—tossed the ball back to the pitcher. "Second out coming up," he called.

On deck, swinging two bats, Patrolman George Humenuik frowned.

"So you're sure Cruz wasn't pushed?" asked Lattimer.

"He fell, damn it," growled the big cop. "Now shut up. I'm watching this guy's delivery. I want to see how I can knock his head off."

Lattimer sighed. The captain of the police team had told him that this annual game in Central Park was supposed to demonstrate the good will between the police and the former inmates who made up the Fortune Society. But Humenuik, the cops' cleanup batter, hadn't been chosen for the team for his feelings of good will. Humenuik liked ex-cons even less than he liked reporters.

"But one woman," persisted Lattimer, "told the *Post* that she saw Cruz, quote, go flying, unquote. 'Flying' doesn't sound like 'fell.'"

"So talk to *her*," said Humenuik. "Not me."

"She didn't give her name to the *Post*," said Lattimer. "That's why I want *your* list of names. The witnesses."

The pitcher threw again. The detective swung—and missed again.

Humenuik spat.

"For instance," said Lattimer, "did you talk to the guy in the token booth?"

"No, for Christ's sake," said Humenuik. "It was out of his line of vision. Why would I talk to him?"

"To find out if he saw anybody leaving quickly."

"Christ, the way the body looked, I wouldn't be surprised if fifty people left quickly."

"Okay, okay," said Lattimer. "Well, how about a key? When you went through his clothes, for his wallet, did you find his keys?"

"Did I list his keys?"

"No."

"Well, what do you think I am? What I find, I list. I didn't find any keys."

The pitcher threw a bit low. The detective almost went for it, then held up. Ball one, strike two.

"Did you look on the tracks?" asked Lattimer.

Humenuik swung his two bats viciously. Lattimer took a step back.

"I spent an hour on my hands and knees looking through all the candy wrappers and crud specifically for a key because I knew how important the key would be to you," said Humenuik.

"Right," said Lattimer. "Well," he persisted, "how about your list?"

Humenuik turned to Joan Scully, who had been watching all this. "You with him?" asked the big cop, pointing his bat at Lattimer.

"Yep," said Joan.

"He's nuts," said Humenuik. "You know that."

"Yep," said Joan.

"Should I give him the list?"

"Give him the list."

Joan Scully couldn't imagine that Humenuik wouldn't give Lattimer the list. For, as she'd been learning, Lattimer seemed to get most everything he wanted. In the hour and a half they'd had before the ball game started, Joan had wanted to eat lunch. Lattimer had wanted to make phone calls. Lattimer had won.

First, Joan Scully had heard him call his newspaper, where he got hold of someone named Ganz and made Ganz promise to Xerox any information that the newspaper had on Oakes-Metcalf and have it sent by messenger to Lattimer's home in Dobbs Ferry.

Next Lattimer had called Oakes-Metcalf, got hold of Dr. Falcone and made the assistant resident promise to look for the lab coat Justin was wearing yesterday—and check if there was a slide in one of the pockets. "Not that I think it'll be there," Lattimer had said to Joan.

Then Lattimer had called his friend Tom Munro, who worked for IBM. Munro was neither at home nor at his office. Finally Lattimer tracked him down at a company father-son outing. Yes, said Munro, IBM did have an electron microscope and facilities to develop the film the microscope's camera used. And, well, yes, he supposed, if it was really important . . . "He'll get the film developed this weekend," Lattimer had said to Joan. And Lattimer had made one more call—to arrange for a messenger to take the film canister up to Armonk.

So now Joan, with an inadequate sandwich inside her, waited for Patrolman Humenuik also to give in. Humenuik, on deck, glowered at the ex-bank robber turned pitcher. The pitcher delivered the ball again. The detective-batter struck out by a foot. Humenuik strode to the plate. He dug in his heels and took a practice swing, as if at the pitcher. Then he looked over at Lattimer and Scully.

"For *you*, pretty lady," said Patrolman Humenuik, "I'll give him the list. It's back at the station house. Tell him to call me there at four o'clock."

"Thanks," said Joan, "I will."

"Such a charmer," said Lattimer to Joan Scully.

They watched as Humenuik lined the first pitch back at the ex-bank robber's head. The ex-bank robber flung himself down on the mound and the ball whizzed into centerfield for a single. They heard Humenuik chuckle as he rounded first base.

Dobbs Ferry, New York

Steve Justin poured the potassium nitrate from its can and measured 8 ounces on the kitchen scale that Kenny Bedloe had "borrowed" from his mother. Then Steve poured the white powder into a pot, mixed in an equal amount of sugar and placed the pot over the Sterno stove.

"Hey," said Kenny Bedloe, reading the instruction book that came with Steve's chemistry set, "it says here that you're supposed to use an electric frying pan that's thermo"—he wrestled with the word—"thermo-stat-ick-ally—"

"Thermostatically controlled," said Steve. "I know." He lit the stove.

"Because," read Kenny, "you can't let the temperature go above 230 degrees."

"Right. But we don't have an extension cord long enough for the electric pan, do we?" Steve started stirring the warming mixture of potassium nitrate and sugar.

"Uh, no," said Kenny. He wondered if it was a good idea to be doing this up in his treehouse. "No, but—"

"But this," said Steve, indicating the candy thermometer he'd put in the pot, "should do fine."

"But," said Kenny, "the book says—"

"My Dad," said Steve, "My *Dad* says a scientist shouldn't always go by the book. A scientist has to be willing to try new stuff. To improvise."

Kenny was silent. He drummed his fingers on the rocket tube, toyed with the attached fuse.

"My Dad," continued Steve Justin, "told me last week he's worked five years on a whole *new* cancer thing. And he said he'd work five more years if he had to."

Steve kept an eye on the candy thermometer. It read 150 degrees. And he kept stirring the mixture. As soon as the potassium nitrate dissolved in the melting sugar, they would pour the liquid into the rocket tube. There it would harden into a solid fuel.

"And if he can't work on it now," said Steve, "then *I'm* going to. So I've got to learn to improvise, too."

Kenny Bedloe was getting nervous. He didn't like this experiment and he didn't like hearing his friend talk about his father, who was sick. Kenny felt that it would jinx Steve's father.

"Hey, Steve," said Kenny, "let's quit this, huh? I'll go down to the house and get some more paper and we'll draw cartoons, huh?"

Kenny had the makings of a good cartoonist. He could draw all of the comic strip characters like Charlie Brown and the Wizard of Id. And, as he and Steve were getting interested in politics, he was learning to copy political caricatures, and even draw his own. This week, up here in his treehouse, he'd been working on some of Governor Reed's rivals.

"Hey," said Kenny, "I think I finally got those things that hang down from Prentice's jaw—you know, on the side."

"Jowls," said Steve. The thermometer read 180 degrees.

"Yeah, jowls. I can do them now. Hey, let's stop this experiment and I'll do Prentice and his jowls. Make him look nasty like he really is."

"He's not all nasty," said Steve, still stirring. "My Dad says he's just an opportunist."

"What does that mean?" asked Kenny.

"An opportunist, my Dad says, is somebody who will do anything to get somewhere. Whether it's good or not. Like he thinks the end justifies the means."

"What does *that* mean?" asked Kenny.

"I don't know exactly," admitted Steve.

Kenny looked at the thermometer. Its climb had slowed and it was still under 200 degrees. But he noticed that the melting mixture was coating the bottom half of the thermometer. For some reason, that made him nervous and he wanted to get down from his treehouse right now. But he didn't want to leave Steve alone. Kenny knew from his parents that what had happened to Steve's father was really serious. And he could tell, from how calm Steve was *trying* to act, that Steve was really upset about it. So he wanted to stick close to him.

"Come on, Steve," he insisted, "let's both go *down*."

"Hey!" cried voices from down below, at the base of the tree. "Hey, can we come up?"

It was Melissa and Laurie Justin.

"No!" cried Kenny.

"Selfish," called Melissa. "You and your old treehouse. Well, we're coming up anyway. Mom says we can't watch TV for a while so we're gonna play with you."

The boys could hear Steve's sisters starting to climb the boards nailed into the tree trunk.

"Hey, go away," called Steve, still stirring. "We're busy."

"Yeah, go away," called Kenny. "It's dangerous." But he saw that the thermometer was holding steady at 205 degrees. And the mixture was almost liquid. They were almost done.

"Busy, busy," mocked Melissa, poking her head into the treehouse. "You're just as busy and grumpy as Mom is."

"She's not grumpy," said Steve.

"Well, she gave us a grumpy meal," said Laurie, joining them. "Shrimp—yuk. You were lucky you got to eat at Kenny's."

"And then she ran around being busy some more," said Melissa.

"Yeah," said Laurie. "And staring off into space again. Wow. I wish Dad would come home. I wish—"

Suddenly there was a *"whoosh."* The mixture ignited. A column of flame shot up two feet out of the pot.

"Ow!" yelled Steve as the flame singed his hair.

"Out!" yelled Kenny as dense white smoke billowed out of the pot.

Kenny, Melissa and Laurie scrambled for the doorway. The girls scampered down the tree. At the doorway, Kenny hung back. He stuck his head inside. All he could see was white smoke.

"Steve?" he asked. The smoke was so thick, Kenny was confused. Maybe Steve had gotten out past him?

Kenny felt a hand come out of the smoke and touch him. "Hey!" he yelped. It was *spooky.*

It was Steve. He was coughing. "What—?" he coughed. "What happened?"

Steve and Kenny made it down the tree. Steve rubbed his eyes and some of his blackened eyebrows came off on his hands. "Gee," he said.

He and Kenny crossed the lawn to the Bedloes' back porch where the two girls had run for cover. There the four of them watched the white smoke billow out of the treehouse—until it faded and disappeared.

"Boy," said Steve, in wonderment, "I'd like to know what caused *that.*"

"I don't care if I ever know," said Kenny Bedloe. *"Now* will you draw cartoons with me?"

"Steve," said Melissa, "you look funny."

"Yucky," said Laurie.

"I'll ask my Dad what caused it," said Steve Justin, still lost in thought.

Houston, Texas

"Homer P. Finley?" read Ryker with mounting incredulity. "Who the hell is Homer P. Finley?"

"A friend," gasped Ash. "The bes' friend Ah eveh had. You wouldn't understan'."

"No, I guess not," said Ryker. "I wouldn't understand leaving a half-billion-dollar fortune to somebody who—listen, when was the last time you saw this Finley? I never even heard you mention him."

"Well, Ah know 'im. An' he's a *good* un. Drank with me all summer in that hot fuckin' hellhole." The old man chuckled in between wheezes. "Drank me under the table, too. Under the floor! Took me in poker, too. Think he cheated. Hell—*musta* cheated. Lost a couple thousand to 'im. All Ah had. Spent it in the whorehouse in Tulsa. Had to drag 'im outta there the night the gusher came in. Was on their mos' expensive whore, as Ah remember. Licking French champagne off her. On mah money. Nothing but the best for Homer." Ash tried to slap his thigh—the I.V. tubes stopped him. "Marvelous bastard," he gurgled. "Goddamn mar—"

"Wait a minute," said Ryker. "Gusher? Outside Tulsa? What the hell year was that?—'27?"

"Nineteen twenty-five," sang Ash. "Ah never forgit mah first strike. August 25, 1925."

"And Homer was with you?"

"Right."

"And when was the *last* time you saw him?"

"Huh?"

"*When?*"

"*Then*, goddamn it!" spat Ash. "Ol' Homer was always movin'. Movin'. Nothin' gonna tie *him* down. No sir. Ah bought out his share an' he moved on."

"Jesus Christ," Ryker swore softly. He looked around the hospital room. Nurse Crippen buried her head in her paperback and tried not to notice. Ryker didn't understand her reaction, didn't realize that Crippen felt responsible. Because she had urged Matt Ash that there must be *some*one he cared for, Ash had dictated the bequest to Homer. Ryker also couldn't understand the reaction—or rather, the lack of reaction—of Virginia Ash. From next door, in the living room of the Presidential Suite, came the drone of the TV set to which she remained glued. Didn't she care, marveled Ryker, that her husband had just left her penniless?

"Jesus Christ." Ray Ryker threw the single-page, handwritten will at his boss. It landed on Ash's stomach, on the site of his operation. "And you're going to leave everything you own to somebody you haven't seen in over half a century? Somebody you don't even know where he is today? Somebody who's probably long *dead?*"

"Homer ain't dead," said Ash firmly. "Ol' Homer'll be hangin' on somewhere. Doin' all right one way or t' other. The lawyers'll find 'im."

"You think the lawyers will let that—that so-called *will*—stand up? Why, your wife and her relatives will get it laughed out of court."

"Doubt it," snapped Ash. "Doubt it, boy. An' what's it to you, anyway? You ain't gonna take a crack at it, are you?" He peered sharply at Ryker. "Claim yore mah adopted son?" Ash let out a cackle that died in a gasp of pain.

Ray Ryker clenched and unclenched his fists. He rocked on the balls of his feet. Homer P. Finley was an additional barb on the wire that was sticking into Ryker. Ryker had thought that if Ash did make a will, he'd leave his money for some ridiculous project—like making a solid gold statue of himself. *That* could be defeated in court. So, at the worst, Texahoma Pipeline would be inherited by Virginia and her relatives. And the relatives were the same as Virginia—stupid and weak. Ryker felt that eventually he could get them to sell to him. But Homer P. Finley? It could take months, years to find him or all his survivors. And what would they be like? If they were anything like Ash described Homer, they'd be ornery as hell.

For despite what he told Ash, Ryker knew the will was lawyer-proof. It was simple, direct—and properly witnessed by Crippen and a hospital porter. And if Virginia's relatives claimed Ash wasn't "of sound mind"—well, hell, the will was the best evidence the old man was still the same bastard, the same M. ASH he'd always been. Leaving a half billion to an old drinking buddy—to, apparently, the only man as ornery as Ash himself—that's the ultimate way to Mash all of us, thought Ryker. Well, at least one nice thing: As long as this was Ash's will, Virginia wasn't about to try to get anybody to pull the plug.

Ryker sighed. He knew the will was also evidence that today was no day to again talk to Ash about selling Texahoma to him. He'd come to the hospital for that reason, hoping that, if he could get a deathbed agreement, Wissenbach would find backers after all. But then Ryker had seen the will, seen the mood Ash was in. So now Ryker realized that Ash would positively delight in turning him down. I need a fucking miracle, thought Ryker. To get the bastard to sell to me, I need him to think as much of me as he does of Homer P. Finley. And for that, I think I really *am* going to have to save his miserable life.

Ryker turned to find Goodhue, to have Goodhue ready for when the cancer-cure people phoned on Sunday.

"Does it hurt, Ray, boy?" Ash gleefully called after him. "Does it hurt so much you want to die? Then you know how Ah feel. Ha-ha!"

New York City

"Manuel, come back here and mind your sister."

"Hey, jump across. Jump across."

"Direct from San Juan, the new singing sensation ... "

It was dark in the entranceway at 236 East 106th, but the glass on the outer doors had long since been knocked out. So as Frank Lattimer and Joan Scully tried to make out the names on the mailboxes, the street sounds still washed over them. Men carried transistor radios blaring Latin music and the chatter of Latin disc jockeys. Women called after their children. Children called to each other and, skillfully directing the spray from open hydrants, sprayed passing cars. The cars honked. On the trestle at the end of the block, a Penn Central train rattled by.

The heat also penetrated the entranceway (the promised rain had not come) and so did the hot smells of some kind of Hispanic food frying. And Joan Scully was enjoying soaking it all in. True, she had a bit of a sense of tagging along after Frank—to the police station, the ball game and now here. And she could hear David Crawford mocking her for "slumming" in Spanish Harlem. But hell, she thought, it's not that. I'm here because I want to be here. Because, in addition to following the trail of Roberto Cruz, it's nice to see a different part of the city I live in. And see it isn't so different from my Upper East Side.

It also pleased her that she could pick up some of the Spanish language. In midtown she had less need to try.

Frank's language was even clearer. "Goddamn it, he isn't listed here anywhere."

The eight mailboxes were rusted, bent and smashed. What few names were on them were scrawled or defaced. Joan peered through the inner door. In contrast to the painfully bright sunlight in the street, the hallway was pitch dark. She rattled the door. It still had a lock, but only barely. Another loose screw and it would fall off.

"It looks like an empty shell," she said to Frank. "Do you suppose anybody still lives here? And why would Roberto live here? He made enough to live better."

Behind her a young woman's voice—English with a heavy Spanish accent—said, angrily, "You want Roberto Cruz?"

Lattimer and Joan Scully turned. They were facing four Puerto Rican teen-age girls in jeans and shiny jerseys. One of the jerseys had "Young Titans" stenciled on it and Joan noticed the same name on a military-looking crest sewn on one girl's black beret. The girls stood with hands on hips or arms folded. They were still kids—one chewed gum, one had acne—but Joan still got a little worried.

"Yes," said Frank Lattimer. "Does he live here?"

"No," snapped the girl with the beret, "he don't live here. He never lived here. *We* live here—this is the People's territory, the People's free medical center, and if you don't get the fuck out of here you're gonna *need* medical care 'cause—"

"Hold it," said Lattimer. "Hold it. If he doesn't live here, we're going. But how did you know that we were looking for Cruz?"

"You say you're going but you're not going," said the first girl, between snaps of gum. "Well, don't say—go! And don't think what you did to Maria scares us, 'cause it don't. 'Cause this time we'll give it back. And worse." The girl took a step toward Lattimer and Joan, her hands open but threatening.

Joan took a step back. The last time she had seen this kind of thing, heard this kind of rhetoric from people, had been on TV news years ago, back when the black and Puerto Rican ghettos were "hot." Well, thought Joan, the news coverage has gone away but I guess the people haven't. She took another backward step and hit the front door. The doorknob went into the small of her back. Frank, she thought, do something.

"Hey, wait," said Lattimer. "Who did what to Maria? We sure didn't."

Another of the girls ran a hand to her cheek. She let loose a burst of Spanish: "Tu amigo me ha batido! Duro! Le dije . . . " Joan struggled to understand it: "Your friend hit me. Hard. I told him not to go inside. Told him there's no Roberto Cruz. But he pushed me. He hit me."

Joan tugged at Lattimer's sleeve. She translated for him. He looked at her, surprised and impressed.

"Tell her," he said, "that the man wasn't our friend."

Joan translated back and forth:

"Your friend," said the girl. "Last night."

"Last night?" asked Lattimer. "You mean a cop? Checking the apartment?"

"No," said the girl. "The cop came later. This man came first. Your friend."

"But why do you think it was my friend?"

"He was a white. You're a white. He was asking for Cruz. You're asking for Cruz."

"Yeah," said the girl with the beret, who seemed to be the leader. "You're asking for Cruz. But what you're going to get is trouble."

And she also took a step toward Lattimer and Joan Scully. But her hands didn't come up open. They came up with a knife.

Oh, Jesus, thought Joan Scully. "Hey," she said weakly. Then: "Está bien. Vamonos. Vamonos." It's all right. We'll go. We'll go.

The girl lowered her knife a bit.

"Por qué esperas?" she demanded, a shade less angrily. Then what are you waiting for?

Joan turned to Frank Lattimer. "It's okay, Frank. We can go."

Joan saw Frank look irritated at the knife, as if he were irritated it had threatened not only his life but also his story. "Thanks," he said to Joan. "But we can't go yet. Ask her—ask Maria—when this man came."

"Frank!" Joan exclaimed. She just wanted to leave.

"Please."

The four girls were getting impatient again. The lead girl slapped the flat of the knife blade in her hand.

"One thing," said Joan, in Spanish. "Please. The man who hit Maria—he's no friend of ours. In fact, we—maybe we can find him for you. But first we have to know: What time did he come?"

Several of the girls looked at Joan suspiciously. But Maria shrugged. "Seven, eight last night," she said in Spanish.

"And ask"—said Frank to Joan—"ask what he said."

Joan translated. Maria shrugged again. She answered in Spanish. "He said, 'Where is Roberto Cruz? I was told he lives here. Where is he?'"

"And what did he look like?" asked Frank.

Joan translated. "Thin," said Maria. "He was very thin. And older"—she pointed at Lattimer—"older than him. Dark face. Frowning. And his nose—" She pinched her own. "Long. Pointy."

"And white?" asked Joan.

The girl nodded. "Blanco. But"—she moved her hands in the air, struggling to express an idea—"but he was more like from around here. Like—how he moved. Very—like shadows. And fast. Like I saw him and he hit me and—gone." She pointed to the street—where a car, a convertible with the top down, was now stopped and honking at the kids manning the hydrant spray. The kids laughed.

"Have a bath."

"Or put your top up."

The driver gestured angrily that the top wouldn't go up. The kids laughed harder.

Joan Scully turned to Frank Lattimer. "Come *on*, Frank. She said a lot. I've remembered it all. I'll tell you. Now let's go."

Lattimer hesitated. The girl slapped her knife harder. The girl chewing gum snapped the gum faster.

"Come *on*."

"Okay," said Lattimer. "I guess that's all."

"No it ain't," said the lead girl.

"Que?" asked Joan. What?

The girl answered in Spanish, "We gave you something. Now you give us something."

Joan didn't have to translate for Lattimer. The girl rubbed her fingers together to make the universal symbol for money.

Lattimer dug into his pocket and came out with bills. He gave the girl a ten.

"More!" she said.

Lattimer gave her another ten. "And that's it," he said firmly.

The girl hesitated. She still hadn't put her knife away.

"You really do have a medical center here?" Joan asked, in Spanish.

The girl looked surprised, then embarrassed. "For the Young Titans," she said in Spanish. Then she got her pride back. "For us and others in the neighborhood. It's a *real* center. Jorge—he was a medic in Nam—he runs it. He helps people who get hurt."

"Can't they go to Metropolitan, to the emergency room?" asked Joan. The hospital was less than a dozen blocks away.

"And wait for three hours while they bleed?" said the girl.

Joan opened her wallet. "Not money," she said, in Spanish. She pointed to her Oakes-Metcalf employee card. "I work at a hospital. I'll get you things. Bandages. Splints. Antiseptic solution."

"No bullshit?" asked the gum-chewing girl.

"I promise. I'll be back."

The girls look dubious.

"Aw, fuck," said the lead girl. "Anyway, we got twenty bucks. Let's go."

And they walked down into the street and disappeared in the crowd.

"Hey," said Lattimer. "Thanks a lot. What'd you say to them?"

Joan Scully told him.

"And *will* you come back? To *this* place?"

"Sure."

"Goddamn," said Lattimer, admiringly. "A working knowledge of Spanish, a fair amount of guts—what else do you have?"

"A hunger for a decent lunch" said Joan, smiling and putting her arm through his. "Come on." It pleased her to direct him down the steps—it certainly wasn't tagging along. But if he only knew how *frightened* she'd been in her guts.

They walked toward the subway at 103rd Street. Joan told Lattimer what Maria said—and Lattimer quizzed her.

"Last night? After Cruz was killed?"

"I guess so. Is that important?"

"Sure. It could be Cruz's killer, trying to make sure there was nothing incriminating in Cruz's apartment."

"Incriminating? Like what?"

"Well, if he really did steal Paul's cure—some notes, letters, anything."

"But why do you say his 'killer'? Couldn't it be just a friend?"

"Unh-uh," Lattimer shook his head. "What did Maria say the thin guy said? 'They *told* me he lived here.' That sounds like somebody *hired* him to find Cruz."

"But where *did* Roberto live? And why did he want people to think he lived up here?"

"I don't know," said Lattimer. "But we sure as hell are going to find out."

They walked down the stairs to the subway, leaving Spanish Harlem behind—a place, Joan Scully realized, that was a bit different from her Upper East Side.

Dobbs Ferry, New York

Until she found the silver satin pillowcase on the floor of her closet, the day had gone fairly smoothly. But then there it was, in a far corner, under an old picnic blanket, along with one of Laurie's T-shirts, wadded up. Barbara Justin turned the pillowcase over in her hands and the monogram appeared. BEJ. "That's in case I forget whom I'm sleeping with," Paul had joked. "I can just read your initials." Then he had kissed her. "Happy birthday, love," he'd said. "Shall we try them out tonight?" And yes, they had tried out the satin sheets and pillowcases that night—and, remembering it all now, Barbara involuntarily wadded up the pillowcase again. And the day had been so smooth, she thought. So ordinary.

Maddeningly ordinary, in fact. Barbara had awakened vaguely expecting momentous developments. After all, yesterday, in a single day, she had learned she possibly had cancer and her husband probably had a paralyzing stroke. But today, she had learned that nothing was going to happen quickly about either illness. The hospital said Paul was the same. And she couldn't get a doctor for herself until Monday. In the meantime, in the Justin home, there was no outward sign that anything had changed. Barbara saw her familiar—if tired—face in the mirror. The kids squabbled as usual over what Saturday morning TV programs to watch—until she threw them all out into the sunshine. The cat, as usual, turned up his nose at the new cat food Barbara tried on him—so she threw him outside, too. And, as for Paul's absence, well, he could just as easily be away at a medical conference. Is this what life is? Barbara wondered. Does life simply go on?

She dusted and vacuumed and did a load of laundry that had accumulated while she was in Boston. And, despite herself, as she went past the TV set, she caught snatches of old soap operas that Channel Five was re-running. At times, it was easier to believe that this was happening not to Paul and herself but to some characters on the tube. *There* the situation would be treated properly. With cries and wails. With tearful embraces. With relatives descending with intended comfort but actually bringing their own crazy problems. Not in this house, thought Barbara. Her only other relative, her sister, Susan, had called from Tucson to say, "Mom told me the news. I'm really sorry. What can I do?" And Barbara had answered, truthfully, "Nothing, really," because right now there *was* nothing. It had been a maddeningly *sane* conversation. Barbara had even found herself asking all kinds of intelligent questions about Susan's efforts at getting a master's in library science and her husband, Curt's, promotion in his food processing company.

The washer was buzzing. She turned it off, emptied it and put in another load. What was there to do now? She realized that if she didn't keep busy, she would start dwelling on things. She stood in the laundry room, frozen for a moment, a box of Tide in her hands, and heard the voices float in from the soap opera. There were so many ways to spin the plot. She imagined herself dead and Paul recovered, raising the children alone. She imagined herself well and Paul permanently paralyzed—and she moving him into a nursing home. Or Paul dead. Or—

Stop it, Barbara, she ordered herself. Do something. Weed the garden.

That's done, she answered.

Go shopping.

Oh, really! she objected. Just to spend money?

Clean out the closets.

Ah.

She marched upstairs and started in the guest room. They still called it the guest room although it had really become Paul's study and her sewing room. And the guest room closet had become a catch-all. Tax records, clay pots, roller skates, an American flag, paper patterns, crutches (from an old skiing accident), photographs (she avoided looking at them) . . . Trying to ignore the past that was conjured up, she sorted, threw away and stored. And then on to the master bedroom. Less clutter in these closets. But then, behind the empty hat boxes and the alligator shoes she always meant to mend, she came up with the silver satin pillowcase.

Barbara wondered where the matching pillowcase was. And the silver satin sheets. Up in the attic, she supposed. Stored for almost two years now. She hadn't put them away right after her birthday, of course. During that summer she had used them maybe a half-dozen times. But each time was like the first time. Bad.

"I feel silly," she had confided to Paul, as they lay on them that first night. "Self-conscious."

"Don't be," he'd said lightly.

"Don't be self-conscious," she had laughed, nervously. "That only makes me more . . . self-conscious."

"Well, we're supposed to feel sexy."

"I don't need sheets to make me feel sexy."

"I didn't say we did."

"I feel tacky," she said.

"Well, *I* think they're cool and slippery," he said.

"That's just it. Like they're *forcing* us to 'slip into each other's arms,' " she said, mock-dramatically.

"Aw, c'mon, Barb," he sighed.

They lay silent and apart. Then he did put his arms around her. Gently, he began to stroke her.

"Paul?" she murmured. "Don't you love me for *me*?"

"Shh," he said, and tried to kiss her into silence.

And they did make love. He took his time and was thoughtful and when he entered her she thought she might come. But only he came. And she felt alone and distant on the satin sheets, trying to decipher a pattern in the small crack on the ceiling.

"Can I do anything for you?" he asked—meaning, "Should I go down on you?" She had been learning to like this.

"No."

"But I thought—"

"No, Paul," she lied. "It's fine." The lousy sheets, she thought. They felt slick and cool-clammy, as she imagined the skin of a snake. She had to restrain herself from squirming.

"Fine," she repeated.

And whenever she used the sheets it was like that. She felt awkward with her body and couldn't come. So finally she put them away for good. Paul didn't say anything. She knew he was trying not to judge her—but she also sensed that, afterward, he made fewer suggestions about trying new things in bed. And she didn't know how to suggest anything.

"Paul," she said now, holding the wadded-up pillowcase. She wished she had that summer back, to do it differently. She wished she had Paul home now—she'd dig the satin sheets out in a minute. Maybe when he's out of the hospital . . . she thought. But when she spun out the plot that way, she saw herself mutilated—one or both breasts cut off—and Paul turning away from her in bed. She twisted the pillowcase in her hands. Opportunities lost. Years lost.

Barbara cursed her timidity. She remembered how shocked she had been last time she had seen Susan, when Susan had mentioned that she and Curt had tried anal—even now Barbara had trouble completing the thought. She envied Susan her freedom to enjoy sex and to go back to work. Until now, Barbara hadn't needed freedom, because she'd had Paul. But what if I have to go it alone? she wondered. What if Paul dies? She tried to imagine herself venturing out with other men, venturing into the job market. She simply couldn't imagine it. What do I know, she asked herself bitterly, besides sewing? What can I—

Downstairs, the back door banged open.

"Mommy! Mommy! Guess what?! Stevie burned his—"

It was Laurie's voice. Then it shifted into a higher, more frantic pitch.

"Oh, Mommy! Mommy! There's a flood in the kitchen!"

Barbara Justin dashed downstairs. Laurie was standing in the doorway, pointing at the water that was coming out from under the refrigerator and now covered most of the room.

"Oh, damn," said Barbara. She suspected what it might be. Pulling out the freezer, she saw she was right. The automatic ice cube maker hadn't shut itself off. It continued to gush water into the already-filled trays. A domestic crisis, thought Barbara. Well, she told herself with some bitterness, you're a domestic—solve it. Get your home running smoothly again.

She sloshed through the water to the rag bin and to call a repairman. Then she saw the satin pillowcase still in her hands.

Barbara had an overwhelming angry impulse to hurl the pillowcase on the watery floor, to use it as a rag to mop up. After all, it was no use as a pillowcase, right? The life, the opportunity it represented was dead—never to come again. Her arm was poised to hurl it.

She checked her arm. She draped the pillowcase over a chair.

Okay, she thought. Against all reason, I'll hope for a second chance. If my body and Paul's body can be healthy again, maybe . . .

"Laurie," she said, "give me a hand." And she tossed rags out of the rag bin and onto the floor. "Now, what," she asked, "did Steven burn?"

New York City

On the TV set in the city morgue, Lou Costello was telling Bud Abbott that there were strange noises in the mummy's tomb. The morgue attendant, a young man with a prominent Adam's apple, grinned foxily at Joan Scully and Frank Lattimer. "Kinda funny, right? For a morgue? Abbott chased by dead people?"

"Hilarious," said Joan Scully.

"What can I do for you?" asked the attendant.

"Roberto Cruz," she said. "The man who died last night. On the subway?"

"Oh, yeah. Sure."

"Well, has he been identified yet?"

"Just a sec."

While the attendant checked his files, Lattimer left Joan Scully for a pay phone on the wall. He called the 19th precinct.

"Nope," said the attendant, looking up from his files. "The M.E. just finished the autopsy. But nobody wants to come in and say they know him."

"Well"—Joan breathed in—"I knew him. I worked with him at Oakes-Metcalf. I think I can identify him."

"You don't have to," said the attendant, overly solicitous.

"I know I don't have to. But doesn't somebody have to?"

"Yeah. But you don't want to. Not if you were a friend. The subway—it didn't just get his body. If you understand me, Miss, it also . . . well . . . his face."

"Oh," said Joan. As part of her Ph.D. work, Joan had taken anatomy courses at Columbia Medical School and had handled corpses. But they had been anonymous. And they had been cleanly dissected—not what she imagined Roberto Cruz looked like right now. She doubted the Medical Examiner had had to make the traditional Y-shaped incision to open his body. The train had probably done it for him.

"Well, could I take a look at his effects, then?" she asked.

This had been Lattimer's plan all along: Ask to see the body, then appear to settle for the effects. And thus check for the keys.

"Effects?" said the attendant. "His effects aren't here. The police have them."

"His clothes, too?"

"Clothes?" The attendant was getting suspicious. "What do you want to see his clothes for?"

"Well," she said, "Roberto sometimes wore very distinctive clothes. I think if I saw them, maybe I could identify—"

The attendant shook his head with an air of superiority. "I doubt it," he said. "But okay."

He disappeared into the next room.

"Good going," said Lattimer to Joan Scully, putting a hand over the phone's mouthpiece.

"Thanks," she said dryly. "How's it going with you?"

"Humenuik's getting me his list of witnesses."

Lattimer went back to his phone conversation. As Joan waited for the attendant, she watched Lou Costello dodge a mummy that kept trying to fall on him.

The attendant reappeared with a box. He dumped out its contents—a mass of red rags.

"Sorry," he said. But Joan could see he wasn't sorry at all. The attendant enjoyed shocking the public with what death looked like. "Sorry. But this is all that's left. Don't know how you can tell anything from them."

Joan Scully methodically went through the ripped and bloodstained pants and shirt, inspecting all the pockets. Then she shook the clothes vigorously. One dime fell out.

"Hey," said the attendant, "what are you—"

"Could anything else have fallen out earlier?" she asked. "Any keys?"

"Miss," said the attendant, now really getting into it, "they put your friend in a body bag down in the subway. Carried him back here in the same bag. Nothing could fall out. Or do you want to see the bag, too?"

Joan Scully was annoyed. She was annoyed that Frank was on the phone while she had to do this. Why couldn't they have switched places? Still, it was better than having to go inside and actually see Roberto. If his clothes look like this, imagine what—

"Well," insisted the attendant, "*are* they your friend's?" His tone was slightly mocking and more than a little patronizing. "Or maybe you *do* need to see the bag. He's still in it, you know."

Joan Scully knew what the man was thinking of her: The weaker sex. Can't bear to see her friend's face so she thinks she's proving something by going through his clothes. Crazy redhead.

"I've changed my mind," said Joan Scully, suddenly. "I will see Cruz."

The attendant leered. His Adam's apple bobbed in delight. "I don't have the time to dress him up for the viewing window like usual," he said. "Soft lights and all. No, you'll have to come back inside with me."

"You don't understand," said Joan Scully. "I don't just want to see him. I want to go through his bag, too."

"This way, then," said the attendant with a wave.

As Joan Scully started after him, she could see that Lattimer was cradling the phone against his shoulder and writing down names. And on the TV set, the mummy was actively chasing Lou Costello. The mummy's wrappings were unraveling.

Houston, Texas

Just before dinnertime, Dr. Arthur Goodhue was in his driveway polishing his car—a new Porsche that he didn't have the nerve to drive very much—when Ray Ryker's goons swooped down on him.

They weren't goons, of course. They were both polite young men in white shirts, narrow rep ties and narrow-lapel dark suits. But they guided him so insistently to their own car—a nondescript Ford Galaxie—that Goodhue couldn't help but sense the muscles under the suits and so he thought of them as goons.

"Mr. Ryker would like to see you right *now*, Doctor," said the young man, deferentially, as he closed the passenger door on Goodhue and got in behind him and the other young man stepped on the accelerator.

And so minutes later they ushered a highly annoyed but impressed Dr. Goodhue into Ryker's presence in the Texahoma offices. But not into Ryker's personal office. Goodhue was ushered into the next-door control room, where Ryker was holding forth to a portly, polished, Latin-looking businessman.

"So he'll call up the level of T-107," Ryker was saying. "And you see—here—he's getting a level of 31.8 feet."

Ryker and the other man were standing in the middle of the living room-size room, looking over the shoulder of an operator seated at a desk with a keyboard console and a cathode ray display. There was no other furniture in the room and no windows. Just three blank walls—and, filling the long wall facing the desk, a hugh schematic diagram of oil wells, pipelines and tanks. Next to each tank symbol was a flow meter, with a pen charting a line on a revolving paper drum.

Ryker nodded to Goodhue. He made a brief introduction—"Dr. Arthur Goodhue—Dr. Hector Cunaho, Brazilian State Petroleum"— and then went on as if Goodhue weren't there. Goodhue got even more annoyed and impressed.

" . . . so now he'll call up all of Section 3," continued Ryker.

Goodhue came closer and watched also. The operator pressed some buttons on the console. The cathode ray display changed from a series of numbers to a more detailed portion of the wall diagram.

"Now, up until this point, Doctor . . . " Ryker was saying.

Goodhue was startled. At first he thought Ryker meant him— until Cunaho nodded. Ryker went on, "Up until this point, our system is no different from yours. You know a tank is almost filled, you know it must be shut down and the flow diverted to another tank in the section. But, at this point, *your* operator must call a man in the field, correct?"

Cunaho nodded.

"And he must drive out to the two tanks and turn the valves by hand, correct?"

"If his pick-up truck is *running* that day," joked Cunaho.

Ryker laughed—his sharp, barking laugh.

"Yes," Ryker agreed, rocking on his feet. "Well, watch what *our* operator can do. Watch what control we have."

Control, thought Goodhue. His goddamn control.

Ryker touched his finger to the cathode ray display, to a half-dozen green and red lights on the diagram. "Green for open valves," he said. "Red for closed. But watch."

Ryker's operator picked up a light pen and touched it to each of the green and red lights. The lights immediately started flashing.

"The valves are now ready for instructions," Ryker explained.

The operator pressed more buttons on the console. Some of the green lights turned red, some of the red lights turned green.

"Just like that," said Ryker, proudly. "We shut down the full tank and start filling the empty one—two hundred miles away, without a man and a pick-up truck." He pointed to the wall. "As the flow meters verify."

"Very impressive," agreed Dr. Cunaho. "And what is the reliability?"

"Ninety-eight percent," said Ryker. "And, of course, it contains a fail-safe system."

"And the cost?"

"In manpower savings, over 20 percent of return on investment."

"And this is the system you would install if you open the La Reza field for us?"

"Yes." Ryker leaned forward, looked up at Cunaho who stood a head taller. Ryker's eyes were bright, his teeth gleamed. Goodhue saw Cunaho shrink to Ryker's size—or, more accurately, Ryker grow to Cunaho's.

"And now," said Ryker, "Johnny—"

The operator turned around. "Yes?"

"—Johnny, would you take Dr. Cunaho to Mr. Farb in Production?"

"But," said the operator, a mild, middle-aged man in steel-rimmed eyeglasses, "who'll run the room? I've got to pump out T-107 and—"

"I will," said Ryker. "I'll call you back in about fifteen minutes."

"Okay," said the operator.

"Talk to you later, Doctor," said Ryker to Cunaho.

Ryker's operator and the Brazilian oil executive left. Ryker took the operator's place at the desk. Arthur Goodhue was still fuming. He suspected Ryker had deliberately made him wait and watch all this to impress him. Well, he admitted, he was impressed. But why?

Ryker ignored Goodhue. He pressed buttons on the console and a new diagram appeared on the cathode ray display. He picked up the phone on the desk and dialed a number.

"Pumping a batch of Scurry out of T-107," said Ryker. "Okay." He hung up.

Finally, he turned to Goodhue. "That was the tank farm," he said. "When they've lined up their system, they'll call back and I'll pump out. In the meantime, we've got a few minutes to talk."

Goodhue thought Ryker made it sound as if he, Goodhue, had wanted to talk to Ryker. As if Ryker were doing him a favor by granting him a few minutes. Goodhue was annoyed at the charade. He remembered his premonition of two days ago: The time would come when Ryker would use him to do more than guard old Mr. Ash. So this was the time. And Goodhue sensed he was powerless to object. He wished Ryker would just get to it.

But Ryker would get to it in his own way.

With a sweep of his hand, he indicated the console, the cathode ray display, the diagram on the wall.

"Can you sense it, Doctor?" he asked. "Hundreds of miles away, that oil was building up in the tank. Thirty-one feet—thirty-two feet—thirty-three. It was obeying the rules, growing like it should. But—it didn't know when to stop growing. Thirty-four feet. Thirty-five. At thirty-five, it would have burst the walls of the tank. Crack it open. Except"—he tapped the display—"we stopped it. Here. We controlled it. Switched it off. Just like that."

"So?" asked Goodhue. It was the first word he had spoken since coming in.

"So, don't you see the analogy?"

"No."

"To cancer," said Ryker.

"Cancer?"

"Unchecked cell growth, isn't it?" asked Ryker. "Matt Ash's stomach cells growing, like they should, filling the space allotted for them, but then—instead of stopping—*continuing* to grow, bursting the walls of the stomach, spilling into the spleen, the liver, uncontrolled."

"Well ... " began Goodhue. "It's not exactly—"

"It's exact enough," snapped Ryker. "It's exact enough to say that what we need isn't radiation or surgery. Those are half-measures, inefficient measures. For losers. What we need is a *control* panel to *switch off* the fucking cells, just like that."

Ryker's eyes blazed. He's actually scary, thought Goodhue. The windowless room was air-conditioned, but Goodhue suddenly felt himself sweating hard. I wonder if I smell, he thought. I wonder if my fear smells. I must use more cologne.

"Well, Doctor," continued Ryker, "it appears somebody is now offering us what we need. A way to switch it off."

"What?" Goodhue didn't understand.

"They're offering a cure."

"What cure? Who?"

Ryker explained the phone call and the claims his caller had made. As he repeated the claim of regeneration, he was stopped by Goodhue's sudden, giddy laughter.

"What?" snapped Ryker.

Goodhue couldn't help himself. He had felt so intimidated by Ryker—the scene at the hospital two days ago, and now the goons and the windowless room—that this was a wonderful release. "Cure," he gurgled through his laughter. "Regener—"

"Shut up," snapped Ryker, louder.

But Goodhue was too amused to stop.

To think that this man, thought Goodhue, this multimillionaire who had pushed him around was himself being pushed, conned, used by some charlatan with another *cure for cancer!* "Is he selling hydrazine?" giggled Goodhue. "Or megavitamins? Or Krebiozen? Or something more recent like Laetrile? Or—"

"Shut up!"

"Or diribohexamephronine. Or—"

"What's that?" asked Ryker sharply. "The diribo—thing?"

"I just made it up!" yelled Goodhue, pounding his fist on the console, his chest and cheeks aching with laughter. "Just as all those other cancer 'cures' were made up! Just as that man on the phone is making it up!" Goodhue struggled to control himself. "Don't you understand, Ryker—you're being taken. Do you know ... in the last century ... how many tens of thousands of people ... poor, suffering fools ... desperate, driven ... have spent how many millions of their hard-earned money on how many cancer cures? Why, as far back as the 1820s—or '30s, I forget which—a Dr. Monton in Marseilles claimed he had a—"

"All right," said Ryker vehemently. "All *right.*" He tried to stare Goodhue down. Having made his point, Goodhue stopped. Goodhue stuffed his hands in his pockets and shook his head dolefully.

"All right," said Ryker, softly but still intently, "you've made your point. And it's a point which—I'm sure you know—I hardly need *you* to make for me. I've considered it at length."

"But then how can you—"

"Which is why," said Ryker, "you *are* here. To prove the claim true or false."

"How?"

Ryker recounted what his caller had said: Goodhue should be ready to go "somewhere" tomorrow.

"I won't," said Goodhue.

Ryker calmly folded his arms across his chest; he showed no surprise. But Goodhue felt very surprised. He realized he hadn't said "I won't" as a pro forma thing, preliminary to giving in. No, he really meant it. To his surprise, he was discovering that his gleeful laughter at Ryker had weakened the smaller man's hold over him.

"It's a fool's errand," said Goodhue. "I'll continue to watch Matt Ash for you—that falls in my realm as a physician. But to go on a wild goose chase . . . " He threw up his arms and turned to leave.

"You're not leaving, Goodhue," said Ryker, evenly.

Goodhue stopped and turned. He felt his newfound strength ebb a bit. "What do you mean, I'm not?" He thought of the goons.

Goodhue tried to stay calm. "You mean—not without giving you the names of some oncologists in town who *might* go? Well, all right . . . there's Lefebvre. There's—"

"There's you," said Ryker.

"No!" said Goodhue. He shook his fist in Ryker's face.

The fist came too close. It grazed Ryker's nose.

The smaller man's reaction was too fast for Goodhue to see. Goodhue's wrist was grabbed and then twisted high behind his back, forcing his face down into the keyboard of the console—and then he was released and he fell to the floor.

Goodhue's mouth was frozen open. It had all happened too fast for pain or even fear. Goodhue felt only shock—and now, lying on the floor, trying to regain his senses, a confusion of emotions. Outrage, humiliation and a deeper fear—not for his physical safety, but for his psychic safety. And a moment ago he had thought Ryker's hold over him had *weakened*!

But it was clear from Ryker's bearing that he was confused, too. He was gasping. "I . . . don't do that again . . . I'm sorry to have lost . . . control . . . but don't do that . . . laugh at me . . . touch me . . . nobody touches me . . . are you . . . all right, Doctor? . . . Get up, damn it . . . I didn't hurt you . . . if I'd wanted to hurt you I could have . . . I'm sorry . . . but you have to . . . have to verify this claim for me . . . "

Ryker's dark eyes were blazing. His thin, slashlike mouth was stammering. He forced his mouth shut. He locked his hands behind his back.

Goodhue picked himself up gingerly. "I think . . . I think I better leave now."

The two men's eyes met. Goodhue lowered his.

" . . . but you know," he said, "where to reach me."

It was established. Goodhue would run Ryker's errand.

The cancer specialist left the control room. The call came from the tank farm. "Ready to receive Scurry," they told Ryker. With pleasure, Ryker manned the console.

New York City

Around 8:30 P.M., Joseph Falcone dropped in at intensive care and asked how Justin was. "The same," one of the nurses told him. "And the lab says he's got normal hemo and electrolytes." Falcone looked at the report. No leads. Even though he knew it was fruitless, he ran through the same series of checks on Justin that the nurses did. He came back to their desk.

"The same," he agreed.

"Hey, what's wrong, Doctor?" kidded Nurse Lopez. "How come you can't cure him?"

"Yeah," said Nurse Abrams. "I mean we've got a great medical center here."

"We've got a *cancer* center here," said Falcone.

"Meaning if he had cancer ... " began Lopez.

" ... we couldn't cure him of that either," concluded Falcone.

The three laughed ruefully.

Fire Island, New York

They rang the front door bell and nobody answered. But soft lights were glowing upstairs in the house. And the door was ajar. So they opened the door the rest of the way. The sweet, unmistakable smell of marijuana smoke floated out from the darkness.

Frank Lattimer and Joan Scully exchanged raised eyebrows: Were they at the right house, at Hugh Underwood's house?

It had been a long, hard time getting here. First, the parkway had been clogged. Then they'd had an interminable wait for the ferry. The ferry deposited them a mile down the island from Underwood's semi-exclusive community and, since the bike rental shop was closed, they'd had to walk. It had been a nice walk. It was cooler here, away from the heat of the city. And the air here was fresh; the stars above shone brightly, unobscured. Joan Scully had breathed deeply of the ocean air, trying to clean the day in the city—the garbage trucks, the Institute, the police station, Central Park, Spanish Harlem and the morgue, particularly the morgue—out of her. Mainly, she had succeeded, although the image of Roberto Cruz still lingered: a tough, green plastic bag filled with meat and gristle and no keys. When she'd emerged from the morgue, she'd washed her hands and arms for a good ten minutes. And she'd let Frank persuade her to come to Fire Island tonight. Frank had said he just wanted to ask Underwood a few simple questions and then they could relax, enjoy themselves. Frank had a friend, Eddie Winslow, who was away this month and had a beach house they could use. First, just a brief meeting with Underwood.

But was this Underwood's house? Where somebody was smoking grass? Joan sensed that both Underwood and his wife were very proper people and their oldest child was—what?—eight years old? Perhaps in the dark, on the unlit wooden walkways through the dunes, Frank and she had lost their way. But Lattimer pointed again at the discreet engraved plaque under the deck light. "Underwood." The plaque harmonized with the restrained, modern design of the house, with the weathered redwood, the tubular deck furniture. Right house, all right. Joan Scully shrugged. Maybe they had a baby sitter who was turning on.

"Hello," called Frank Lattimer into the dark living room.

On the living room floor, they could make out a dark mass. The mass now untangled itself and one of the people came toward them, naked, holding panties over her crotch.

"Hello," said the black woman, whom Joan Scully immediately recognized from the picture on her boss's desk as Mrs. Underwood.

"Hello? Yes? Whom are you looking for?" she asked.

Lattimer was impressed that the naked woman—slightly sagging in the belly but still attractive—used "whom" instead of "who."

"Uh," Lattimer cleared his throat. "Hugh Underwood," he said.

"Well," the woman laughed. "He's gone to a party. Not this one. But a very proper party. It's"—she looked at her watch, the only thing she wore—"just before ten. I don't expect him till after eleven. Would you like directions? Or would you—" She looked Lattimer and Joan Scully up and down. She hesitated—and then indicated the dark mass on the floor. Joan Scully distinguished two young men, both white. They were kissing each other on the mouth and now one was moving his lips down toward the other's crotch. "Or would you care to join us?" asked Mrs. Underwood. "We could use a fourth at bridge. Or a fifth."

Joan Scully felt a quick shiver. Of both excitement and revulsion. Lattimer sensed it in her. He looked at her sharply.

"But then I don't know your names," said Mrs. Underwood. "Perhaps I shouldn't invite strangers to—"

"Joan Scully," Joan said. "I work with your husband at—"

"Of course." Mrs. Underwood waved a hand. "Hugh has mentioned you. He never mentioned, of course, that you're beautiful. No. That wouldn't interest him. Only his work. Only cancer. A wonderful disease, cancer."

"Well . . . " said Joan.

"Well, while he's wasting his life on goddamn crawly tumors," spat Mrs. Underwood with quick fire, "and sucking up to crawly people at the Helwigs' party, *I'm* doing what interests *me*. And he's so fucking stupid that he doesn't even *suspect* it. And isn't that the worst of it, isn't that the worst?" And she started sobbing.

One of the young men called languorously from the floor. "Hey, Ceil. Hey, Ceil."

"Oh, fuck you," she snapped at him, pulling herself together.

"Please do," laughed the other young man softly.

"Go fish or cut bait," announced Ceilia Underwood to her visitors. She put her hands on her hips and her panties fell to the floor. "Join in or get out."

"Out, I think," said Lattimer politely. "Perhaps we could see your husband in the morning?"

"Tomorrow," announced Mrs. Underwood, "is family day. The Hugh Underwoods and their two children will be fishing for porgies and cannot be disturbed."

Lattimer couldn't tell if she was kidding or not. "Well, then," he said, "where is—"

"Back the way you came. Second right. Third house on the left. Japanese rock garden all around it. Helwig."

And she slammed the door in their face. They heard the locks being thrown.

"Well," said Frank Lattimer to Joan Scully.

"Well," said Joan Scully to Frank Lattimer.

They both laughed and started down the walkway.

"You weren't . . . ?" began Lattimer. "When she asked—?"

"Interested?" said Joan Scully. She grinned at him.

"Yes."

"Why?"

"I'm interested."

"If I'm interested in . . . " she teased.

"Yes, damn it," said Lattimer. "Group stuff."

"Not now."

"But you have been."

"Unh-uh," she teased, "you're getting possessive. And not just possessive of my present or future but possessive of my—"

"Past. Past, wise-ass," he laughed.

"That's all right," she said. "I'm flattered. I think it's nice you feel possessive of me."

"Really?"

"Sure," she said, matter-of-factly. "I feel possessive of you."

"After just one day?"

"It's been a good one day. Mainly."

"It has, hasn't it," said Frank Lattimer. He put an arm around her. "I hope," he said, "that Hugh Underwood doesn't feel possessive of Mrs. Underwood. Or someday he's in for a big unhappiness."

"Umm. We turn right here."

"Right," said Lattimer. But instead he took Joan Scully in his arms. They embraced warmly in the middle of the walkway junction. Their mouths sought each other.

"Mrs. Underwood turned you on," whispered Joan Scully.

"*You* turn me on."

"Well . . . okay." She ran a hand up his leg. "But if we stay here, you won't get to meet Dr. Underwood. And he's even more of a turn-on." Her hand started to grip his crotch.

"At this moment, I don't care if I ever meet—"

On the walkway, next to them, somebody cleared his throat. "Excuse me, but—"

"Oh, Dr. Underwood," said Joan Scully. "I didn't expect to see—"

"Joan? Is that you, Joan? What are you . . . ?"

They stopped in mutual confusion.

"Well," said Joan briskly. "This is Frank Lattimer, a friend of mine and a reporter—"

"A reporter?" Underwood bristled.

"And a friend," she said reassuringly. "And Frank, this is Hugh Underwood—a good boss and also, I hope, a friend."

The two men shook hands. "I thought," said Joan Scully, "that you were at a party."

"I was. Am. I'm just going back to my house to get something I forgot."

"Oh," said Joan. She felt a pang of sympathy for him.

"And what are you doing here?" asked Underwood.

"We came to see you, Doctor," said Lattimer.

"Me? Why? Can't it wait till Monday, Joan?"

"I don't think so," she said. "You see, we're worried about Paul."

"Paul. Well, yes. So am I. But why—?"

"Because. Because when you put that together with the way Roberto died and—"

"Roberto? Our Roberto? What—?"

"You didn't hear?"

"No."

So she told in a rush about the subway accident and Frank's suspicions about Justin's notes and slides being missing and the fact that Roberto didn't live where he was supposed to . . . and all the while Underwood's face seemed to go through quick changes (his black face, in the dark, was hard to see, so she wasn't sure) from shock to puzzlement to impatience to a half dozen other emotions.

"... and so we wondered if maybe Paul had really—really— found a cure, or at least if somebody else thought he did ... " she was saying, and she was aware of Lattimer trying to put a word in edgewise, to shut her up, because she knew this was no way to get information out of her boss, but she suddenly realized that she had to keep on talking because she was flustered that Underwood had discovered her kissing Lattimer and because she didn't, for Underwood's sake, want Underwood to go past them and discover Mrs. Underwood.

My God, thought Joan Scully. From being a grown-up a minute ago, I'm now acting like a little girl. A little girl who wants to win approval from Daddy and give protection to Daddy. Frank's right— I've got a complex.

So she shut up.

"Joan," said Underwood in his calm, southern voice. "Forgive me, but I just don't draw the conclusions you do. Roberto's death is—why, it's a tragedy, of course. But as for Paul's notes and slides, I'm sure they're around somewhere. I don't think we need conspiracy theories to explain it. Perhaps," he said, mildly, "if we applied a bit of the scientific method ... " His soft words hung on the warm night air.

Underwood shot his cuffs and looked at his watch. "And now I really should get home and then get back to the party. I'm sorry you both came out here for nothing. I'd invite you over tomorrow but we're all going out."

Yes, going out fishing, thought Joan Scully. She was willing to bet Underwood was the only man at the party in a suit. And if he was too formally dressed for the party, imagine how formally dressed he was for the scene he was about to witness at home. Well, she thought, maybe the two young men are gone by now?

"One question, Doctor," said Frank Lattimer.

"Yes?" Underwood turned to him.

"The private grant that Virology got two years ago. Who gave it?"

Underwood looked at Joan Scully, then back to Lattimer.

"Well," he said. "I don't know why Joan got into all this with you, and I hope as a reporter you have more real news to report—but the grant is hardly a secret. Or important. It was the Endicott Foundation."

"Did you apply for it?"

"No. It just came."

"You didn't think it was unusual?"

"Of course. But not unprecedented."

"Oh," said Lattimer. "Well, did you follow it up? Try to find out why your section was so favored? To see if you could get another?"

"Of course."

"And?"

"They didn't give any reason. Sometimes foundations don't *have* reasons, you know. They simply have to get rid of X amount of money to balance their budgets."

"Oh," said Lattimer. "Thank you."

"Not at all," said Underwood. "Good night. See you Monday, Joan." And he shook Lattimer's hand again and walked off, limping. As he did, Joan Scully saw him shake his head, as if in wonderment.

"I really fucked it up, didn't I?" said Joan to Frank Lattimer.

"No," said Lattimer. "I was watching his face as you talked. I think I saw something."

"Yeah, you saw he thought I was nuts."

"Nope. I saw guilt."

"Guilt?"

"Yes, indeed. The good doctor has done something having to do with Justin that makes him feel very bad."

"*Hugh Underwood?*"

"Uh-huh."

"Do you think he—? Could—? What do you mean?"

"I don't know yet."

Joan Scully ran a hand through her red hair. She looked up at Lattimer. "Whew," she said, "you sure try to build a lot from asking just a 'few simple questions.'"

"Well," said Frank Lattimer, "when you start out, you never know what you'll find."

"Yeah," agreed Joan. She found herself playing with a button on Lattimer's shirt. "And imagine," she said, "what Underwood will find—when he goes home looking for whatever he forgot and finds his wife's friends."

"Maybe she'll invite him to join," suggested Lattimer.

"A fourth at bridge," said Joan.

"Deal him a hand," said Lattimer, cupping his hands behind her neck and pulling her slowly toward him.

"Uh-huh," she agreed.

"You know," he said, "I think *we* could play bridge over at Eddie Winslow's."

"So far to go," said Joan, putting her hand back on Lattimer's crotch, "just to be dealt an ace."

"Hmm," said Lattimer.

"There're no more deadlines, tonight, Ace," she said, as they stepped off the walkway. "Nowhere to rush to. And I bet the sand feels nice."

"Softer than Eddie's bed, as I remember," he said, as they started to lie down in the dunes. High above them, clear and bright, the constellations wheeled.

Los Angeles, California

For Christmas, one of Senator Prentice's teen-age sons had given him a transparent plastic ashtray in the shape of a human lung. The more Prentice smoked and used the ashtray, the darker it got and the more it reminded him to quit smoking. But he hadn't been able to quit yet. In fact, since April, since he had started his increasingly hectic travels around the country, he had gone up to two packs a day. To-night, far from his Indiana home, Prentice ground out another ciga-rette in frustration.

"... and we've got to find a way to reduce unemployment in the central cities. Why, just this afternoon, in Watts ... " he heard him-self saying. He paused and gave the cigarette butt another vicious turn.

He looked at the crowd around him. He had been speaking less than five minutes, but he knew he was already losing their attention. At the fringes, many guests were turning away to get another drink at the bar and more hors d'oeuvres. Others were starting to talk to each other or gaze at their reflection in the room-wide sheet of glass that faced the beach and the dark expanse of the Pacific Ocean.

Unemployment. Watts. Prentice mentally snorted. The crowd was rock-star Hollywood with a few movie people thrown in. He doubted that this Malibu crowd—casually but expensively dressed, wandering around this $1.5 million beach home—worried much about blacks on welfare. Well, change your emphasis, he told himself.

"... but while we've got to stimulate the economy to create jobs, we can't let industrial pollution destroy ... "

On the floor in front of Prentice sat a very famous actress, her arms drawn up around the knees of white silk pants. Gucci shoes below. Prentice had been briefed that she was very active in the Sierra Club. But at his mention of "pollution," she let a little sigh escape. As if to say she'd heard it all before.

Oh, God, sighed Prentice to himself. How could he reach people? How could he get himself across? He was having no more luck with this group than he'd had this afternoon with the twenty-year-old blacks shooting endless baskets on cracked concrete courts. They also didn't know who he was—or care to find out.

It was embarrassing. It was galling. Back home in Indiana, Arthur Prentice was the most powerful—and yet probably best-liked—politician of the last two decades. In Washington, in the Senate, he was a member of the powerful inner club. But in the rest of the country, in the eyes of all the other people whose support he needed in order to become President . . . Arthur Prentice was, well, just another serious-faced man in late middle age in a pin-striped suit. They didn't know, reflected Prentice, how deeply he cared about his country, about where it was going, about what he felt he could do for it—if he could only better express those feelings. An hour ago, when he stepped through the doors of this mansion and was ushered in to meet its owner—meet the rock star's cool eyes—Prentice had again sensed that impossible gulf.

"Mr. Maxwell?" Prentice had said, offering his hand.

"Just Maxwell," said the young man, looking up briefly, flashing a grin. He went back to concentrating on the pinball machine he was playing. It stood amid a bank of two dozen other machines in a huge room. Maxwell played it well. He slammed the last ball around, making lights flash and bells ring. "Five free games, six free games," he chanted. "Aw-wright!" The ball finally fell out of play.

Maxwell turned to his visitor. "Okay, Mr. Prentice, the party's about to begin. But I hear there's something else you're going to ask me to do. What is it?"

Prentice had felt lost. Who was Maxwell? How did he live? Prentice's teen-age daughter had explained that the young man had been born with a tongue-twister of a Hungarian name and that he had adopted his new name—and the name of his band—from the Beatles' song, "Maxwell's Silver Hammer." And as Prentice and Jack Lynch—Prentice's top aide—had walked through the rambling, custom-built, crazy-quilt home, Lynch had explained that the music reverberating around them came from Maxwell's latest album. "A platinum seller," Lynch had said. "What we want is some of the platinum."

What Lynch wanted Maxwell to do was give a concert for the Senator and donate the gate receipts—a neat way around the legal $1,000 limit for individual donations. Prentice had planned to ask Maxwell after the party. But he was being forced to ask now. So he did—as smoothly as possible. And Maxwell turned back to the pinball machine.

"Nope," he said, hitting a button to start one of his free games. "You're welcome to this party." That grin again. "Welcome to talk to my friends—ask them. But I don't sing for anyone but me."

So the party had begun and Prentice had tried to reach Maxwell's friends—and Prentice was failing. Oh, thought Prentice, to reach people easily and as powerfully as Maxwell's music did, as did the music and movies made by these friends of his. And then to be known and loved across America, as they were . . .

Prentice lit and drew on another cigarette. He tried again.

"And even as we build a better society at home, we cannot forget we live in a larger world. And while we cannot always lead the world, we can cooperate to . . . "

Lousy, thought Prentice. He saw, across the room, Maxwell looking blankly at him. If . . . thought Prentice, if it were only rock stars and blacks who didn't care. But two days ago, in New York City, Prentice's speech on "A Post-Détente World" had similarly failed to stir the Council on Foreign Relations. So how could he fire people up? Time was running short. Prentice was going to officially announce his candidacy within the month and when he announced, he wanted to do it with pledges of support, financial or otherwise. To show some momentum. Because right now his momentum was zero.

" . . . so America cannot defend every place on the globe," he said, looking at the very famous actress, "but certainly if the Cannes Film Festival came under attack . . . "

Prentice played for a laugh, got a very mild one. The actress shook her head, unfolded her silk legs, got up and went toward the bar.

Okay, thought Prentice. Fuck you, too. He took another puff. So how *do* I distinguish myself from the two dozen other declared and undeclared candidates for the Presidency? He had told his aides that he would risk taking an unusual stand, making an unusual promise, if they could think of one. Cure cancer by 1988? Lynch had suggested, half-facetiously. Prentice had smiled. It had helped him to get his Cancer Control Act passed, but it wasn't the kind of thing you could run on. No, give me something else. I'm thinking, Lynch had said, I'm thinking. Ah—how about telling them the *real* reason you want to be President?

You mean, Prentice had replied dryly, my lust for power? My greed? My megalomania?

Something like that, Lynch had said.

Yeah, thought Senator Arthur Prentice, now grinding out this cigarette also, this crowd would understand power and greed. But instead what he told them was " . . . and I thank you for this opportunity to talk to you tonight. Are there any questions?"

There were a few desultory ones. Prentice fielded them with as good humor as he could summon. He scanned the crowd for his host, but Maxwell had disappeared. Back to his free pinball games, Prentice supposed. Or maybe to screw one of the nubile young things whom Prentice had seen drifting vaguely through the beach house before the party started. These people! thought Prentice. A long-haired young man walked in front of him, obstructing Prentice's view of whoever was trying to ask him a question. Prentice saw the little spoon on the silver chain around the man's neck. I'm not dumb, thought Prentice. (He had served on a Senate subcommittee on drugs.) I know it's for coke.

The questioner was the very famous actress, returned from the bar. She was asking about capital punishment. The question was turning into a drunken harangue. Ducking his head for a moment, Prentice's eyes fell upon the ashtray. God, are all those butts mine? he marveled. I wonder what my lungs look like. The irony of his Cancer Act and his chainsmoking was not lost on Prentice.

" . . . yes, well, capital punishment—" he tried to interrupt.

"Excuse me, Senator, ladies and gentlemen . . . " Lynch was coming to his side. "But there's an important phone call for Senator Prentice."

Prentice was grateful for the lie. He waved to the crowd and allowed Lynch to lead him off into a butler's pantry—which was as large as most people's living rooms. There he discovered that Lynch had been only half-lying. The caller had hung up—but his message *was* important.

"Wozinsky in New York—" explained Lynch.

Prentice nodded. Wozinsky was a Park Avenue lawyer and a Prentice supporter.

"—he got a call from Warren Brown—"

"Not again," sighed Prentice. Brown's testimony had helped Prentice get his cancer bill passed. Now, in the last month Brown had been trying to get Prentice's help with the Institute's HEW problem. But as Prentice told Brown, HEW couldn't be budged.

"—and Brown says that the head of one of his sections, a researcher, a black man named Underwood—"

Prentice shrugged. He'd never heard of the man.

"—is working under one of your grants—" continued Lynch, his eyes growing brighter.

"So?" asked Prentice. "Look, I told Brown that no—"

"—and Underwood told Brown this morning that he's just discovered what causes cancer."

Prentice paused a beat. "Yeah?" he asked carefully.

"Yeah. And Underwood also says—"

A butler came in with a decimated hors d'oeuvre tray. While the two politicians waited, the butler filled the tray. They listened to the sounds of the people in the next room. It seemed to Prentice that, in his absence, the party was getting livelier.

The butler left. Lynch continued: "—says he's only six to nine months away from a cure. *The* cure."

Prentice again caught himself. "The ... cure for cancer?" he asked carefully.

Lynch nodded.

"You think it's real?" asked Prentice.

"Wozinsky says Brown does."

The sounds in the next room suddenly seemed far away to Prentice. Insignificant. The babble of children. Silly, spoiled children he had wasted time trying to please. Southern California was unreal, he concluded. Reality? Reality was a lab in New York City and a discovery there and the impact that discovery—and his connection with it—could have on people. All people. From Watts to the Council on Foreign Relations to the farmlands of his native Indiana to ... yes, even to Malibu Beach.

Prentice smiled at Lynch. "Well, if Mrs. ——," and he named the very famous actress, "in there happens to get cancer, she *doesn't* get the cure. And that goes double for Maxwell."

Lynch laughed. And then they got down to business.

SUNDAY

Fire Island, New York, and New York City

Joan Scully lay on her back on a bench of the little ferry boat. She gazed at the pale sky, sun stripping away the morning mist. She enjoyed the simplicity of her world. All she could see was the sky and part of Lattimer's forearm just above where his hand touched her arm. All she could feel was his hand on her and the sun above, and under her the wooden bench and the gentle movement of the boat through the waves. She liked being motionless and yet moving. Her mind also felt stripped to simplicities. None of yesterday, running around, made sense. Yet it had made sense to be with Lattimer, to make love to him last night. And it made sense to be with him today, to take the first boat out of the island because he had to be in the city by early morning. It wasn't a commitment. It didn't mean she would want to be with him tomorrow. It meant she was glad to be here now, feeling what she did. It surprised her a little. She had never let her defenses down so much, so much lived in the present. Tomorrow she would go back to the lab and her research. Now she would listen to the gulls' calls and the throb of the ferry-boat engine.

In the city, Paul Justin also lay on his back in a simple, motionless world. He had no defenses. He gazed straight up as the nurse rolled back his eyelids and checked his pupils. For a moment he saw her face—clear through the left eye, still blurred through the right—and then blackness again. He felt her hold his wrist to take his pulse, felt the blood pressure cuff tighten around his arm, heard the *whoosh* of escaping air as the cuff loosened. He felt her put her finger in his palm and heard her call his name and her request to squeeze her finger. He could not. Then there was the terrible tickle in his throat and the need to cough as she suctioned out his mucus. And then the ignominy of the thermometer up his rectum. The nurse rolled him onto one side and left him there. Time passed. He floated in time, in an unchanging present. He heard a man come in. The man opened Justin's eyelids. A pinpoint of light shone in each eye and he briefly saw it was Falcone. Falcone closed his lids again. Justin felt Falcone bend his arm and felt it flop down on the bed, lifeless. He felt Falcone scrape the bottoms of his feet—but they didn't move. He felt pain as Falcone pinched his stomach—but he knew he didn't show it. And then he heard Falcone mutter, "So what the hell is it? A blood clot? A viral infection?" And felt terror as Falcone said, "Maybe tomorrow we should try a brain biopsy."

Houston, Texas

Every Monday, Wednesday and Friday morning, Ray Ryker did the Royal Canadian Air Force exercises. Every Tuesday, Thursday and Saturday morning, he did isometrics. Sundays he rested. But not this Sunday. This last week, Ryker was concerned that things were getting away from him. So this morning, in his small, private gym, he was going after them.

First, he had put on eight-ounce gloves and worked combinations on the punching bag for twenty minutes. He had boxed at Penn and he was still good. Now Ryker was running on the motorized treadmill, running two miles, three miles . . .

The phone rang. Annoyed (he'd wanted to do five miles), Ryker stepped off the treadmill and answered the phone.

"Hello?"

"Pay attention," said the man with the gravelly voice. "Your cancer expert should take Braniff Airlines flight 436 . . . "

Ryker jabbed a button on another phone. It rang a bell in local switching office no. 5 of Southwestern Bell. The trace began.

" . . . leaving Houston this morning at 9:20."

"What?" asked Ryker, stalling for time. Ryker knew one of the directors of Southwestern Bell. A few strings had been pulled. A separate line had been run to local switching office no. 5, where Ryker's phone was connected. And the office had been given a standing order: keep ears open for the bell, keep eyes on the primary side of line link frame no. 7, switch no. 8. That switch was Ryker's phone.

In the switching office, Fred Hisiger heard the bell ring. He looked at switch 8. Yes, the magnet was closed—there was a call. He looked up the line above the switch to see which of the ten contact points was closed. It was the contact point on level 3.

"Braniff 436," repeated the gravelly voice.

"When?" asked Ryker.

"You heard me," said the voice.

"But where does he get off?" asked Ryker.

Hisiger turned to the secondary side of the line link frame. He looked for the converse of switch 8, level 3—switch 3, level 8. He found it.

"It only goes one place," said the voice. "Good-bye."

"Wait a minute," said Ryker. "If I do send someone, when do I hear from him?"

"Later today."

"And when—if you really have the cure—when does he call to confirm it?"

"I told you: Tuesday."

"And when do I deliver the money?"

Hisiger looked at the line on switch 3, level 8, to see which magnet was closed. He saw it was magnet 4 right. He consulted the adjacent chart to see where that magnet went.

"I told you that, too," said the gravelly voice, increasingly annoyed. "The first nine million on Tuesday."

"Wait a minute," protested Ryker. "That means I've got to raise the money *tomorrow*—before I know whether I'm going to pay it or not."

"I told you that before," said the voice. "And believe me, you'll want to pay it. Now, good-bye, Mr. Ryker."

"But how can I convert to cash in just one day?"

The chart said magnet 4 right went to trunk link frame 9. Hisiger quickly walked there.

"Don't shit me, Ryker," said the gravelly voice, "you can do it."

"But how do I deliver?"

"I'll tell you Tuesday."

"But—"

The chart on the trunk link frame said magnet 4 right connected to switch 5, level 7 on the primary side of the trunk link frame. Hisiger turned to the secondary side of the frame. He looked for the converse—switch 7, level 5. He found it.

"Don't 'but' me, you son of a bitch," said the gravelly voice. "You want Ash to live, don't you?"

Good, thought Ryker. I've got him pissed off enough so that *he's* trying to score points. Now I can keep him from hanging up.

"Well, I don't know," drawled Ryker. "I don't know if he deserves to live. Have you ever met the buzzard?"

"No."

"Well," said Ryker, laying on an even slower drawl, "he's the goddamn ... orneriest ... "

Hisiger consulted another chart. It said switch 5, level 7 was incoming trunk 5024 from Colorado Tandem. Hisiger picked up a phone to call Colorado Tandem, to have them continue the trace.

"Yeah, well, he's your meal ticket," said the gravelly voice. "So get ready to get the money." And he hung up.

"Damn," said Ryker. He ground his teeth. He doubted the connection had gone on long enough. He doubted the phone company had used even that time well. Ryker envisaged some anonymous maintenance man at the phone company, some drone, only halfheartedly tracing the call. Ryker wished *he* could have done it. *He* would have sped from switch to switch in a blaze of efficiency. *He* would have gotten the caller's number. *He* would have run the system. But as it was, things were beyond Ryker's control. He clenched and unclenched his teeth in frustration.

Ryker's phone rang. Ryker grabbed it.

"Yes?" he barked.

"Uh, Mr. Ryker?"

"Yes?" Short. Curt.

"Uh, this is Fred Hisiger at the phone company. I just traced that call of yours—"

"Yes? Yes?"

"—back to the Colorado Tandem."

"What does that mean?"

"It's a big relay station in Colorado."

"But you don't have the caller's number?"

"Uh, no. Uh, you were only on a little over a minute, I think. Uh, frankly, I think we got pretty far in just that—"

"Well I don't think you got far at all, Hisiger," snapped Ryker.

"Uh, well—"

Ryker hung up. Colorado? he thought. He called Braniff Airlines. They said flight 436 went to Chicago. Chicago? thought Ryker. He made three reservations on the flight. He called Goodhue and told him to get his ass down to the airport. He called the two people whom he'd assigned to shadow Goodhue and told them to be on that flight also. He called the director of Southwestern Bell and asked that he be hooked up to Colorado Tandem so that when the man called on Tuesday, the trace could be confirmed.

"That's impossible," said the director.

"Why?" snapped Ryker.

"There's nothing—no switch—nothing that Colorado Tandem can watch that will tell them what call is going through to *you*. The Houston switching office has to *tell* them what trunk it is."

"Well," said Ryker, not quite understanding. "Tell Colorado to watch the same trunk as today."

"But on Tuesday the call could—and probably *will*—come in on another trunk. There are about 10,000 trunks."

"Shit," said Ryker.

"In fact," said the director, "there's no guarantee the call will come through Colorado Tandem. It could go by way of Los Angeles or Miami or damn near anywhere."   ○

Ryker was up behind his desk. He rocked back and forth on the balls of his feet. "You mean," he swore, "that just because it came through Colorado today doesn't mean my man is *in* Colorado?"

"Well, it's probable," said the director. "The computer always tries just to put the call on the most direct route. But it could be, well . . . "

"Anywhere," said Ryker. Little Ray Ryker felt suddenly isolated in his huge house.

" 'Fraid so," said the director. "Look, Ray. I shouldn't have even done this for you. It's illegal, you know. Hell, why don't you just *pay* your blackmailer. A hundred grand is not much to you. Or let him try to publish the damn pictures. How much can they hurt you? You got an understanding wife."

That was the story Ryker had given the director.

"Yeah, okay, Phil," said Ryker. "Maybe you're right. Thanks."

He hung up. Damn it, he thought, if only it were a hundred grand.

Ryker got back on the treadmill. He turned it on again and resumed his chase—trying to catch up with Matt Ash.

New York City

"Down this way a little more, I think," said the subway token seller. "Right in front of 'fuckers.' "

"Here?" asked Frank Lattimer, positioning himself opposite the graffiti.

"Yeah. About there."

"About? You're not sure?"

"No, I'm not sure," the token seller shot back. "Whatta you want? A big 'X' to mark the spot?"

"It would help," said Lattimer. He stood in the middle of the uptown local track in the 77th Street/Lexington Avenue station. The token seller was up on the platform. Joan Scully was there, too. And a small crowd. They were watching the crazy man down on the tracks.

And he *was* crazy, Joan Scully decided. At dawn, Frank had told her he wanted to get into the city early, to meet with the Transit Authority employee who was in the token booth on Friday when Cruz was killed. So Joan assumed Frank simply wanted to ask the man if he saw anybody push Roberto. But no, Frank had given the man—a Mr. Theophilidis—$50 to point exactly where on the tracks Roberto had been hit, while Frank searched the tracks for Roberto's missing keys!

The token seller on duty *this* morning said Frank didn't belong down there and was going to get killed and he was calling the Transit Authority cops. The token seller with the $50 already in his pocket said go ahead and call. And Joan wished the cops *would* arrive.

"Frank!" she yelled. "Get out of there now. I'd like to have another whole day with you. A *whole* day." She remembered how Cruz's body looked.

"Relax," said Lattimer. "It's Sunday. It's fourteen minutes between trains. Right, Mr. Theophilidis?"

Theophilidis said yes. Then he looked at his watch and decided Lattimer's $50 entitled him to more information. "But the next one," he added, "is in just four minutes."

"Frank!" yelled Joan Scully. "Get out of there. Call your friend, Whitcomb. Have him get the *subway* men to look for you."

"Tried it," said Frank Lattimer, bending down, looking in between the ties. "He said no."

Actually, when Lattimer had pulled off the clogged parkway last night and managed to reach Whitcomb on the phone, the police lieutenant had said more than "No." Whitcomb had said—after Lattimer had related what he'd discovered thus far about Cruz and what he wanted to do next—"No, no. Damn it, no. Not with nothing to go on."

"Well," Lattimer had replied, "if you call what I have 'nothing,' then *you* get me some information on Cruz. Like from his fingerprints. I know they took them at the autopsy. That's S.O.P. Now why don't you check them through the FBI today and see if he's got a record. I'm betting on it."

"It's a lousy bet."

"Hell, Whit, Cruz set up a phony address and he's got some wise guy—probably his killer—trying to track it down, to clean up loose ends. He was somebody's hired help—and maybe the FBI can tell us whose."

"It's a weekend," Whitcomb had said. "On this one, the FBI will not work weekends."

"Well, I will," said Lattimer. So today he was down on the subway tracks. He'd already been looking for over twenty minutes. He'd jumped down as soon as a train pulled out of the station, looked for about thirteen minutes and then, when he saw the light in the tunnel, he'd stepped into the narrow safety strip between the third rail and the graffiti-covered wall. The train had pulled in, pulled out—and Lattimer was looking again. But there was so much to look at—so much silvery, key-like glitter. Gum wrappers, pull tops from soda cans, countless other pieces of waste. Several times Lattimer had dropped to his hands and knees, thinking: This is it! only to see it wasn't.

"You're sure Cruz was hit here?" he asked Theophilidis.

"Maybe further down," shrugged Theophilidis. He waved Lattimer 30 feet along the wall that separated the uptown and downtown tracks. Lattimer now stood in front of "Skulls" in the spray-painted slogan "The Skulls are shit-eating motherfuckers."

"Here?" he asked.

"Maybe," said the token seller. "Some people say the train hit him in mid-air, carried him along. I think maybe he only *landed* in front of 'fuckers.' "

"Swell," said Lattimer. "So his keys could have fallen out anywhere." He bent down again and kept looking. He tried to ignore the growing heckling from the crowd on the platform—and Joan's pleas. Concentrate, he thought. Concentrate. He had once gone with a girl who had the knack of finding bobby pins on the street. Not money or jewelry but bobby pins. "And I don't even *wear* bobby pins," she would complain. Since the girl's hair was a mess and Lattimer felt maybe she should pin it up, he considered telling her finding bobby pins was a sign. And what, he wondered now, is finding pull tops a sign of?

There! . . . Just in front of him, on the splintered wooden tie, plain as daylight, was a set of keys. He stooped to pick them up.

"Train's coming," Theophilidis said, loud but calm.

Lattimer turned to look down the tunnel. Far away there was a hint of light.

"Okay," said Lattimer. He scooped up the keys.

A voice shrieked in his ear. "Mister! You get killed!"

Startled, Lattimer dropped the keys. Bending over the platform, her contorted face only a few feet from his, was an old woman with shopping bags. "You get killed!" she shrieked again.

"Yeah," Lattimer muttered. The light had now become a steady beacon, moving toward him. Lattimer looked for where the keys had fallen, to pick them up—or, he realized, maybe just to spot them. He should really hurry and get to the safety strip, and retrieve the keys after the train left.

He spotted the keys. They were now on top of a rail, the rail closest to the platform. The train would flatten them. He saw the train gathering bulk as it roared at him. He had to retrieve the keys now.

He did—and started to cross the tracks to the safety strip. But he couldn't move. Taloned fingers dug into his upper arm.

"This way, mister!" shrieked the woman, trying to drag him

back. She was down on her knees on the platform, leaning over the edge, off balance, clutching him.

Lattimer was aware of a number of things all at once: That Joan and Theophilidis were grabbing at the woman, trying to pull her off him. That the train was maybe only fifteen seconds away from killing him. That he couldn't climb up to the platform in time. That if he lunged for the safety strip he might pull the woman with him—and they all might die.

Lattimer chopped at the woman's wrist. She let go, shrieked and started to fall on him. This, thought Lattimer—the train roaring into the station, only fifty yards away from him—is a totally insane, but somehow perfectly reasonable, New York City way to die.

He hurled the woman back onto the platform, into the arms of Joan Scully and Theophilidis. There was no time for him to get to the safety strip. He threw himself under the overhang of the platform, hoping there was room next to the inside rail. He wondered how Roberto Cruz felt in his own last seconds. The steel wheels thundered past him, six inches from his face. He shut his eyes. He tried to drive himself into the wall. He heard, felt, the train slow down. His ears roared with a confusion of metal sounds and air brakes and human screams.

The train stopped. Above him, he knew people were screaming questions and orders, but he tried to blank them out. He concentrated on burrowing into the wall, hoping the train would start *now* and pull out of the station, fearing that if it didn't start *now* a part of him—a foot, hand—might somehow flop out on the rail. He couldn't stay in this tight ball forever.

The train didn't move. It didn't move. His right foot twitched. Did it . . . ? Where was his foot now? Had it . . . ?

The train wheels shuddered. Lattimer bit hard. His mind shoved his body down the smallest crawl tunnel in the deepest coal mine in Pennsylvania. The train started to move.

The train pulled out of the station and Lattimer fell onto the rail behind it, unharmed. Still clutched in his hand were Cruz's keys. He had forgotten all about them. The only blood on Lattimer was where his fingers had driven the keys into his palm.

"I hope for Christ's sake it was worth it," said Theophilidis.

"No way," said Joan Scully.

And the Transit cops arrived and started questioning him.

Dobbs Ferry, New York

O rocks and rills
O soft green hills

These do our spirits raise
Renewing life
Through troubles rife
O Nature let us praise

Barbara Justin finished singing, closed the hymnal and sat down in the pew. She was very dissatisfied. She looked around at her fellow worshipers but saw only smiles and attentiveness. Apparently they *liked* these pallid hymns, this dull service.

She wanted something more. She had not been to church for many years—since her wedding day, she reflected. And even before that she had not gone often. The Yateses of Boston were part of the self-reliant Yankee aristocracy ("The Lowells speak only to the Cabots and the Cabots speak only to God.") who addressed the Deity on equal terms. Naturally, they were Unitarians—and not very regular ones at that. But Barbara had awakened this morning feeling miserable and rudderless. And it was Sunday. The idea of going to church struck her as a wonderful idea, a great boon. She even asked the children if they wanted to come. She envisioned all of them suffused by a new hope. But Melissa, who had gone once or twice with her grandmother, said church was "yucky." And Steve said he didn't want anyone to see him for a while (Barbara had to admit he did look funny with only the remnants of eyebrows). Only Laurie, who didn't know very well what church was, agreed to come. So now they were in the Dobbs Ferry Unitarian Church. And Barbara felt just as miserable as before.

Where was hope? she wondered. Where was it? Instead of speaking as a man of rugged faith and certainty, the minister spoke like a cross between a Rotarian and a Ph.D. in psychology. Instead of praising God, the hymns praised a depersonalized "Nature"—set to music more suited to an "easy-listening" AM radio station. Barbara thought of "Rock of Ages/Cleft for me/Let me hide/Myself in Thee." That's what I need, she thought, a place to hide, arms to enfold me. Too late, she remembered the jest about the Unitarian faith: "Where Christ is out and God is optional."

Barbara Justin didn't believe in God, but just for now, for this morning, she wanted to.

The smooth-faced minister took to the podium and began his sermon. Instantly, Barbara saw the tie-in with the last hymn. The minister never mentioned heaven. Instead he talked about the soft green hills of *this* world and our place in it. He talked about ecology and—God help us, thought Barbara—recycling. He declared, "Death, be not proud. Because when we die and are consigned to the earth, our bodies enrich those hills and, in the grass and trees that grow on those hills, we defy death and live forever."

Barbara could hardly disagree. But it was not what she had come to hear today. Goddamn it, she yelled inside, I'm *not* a tin can to be picked up on Saturday morning and taken to the collection site behind the Dobbs Ferry High School for recycling. Not this weekend. She knew only too well that her body was mortal, that it would decay. She folded her arms tightly across her breasts. Where was the hope of *resurrection*? Where was "whosoever believeth in Him shall not perish, but have everlasting life"? The minister talked about the oneness of each person's relationship to the earth, of the oneness of each person's relationships to his or her self. " . . . for as Walt Whitman put it . . . " said the minister.

Barbara looked at Laurie. She hoped her daughter was fretting; it would give her an excuse to leave. But Laurie was content tracing the whorls of wood in the back of the pew ahead of them.

" . . . I have said that the soul is not more
    than the body
And I have said that the body is not
    more than the soul
And nothing, not God, is greater to one
    than one's self is."

So proclaimed the minister, reading from *Leaves of Grass*.

That does it, thought Barbara. She took Laurie's hand and edged her way down the pew, stepping over people's feet. They looked up at her, slightly annoyed at being distracted from the poetry.

Barbara reached the aisle and stared at the minister. She knew Whitman, too, and loved him. At Smith she had written a paper on him. She had a sudden urge to scream at the minister—scream right here, in this polite, decorous church. Agnostic that she still was, she wanted to scream, "Where is *God*? Don't you know that Whitman also says that grass is the handkerchief of the *Lord*?"

Barbara Justin opened her mouth. The anger and pain welled up inside her, seeking release. Soundlessly, Barbara Justin closed her mouth. She and Laurie walked out of the church.

New York City

There were eight keys on Roberto Cruz's key ring. One was a car key—it said GM. Two were mailbox keys—but not identical, and Lattimer wondered why. Three others, he figured, were apartment keys. One key matched one of Joan Scully's—it opened the door to the virology section of Oakes-Metcalf. Lattimer and Joan Scully went in and tried the last key. It smoothly opened Paul Justin's filing cabinet.

"For the first time," said Joan, "I believe I'm beginning to believe."

"Nothing more than 'beginning'?" asked Lattimer.

"Yes. Because I can't figure out what the rest of it means. Roberto steals Paul's notes? Okay. Somebody has Roberto killed? Okay. But what does that 'somebody' *do* with the notes?"

"Well," said Lattimer, "if they're not just notes—if they're the cure for cancer—I know what I'd do. I'd find the richest people in the world dying from cancer. And I'd sell them the cure for a large cut of their riches."

"Frank!" said Joan Scully. "But could they keep that a secret?"

"They may have so far," said Frank Lattimer. He bounced the keys in his palm. "But if I could find the two mailboxes these went to," he said, "and the car, and the apartment . . ."

"Well, I don't know how to do it," said Joan. "And I hope—at the moment—that you don't know either?" She arched an eyebrow to question him. "That it can wait till tomorrow?"

Lattimer sighed. "Tomorrow," he said. "Tomorrow I'll check the Motor Vehicle Bureau and find out what car Cruz owned. Maybe I can trace him from that. Plus I'll check this place's personnel records. Maybe Cruz slipped up and wrote something interesting in his records. *That* could help us find him."

"But that's all tomorrow," pointed out Joan.

"Yeah. Sunday the bureaucrats sleep. It's their religion."

"Smart bureaucrats," said Joan, "because that's what I'm going to do, too. I'm going to get out of these clothes I've been living in for two days—and, Frank"—she jabbed a finger at his chest—"you ought to do the same, you've got a subway track down your shirt. Then hop into a tub and then a bed and then—"

Frank Lattimer snapped his fingers. "Clothes," he said. "Dry cleaners."

"What?"

"In Cruz's wallet. Yesterday, in the police station. Cruz had a receipt for dry cleaning."

"So . . . " Joan began.

"So I think it was the kind that gets torn in half. Dry cleaner keeps the top half. And I bet that the top half has Cruz's address. The cleaners would have written it down!" Lattimer reached for the phone on Justin's desk and dialed an outside line. "Good morning," he said. "Is Detective Prosser there?"

"But wait a minute," protested Joan. "The cleaners won't be open today, either."

"Right," said Lattimer. "But unlike bureaus and offices, an individual businessman can be *persuaded* to be open."

"Swell," said Joan Scully.

"Lieutenant," said Lattimer into the phone, "this is Frank Lattimer again. The reporter. You know, Whitcomb's friend? Right. Listen, about that guy, Cruz, killed on Friday... I wonder, could you possibly take another look in his wallet and read me the name of... " Lattimer stopped. "Hell," he said. "It's gone to the property clerk's office?" he said. "Well, could you possibly ask someone down there... yes, I realize it would be stretching things... but I'd appreciate... " And Lattimer kept talking.

Fire Island, New York

After they were out of sight of land and had finished their first round of gin-and-tonics, Wozinsky suggested they go below. Underwood understood this meant they were finally going to get down to business—whatever that might be. All day, Underwood had been trying to figure it out. It had started with the trim, Ivy League-looking young man ringing his doorbell early this morning. "Sorry to bother you, but would you and Mrs. Underwood be free to join Mr. Samuel Wozinsky—he's a friend of Dr. Brown's—on his boat around noon?" Underwood, bleary-eyed from lack of sleep after fighting with his wife, had mumbled a few questions, got some vague answers and had agreed anyway. But Ceilia had refused. "You go with your fucking important people," she had spat. "Maybe *I'll* get myself *laid* today—by one of those people who were over last night." Underwood had immediately gotten defensive. "I didn't say you had—ah—*done* anything. I just wanted to know why two men were leaving the house—" But his wife had interrupted, accusing him of accusing her and they were back at it again, this time in front of their shocked children. By noon, Hugh Underwood was glad to get out of the house and go on the mysterious Mr. Wozinsky's boat.

He immediately saw that "boat" was an understatement. "Yacht" was the right word, a 52-footer with a crew of three. As Wozinsky and Underwood now settled in what Underwood could only regard as a large, opulent living room, the white-jacketed steward refreshed their drinks, set out a tray of hors d'oeuvres and withdrew, shutting the door behind him. The living room rocked gently. Underwood sipped his gin. Wozinsky was a tall, older man with white hair, bright blue eyes and a firm jaw. He wore the casual, subdued clothes of old-New-England money. Underwood felt out of place. His stomach was slightly queasy. Calmly, Wozinsky proposed it to him: Senator Prentice would declare his candidacy tomorrow in Washington. In his statement, he would call attention to his Cancer Control Act, explain that Underwood had received a grant from it and announce that because of the grant, Underwood—with Dr. Paul Justin, now unfortunately stricken—had just achieved a breakthrough that would lead to a cure within a year.

"Just in time for the convention," said Hugh Underwood, dully. His remark surprised himself. He had listened to Wozinsky with a mounting sickness. He had felt embarrassment, anger, excitement, shame. He had thought to protest—as he had tried to protest to Dr. Brown yesterday. But by the time Wozinsky had finished his self-assured proposal, Underwood felt the inevitability of it. He was in another world, in a rich, floating living room far from shore, and the waves and the alcohol were doing him in. He couldn't stand. He didn't even have Ceil to lean on.

Wozinsky smiled at him. "Well, if need be, in time for the election. Can you manage that?"

"Can you manage the people in my section—who know this is a lie?"

"Dr. Brown and you will talk to them."

"Yeah. Sure we will," said Underwood, dully.

Wozinsky looked at him sharply. "You're going to have to be more positive, more *animated* tomorrow when the reporters descend on you."

Hugh Underwood remembered his fantasy of the reporters descending for anecdotes about the great Justin. Well, at least this would be better. But it still wasn't what he wanted. He simply didn't have the—

"Ambition," said Wozinsky, raising a fist. "Fire yourself up, man. Act humble, of course. But with an obvious, secret pride. You'll be a Nobel Laureate soon. You're entitled."

Ambition? No, thought Underwood. He had been too cautious to have ambition. Instead, what he'd had was determination to succeed, to—more importantly—be accepted. Accepted as Wozinsky was accepting him now. It would be nicer if Wozinsky were a WASP—but, no, perhaps he was actually more impressive this way: A Jew who had transformed himself into a WASP. If Wozinsky could do it, so could black Hugh Underwood. And if going along with Wozinsky and Brown's deception would finally get him accepted . . . then all right. He would do it for *that* reason.

"All right," said Hugh Underwood.

"Fine," said Samuel Wozinsky. "Here, let's drink to it."

Underwood raised his nearly empty glass and stared into its bottom. Through the ice cubes and the glass, Wozinsky's patrician face was twisted, distorted. The distortion showed Underwood the truth: Underwood wasn't being accepted as a white man. He was being used as a black man—to appease HEW for Dr. Brown and win black votes for Senator Prentice.

Hugh Underwood's stomach turned. The yacht rolled. He stood up and took one faltering step on his bad leg, staring wildly for a bathroom. His stomach heaved. His half-digested lunch rose in him and spilled out of his mouth onto the rich carpet. He gagged and vomited, gagged and vomited.

But he couldn't vomit it all.

Chicago, Illinois

Braniff flight 436 arrived at O'Hare as scheduled, at 11:25 local time. Dr. Arthur Goodhue got off and joined the crowd of his fellow passengers walking toward the main terminal. Somewhere close to him, he knew, were two of Ryker's people. "I don't want you to know who they are," Ryker had said, "or you'll look at them and give them away. But *they'll* always be watching you. And when Mr. X picks you up—however he does it—they'll follow."

Nervously, Goodhue glanced around anyway, trying to identify his shadows. He entered the main terminal and hesitated. He wished whatever was going to happen would happen now. He gripped his small suitcase even harder. He headed toward an empty seat.

"Dr. Goodhue. Dr. Arthur Goodhue," called the public address system. "Please report to Braniff Information Desk, main lobby."

This must be it, thought Goodhue. But what?

"A message for you, Dr. Goodhue," said the man at the desk. "Your meeting's been moved to St. Louis."

"St. Louis!"

"Yes, sir. Your office says to catch United flight 716 leaving at noon." The man pointed to the United ticket counter. "I think you can just make it."

"Thank you," said Goodhue. Shaking his head, he started toward the ticket counter. So Mr. X figured Ryker would try to have me followed? he wondered. But how can having me go to St. Louis shake my shadows? Mr. X can't possibly have arranged to have just one seat left on flight 716!

A few people joined Goodhue in line at the counter. He assumed at least one was Ryker's man. "One seat on flight 716," said Goodhue, loudly, to the ticket agent. He held out his American Express card. "First class, if you have it."

"We do, sir," said the agent, quickly making out the ticket.

Good, thought Goodhue. I need to relax—and make Ryker reimburse me.

"Gate 6," said the agent. "West arcade. Boarding now." He indicated the clock behind him. It read 11:41.

On the way to the gates, Goodhue turned in at a men's room. "My people will have you in sight all the time," Ryker had said. "There isn't a single damn place they won't follow—until I know where that goddamn so-called cure is." Goodhue relieved himself but couldn't relieve the tension. He glanced at the man washing his hands next to him.

Beyond the men's room was the security check leading to the west gates. It was 11:49. Goodhue waited his turn and then set his suitcase on the conveyor belt. One of the airport guards motioned him through the electronic scanner. The scanner beeped. The guard held up his hand. Sheepishly, Goodhue stopped and dug into his pants pockets. He handed the guard his keys and his change. The guard motioned him to come through again. The scanner beeped again. This time the guard motioned him all the way through. He had Goodhue raise his arms and move his feet slightly apart. With a light touch, the guard ran his hands over Goodhue's whole body.

"Pacemaker?" he asked.

"No," said Goodhue, puzzled. "And hardly any fillings." He tried to joke but he was very nervous. Back in Houston, Ryker had given him a tiny piece of paper. The paper listed all the U.S. states with a number next to each one, and additional coded information. When Goodhue reached wherever he was going—and the people there allowed him to call Ryker, as Ryker said they'd promised—Goodhue was to use the code to tell Ryker where he was. Goodhue had put the piece of paper in his wallet. He couldn't believe that the guard suspected him for *that* but, in this weird situation, he could believe almost anything. Why else was the guard checking?

The guard finished running his hands over Goodhue. He nodded slightly to the state trooper who, Goodhue now realized, had been watching all this from a few yards away.

"Excuse me, sir," said the trooper, politely but firmly. "Could you come with me for a moment?" Unlike the guard, who merely had a uniform, the trooper had a holstered gun.

"Well ... sure ... " said Goodhue, allowing himself to be directed to a door that led off the corridor. "But my plane—"

"We'll hold the plane," cheerfully called one of the uniformed girls at the conveyor belt. She held Goodhue's suitcase. Beyond the girl, a middle-aged woman—who had been two persons back of him in the line to buy tickets for this flight—looked suddenly alarmed. And waiting to go through the scanner, but stopping, was the young man from the adjacent washbasin who had also been—Goodhue now remembered—on the flight from Houston. The young man started to make a move toward Goodhue and the trooper, then thought better of it. The trooper ushered Goodhue through the door marked "Authorized Personnel Only."

The door shut.

"Do you really think . . . ?" began Goodhue. "Or are you really . . . ?" he stammered.

They were in a small, nondescript room. Bare, concrete walls. Metal table and chair. The trooper pointed to the door in the opposite wall. "Go through there," he said, still politely and a bit more friendly.

"But my suitcase," said Goodhue. "My clothes, toilet kit—"

"I'm sure they'll have stuff," said the trooper.

Goodhue went through the door and found himself out on the airport tarmac. A car was waiting. The passenger door was open. The driver, a freckled-faced young man, leaned across the seat and beckoned him. Goodhue got in. The car started moving.

"Dr. Goodhue, I presume?" asked the young man. Goodhue nodded. He still wasn't sure how it had all been done—did the trooper have a device to trigger the scanner?—but he was sure he was leaving O'Hare and his two shadows far behind.

New York City

Turtle Bay Cleaners, on Second Avenue between 49th and 50th streets, was closed. The man who ran the newsstand across the street said he knew who owned the cleaners. But he said he didn't know why he should tell Lattimer and Joan Scully.

"I've got a suit in there," improvised Frank Lattimer. "A tux. And I've got a formal dinner tonight. So if, I figured, the owner lives nearby . . . maybe he'd open for me."

The newsdealer surveyed Lattimer's clothes, filthy from the subway.

"A tux?" he asked. "You don't look like you ever wore a tux in your life."

Lattimer dug into the pockets of his filthy pants and produced a five-dollar bill.

"That'll buy you six copies of the Sunday *Times*," said the newsdealer. "Plus change."

Lattimer pulled out a twenty-dollar bill.

"Frank!" said Joan, "that's too much." Frank's purchases of information were going to bankrupt him.

The newsdealer grinned. "Jesus. That's—what?—more than thirty *Times*? I don't have that many." The newsdealer pocketed the twenty-five dollars. "His name's Lewis Schwerin. But I don't think he lives around here." He laughed. "See what you'll have to pay him to come in from Queens."

Lattimer used the pay phone next to the newsstand. The operator said there were six Lewis Schwerins in Queens. Lattimer started calling them. Joan stood next to him, wilting in the heat. It was early afternoon but the sky was darkening; the air was close and sticky. God, I hope it rains, she thought. Or God, get me into someplace that's air-conditioned.

After five phone calls, Lattimer reached the right Lewis Schwerin. "Yeah," said his wife. "But he's not here. He's in the city, visiting his uncle."

Lattimer, claiming he was a close friend, asked for the uncle's phone number. Schwerin's wife gave it to him. "And remind him he said he'd bring home my diet book he borrowed."

"Sure," said Lattimer. He called the uncle and he got Schwerin on the phone. The newsdealer eavesdropped. "I've got a suit in your store . . . " began Lattimer.

"*Not* a tux?" the newsdealer interrupted, sardonically.

" . . . and I need it for tonight, so I wonder if you'd . . . " Lattimer continued. "It'd be worth an extra ten bucks to me," he concluded.

"Only ten?" snorted the newsdealer.

"Oh, hell," sighed Schwerin, "you don't have to pay me anything. You're a customer. Besides, I have to stop by anyway and get something. Can you wait a half hour?"

Lattimer hung up and turned to the newsdealer. "Schwerin's coming for nothing," he said.

"So some people are bighearted," shrugged the newsdealer. "Me, I'm in business. How'd you like to buy a *Times* to read while you wait for Schwerin? For you, only seventy-five cents."

"I think we'll take our business elsewhere," said Joan Scully.

They bought a *Times* at another newsstand and read it in a cool and dark coffeeshop across the street, where they could keep an eye on Turtle Bay Cleaners. Or rather, Joan Scully read it. Frank Lattimer found another pay phone and started making calls again. So far, from Humenuik's list of eyewitnesses, Lattimer had reached the train's motorman and conductor, neither of whom had been of any help. Now he began calling the people who had been on the platform.

He got results, but they, too, were of little help:

Keith Dugdale said he only saw the man in mid-air. He didn't see what had *propelled* him. Lattimer thanked Dugdale for his precision.

Alan W. Kappel said he thought the man was drunk.

Louise Lezyniak still wasn't in.

Neither was Brian O'Neil.

Richard Saradjian said that New York subway platforms were a filthy disgrace and that the man had no doubt slipped on something.

Nancy Todd said she bet it was suicide and Lattimer had a cute voice and hey, would he like to get together?

And Teresa Vitiello said she didn't know. She was right behind the man, almost touching him, but she didn't know. Lattimer pursued this: Had she seen anybody *else* touching the man? Anybody on either side of her? Anybody she could identify?

"No," said Teresa Vitiello. She was very sorry, but she had seen nothing. Before Lattimer let her hang up, he checked his list again. Yes, in addition to this home number of hers, he also had the place where she worked—the Gem Flower Shop on Third Avenue near Seventy-fifth.

"Thank you," he said, hurriedly. Joan Scully was trying to get his attention. Across the street, Lewis Schwerin was opening Turtle Bay Cleaners and looking around for the people who'd asked him to do this.

Schwerin was a heavy-set, amicable man. But when Lattimer said he'd lost his receipt, Schwerin began to frown. "I remember the number, though," said Lattimer. "166."

"Why?" asked Schwerin suspiciously, "would you remember the number?"

Lattimer knew the number because a clerk in the police property clerk's office had read it to him over the phone an hour ago. (The clerk had balked at actually giving the receipt to Lattimer—Prosser didn't have *that* much clout.) But what Lattimer said to Schwerin was: "Easy. It was my brother's I.Q. He would never let me forget it."

"Huh," snorted Schwerin. He looked through his file for the top half to 166. He kept glancing up at Lattimer and frowning more.

"Are you sure you're a customer?" he asked. "I thought I knew all my customers."

"Well," began Lattimer, "I—"

"Because," said Schwerin, finding the top half of 166 and pulling it out of the file, "this says Morales. I wrote Morales here. And you don't look like any Morales."

"Not Cruz?" asked Joan Scully.

"Cruz? What Cruz?" asked Schwerin. "Cruz. Morales. He can't be either."

"Roberto Morales is a friend of mine," said Lattimer smoothly. "He asked me to pick up his suit for tonight but he's out of town right now and I thought that if I tried to explain all that you'd never open up, so—"

"I sure wouldn't have," said Schwerin, "because I think I remember Morales." He snapped his fingers. "Got it. It's *Luis* Morales, not Roberto. So *you're* no friend." Schwerin's eyes roved worriedly back and forth. "So what are you doing with his receipt number? Why are you here?" He began reaching under the counter.

"Uh, you didn't write down his address, did you, by any chance?" continued Lattimer.

Schwerin brought out a revolver. "I've got a license for this," he said.

Lattimer took Joan Scully's elbow and began moving quickly away. "Uh, thanks, Mr. Schwerin," he said, "I guess—"

There was a sudden clap of thunder—and Joan Scully jumped.

"—guess I don't need the address after all."

Joan looked behind her. Rain was pelting the street so hard she couldn't see across to the other side. And then the thunder came again. Lattimer opened the door and he and Joan Scully went out into the downpour.

As they left, just before the sound of the rain surrounded them, they heard Schwerin mutter, "So why *did* I come over? Hell, I bet that dumb diet book isn't even here."

Lattimer and Joan Scully ran across Second Avenue, getting immediately soaked to the skin. "Luis Morales?" Joan asked Lattimer as they ran. "Do you think he's a friend of Roberto's?"

"I think he *is* Roberto," said Lattimer.

They passed the first newsstand and the dealer called after them, "Hey, you didn't get your suit."

"I got something better," said Lattimer. And they ran to the coffeeshop, dodging the fast-filling puddles.

Houston, Texas

"Well, what *happened* to the state trooper, damn it?"

"He . . . he disappeared, too."

"How?" yelled Ryker over the phone. "Where?"

"He . . . he didn't come out of the room where he took Goodhue."

"So he was a phony."

"I guess so."

"You guess so," said Ryker sarcastically. "Did you check?"

"Yeah. Yeah. We checked with the airport security guard. *He* said sometimes a state trooper is around, sometimes not. And different troopers are different. He'd never seen this guy before—but that wasn't unusual."

"Well, what about the security guard, damn it? It was his scanner that went off."

"Legit, as far as we could tell."

"Sandahl," snapped Ryker. "You're a real fuck-up. You know that?"

"Uh ... "

"Do you know that?"

"Uh ... I guess so."

"Jesus," said Ryker. "You and Liz Davis get a free plane trip to Chicago, Liz gets drunk on the plane, you feel up the stewardesses and you both—"

"We didn't ... do anything like ... "

"—and you both lose Goodhue! Well, you can both goddamned well buy your *own* tickets back. Or better yet, Sandahl, better yet ..."

"Yes?"

"Don't come back at all."

Houston, Texas

Sunday morning, naturally, Virginia Ash went to church. The service so uplifted her that, on the way back to the hospital, she stopped and had a banana split. She felt enthusiastic for life. She wanted to *gobble* life. For today was the day the Reverend Trumbull was coming to heal and save Matt.

Entering the hospital, passing the reception desk, Virginia heard a voice behind her ask the nurse for "Mathew Ash, please?" That rich baritone! she thought. It was him. Trumbull stood there, tall and handsome, in an expensive suit, his face serious.

"Oh, Reverend Trumbull," she cried, flying to him. "I'm Virginia Ash." She grabbed for his hands, but they encircled hers, holding her in a strong, comforting grip. His eyes gazed steadily, deeply into hers. They seemed tired, as if they had been wrestling with all the problems of the world.

"Thank you, Virginia," said Reverend Trumbull. "Thank you for sending for me. With your faith and mine, I'm sure we can help your husband. Will you take me to him now?"

Virginia was overwhelmed with love and gratitude. "Why, certainly. This way, Reverend ... and ... ?" She gestured at the man who was accompanying Trumbull.

"Del Erskine," said Trumbull, introducing him. "One of my most beloved friends in Christ. He's flown with me all the way here to help your husband."

"Thank you, Mr. Erskine," said Virginia.

"Yes, ma'am," said Erskine, who was along as Trumbull's baby sitter. It was his job to keep Trumbull dry this weekend.

"Yes," said Virginia. "Well. This way." She led them toward the Presidential Suite.

Before they even opened the door, they could hear the screams.

"Goddamn it, Ah *know* it's one o'clock. Give me ma shot! *Give* it to me!"

Virginia hesitated at the door. "I'm really sorry about... Matt..." she said. "He hurts so much."

Trumbull shook his head with compassion and they went into the living room.

Virginia looked at her watch. "Well, it's almost one," she said. "Why don't we wait here till *after* one..."

The screams continued: "Ah can't take it! Ah can't!"

"Then," continued Virginia, "then he'll be easier to see."

"No," said Trumbull. "He's seeing me now." And he marched into Matt Ash's room.

Virginia and Erskine went to the doorway to watch. They saw Matt's eyes latch onto Trumbull.

"Who the hell are you?" he demanded. "A doctor?"

To her surprise, Virginia saw Trumbull nod slightly.

"A doctor?" screamed Ash. "Then tell this nurse to give me ma *shot!*"

"It's not one o'clock yet," Nurse Crippen said to Trumbull.

"That's all right," said Trumbull softly. "He's not getting his one o'clock shot."

"Not getting ma shot?" exploded Ash. "But Ah hurt. Ah hurt."

"You're going to have to live with it," said Trumbull softly.

"Live with it?" Ash yelled. "What kind of doctor are you? What kind of lousy—"

Trumbull let Ash rave on, the screams washing across him, not moving him.

When Ash had to pause for breath, Trumbull said softly, matter-of-factly, "Mr. Ash, do you know why you have this hurt, this cancer?"

"What?" asked Ash. He had been yelling so loud, he hadn't heard Trumbull.

"Do you know *why* you have cancer?" asked Trumbull, even more softly. He made Ash strain to hear.

Ash shook his head as if he hadn't heard right. "*Why?*" He said the word wonderingly. "What does that mean?"

"It means," said Trumbull, softly, "why are you lying here dying of cancer? Why aren't you healthy instead? Why aren't you in the Cattlemen's Club enjoying a tender young steak. Or why aren't you in another bed, enjoying a tender young piece?"

Virginia Ash was shocked. Not just by the Reverend's language. But also by his abandonment of his rich, deep voice for these soft, matter-of-fact tones.

"Huh!" snorted Ash. "For a doctor, yore pretty dumb. Ah got cancer 'cause—'cause Ah got it. 'Cause you *get* it. Like gettin' a cold, or gettin' hit by a car."

"Wrong," said Trumbull. "As a doctor, I know you get cancer because your body turns on you. Because a few cells go wild and start eating up your whole body. Eating you alive."

Trumbull let that hang in the air.

"All right," said Ash. "So that's what happens. Ah've heard that. So what?"

"So *why* do you think your body has turned on you? Why do you think some people get hit by a car? And other people live to a hundred? But *you* get eaten alive?"

"Hell. *Ah* don't know."

"Why would your body—your own body—punish you like that, try to destroy you like that?"

"Who knows?" yelled Ash.

"Why would your own body," asked Trumbull softly, "try to Mash you like that?"

"Huh!" Ash snorted. He smiled. "Mash me, huh? Mash *me*."

"Yeah," said Trumbull. "Mash you."

"You gonna tell me it's punishment for ma sins?"

"No one else left to punish you," pointed out Trumbull. "You Mashed 'em all."

"Ah did indeed," smiled Ash.

"And you're proud of that?" asked Trumbull, still softly. "Proud of cheating Wade Kilbourne out of those leases in Oklahoma in '32? Proud of bribing the Railroad Commission in '39? Proud of gouging the Navy Department on oil for the war—for the *war*, mind you—in '42?"

To each of these, Ash had nodded.

"Proud of Mashing Betty Sue Witte in 1923?"

"What?" asked Ash.

"You remember Betty Sue," said Trumbull, "nice little thing. Gave you head in the balcony of Chase's Trans-Lux? Gave you her pussy in the back seat of your buddy George Ordal's Model A? Gave you a son—or was going to give you a son, was going to make you a daddy, have you be her husband, until you fixed all that." All recited casually.

"Ah don't want to *hear*!" screamed Ash. "Ah want ma *shot*!"

Virginia didn't want to hear either. She knew people said Matt had done bad things—and maybe he had—but she'd never heard about any Betty Sue Witte or any child. And she didn't want to. But Trumbull went on.

"Sure. You fixed it. The week Betty Sue told you she was carrying your child and wanted to marry you, you took her to the county fair in Waterboro. Took her over to the Bump 'N Roller that your buddy George was running. Waited until last thing at night, until George had closed the thing down. Asked Betty Sue if she wanted a ride by herself, for free. You said you had a stomachache."

"Nurse!" Ash was screaming. "Nurse!" But Crippen was transfixed by the story.

"So Betty Sue went on alone. And George jacked that Bump 'N Roller up to three times its normal speed and George went off yelling that the thing was out of control and you stood there watching while Betty Sue screamed and that child of yours was bumped and rolled right out of her."

Virginia's own stomach, full of ice cream and bananas, turned over.

"Except that wasn't the end of it, was it, Matt? Because you didn't count on Betty Sue hemorrhaging on that machine and coughing blood, did you?" Trumbull paused. "Did you?" he asked casually, the way someone would ask if you'd paid this month's phone bill.

"No!" screamed Matt Ash.

"But she did," continued Trumbull. "And she died in the hospital the next morning, didn't she?"

"No!"

"But she did," said Trumbull. "She died with her belly torn and bleeding and now you're dying the same way. Because even if your mind denies it, your *soul* and your *body* know it—and they're paying you back with pain. Paying you back for killing a woman who loved you. And for killing the child you've always claimed you wanted. So you're not going to escape that pain through shots. And you're not going to escape through suicide. You're going to *live* with that pain."

"Doctor!?" screamed Matt Ash. "What *kind* of doctor are you?"

"Doctor of the soul," said Trumbull softly. "I talk to people and try to heal their souls and their bodies. I talk to people and they talk to me. Sometimes they make confessions."

"That son-of-a-bitching George Ordal," screamed Matt Ash. "I'll get him. I'll Mash him if it's the last thing—"

"No you won't," said Trumbull. "He died last September."

"I hope he died like this!" yelled Ash. "Hurtin' like this!"

"No. He went in his sleep. Real peaceful. At peace with himself. Died of natural old age, his doctor told me. I'd helped heal George of cancer seven years before."

"You ... you ... " Ash's eyes went wild. "You're that phony

cancer healer, goddamn it. That phony Reverend whatsis. Virginia!" he roared. "You did this. You sicked this phony ... phony ... "

"Phony what?" asked Trumbull softly. "Didn't I speak the truth to you?"

"Phony preacher," spat Ash. "Like my uncle. Spoutin' God. Spoutin' Christ."

"Did you hear me mention God or Christ, Matt? The only person I mentioned was you. Whatsoever a man soweth, that shall he also reap. That's you. You're killing yourself with cancer—and you're the only one who can stop it."

"How?" screamed Ash. "How?"

"Think about it," said Trumbull. "You think about it and I'll be back." He turned and started walking back to Virginia and Erskine. Virginia marveled at the glory of the man. But Erskine saw his fatigue. He knew that after a sermon like this, Trumbull would want a drink real bad.

"Back to sell me Christ!" yelled Ash, shaking a fist at Trumbull's back.

"Back to sell you yourself," said Trumbull softly. This time the softness wasn't a rhetorical trick. It was the softness of a man who believed. Erskine marveled. He knew that Saving Grace, Inc., was a business and the Reverend Richard Watson Trumbull was a money-hungry businessman. And an alcoholic. And maybe, depending on how you looked at it, a phony. But Erskine also knew that Trumbull didn't look at it that way. Trumbull believed.

"You can give the old man his shot now," Erskine told Nurse Crippen.

New York City

"Frank," objected Joan Scully, "it *is* trespassing."

The telephone operator had said that near Turtle Bay Cleaners there was only one Luis Morales—at this address on Forty-ninth Street. In the vestibule, the mailbox for 3C bore it out. And a key from Roberto Cruz's key ring opened the mailbox. Its only contents—a circular about a new liquor store opening, addressed to "Occupant." Lattimer used another of Cruz's keys to open the downstairs door. And still two more keys fit the locks on apartment 3C.

"Well," said Lattimer, "yeah, trespassing. But it gets us in out of the rain. Besides, if we wait for Prosser to get a search warrant"—he opened the door to 3C—"we'd wait a week to look at this."

"But what are we looking for?" asked Joan.

They walked in and stood dripping water in the middle of the living room.

"We'll know when we find it," said Lattimer.

Cruz's-Morales's apartment was in the rear of an old brownstone. The curtains, on windows facing a dark and narrow courtyard, were drawn. Lattimer got the sense that even when the sun was out, little light came in here. Now, with the gray rain pounding the courtyard, the apartment was also gray. It was a drab, small place: living room, sleeping ell, bath (with room for only a shower—no tub), kitchenette. And, unfortunately, thought Lattimer, it was as clean and neat as you'd expect of a man who had made his living washing and stacking test tubes. There was no scrawled list of anything on top of the bureau nor in any drawer. Nothing interesting had fallen between the cushions of the battered couch. And the wastebaskets were empty.

"God," said Joan Scully, opening and closing cabinets above the sink, "almost *any*body could have lived here. There's almost nothing of Roberto."

"Almost nothing?" asked Lattimer, from the living room.

"I remember this book"—she held up a paperback—"*Lives of Great Scientists*."

"That's interesting," said Lattimer, walking over.

"It's sad," said Joan Scully. "I think maybe he wanted to be like Paul."

"Hmm."

"Frank," she asked, "why *did* he live here and not in Harlem like he said? I mean, sure, this neighborhood, this building is nicer. But why did he *say* he lived up there? And why the two different names?"

"I think maybe he wanted some distance from the people he worked for—a place they couldn't find him."

"The people he worked for?"

"The man who went up to Spanish Harlem looking for his apartment."

"But you think the people he was working for killed him. So then why would they go to his apartment afterward?"

"To do what we're doing?"

"To look for—?" began Joan Scully, puzzled.

"Stuff he left behind," explained Lattimer. "Stuff they didn't want anybody to see." He went back to the living room, to turn over the threadbare rug.

Joan sighed. "Well, they needn't have bothered. There's nothing *to* see." She opened a plastic soap dish beside the sink—she was curious, because there was already a bar of soap stuck to the metal dish that came with the sink—and a savings account book fell out.

"Frank!" she called.

They flipped through its pages. It said that starting in May of last year, Luis Morales had made a deposit of $300 every week, with the last deposit last Monday. That, plus interest, gave him a total of—Joan read in amazement—$18,520.20. "Where did he get that money? Three hundred a week? The lab paid him only half of that."

"He got it from the people he worked for—for snooping in Justin's file cabinet."

"But what people? How can we find out? Would the bank keep records—you know, photostats of the checks?"

"I'm sure they paid him in cash."

"Okay. Well, how did he get the cash—if they didn't know he lived here? He never got mail at the Institute."

Frank Lattimer held up the key ring. "This other mailbox key," he said. "I just realized—it's got to be to a post office box. That's how they paid him."

"Well, then . . . " she began eagerly.

Lattimer shook his head. "But I doubt the box is in Cruz's—or Morales's—name. His employers wouldn't have left that lying around in post office records." Lattimer held up the key. "Look, it doesn't even have a number. They must have opened the box for him, made a duplicate of the key and given *him* the duplicate."

"Why?"

"Because even back then they must have known they'd eventually kill him. And they didn't want even the slightest chance the box would be traced."

"They thought of everything," said Joan, bitterly. "Cold-blooded. Cold-blooded killers."

"I wouldn't shed much of a tear for Roberto," said Lattimer. "I think he tried to kill Paul Justin. And I think that next Monday—tomorrow—he expected to go to his post office box and collect a nice bonus for it, on *top* of that twenty-two thousand."

Joan Scully looked around the small apartment. Just standing in the kitchenette, she could see all of it. "And I thought I knew Roberto," she said, thoughtfully. "I saw him every working day for a year and a half, and every day he came back here to his hiding place and—and what? Got his bankbook out of *its* hiding place—why'd he hide it? shame? dirty little secret, even from himself?—and checked how much he'd made by betraying Paul? And how he was going to spend it . . . ?" She shook her head. "Let's get out of here, Frank."

Lattimer put an arm around her and squeezed briefly. "Right," he said.

They went out the front door of the brownstone—into bright

light. As suddenly as the rain had begun, it had ended. And, after the darkness of Cruz's-Morales's apartment, they had to squint against the re-appeared afternoon sun. The sun burned just as hot as before; the shower had cooled nothing. The air was still hot and sticky, and now full of the smell of moist dog droppings. The asphalt of Forty-ninth Street boiled up wet and smoking. In front of the house, a lone, scrawny sapling dripped limply.

"How'd you like to get out of here," began Lattimer. "Go up to my place in Westchester. I can get out of these clothes and into something clean and pressed. We can sip some gin-and-tonic in the backyard, watch the grass grow. I'll cook you some coq au vin for Sunday dinner . . . "

Joan took his hand. "Sounds great," she said. "Just let me—"

"Wait," said Lattimer. He stopped on the sidewalk. He was looking at the garbage cans and garbage bags piled against the brownstone.

Joan Scully, who was coming to know Lattimer—only too well, she thought—understood at once. "No, Frank!" A cry of despair. "Not pick through the *garbage* . . . "

"Cruz attacked Paul on Friday morning, right?" he asked. "So maybe, if we buy your idea that he hid stuff from himself, wanted to get stuff out of the way . . . what better time for a housecleaning than Thursday night? And if so"—he pointed at the rain-slick cans and bags—"it's right in there."

So Joan Scully sat on a small dry spot on the stoop of the brownstone and told those passersby who asked that her husband (the lie set off odd reverberations in her head) was looking for her wedding ring that had probably fallen into the kitchen wastebasket when she took off the ring to try to fix the sink drain. She didn't have to use the explanation on many people; most took one glance and quickened their pace past the brownstone in disgust. But when one resident of the house—an angry old woman in blue hair and a faded kimono—came out, Lattimer had to try something else.

"Hi," he said, "I'm a friend of Luis Morales. He called me—he's out of town, you know—and said he thought he accidentally threw out a very valuable—"

"Claude!" shrieked the old woman. "Claude!"

Frank Lattimer continued quickly but methodically going through the garbage. He had already emptied, checked and refilled two of the three large, green plastic bags. The contents of the third, smaller bag were now spread out on the small concrete area between the house and the sidewalk. They were soaking up water from on top of the concrete. Lattimer picked through a sodden, smelly mess of food, paper, tin cans. . . . Joan Scully averted her face.

The woman reappeared, now with a young, pouting, baby-faced man whose T-shirt bulged with rolls of fat.

"What the hell do you think—" he began to roar in a falsetto.

"Hi," said Lattimer, calmly. "Say, do you know if Luis wraps his garbage in little plastic bags or not? It would sure save my time looking. I would have bet plastic bags, but so far—"

The fat young man came pounding down the steps, jostling Joan, who tried to retreat into the wilting tree. "I know karate!" he yelled. "I know all of Bruce Lee's—"

"Ah!" said Lattimer. He held aloft a smeared piece of wet, brown wrapping paper. "What I'm looking for."

The young man stopped a yard away from Lattimer, one hand raised for a karate blow. A bad imitation of a blow, thought Lattimer.

"I swear," said the young man, "my hands are deadly weapons. They can chop you into pieces."

"I'm sure," said Lattimer. "But I don't want to get *my* hands on *you*." He held them palms up. They dripped garbage. "Kinda messy, huh?" said Lattimer, in a conciliatory voice. "Now, I've got what I need. So why don't you just let me pick up this bag and I'll leave. Okay?"

The young man's hand quivered in the air. He panted. The old woman leaned over the railing of the steps and yelled, "Claude, stop him!"

Lattimer stuffed the wrapping paper in his pocket. Under Claude's awkward, would-be menacing stance, Lattimer quickly re-filled the garbage bag. "There," he said. He wiped his hands on his pants and walked past Claude. Joan Scully took his arm and they walked away, down the street.

Behind them, halfway down the block now, they could hear the woman's wail of "Claude! All those *lessons!*"

Joan Scully broke into hysterical, gasping laughter. "Karate! Garbage! Defending the honor of his apple cores! Oh, Frank, you were so brave to face him—" She doubled up laughing, clutching his arm for support. "Oh, God, you stink. Oh, you're crazy. Oh, I'm crazy to be with you. Oh." She wiped tears from her eyes. "Okay, so what trea-sure did you rescue from the clutches of Claude, from the uncaring minions of the sanitation department, from all the—?" She broke up again, helpless.

Frank Lattimer took the brown paper out of his pocket. He read " 'Mr. Jose Santiago, Post Office Box 4803, Grand Central Station, New York.' There was no Santiago in that building. That's got to be our Roberto."

"So you *can* trace the box," said Joan Scully.

"Yeah," said Lattimer, "to whatever phony name Cruz's employers used when they opened the box. No, even with the box number, it's still a dead end."

"Then all that—garbage—for nothing?"

"No," said Lattimer, "not nothing." He pointed to the wrapping. "A postmark. Denver, Colorado."

"I wish I were in Denver now," said Joan Scully. She and Lattimer had reached the corner of Second Avenue. A huge truck roared by, spraying water out of the gutter. They jumped back just in time. "Anywhere far from here," she added.

"Will you accept Dobbs Ferry?"

"It'll have to do."

Los Angeles, California

"Why tomorrow?" asked John George Lapidus.

"Because," explained Senator Arthur Prentice, "we learned that Reed is going to announce this Thursday. We want to beat him to it."

"Why?" asked Lapidus.

"I would think that's obvious," said Prentice. "From now on, for the next year, I can make the point that I announced first, before anyone, that I was the first to present myself to the American people, for their scrutiny."

"Ah," said Lapidus. He sank his considerable bulk further back into the deeply padded seat of the limousine. The limousine was speeding south on the San Diego Freeway to Los Angeles International where Senator Prentice had a plane to catch. His aide, Lynch, had persuaded Prentice that before he left he should really talk to Lapidus, who was the top political campaign and image consultant on the Coast, perhaps in the whole country. So, Prentice had fit Lapidus in. Thus far, he wasn't impressed. He didn't like Lapidus's own image; the man was a fat slob. And now Lapidus didn't even realize what a coup it was to beat Reed to the draw.

"And why the Senate Caucus Room?" asked Lapidus.

"I would think," said Prentice, a bit of edge in his voice, as he ground out another cigarette in the ashtray, "that that's obvious, too. It's become *the* place for senators to declare. JFK declared there. So did Bobby. It puts me in their tradition, helps me emphasize my stance as a national Democrat—as opposed to the limited, *state*wide experience of Governor Reed."

"Ah," said Lapidus.

Good Lord, thought Prentice, the man is really thick. "You *do* see the benefit of having this researcher—Underwood—there with me, don't you?" asked Prentice. "The impact of tying my announcement to this cancer cure thing?"

"Oh, yes," said Lapidus, gazing at the ceiling of the limousine. "Very good idea."

There was a glass partition between the back seat and the chauffeur. It prevented the chauffeur from hearing—a day too soon—about the cancer idea. Prentice wondered if it would also prevent the chauffeur from hearing Lapidus's cries if Prentice strangled him. Assuming he *could* strangle him—get through that fat, flabby neck. If Lapidus was any example of the new political wisdom, of California style, of images over issues ... well, Lapidus was a lousy example.

"It's too bad it's tomorrow, though," said Lapidus calmly, pinching his nose. "If you could put it off a week or so, I think you could improve it."

"What do you mean?" asked Prentice. He was getting even angrier. He could swear Lapidus was pinching his nose as a cover for picking it.

"I mean," said Lapidus, "that you're about eight to twelve years out of date, Senator. First of all, people today don't care who announces first. If anything, they get tired of people who've been campaigning forever. Look at Humphrey. On the other hand, look at Jerry Brown. He came in late in the spring of '76 and everybody said, 'Hey, a fresh face.' Gave Carter fits. Secondly, Senator, Camelot is gone. And Washington isn't loved. So, do you really have to announce in the Senate Caucus Room and look like another Washington politician?"

Prentice bristled. "But—"

"So if you could wait a few weeks—"

"I can't," said Prentice, "and you know it." He lit up another cigarette, drew in on it decisively. "After Washington tomorrow, I fly home to announce in Indianapolis and in Purdy's Falls—my hometown. And Wednesday I announce in New Hampshire to demonstrate my commitment to the first primary. Those are commitments—auditoriums and hotels booked, people giving their time to me. I can't let them down."

"I'm not asking you to break *those* commitments," said Lapidus. "Just don't put yourself and this guy Underwood in Washington. Don't associate yourself with that. Associate yourself with something better, more dramatic."

They were going off the freeway now, onto local streets. Prentice checked his watch. It would be close but he'd catch the plane to the capital.

"Associate myself with what?" he asked.

Lapidus held his pudgy hands in the air, as if framing a picture. "I see you and Underwood in front of the Oakes-Metcalf Institute at one o'clock tomorrow afternoon. I see white-coated doctors and nurses going in and out of that tower of healing. I see crowds of people—office workers and construction workers on their lunch hour, women shoppers with babies in arms, young, old, rich, poor—gathered in the street because they've been told on the news tonight that something important is going to happen. And I see you declaring your candidacy there, and announcing the imminent cure, then going inside, followed by TV cameras, to Underwood's lab—where it happened, where you *made* it happen—and then back over to the hospital, to a ward where you will visit a little girl dying of leukemia—which you will—"

"That's really too ... too ... " sputtered Senator Prentice.

"Too good, isn't it?" smiled Lapidus. "And I could help you do it, you know. We should have a week to set it up—but even for tomorrow, twenty-one hours from now ... " Lapidus thoughtfully rubbed the side of his jaw, stopped and squeezed as if he had found a pimple. " ... Yep," said Lapidus, "I could do it."

"I'll have to think about it," said Prentice stiffly.

"You've got just from here to your plane, Senator. I've got to know."

They rode into the airport in silence. Prentice smoked thoughtfully. There were all kinds of smartness, Prentice knew. For instance, look at his ninety-nine colleagues in the Senate. Few of them were really brilliant. Most of them, he felt, indulged in ridiculous public posturings. Many of them, he guessed, indulged in private foibles—drink, adultery and worse. But all ninety-nine were damn savvy. And Prentice had learned to learn from all of them. Come to think of it—thinking of all the people, from low-level bureaucrats to four-star generals, whom he dealt with, whom he'd learned to use for his purposes—he knew smart men even cruder than John George Lapidus.

The limousine stopped at TWA.

"Yes," said Senator Arthur Prentice, "we do it."

"Fine," said Lapidus.

They got out of the limousine together, to find Lynch who was waiting, and to change planes from Washington to New York. "One thing though, Senator," said Lapidus, as he waved Prentice ahead of him, through the terminal doors, "it's a *hell* of a risk."

"Doing it in New York?" asked Prentice sharply, puzzled.

"Doing it at all," corrected Lapidus. "Hanging it on this cancer thing."

"Come on, Lapidus," said Prentice, "what's the worst that can happen? So a year from now Underwood doesn't produce a cure? So who'll blame *me*?"

"Yeah," said Lapidus. "You're right. It's the send-off that counts." He smiled broadly. "Jesus—this week is going to be beautiful." He patted his stomach and belched. "All *right*."

Lander, Colorado

From O'Hare, the freckle-faced young man drove Dr. Arthur Goodhue through Chicago to the older, smaller, but still used Midway Airport. They arrived just in time for United Airlines flight 230 to Denver, for which the freckle-faced young man had two first-class tickets. Dr. Goodhue's ticket was in the name of Eugene Hallett. The young man warned Goodhue to speak to no one. On the plane, when Goodhue had to go to the lavatory—he had emptied his bladder only an hour and a half ago but he was nervous—the man followed Goodhue to the lavatory. He stood outside while Goodhue relieved himself, then went inside to make sure Goodhue hadn't left a note, and then accompanied Goodhue back to their seats. Goodhue had the window seat. He stared out, wondering what he was doing here. All the way to Denver, clouds blocked his view. He felt disoriented.

In Denver he didn't get to see any of the country either. The young man led Goodhue through the airport parking lot to a van, had Goodhue climb in back and locked him in. There were two men inside, both looking as worried as Goodhue felt. Goodhue joined them on the comfortable seats.

"Welcome to the CCC," said one of the men, with a rueful smile, extending a hand.

"CCC?" asked Goodhue, shaking the man's hand, certain he'd met him before.

"Colorado Carcinogenic Colloquium," said the second man cheerfully in heavily accented English. "I'm Dr. Piers Hansum and this is Dr. Joseph Merewitz."

"Oh, yes, Dr. Merewitz," said Goodhue, now placing the man. "We met last year in Miami, at the National Cancer Institute meeting. And of course, Dr. Hansum, I know of your work." Goodhue introduced himself. "But what are you both doing—?"

"The same thing you are, I expect," said Merewitz. "Checking out this so-called cure. Do you know Lillian W. McKinney?"

"No," said Goodhue.

"Well, she owns half of downtown Vancouver. Only she's dying of lung cancer and she sent me here to see if she could get saved. Poor rich old lady. Desperate."

"Not half as bad as my case in Amsterdam," said Hansum, "Sixteen-year-old boy. Chronic leukemia. His parents are in pieces."

"It's all a con, of course," said Merewitz, waving his arm around the carpeted, softly lit interior of the van. "There's no cure. But we might as well make the best of it—have a colloquium, eh? Now, Dr. Goodhue, what do you think of this Munich study linking menopause to an increased ... "

Arthur Goodhue, who was not of their rank, was flattered to be with the other two doctors. They sat in the van in the parking lot of the Denver airport and talked shop. Every ten or fifteen minutes, as more flights arrived, they were joined by another oncologist. From Atlanta, Buenos Aires, Turin. After Dr. Ahmed Khoury from Cairo was locked inside, the van started to move.

The van moved along what felt to Goodhue like a highway and then slower, with more stops, on what must be city streets. Then a highway again. Goodhue tried to do as Ryker had instructed him: Keep track of the turns, listen for identifying noises. But it was no use. When the van started climbing, Goodhue felt they must be heading west, into the Rockies. But then, there were so many turns, he became confused. Arthur Goodhue had been on the move for the last six hours, in and out of various planes and vehicles. He just wanted to rest.

The seven oncologists speculated where they were going and compared notes on how they had gotten here. Dr. Emilio Vezacino had flown from Turin to Rome to JFK International. He had been met at JFK and been driven on the Van Wyck Expressway toward La Guardia. On an exit ramp short of La Guardia, Vezacino turned to see a slick of oil laid down on the road. The three cars behind them piled into each other. Vezacino's driver then doubled back to JFK and the two men had flown to St. Louis and then Denver.

"Ingenious," said Dr. Roger Brua of Atlanta, "and disturbing. They seem willing to hurt people."

"It was slow on the exit ramp," said Vezacino. "I doubt there were injuries. Just dents in the cars."

But the story worried Goodhue. The van turned off onto what Goodhue felt must be a secondary road. The angle of climb increased, the van went into lower and lower gears. The doctors sat in silence for a while.

"Well, *my* 'escort' caused a broken arm in New Orleans," said Dr. Anton Jaroslawicz. "I had flown in from Buenos Aires and ... "

Goodhue tried not to listen. He hoped his fear wasn't showing. He hoped he'd used enough cologne. He focused on the laboring of the van's motor. The turns became sharper, the van went even slower.

" . . . in a men's room in the airport," said Jaroslawicz. "They led me into a stall and—would you believe it?—there was a man already in there, dressed just like me! My height. My build. Well, my double went *out* the door of the stall and when—"

The van stopped. Jaroslawicz stopped. Something heavy—a garage door? wondered Goodhue—slammed shut behind them. They waited. Then the van doors were opened and Goodhue and his six colleagues were herded out. . . .

They were in a large garage, empty except for the van. Two men in coveralls pointed toward a corridor and the oncologists obediently followed one of the men that way. Goodhue turned around swiftly to check the van's license plate—Ryker would be proud of him, he thought—but it was covered up. Goodhue fell into step down the corridor. They turned several times, climbed a stairway, turned again. White walls, closed doors marked only with numbers. Goodhue got the impression of a small hospital. Several times they passed windows, but these were covered with opaque plastic. Goodhue had no idea where they were.

The guide led the seven oncologists into a room the size of an average living room. He left them and locked the door.

The room was dominated by a huge rear-projection screen, wider and taller than a man's height. Facing the screen were a dozen armchairs.

"Home movies?" Merewitz muttered. "Where's the popcorn?"

"Do you think—" began Brua.

"Good afternoon, gentlemen," boomed a voice from the speakers on either side of the screen. "Please be seated. I know you've all had long trips here and I know you're eager to get on with this."

The seven oncologists cautiously sat down and regarded the blank screen with varying degrees of suspicion and anticipation. Goodhue felt plain worried. Khoury took out an evil-looking black cigar, started to light it and then hesitated.

"Quite all right, Dr. Khoury," said the voice. "Please feel at home."

Now Goodhue noticed the two small TV cameras trained on them from high on either side of the screen. Feel at home, laughed Goodhue nervously to himself. How?

"Gentlemen," continued the voice, in confident, pear-shaped, scholarly tones, "as we promised, we *do* have what admittedly sounds difficult to believe—the cure for cancer. We have found the cure because, first, we have found the 'C' particle."

The huge screen was filled with what Goodhue recognized as a human muscle cell. "If we go within this cell," said the voice, "we find . . . "

In the adjacent room, Ed Murdoch and Christopher Ives sat at a control panel. As Ives ran through an illustrated description of Justin's findings, Murdoch looked back and forth across the monitors—showing the oncologists and the slides they were watching. This was the fifth such show Murdoch and Ives had put on today and they had five or six still to go. Murdoch felt ambivalent about the shows. His original plan had been to keep the oncologists ignorant, not only of where they were, but also of each other. To transport each of them separately to the sanitarium and then to put each in a separate room with a closed-circuit TV monitor. That way, when each oncologist returned to his millionaire client, no client would know the identity of any other client. So the millionaires couldn't pool their resources to track down the men who'd stripped them of millions. But when Cruz discovered that Justin's notes were gone and Murdoch had had to move ahead of schedule, there had been no time to set up individual transportation and individual TV monitors. Instead, Murdoch had been forced to go with these groups of six or more oncologists. But Ives had said it was actually better this way. "Let them be with their colleagues," he'd argued, "and they'll feel stronger, less coerced. They'll be less likely to dig in their heels just for the *sake* of resisting us. That's what I'd do, if I were in their shoes."

Maybe, thought Murdoch. Ed Murdoch had a constantly working, constantly dissatisfied mind. Twenty years of police work on the street—in dark alleys, lofts, docks and warehouses—had taught him that things went wrong very easily. And the more people involved, the easier. Today the sanitarium had seventy-three oncologists, representing the seventy-three multimillionaires who had accepted Murdoch's offer. Seventy-three out of one hundred. Not bad, thought Murdoch. But also hard to handle. Murdoch thought of the dozens of monkeys on the hillside on Thursday, chattering, running amuck. He'd rather deal with one man at a time: Strip that cigar from Khoury's kisser, forcibly uncross Merewitz's arms. Break each man down, one by one. Get each to send for his client's dough and then split. Split to one of several Central American countries where, knew Murdoch, a norteamericano could buy a secluded villa and live unmolested by the local policía. And where, if the norteamericano's tastes happened to run to twelve-year-old girls . . . well, money bought that too in that relaxed climate.

Ives's presentation went quickly. The identification of the "C" particle. The injection of "C" particles from cancerous lab animals and then cancerous humans to produce cancer in healthy animals. The injection of the D4 serum into cancerous hamsters. Photographs of the hamsters and their "C" particles before and after the serum (the most recent autopsies having been done this morning—showing a cure in only four days). Plus photographs of cell samples before and after.

And now the objections that Murdoch had already heard so often today.

"But of course," said Merewitz, looking one of the TV cameras square in the eye, "you could have faked all this."

There were nods from the six other specialists.

"Of course," Ives admitted cheerfully. "We haven't—but we could have. This is only background. We don't expect you to accept this as proof."

"What then?" demanded Jaroslawicz.

"What would *you* suggest?" asked Ives.

"Clinical proof, of course," said Hansum. "Specimens."

"Even specimens," pointed out Ives, "could be suspect. Suppose we showed you live animals that are now recovering from cancer because of our serum? In the two short days you have here, you could follow their rapid recovery. But you'd suspect natural remission, of course."

The oncologists nodded again.

"So what would you suggest?" asked Ives.

"Well . . . " Vezacino considered it. "*Hundreds* of specimens. I doubt even you could have assembled that many animals simultaneously undergoing natural remissions. Then we"—he gestured to include his colleagues—"we could select which to follow in the next two days."

"With proper lab equipment, of course," said Khoury.

"But without a clinical history of these animals," objected Jaroslawicz, "it's *not* enough."

"Suppose they gave us histories," said Brua. "Slides. Dated slides."

Ives's smooth voice intruded. "But how could you trust our dating?"

"How indeed!" Merewitz laughed cynically.

"No," disagreed Vezacino. "I for one would settle for just the animals."

"But you should have more," said Ives. "Are you familiar with the decay of Newtonium-9?" he asked.

Ives and Murdoch got blank looks on the TV monitors.

"It's a transuranium compound with a half-life of forty days," explained Ives. "If one were to paint it on a slide—or on anything—it would effectively date that slide. And that is what we have done."

Khoury chewed his cigar. "I don't know," he said. "It would date when the painting was done—not when the slides were made."

"A con," agreed Merewitz.

In the control room, Murdoch shook his head. He'd busted many con games, from Gypsies "burning" cursed twenty-dollar bills (while actually stealing them) to corporations manipulating millions in phony stock. Now he had the problem of proving that something that *looked* like a con *wasn't* a con. But, as in earlier shows today, Ives was proving right: By raising the objections himself (a stroke of genius, felt Murdoch), Ives was forcing the specialists to suggest what proof would be sufficient. And to agree on it. They were convincing *themselves*. Only Ahmed Khoury and Joseph Merewitz—the Egyptian and the Canadian Jew—were holding out.

"Ahmed," appealed Hansum. He gestured at the TV cameras. "They're offering us the best evidence they have."

"Yes," said Brua. "Let's at least *look* at it."

"Well ... " Khoury waved his cigar in a shrug.

Ha! thought Murdoch. Even the Egyptian was weakening. Now was the time, felt Murdoch. He looked at Ives. Ives nodded. Murdoch pressed a button.

The door to the room was unlocked and two white-coated assistants wheeled in a huge lab table. On it were dozens of cages, each containing dozens of mice or hamsters. And in front of the cages were files full of slides.

A murmur of interest went up from the oncologists. They rose from their chairs and surrounded the table.

"All the animals are tattooed with numbers that match their slide files," explained Ives. "Pick the ones you want and our technicians will take them back to your rooms for you. There you will find all the equipment you need to work with."

He and Murdoch watched, satisfied, as most of the seven oncologists fell upon the lab animals like eager children. It was another stroke of Ives's—Murdoch saw again, for the fifth time today—to withhold the animals until the end, to make the specialists appreciate them as some wonderful gift.

"Chris," rumbled Ed Murdoch, "you've done it again." The ex-FBI man leaned back in his chair and stretched his arms wide. He didn't notice Ives's look of concern as his shoulder-holstered pistol came into view—he was thinking about young mouths and hands on his drooping, fleshy body. He was also thinking it was time that Ives and he look at their *own* hamsters.

Inside, in the room with the animals, Arthur Goodhue—who had said nothing for the past half hour—was thinking he was a lot less worried than he was before. The Colorado Carcinogenic Colloquium looked like it would be very interesting. And informative. Ryker would be pleased.

New York City

Paul Justin was not scheduled to have his temperature taken again until eight o'clock. But when Nurse Abrams looked in on him around 6:30, she noted his face was sweaty. She touched his forehead. It was hot. She immediately turned him over and stuck a thermometer in his rectum. While she waited, she consulted his chart. The last reading, at 4 P.M., showed a temperature of 99 degrees. She removed the thermometer. It read 104.1.

"Dr. Falcone," she paged, "Dr. Falcone to intensive care."

Falcone, who'd had only eight hours of sleep since Friday morning, had been catnapping in the doctors' dorm of Oakes-Metcalf. He arrived rubbing his eyes.

"It shot up," said Abrams. "Just like that."

Falcone nodded grimly. He checked Justin's abdomen. It was soft—so the fever wasn't peritonitis. He flexed Justin's neck. It was normal—so the fever wasn't meningitis. He pressed his stethoscope to Justin's chest.

The right side sounded normal. But on the left, Falcone heard the familiar, cellophane-like rustle.

"Junk in the base," said Falcone. "I think he's got pneumonia."

It didn't surprise the assistant resident. The tube in Justin's mouth was an efficient conduit for bacteria to get into the lungs. And even with the respirator, Justin's lungs weren't expanding properly. They were developing areas of partial collapse. So once the bacteria got in, the lungs couldn't clear them out.

"Let's get a chest X-ray," said Falcone to Abrams. "Plus a blood culture and a sample of sputum for culture." The sputum was the stuff they were suctioning out of Justin's throat every two hours. "Then start him on penicillin—600,000 units every six hours. And let's get his temperature down. Aspirin suppositories and a cooling blanket."

While Abrams went to call for the portable X-ray machine, Falcone took Justin's blood pressure. The last reading on the chart said it was 115/65—very close to normal. But now Falcone got 90/60.

"Shit," he swore. There were now at least three lousy possibilities. The pneumonia (Falcone was almost certain it *was* pneumonia) could get worse and Justin could drown from the fluid in his lungs. Or the pneumonia could lay Justin open to superinfection. Or the pneumonia could push the blood pressure still lower and Justin could go into septic shock.

Of the three possibilities, the last one worried Falcone the most. Any infection—such as pneumonia—releases toxins into the bloodstream, toxins that interfere with the body's ability to maintain the "tone" of the small blood vessels. So these blood vessels dilate and blood pressure drops. As the body's organs are deprived of blood, the body can go into septic shock. This risks death due to total body failure—everything stops functioning at once. In a typical forty-year-old man, the chances of pneumonia causing septic shock are low. But what concerned Falcone was that, since Justin's comatose state had made his muscles flaccid, the tone of his blood vessels was already poor. And once in septic shock, Falcone put Justin's chances of survival at only 50-50.

Nurse Abrams returned and Falcone had her begin feeding Justin an I.V. of Levophed, a solution of 2 amps per 500 cc's, going in at five drops per minute. The Levophed, designed to constrict the blood vessels, would help get Justin's pressure back up. Then Falcone called Dewing at home. Dewing, who was about to go out for the evening, was annoyed but said he would come over. As Falcone hung up, the technician appeared with the X-ray machine. "I have a feeling," said Falcone to no one in particular, "that we're going to lose this guy. And we're not even going to know what caused it to begin with."

Dobbs Ferry, New York

As Lattimer had promised, Joan Scully got to sip a gin-and-tonic in his backyard. But she didn't get to see the grass grow. The grass—patchy, burned and now damp—was busy being crushed underfoot as Steve, Laurie and Melissa Justin hurled boccie balls across it. I shouldn't be surprised, Joan thought. Apparently, Frank could no more let go of a story than ... she struggled for an analogy ... than Steve, Laurie and Melissa's father could let go of looking for the "C" particle.

She smiled ruefully. So much for a quiet evening alone with Frank. It had started going wrong when they arrived at Grand Central at 3:37 and were rushing across the concourse to catch the 3:40 to Dobbs Ferry. Suddenly, Frank had stopped and said, "Why rush? I'll make a few phone calls and we'll get the 4:10. Okay?" Joan Scully had laughed. "Take you away from your favorite place—a phone booth? I wouldn't dare." So Joan had flipped through magazines while Frank had called the two remaining people on Humenuik's list. He emerged from the phone booth to say he'd reached both of them: Louise

Lezyniak said she thought the man had slipped. And Brian O'Neil said he had talked to the police in *confidence* and was going to lodge a complaint about his name being given to a reporter.

Having received this "really vital bit of news," as Joan referred to it, she and Lattimer were able to catch the 4:10. They arrived at 4:42 and headed to Frank's house on his motorcycle. And at about five o'clock, going past the Justin home, Frank—with his damn reporter's eye, thought Joan—had spotted what would not have been there a half hour earlier: Mrs. Justin going out the back door with a box of groceries, headed toward her car. She was followed by all three of her children, each with his or her own box.

Lattimer had stopped his motorcycle. "That's funny," he said, "carrying groceries *to* the car?"

"A picnic?" Joan suggested.

"I see TV dinners, milk, ice cream. That's not a picnic."

So they had walked over and said hello. Barbara Justin had been wary with Frank. But after Joan introduced herself as Paul's co-worker, Barbara warmed up. She looked as if she needed a friend. It had started with the ice cube maker, she explained, but now the whole refrigerator and freezer was on the fritz. So she and the kids were taking the food to a couple of neighbors' houses, so it wouldn't spoil.

"Hey," Frank had said, "no reason to drive all around. My refrigerator's almost empty." He put the cartons in the Justin station wagon. "Come on over to my place."

"I'm really sorry about Paul," Joan added, almost on cue. "I know how much he ... and you ... " Joan brought her hands together. She wanted to express the sympathy she felt—but she also hated herself for expressing it. She knew that it would help persuade Barbara to come with them.

It did. Barbara Justin's lips had formed a tight, trembling smile. "Thank you," she had said.

And of course, once the food was in Frank's refrigerator, Frank had insisted that Barbara and the kids stay for dinner. Barbara's pro forma protest that they could very easily eat out was overwhelmed. Frank produced ingredients for coq au vin and talked enthusiastically of hamburgers with a sauce that would make the kids forsake McDonald's forever and ...

So now Joan Scully sat in the backyard—banished there by Frank and Barbara as they prepared dinner inside—and chewed on a gin-flavored ice cube. Joan wondered how Frank was doing pumping Barbara for information about Paul. God, the man was incorrigible.

But when the cooks emerged onto the patio bearing trays of food, they were talking of Dobbs Ferry road repairs and bond issues.

"... twisted the mayor's arm?" Barbara was asking, surprised. "And *that's* why he voted against it? Frank, I had no idea you knew this town."

"Barbara," said Frank Lattimer, "my sneaking desire is to give up going into the city and just open a little newspaper here. Be a country editor, sit in a rickety, old wooden armchair..."

Softening her up, thought Joan. The disarming Frank Lattimer. Over the coffee, he'll go in for the kill: Tell me, Barbara, if Paul dies tomorrow, will his cure be lost forever? Or do you know anything about it?

But coffee was a long ways away. Frank expertly tossed a salad, shook and poured some dressing into it.

"Mm," said Joan, starting to eat. "What's that?" She pointed at a vegetable in the salad.

"Endive," said Frank. "I had some lying around."

"Fabulous," said Joan. "And what's the dressing? It's sure not Kraft."

"My version of a vinaigrette."

"Nice," said Joan.

The coq au vin was just as good. And the wild rice that went with it. Frank served everybody and kept up a lively conversation—about the Justins' cat and a dog he had once owned and cars it had chased and an old car with a hand crank his grandfather once had and how his grandfather talked to the car—a conversation that included everybody and had everybody happy. Frank even cut Melissa's hamburger for her.

He's not just softening Barbara up, thought Joan. He's also doing a pretty good job on me. She liked seeing how Frank was with kids. If I ever marry, she thought, if I ever live like this, with a house, and a backyard, and kids, I hope my man is as good.

Then it was time for dessert—a fresh pear with some kind of fabulous sauce. And not coffee, but espresso from Frank's little machine. Melissa and Laurie ran off to play boccie again. Steve said he had to go home because Kenny Bedloe was coming over and they were going to draw cartoons. So the three adults were alone. They settled back in their chairs under the elms, in the soft, dappled light of early evening. Joan was tense. The little sliver of lemon peel for the espresso spurted from her hands. Here it comes, she thought. Frank's attack.

But Frank got up. He said, "Excuse me." Left his espresso half-full and strode off to join the girls on the other side of the yard. They stopped their arguing over whose boccie ball was closest. Joan watched Frank pick up a ball and show them how, instead of hurling it, they could gently *swing* . . . like this. The girls paid rapt attention. They tried to imitate Frank.

The two women watched Frank. His calm, encouraging voice floated across the lawn.

After a bit, Barbara said, "He's quite a guy."

"I guess so," admitted Joan. She was really surprised he'd left them.

"You know, he's lived down the street from us for over two years and I've never really . . . until this . . . really met him."

"I just met him myself," said Joan.

"I think Paul would like to meet him . . . did meet him, I guess, they rode in together on Thursday, he said . . . I mean, would like to *know* him. In some ways"—Barbara Justin's voice was getting thick—"they're very much alike."

Joan Scully regarded the woman next to her. Barbara Justin's pale aristocratic face looked like ice on the verge of cracking. Her face was all planes and angles—patrician nose, fine cheekbones—barely held together at fissure lines. Barbara flushed. A tremor ran under her jaw line. She flinched, turned away so Joan would not see the tears well up in her eyes. Joan reached out a hand to touch Barbara's wrist. Barbara's face fell apart.

"Oh, God. Oh, God, I need him so much," she cried. "So much. And I'm so afraid. Our life—what's going to happen to it? What—" Barbara fought to stifle the sobs.

Joan awkwardly leaned across the table, across the mess of pears and espresso cups, to half-embrace Barbara. "Hey, no," said Joan. "Let it out, let it go, it's okay, okay to cry."

And Barbara did. Vast, racking sobs shook her tall, frail body. Joan clutched her.

"I don't even care . . . about me . . . I'll live . . . I think I'll live. But Paul . . . all those years . . . tender man . . . loving man . . . driving himself in that lab . . . for nothing . . . for a stroke . . . dumb hamsters . . . dumb 'C' particle . . . never found anything . . . found happiness . . . nothing . . . stupid . . . stupid waste . . . our lives together . . . wanted so much more with him . . . now never . . . never . . . never . . . "

"Okay," said Joan, "it's okay."

"No." Barbara started to come out of it. She sniffled into a napkin. "No. Silly. Shouldn't."

"It's okay. Really. Okay to cry."

From across the lawn came the *thwunk* of two boccie balls hitting and Melissa's innocent laughter. "Great, Melissa," the women heard Frank cry, "I think you're the closest."

"The children," said Barbara, wiping her face with the napkin. "I don't want them to see me this way." Some of her blond hair was plastered by tears to her cheek. She brushed it back. She shook her head. "I think I'll go ... inside," she said. "Straighten up." She stood, a bit shakily, and Joan Scully stood with her, solicitously. "No. I'm all right," said Barbara. "Be all right ... be right back." And she went inside.

Joan Scully stood by the table. She watched, across the lawn, Frank Lattimer laughing as he paced out the distance between two boccie balls, heel to toe, heel to toe, teetering like a man on a tightrope. Frank was exaggerating his precarious balance and the children were laughing with him. He reached the ball and feigned a slump of relief. The girls applauded his achievement. But as she watched him, the good feeling Joan had had at dinner was slipping away. A somber suspicion grew on her. She felt she knew why Frank had suggested this get-together. She felt cheap, used. And angry.

New York City

With his fever, Paul Justin was having a fever dream. He was in a hot, steaming jungle. But the vines pressing in on him were not green plants. They were transparent plastic tubes. And the snakes slithering on the vines were electric wires. The tubes and wires tried to wrap themselves around him, tried to choke him. He slashed at them with a machete. But as the blade cut, he realized he was cutting his own life. He tried to scream. He felt short of breath. He ... he felt himself being lifted, felt something ice cold on his back.

Justin woke up with a start. He saw the machine over him, the medical people around him. He felt lightheaded again. What now? he wondered.

Nurse Abrams pulled the cold X-ray plate out from under Justin. She gave it to the technician, who sped off with the plate and the machine.

While Falcone and nurses Abrams and Lopez waited for the X-ray results, they lifted Justin again and put a cooling blanket under him. They ran all their checks of his functions and then shoved in an aspirin suppository and put him on penicillin. Fifteen minutes later, the lab called up the X-ray: "Left lower pneumonia."

Dewing arrived a minute later. "Tickets to *La Bohème*," he swore. "Planned it for a month—and now *this*. Shit. Now pneumonia." He addressed them all: "Tell me some good news."

He meant it facetiously, but there *was* some good news. "His right pupil is starting to react to light," said Falcone.

"Swell," said Dewing, sarcastically.

"It means something," insisted the assistant resident.

"And if you can save him from dying from pneumonia," said Dewing, "we'll worry about it. But not now. Christ, I said I wanted him *awake* by Monday—not dead."

Falcone noted that Dewing had said "you" are in charge of saving Justin—not "we." Thanks, thought Falcone.

"Should I call his wife?" put in Lopez.

"Yes," sighed Dewing. "Tell Mrs. Justin."

On top of the cooling blanket, Paul Justin was burning and shivering—and now starting to shiver with fear as well.

Dobbs Ferry, New York

The phone rang in Lattimer's house. Barbara Justin answered it. It was Steve Justin. The hospital had called and wanted her to call them. She did. Then she came out and told Joan Scully the news. Barbara, who had just put herself back together, looked as if she was ready to go to pieces again. Again, Joan hugged her.

"Are you going to the hospital?" Joan asked.

Barbara nodded.

"Would you like some company? I'll be happy—"

"Yes," Barbara nodded. "And maybe Frank, too?"

"Well ... " said Joan. "Maybe you'd rather have him stay with the kids ... shouldn't somebody baby-sit?"

"No ... it's easy enough for me to call a sitter. And I'd like ... like Frank with us. . . . I know he cares about Paul."

Joan nodded, tightly, the anger in her growing. She was careful not to show it.

Barbara Justin went inside to phone a sitter. Joan called Frank over to her. The girls were reluctant to let him go. Because they weren't just playing boccie—they were talking about all kinds of interesting things. Melissa was trying to guess Frank's zodiac sign (she was relieved to have established that it *wasn't* Cancer) and Laurie was explaining why their cat was a no-good pet ("he runs away all the time") and that they still wanted a hamster. "Hey," Frank told them, as Joan kept calling, "be right back. You keep playing."

He joined Joan Scully at the patio table. There, Joan told him two things. First she told Frank about Paul's pneumonia. Then she told Frank he was a bastard.

"What?"

"You heard me. A bastard."

He had started to clear the patio table of the dinner dishes. He put a tray down. "What brought this on?" he asked.

"Would it be a clue," asked Joan, "if I told you that Barbara doesn't know anything about Paul's research? That if he *was* on to anything, he didn't tell her?"

"Oh," said Frank Lattimer. "Barbara told you that?"

"Don't look surprised." Joan picked up the tray.

"Huh? And how does that make me a bastard?"

"And don't look *dumb*. You planned it, Frank. Just because you can be so charmingly subtle doesn't mean—"

"Planned what?" Frank Lattimer looked puzzled.

"Left Barbara and me alone together like that. Made sure there was a woman's shoulder she could cry on. So she could let it all hang out. Very neat."

"I swear I didn't—" A smile crossed Frank Lattimer's face. "Unless my subconscious—"

Joan slammed the tray down. "Subconscious, hell. You were consciously using me. Just because I talked us out of getting knifed yesterday doesn't mean that every time something—"

"Barbara cried on your shoulder. That bothered you?"

"That's not the point, and you know it. I'm just glad she *didn't* have secrets to spill about Paul."

Frank Lattimer threw up his hands in mock dismay. "Okay. Okay. Enough. I'll clear the table later." He turned to go inside.

"But she *did* invite you to the hospital with us," called Joan, "so the dinner wasn't a total waste. You can come with us and watch Paul die and hope he'll make some kind of deathbed statement. Or maybe you can *force* one out of him!"

"Women," sighed Frank Lattimer.

Women, indeed, thought Joan Scully. She understood why Frank's wife had left him. She felt that if she were his wife she might be tempted to hurl some dinner utensil at him (wives did that, didn't they?)—but he had closed the screen door behind him and disappeared.

Melissa and Laurie, hearing the angry tone in Joan's voice, had grown silent. Joan now smiled at them and they went back to play. Joan wondered what she should do. An hour ago, over dinner, she had looked forward to spending the night with Frank in this house. She had imagined herself waking up here tomorrow morning, looking out the windows to the elms, hearing birds sing. . . .Well, not tonight. Tonight she'd sleep in her own apartment, and alone. And did she even want to go in with Frank to see Paul? Well, yes. Barbara wanted her to. And she wanted to, also. It would be good to look in on Paul. After breathing life into him on the floor of the electron microscope room and all the way over to the hospital, Joan felt she had a bond with him.

And a bond still—damn it all—with Frank.

Houston, Texas

"Hard to tell so far, Mr. Ryker," said Goodhue over the phone. "It's a big place. Full of hamsters, chimps. It's impressive twenty-nine ways from Sunday."

Ryker ran his eyes down the list of states in his atlas. Twenty-nine. New Hampshire. A surprise. But all right. A small state, easier to check. He flipped to the New Hampshire map.

"But do they have the cure?" he asked.

"Really won't know till day after tomorrow," said Goodhue. "They've got these chimps with leukemia. They're giving them a shot. If the white blood count goes down on all of them, it can't be a fluke. Two chimps, maybe. But not if it's *all* of them."

Beautiful, Goodhue, thought Ryker. "Two." That meant the northeast quadrant. No big towns, he saw. Just Berlin. And the White Mountains.

"So what would you advise?" asked Ryker.

"Well," said Goodhue, "I know it sounds maniacal with a capital 'M'—but I'd raise that money. I mean, there's no way they can fake this demonstration."

Ryker looked more closely at the map. "M." A town beginning with "M" was . . . there was one! Milan! A tiny town on the Androscoggin River. This would be a cinch!

"Thank you, Dr. Goodhue," said Ryker.

"Of course," said the man with the gravelly voice, "you might also like to try the numbers thirteen and four—and the letter W. Although many prefer thirty-seven and three—and the letter A. 'A' is for amateurs, Mr. Ryker. And that's what you are—and we aren't." He gave a rumbling sort of chuckle. "We found your code on the good doctor. I caught him sneaking a look at this little piece of paper . . . "

"Goodhue!" shouted Ryker. "They made you say those numbers—for New Hampshire? All that?"

"Yes," said Goodhue unhappily.

"What about the rest of it?" Ryker demanded. "Is it fake, too?"

"No," said Goodhue. "There really are these chimps and—"

"And that's all you get, Mr. Ryker," said the gravelly voice. And the line went dead.

Ryker waited. The local switching office called again. Not

Hisiger—another man. "Went back to the Ozark Tandem this time," he said. "You know, that's Missouri—Arkansas. Sorry, no further."

Ryker cursed.

Lander, Colorado

It was 6 P.M., mountain daylight savings time. In the sanitarium near Lander, Colorado, in small but cheerful rooms that formerly housed psychopaths, schizophrenics and manic depressives, seventy-three level-headed oncologists were locked in, eating gourmet dinners. In the adjacent wing of the building, Ed Murdoch was laughing as he described to Christopher Ives the phone call he had just made.

" . . . and you should have seen Goodhue's face! When I hung up and led him away to his room, he looked so poorly, I doubt he has any appetite at all." Murdoch's rumbling laugh hawked up some phlegm. "Ha!" he said, spitting it into his handkerchief. "So I bet there's an extra roast pheasant for you, Chris, if you like."

"No, thank you," said Ives.

"Just as well," said Murdoch, his laugh abruptly stopping. "Because what we're going to do now is count those white blood cells."

"But I—" began Ives.

"They're all locked in tight for the night," said Murdoch firmly. "We've got nothing left to do. Except this."

Ives swallowed hard. It was finally here. The moment he had dreaded and postponed. He had been so proud convincing the world's top cancer specialists that he possessed the cure for cancer. Now he was terrified to convince himself.

"All right," said Ives.

They went into the animal room. Ives took the first leukemic hamster out of its cage. He tied a tourniquet around a leg and a vein bulged out. He stuck a syringe into the vein and withdrew 0.5 cc of blood. He put a drop of the blood on the end of a pipette. He repeated this for the other four hamsters. Then he put the first pipette into the Coulter counter, a machine about the size of a TV set, sitting on the table. He turned on the counter. They waited. Thirty seconds passed. Ives wished it would take longer. Then the windows of the counter lit up with numbers.

"7,336 white cells per cubic millimeter," said Murdoch, showing off his newly acquired knowledge. "That's the same as yesterday. This hamster is cured." Then Murdoch pointed to the window for the hemoglobin level. "15.1 grams," he read. "That's normal, too, right?"

"Right," admitted Ives.

Ives ran the other four pipettes through the counter. All showed in the normal range.

"That's it then," said Murdoch.

"No. Wait," said Ives. "We've got to test for infections."

Murdoch smiled patronizingly. "Sure, go test," he said.

From each of the five syringes, Ives squeezed a drop of blood onto five slides. He let the blood dry and then stained it with Wright's stain. He put the first slide under the microscope.

Slowly moving the slide back and forth, he counted the first hundred white cells he could see and noted whether each was a poly or a lymphocyte. The temptation to cheat was overwhelming. He could tell Murdoch that there was an abnormal differential. That when used on leukemia, Justin's vaccine left the patient open to a massive infection. That therefore it could be dangerous when used on any form of cancer.

Ives counted seventy-one polys, twenty-nine lymphocytes. About the same as yesterday. A normal differential. I could lie, thought Ives. But no—Murdoch would take the microscope and count them himself. And even if he didn't count accurately, he'd see it was roughly a 70/30 distribution. Normal.

At least, thought Ives, at least it's out of my hands. It's the machine and the microscope that are sentencing Justin to death—it's not me.

"Normal differential," said Ives.

Murdoch rubbed his patchwork face. Within the drooping folds of skin, his eyes lit up.

"I'll call my man in New York," he said. "He'll do it tonight."

"Will it be . . . ?" Ives let the question hang.

"Oh, very painless," said Murdoch. "Not like Cruz at all. A middle-class death." He smiled and left the room.

Dr. Christopher Ives looked around him, at the caged animals, the lab equipment, the syringes. He felt caged. He felt he *deserved* to be caged, for he was guilty. He popped another Valium but it seemed to have no effect. Ives played with fantasies: He considered flight—skiing down off this mountain. He considered suicide—he picked up a syringe. He could easily find his own vein. An air embolism. Death in under a minute. Ives set the syringe down and reached for his pipe. It took five minutes for his nervous fingers to light it. He inhaled. Ah, nourishment. But he knew it would not last. The syringe wasn't needed. Here, now, in this room, he had a premonition that this whole thing, this whole scheme they had set in motion, would itself cause his doom. Did he want that? Did he fear it more?

Christopher Ives went to try again to call his psychiatrist.

New York City

By the time Barbara Justin, Joan Scully and Frank Lattimer reached the Oakes-Metcalf Hospital, Dewing had long since gone—to catch what he could of *La Bohème*. So Falcone, who had been called away to the OR, came down to meet them. Seeing Lattimer, Falcone shook his head as if to say, "What are you doing here again?" Then, looking somberly at Barbara Justin, he told her that her husband had taken a turn for the worse. Falcone tried to present a balanced view: He said that the pneumonia was a serious threat to Paul's life but that the staff was doing everything it could. For instance, they had managed to bring his temperature down to 102 degrees. Still, given Paul's overall condition, he might not recover. But with antibiotics and luck . . .

"Can I see him?" asked Barbara Justin.

"Sure," said Falcone. It was just after 9 P.M. and according to regulations they'd normally have to wait till 10 P.M. for five minutes of visiting time. But Falcone wasn't going to enforce that.

"Go right in," said Falcone. He left, unhappy.

"But please be quiet?" asked Nurse Abrams. "Mr. Ziebarth has *just* gone back to sleep."

"We promise," said Barbara Justin. "I won't talk."

And Paul can't, thought Frank Lattimer.

The three of them went in and stood silently around Paul Justin's bed. Each was alone with his or her own thoughts.

Barbara Justin's thoughts were very simple. She was thinking how much she wanted Paul home.

Joan Scully, who had not seen Justin since he'd been put in intensive care, was actually more shaken. She'd somehow imagined that the hospital would do something for him. But he looked no better than when the crash team had grabbed him away from her more than two days ago. And the array of wires attached to him and the tube down his throat gave the impression that he was just being . . . maintained. She looked away.

Frank Lattimer was not shaken. But he was a bit confused. He was confused about what he was doing here. Driving them all in Barbara's car from Dobbs Ferry into the city, he had thought about Joan's angry accusations back at his house. They were uncomfortably like those his wife had hurled at him. How much *did* he, he wondered, care about Paul as a person and how much did he just care about him as a story? *Had* he come along to the hospital to give Barbara emotional support—or to try to wring something out of Paul or the doctor?

Worrying about this, Lattimer was relieved, in a way, to see that there was nothing to wring. His thoughts moved on to more productive areas: Would the FBI find Cruz's fingerprints on file and, if so, who really was he? Would the electron microscope photograph of the hamster reveal anything? (He'd call his IBM friend in the morning.) Who supports the Endicott Foundation? (He'd go to the library in the morning.) And what the hell was Underwood feeling guilty about? (He'd ... he'd ... he didn't know how to tackle that one.) Lattimer wished it were morning; there was nothing to learn here. He looked away.

Barbara Justin was the only one of the three who did not look away. So she was the one who noticed Paul Justin's eyes.

"They're open again," she said.

"What?" said Lattimer.

"His eyes—just staring like that. When I was here before, the doctor closed them. Now they're open again. It's very ... " She turned away, unable to face her husband.

"I'll close them, Barbara," said Joan, moving to do it.

"No," said Lattimer. "Wait."

"Why?" asked Joan.

Lattimer held up a finger. "Why *are* they open?" he asked.

"A simple reflex?" suggested Joan. She thought of a frog's leg twitching after it was cut off or a dead shark snapping its jaws. So, she realized, I view Paul as already dead.

"Suppose he's not in a coma," suggested Lattimer. "Suppose he heard us outside and wanted to see us and was able to force his eyes open."

"But he *is* in a coma," protested Joan Scully. "He's unconscious."

Barbara Justin was looking back and forth in wonderment between Joan and Frank. Her face showed hurt and hope. Joan touched her arm. "Barbara, I'm sorry to talk like this. It's just that—"

"No," said Barbara. "Go on, Frank."

"What if," said Lattimer tentatively, "what if the doctors are making the wrong assumptions. They assume he's had a stroke so they assume he's unconscious. But what if he's—"

"Paul," said Barbara feverishly, leaning over him, her whole body taut, intense, "Paul, can you hear me?"

Lattimer gently took her arm. "Barbara, there's a simple way to find out." He pulled the curtain around the bed, shutting the four of them off from the rest of the darkened ward. He looked down at Paul Justin's frozen face. "Paul," he said slowly, distinctly, aware that he was probably making a fool of himself—"Paul, I'm going to ask you a few questions. You can answer them with 'yes' or 'no.' For 'yes,' try to blink your eyes once. For 'no,' blink them twice."

Lattimer took a deep breath. "Okay," he said under his breath, "here goes."

"Frank—" began Joan, softly.

"Paul," said Lattimer, addressing the frozen, burning face with the black respirator tube, "are you conscious?"

Lattimer, Joan Scully and Barbara Justin waited. There was only the steady "*whoosh*" of the respirator filling Paul Justin's lungs and then the air escaping out his nose. Justin's eyes stared blindly at them. His pale eyelashes quivered. They fluttered. Drops of sweat fell from them.

He blinked once.

"Paul!" exclaimed Barbara joyously.

"Wait," said Lattimer. "Maybe it was a fluke." He looked again at Paul Justin. "Paul," he asked, "are you conscious?"

They waited. They waited longer. Justin blinked once. Barbara threw her arms around his head.

"Frank," said Joan Scully, "it looks like it's so hard for him. Maybe—"

"Just two more questions," said Lattimer. He gently pushed back Barbara's arm so he could see her husband's eyes. "Paul, did Roberto Cruz do this to you?"

"Roberto Cruz?" asked Barbara. "Do what?"

"I'll explain later," said Joan.

Justin blinked once. He blinked again.

"No?" demanded Lattimer. "What the hell?" He had been leaning over Justin. He stood up. "But if Roberto didn't—" And I was so *sure*, he thought. "*Not* a drug?" he marveled. "A real stroke? But then why is he—" He whirled on Justin. "Paul, why the hell are you conscious?"

"Shh," said Joan. "You'll have us thrown out."

"Frank," said Barbara, totally confused. "What—?"

"Paul," said Lattimer, his voice still loud, "I'll ask you again. Did Roberto Cruz—"

The curtain was pulled back. Nurse Abrams stood there, hands on hips.

"You said you wouldn't talk at all. And now you're practically yelling. Don't you realize the condition he's in?" She faced Barbara. She softened a bit. "I'm sorry, Mrs. Justin, but you and your friends will have to leave."

"Just one more—" began Lattimer.

"Now," said Abrams firmly.

"Listen," hissed Lattimer, "this man is *not* unconscious!"

"What?" asked Abrams. She approached the bed. "Nonsense," she said.

"He blinked his eyes," insisted Barbara. "He did."

"Mrs. Justin," said Abrams again with compassion, "sometimes that happens involuntarily. I'm sorry, but it means nothing."

"But he blinked in answer to my questions," said Lattimer.

"What questions?" asked Abrams.

"About how he got here," said Lattimer.

Now Abrams knew she was dealing with a nut. "Do I get an orderly," she asked, "to escort you out? Or will you leave now?"

"Better get the orderly," said Lattimer. And in one smooth motion, he pulled the curtain closed, leaned over Paul Justin and said, "Last question, Paul. Have you discovered the cure for cancer?"

Abrams stalked out.

Barbara Justin's mouth hung open.

With what seemed to them a great effort, Paul Justin's eyes blinked once.

"Yes! Damn it, yes!" Lattimer pounded his fist into his palm in triumph.

"The cure—?" began Barbara.

"Now, Paul—" began Lattimer.

Joan Scully tried to pull Lattimer up. "No, Frank. Tomorrow. It's too much for him. And besides, if you keep this up the nurse will never let you back."

"Paul," said Lattimer. "Did—?"

"You *had* your three questions," Joan insisted. *"Please."*

Lattimer straightened up. "Okay," he said.

Lattimer, Joan Scully and Barbara Justin walked out of the room. Barbara was going to pieces in a half-dozen different ways. "A cure?" she stammered. "Roberto Cruz? Is it a stroke? Will he—? What—?" Joan put an arm around her.

At the nurses' desk, Abrams sternly confronted them, a phone in her hand. She nodded sharply at Lattimer. "You just saved me a call to an orderly," she said. Far away, coming down the long corridor, Lattimer saw a man in a white coat. "We're leaving," said Lattimer, pressing the button for an elevator, "thank you."

Houston, Texas

The game was Petropolis. It was a board game like Monopoly except that instead of playing for control of Atlantic City real estate, you played for control of the oil wealth of the world—for tankers, pipelines, oil fields, entire oil-producing nations. And instead of being made of cardboard, the Petropolis board was made of ebony, with markers of real ivory. Petropolis cost $500. Three Christmases ago, when it came out, Harry Wissenbach had given the game as a gift to a dozen of his friends in the oil business. Most had smiled at Petropolis, played it once and put it away in a closet to gather dust. Ray Ryker hadn't smiled. Doesn't Harry know, Ryker had thought, that oil isn't a game? It's a business. And I don't let *my* business get decided by the roll of the dice. He wouldn't play even once.

Now Ray Ryker rolled the dice.

"Six," said Wissenbach. He counted off squares on the board. "Why, Ray, Ah'm sorry to say, yore tanker is stuck on a reef. It ain't gonna get to the sheikdom in time. Ah think Ah'll get the contract."

Ryker glared at the ebony board. He had been playing for only ten minutes, but he despised the game. Dice! Drawing cards! It gave him no control of his fate. He felt like overturning the board and all its markers into the laps of the other three players. But he got control of himself.

"I tell you, Harry," Ryker forced himself to say, "since I'm on that reef, not doing too well, maybe somebody else could do better." He glanced around the long porch. "Do you think somebody could sit in for you and me a few turns while we talk?"

Wissenbach looked unhappy. Like his barbed-wire hunts, Petropolis was his passion. Ryker had been calling Wissenbach all day long, all around town. Finally he got him here, at the River Oaks Club. Wissenbach had installed himself at a table on the clubhouse porch, overlooking the first tennis court, and was hustling up a game of Petropolis. "For friendly," he'd say. "Or a tenth of a mill to the dollar." Since ten million of play dollars could change hands in one Petropolis game, that meant you could still drop a thousand dollars to the president of the third largest bank in Texas. "Sure, we'll talk," Wissenbach had told Ryker over the phone. "Come on over and play and we'll talk."

So, like the barbed-wire hunt, Ryker had allowed himself to be roped in. But enough was enough. There was polite applause from the audience on the porch as two young men—the club's two top players—came off the court. Ryker roped *them* in. It was past eight o'clock, the end of the day. The two tennis players wanted to shower and relax. But they knew who Ryker and Wissenbach were. They couldn't say no.

Ryker cut Wissenbach short as Wissenbach tried to explain the whole game to them. He dragged Wissenbach inside to a quiet table in a corner of the bar.

"Now, Harry," he said, "listen to me. I want to sell my share of Climatron."

"The whole thing?"

"Yes. And I want to do it by tomorrow."

"Jee-sus," said Wissenbach. He took a long drink of his scotch. Ryker drank a Virgin Mary—he didn't like alcohol.

Wissenbach looked at his friend. "Whatcha doin', Ray-boy? Charlie Shaub called me this afternoon, wanted to know if he should buy up yore share of OFI." He eyed Ryker keenly. "So you really found some other partner to help you buy Texahoma? Tryin' to raise cash to go in with 'em?" He clasped Ryker on the shoulder. "Well, congratulations, boy. Ah knew you could do it."

"That's not it," said Ryker.

"No?" Wissenbach shrugged. "Well, none of my business, of course. So how much do you want for your Climatron?"

"What do you mean, how much do I want?" asked Ryker. "Book value, of course."

"Ordin-ar-ily," said Wissenbach. "But by tomorrow? Sounds like a forced sale to me, Ray. Seller gotta be willin' to take less."

Ryker flushed with anger. "What kind of a friend—?"

"A friend an' a businessman, Ray. You own 16.5 percent, right?"

Ryker nodded. He was impressed with the banker's memory for numbers.

"Right," said Wissenbach. He traced numbers in the ring on the table left by his glass of scotch. "Give you a million an' a half."

"Book value is two point three million," snapped Ryker. "*Real* value—hell, in a couple of years, my share'll be worth ten million."

"So keep it," said Wissenbach.

Ryker gripped his glass of tomato juice. It had been a bad day, but this was the worst. After the first phone trace had failed and after the tail on Goodhue had failed, Ryker had totaled up the holdings that he could dispose of quickly. There were three types: $6.2 million (current market value) in municipal bonds in his safe deposit box in Wissenbach's bank. $8.6 million (current market value) in common stock certificates in the safe in his own office. And about $4 million, also in his safe, in stock certificates for two privately held companies—two small companies that Ryker had helped build. For a grand total of $18.8 million. And the price of the so-called cure was $18 million. Ryker had been angry. Paying the price meant stripping himself of almost all his ready resources.

Then Ryker had made a few calls: A call to his broker, telling the man he wanted to sell all his bonds and common stocks tomorrow—and get cash within twenty-four hours. And calls to some of his partners in the two privately held companies, asking them if they wanted to buy his shares. He got a tentative agreement on his shares in OFI—the sportswear company, Owens Fashions, Inc. But of the six other partners in Climatron, none of the five he reached had money handy. So once again, Ryker knew he needed Wissenbach.

And then, at dinnertime, after the code with Goodhue had failed and the second phone trace had failed, Ryker knew he needed Wissenbach desperately. And now Wissenbach was trying to hold him up!

"Climatron," Ryker said levelly, wishing he had Wissenbach's scotch in him, wishing he didn't have to be rock-steady, "is a gold mine. Nobody has their control system, nobody . . . "

It was true. Climatron made the only true computer-controlled energy conservation system for office buildings. As the energy crisis got worse, buildings would increasingly turn to Climatron to reduce the costs of their heating, air-conditioning, lighting and electricity. Ryker loved Climatron because coupled with Texahoma's oil, it allowed him to make money off both ends of the energy crisis. And because, unlike Owens Fashions, which made mod clothing that Ryker personally hated, Climatron was in the business of *control*.

So he didn't want to sell. And he certainly didn't want to sell for only $1.5 million. Yes, the $1.5 million here would give him—barely—the $18 million he needed. But he was angry over the principle of the thing.

" . . . so two million dollars is fair," he concluded.

"One point five," said Wissenbach. "Take it or leave it."

Ryker snapped his plastic swizzle stick. "I'll take it," he said.

"Fine," said Wissenbach.

The two men agreed to meet tomorrow to transfer the stock certificates and for Ryker to get his bonds from his safe deposit box. Then they walked back to the clubhouse porch. Wissenbach had his arm draped around Ryker, exuding down-home friendship. Ryker wanted to shrink from his touch.

"Wa-hl," boomed Wissenbach to the Petropolis players. "How you boys doin'?"

"I took over Kuwait for you, Mr. Ryker," said one of the tennis players, pleased with himself. He fanned the paper money. "Made you five million dollars richer."

If it were only that easy, thought Ray Ryker.

New York City

Barbara Justin, Joan Scully and Frank Lattimer had gotten in the elevator and Lattimer had pressed the button for Lobby. The doors were just starting to close when he realized there was something wrong about the man in the white coat.

The man said to the nurse, "Dr. Dewing asked me to look in on Mrs. Hahn, to see the progress of her radical mastectomy." And then he went into the room where Lattimer had just been. But it struck

Lattimer that the man's words and his tone were stilted . . . as if . . . ?
Lattimer strode quickly between the closing elevator doors, leaving
the two women confused as the elevator descended without him. As if,
thought Lattimer, going into the room after the man, one minute
behind him . . . as if somebody had coached the man to say it.

"Hey!" said Nurse Abrams, as Lattimer strode past.

"Hey!" said Lattimer, as he whipped back the curtains that had
again been drawn around Paul Justin. Next to Justin's bed stood the
man in the white coat. He had unhooked a bottle feeding one of
Justin's intravenous tubes. Into the bottle, he was about to pour the
colorless contents of a small vial.

"You son of a bitch," said Lattimer evenly. He hurled himself at
the man.

The man was slight and dark. His face was impassive. His hands
and feet were very fast. Frank Lattimer had once taken a few karate
lessons, enough to know that Claude's threats this afternoon were a
joke, enough to know this man was for real. With a flurry of a *tsuki* to
his heart, an *uchi* that snapped back his chin and a *keri* that felt as if
the thin man had put an entire leg through his stomach, Lattimer
went down. The man leaped over Lattimer, trying to get past the bed,
to make it to the door. Lattimer gasped and moaned. As the man went
over him, Lattimer caught one of his feet. The man crashed down
into the curtains, ripping them off their tracks, down around Justin
and both of them.

The darkened room was full of patients' startled cries and shouts.
Nurse Abrams was coming in, yelling. The thin man burst out of the
tangled curtains and dashed for the door. Lattimer was only a step
behind him. The nurse filled the doorway, transfixed. The man chopped
her on the side of her neck and she toppled, as Lattimer had seen
cattle do when the slaughterhouse knife went into them. The man
sprinted down the corridor. Lattimer tried to scream, "Stop him," but
there was no breath in him to form the words.

For a wild moment he thought of pursuing the man. Physically,
the man had him beat. But Lattimer thought he had enough pure
hatred in himself to catch up. He started. He stopped. He stumbled
out of the room. He saw Nurse Lopez at her station, half-rising out of
her chair. "Get help!" blurted Lattimer. He sagged against the wall.

Ten minutes later, it was all over. Lopez got an intern and the
two of them took Abrams away—"only unconscious," the intern said.
More nurses, interns and residents arrived. Barbara and Joan came
back up. The staff quieted the patients in intensive care and pulled
the curtains off Paul Justin's frozen form. Falcone attended to him.
Lattimer wondered if Justin had seen the battle, understood he'd
nearly died. Joan led Barbara away from the chaos inside, then came

over and hugged Lattimer. He tried to tell her—and tell two hospital security guards—what had happened. The guards put out an alert for the fake doctor, but Lattimer's gasping description was too vague and there were too many exits. It was clear the man had escaped.

Lattimer asked people to see if the small vial was still there. No, it was gone. "Well, it was open," Lattimer gasped. "Even if he pocketed it, he had to have spilled some. Can you see if there is any on the floor, on the sheets? Take samples, analyze it?" The nurses said they would. Then Lattimer confronted Falcone: "Justin *is* conscious," Lattimer told the assistant resident. "He blinked his eyes, tried to communicate with us. And somebody's trying to kill him so he *can't* communicate." Falcone shooed Lattimer away—into the arms of the police. All kinds of police, squad patrols and then officers from homicide, were pouring into intensive care and Lattimer had to go through the whole thing with them again, from the beginning. He hurt like hell. His head and body were on fire from the blows he had received. But what burned even more was his anger.

New York City

Only when the curtains came down around him, covering his face, had Paul Justin panicked. Before that, he had calmly watched his execution. He realized—when the thin, dark man came in and unhooked the I.V. bottle—that it *was* his execution. He realized this because of Lattimer's question about Cruz. Now he saw the connection: Cruz *had* paralyzed him and this man was here to finish him off. There was absolutely nothing he could do about it. But after two days of paralysis, Justin was used to being unable to do anything. So he had calmly, almost abstractly, watched the man make ready to poison him. He had imagined the poison flowing through the I.V. tubes and into his body. He suspected it would be a death he would not feel, simply an unconsciousness that this time he would not recover from. Of course, he had felt many emotions. Regret at dying. Curiosity over how Lattimer had figured out he had found the cure. Curiosity over whether Cruz had somehow stolen the cure. Hope that somebody else would duplicate it. Love for Barbara. For his children. Some fear, yes. But mainly—in the midst of his fever and his chills—a calmness. He had been trying to learn to accept the living death of paralysis. If it was permanent—as the doctors at his bedside believed—then real death might be better.

So he had been calm. He had been calmly drifting on waves of fever. He had even been calm during the brief fight between his would-be executioner and Frank Lattimer. (Mostly, the fight had been out of his line of sight. While it was difficult to move his eyelids, it was impossible to move his eyes.) But then, when the curtain came down over his face, he had panicked. I'm going to suffocate! he thought. I'm going to die! The poisoning would have been an abstract death but this was *real*, the plastic curtains pressing hot and sticky on his face, covering his newly won sight with a white shroud. Help me! Help me! his mind had shouted.

And then, as quickly as he had panicked, Paul Justin had started laughing at himself. He mentally shook the head that he was physically unable to shake. Suffocate! He laughed. He was one of the few men in the world whom no plastic curtains *could* suffocate. Because he wasn't breathing through his nose or mouth—he had a goddamned *respirator*! As the interns and nurses came in and pulled the curtains off him, he was laughing that they needn't have bothered. His *respirator* would save him! Didn't they see that laughter in his eyes?

It was quiet now in intensive care. There was only the *whoosh* of the respirator and the *beep-beep* of the monitor and sometimes the faint moans of Mrs. Hahn. Paul Justin wasn't laughing to himself anymore, but he was smiling. He was smiling because the laughter had made him feel alive again, had given him hope. When Lattimer came back tomorrow—as Justin knew he would—they could continue the dialogue with the eye blinks. They'd figure out a way to get him out of here, to get his life back. Justin lay awake. With his precious eyes he stared up into the space where the thin man's head had been. For as long as twenty seconds his eyes had been locked on the man. And his eyes—including his previously blurred right eye—had been clear. So they had devoured every detail of the man's face. The small bump in the nose, the exact color—charcoal gray—of the eyes, the slight turndown at the right side of the mouth. In the empty space above his bed, Justin reconstructed the face of the man who almost killed him.

New York City

"Mas larga," said Maria.

"Longer," translated Joan.

"Not longer, exactly," said Frank Lattimer. "More pointed."

"Mas pica," translated Joan, back to Maria.

Maria shook her head. She touched her nostrils. She talked and Joan translated. "His nose is more pointed, yes. But his nostrils flared. He was angry."

Lattimer allowed some exasperation to show. "Of course. *Everybody's* nostrils flare when they're angry. But normally—when I saw him—this man doesn't have flaring nostrils."

The police identi-kit man patiently removed the nose, thoughtfully shuffled through some other noses, selected one and put it down on the blank face.

"Sí," said Maria.

"Maybe," said Lattimer.

"Look," said the identi-kit man. "That's the tenth nose. Let's say it's a buy for now, okay? Now—how about the mouth?"

"Mal," said Maria.

"Evil," translated Joan.

"Tell her," said the identi-kit man, "that all my mouths are evil."

"Thin," said Lattimer. "Not fleshy. Bloodless."

The identi-kit man considered this. He selected two mouths and placed them—first one, then the other—below the nose.

"Eso," said Maria, pointing to the first mouth.

"No," said Lattimer, pointing to the other. "*That* one's closer."

"Then how about . . . ?" began the identi-kit man, reconsidering his stock of mouths.

Frank Lattimer sighed and looked up. Outside their little glassed-in cubicle, across the room, Detective Carl Mathes of Homicide shook his head at Lattimer and returned to his deskful of paperwork. Lattimer knew Mathes was humoring him. Back at the hospital, Lattimer had picked out Mathes as the most intelligent and experienced of all the cops questioning him, and so had drawn the man aside.

"This is more complicated than it appears," Lattimer had said.

"It is, huh?" Mathes was skeptical.

"Let's call a friend of mine," Lattimer had said. "A Lieutenant Whitcomb."

Mathes had found an examining room with two phones. He tracked Whitcomb down to a stake-out in the depths of Brooklyn.

"Make it fast," said Whitcomb.

Lattimer brought Whitcomb—and Mathes—up to date: Cruz's keys that fit Justin's file cabinet. Cruz's secret apartment. Cruz's big bank balance. All his different identities—Cruz, Morales, Santiago. And now the attack on Justin by a man who looked very much like the man who went searching for Cruz in Harlem on Friday.

"How do you know he looks like him?" demanded Whitcomb.

"The girl I met in Harlem," explained Lattimer. "She described the man who was searching for Cruz, the man who hit her. And her description tallies with the guy I saw."

"Simple enough then," said Mathes. "We'll send somebody up there, bring her down. You can both try to build a face."

"Okay," said Lattimer. "But what if we don't find him? Or what if they send somebody else after Justin?" He jerked his thumb toward the room where Justin lay. "I'd like some protection for my friend."

"Protection?" asked Whitcomb.

"Somebody's trying to kill him," said Lattimer. "I want some of your men"—he looked at Mathes—"here in intensive care. Around the clock."

"Jesus," said Mathes. "We've got better things to do than baby-sit—"

"Better things to do than protect a paralyzed man?"

"The hospital has guards."

"You saw how effective they are," said Lattimer.

"You don't give up," said Mathes.

"Nope," said Lattimer.

So Mathes and Whitcomb discussed it. "Okay," said Mathes finally. "We'll guard him. Now let's you go identify your guy."

"One more thing," said Lattimer.

"I can hardly wait," said Mathes. "What?"

"What about some action on Cruz?" asked Lattimer. "What about those fingerprints from the FBI, Whit? Will you tell me if they show Cruz had a record?"

"What's your point?" asked Mathes.

"I think there's a tie-in," said Lattimer, "and the records are the place to start looking for it. I think Cruz and this other guy—the one who tried to kill Justin—were both hired by somebody else, hired for the same job."

"I've heard some pretty cockamamy theories—" began Mathes.

"But you will tell me anyway?" insisted Lattimer.

"Is he always like this?" Mathes asked.

"Unfortunately, yes," said Whitcomb.

The two policemen discussed this request. "Okay," said Mathes finally. "When we know on Cruz's fingerprints—probably tomorrow—you'll know, too."

"Thanks," said Frank Lattimer.

"Now I've got a request for you," said Carl Mathes. "Tell me—what the hell is this all about?"

"Yeah," said Whitcomb, "what *is* this 'job' they're hired for?"

Lattimer hesitated. So far, he'd told Whitcomb only that he suspected Cruz of being after some "valuable medical data," deliberately undefined. Now Lattimer figured he'd better say more.

"Would you guys believe the cure for cancer?" he asked.

Both policemen laughed. "Nope," said Mathes. "But we'll still work with you on what you got."

Only it seemed to Lattimer that all the work was being done by Maria and himself. The police had gone to the house on East 106th

Street and brought Maria to join Lattimer and Joan Scully at police headquarters at One Police Plaza. Once Maria understood what it was all about—that she wasn't being arrested for something—she had participated eagerly. But after a solid hour, what did they really have? Maria and Lattimer agreed that the man was slight and dark. But beyond that... ? The man had moved so fast, he had hardly seemed to be there at all. If he was remarkable for anything, it was for his nondescriptness. Lattimer struggled to assign specific features to him; Maria remembered him in terms of emotions.

"Hooded eyes," Joan Scully translated her as saying. "Like a snake."

"Like this?" suggested the identi-kit man, putting a pair of eyes in place.

"Too heavy," objected Lattimer. "More like... " He spread the identi-kit eyes across the table. They stared up at him, blank, disembodied. Lattimer rubbed his own eyes. He poured himself more black coffee. God, he was tired. Too little sleep last night. Too many things happening today.

"... like these," he suggested.

"No," Joan translated Maria as saying. "Too large." Maria now started rummaging through the eyes.

"Hey," said the identi-kit man, "let's put some order back in this." He scooped up the eyes. "Now. More like *this* ... ?" He selected one pair. "Or like this ... ?" He selected another.

Again, Maria and Lattimer chose differently.

"Well," sighed the identi-kit man. "How about... "

God, it was hard, thought Lattimer. Part of his success as a reporter was his ability to read people's faces. To detect in a press secretary's steady gaze the phoniness that announced he was being fed a lie. But *this*, this constructing a face out of whole cloth...

"Okay," said the identi-kit man, "let's try chins."

It was not until almost another hour later—the clock on the green, flaking wall said one o'clock—that they had put together a face. Lattimer didn't feel it was exactly the face of the man who'd tried to kill Justin. Maria didn't feel it was exactly the face of the man who'd slapped her. But it was close enough. And neither of them could specify how to improve it.

Lattimer stood up, stretched and waved Mathes over. Mathes looked at the composite and grunted. "Okay," he said, "we'll make copies of it and put it out on the street. Now let's see if you can pick him out of the mug shots."

When they'd started all this, Mathes had explained his theory: People who began by looking through mug shots got too easily discouraged. Worse, seeing all those faces, they forgot what the one they were searching for looked like. But now that Maria and Lattimer had a face in front of them, it should be easier.

It was still going to be hard. Mathes pulled a set of huge, heavy books off a shelf and let them thud on the table.

They looked at the books. "How many pictures are in there?" asked Joan Scully.

"Only about ten thousand," said Mathes.

"That many crooks," said Joan dryly.

"That we have pictures of," said Mathes, just as dryly.

"Organized by age, race?"

"Are you kidding me?"

"Okay," said Lattimer. He drank more coffee. Joan Scully translated what Maria had to do. Lattimer and Maria sat down with the books.

So many men, thought Lattimer, as they turned the pages. So many sullen faces. Front view, side view. Front view, side view. The men stared off into space. To Lattimer, it seemed as if many of them were *willing* their faces blank, trying to smudge their features. And many succeeded. Halfway through the first book, the faces started running together. Lattimer doubted he could have picked out his own. He understood why Mathes had had them do the identi-kit first. Maria and Lattimer kept trying to find a match for the composite they had made.

Time dragged on through the small hours of the morning. Beyond their cubicle, uniformed and plainclothes policemen came and went, exchanged information and gossip, answered phones, wrote reports, read newspapers. Once, an old woman in a nightgown barged in, demanding to swear out a complaint against a Peeping Tom. The cops directed her to another room. They seemed pleased by the break in their routine and, after the old woman was gone, told Peeping Tom stories. Maria and Lattimer finished one book of photographs, began another.

Around three o'clock Joan Scully, who had dozed off in a hard, wooden chair, woke up and said, "Hey, this is crazy. Why am I here?"

"Why *are* you here?" asked Lattimer, kindly.

"Loyalty?" she asked.

"That is crazy," he said. "Go home. Go to sleep. You don't have a deadline to make."

"Neither do you," she pointed out.

"Habit," he said. "My habit. You haven't formed it yet. You go to sleep."

"But if I go to sleep, you'll wake me up when you come in. I don't have an extra key for you."

"I'll find another place to sack out. Barney James's."

"You're sure?"

"Sure."

"Okay," she said reluctantly, yawning. She kissed him on the forehead. "It's been a peachy day," she said. "Let's do it again soon."

"We will," said Lattimer.

"That's what I'm afraid of." She smiled. "Call me tomorrow, Ace." She waved good-bye and drifted off through the room and out the door, unseeing. Lattimer turned more pages.

Sometime after four o'clock Maria said something in Spanish and huddled up in the chair Joan Scully had occupied. She fell asleep immediately. Lattimer finished the second book, plowed on through a third. The garbage bags this afternoon, he thought. And now the garbage of people's lives thrown away, here in these books. I'm a garbage collector, he told himself. And a tired one. He rubbed his eyes. His stomach sloshed with too much coffee. His head and chest ached from the karate blows. He propped his head on his elbows. He looked again at the identi-kit face that Maria and he had assembled. Not quite, thought Lattimer, but it's a help. After all the faces on the pages in front of him, it *was* hard to remember what the man in the hospital had actually looked like.

Him, thought Lattimer. He looks like *him*.

Right-hand page, third row from the top, second from the left. *That* man. Lattimer stared at him, front view, side view. Under the pictures was printed "Janko Velic"—and some reference numbers. Lattimer considered Velic. The police lighting flattened out the man's face, making it broader than Lattimer remembered. And the hair was different somehow. Maybe the part? Lattimer looked at the identi-kit face. But... yes... "Hey, this is him," said Lattimer.

"It's him!" he repeated, shaking Maria. "We got him! We got him!"

"Qué?" She woke groggily, fighting off Lattimer's hands shaking her shoulder.

"The man who..." English was useless. Lattimer shoved the book under Maria's nose. He started to point to Velic, then thought better of it. Don't influence her, he thought. Let her pick him out.

She did.

She jabbed her finger into Velic's face as if she could crush him, and unleashed a torrent of angry Spanish. Lattimer wondered if Joan would have been able to translate. He wagered he was now hearing some interesting phrases that Joan's high school and college Spanish courses hadn't covered.

Maria looked up at Lattimer and asked him something in Spanish. She pointed back and forth between herself, Lattimer and the photographs of Velic—looking for agreement from Lattimer.

"Yes," said Lattimer, nodding. "Me, too. He's the man who attacked me also." He grinned at Maria. "We got him," he said. "We got him."

Lattimer made a fist and gave Maria a short, light tap on the shoulder. He stuck his head outside. "Mathes," he sang out, "come on in here."

Detective Mathes was on the phone. After what seemed to Lattimer like forever, Mathes came in, looked at Velic and shrugged. The man didn't ring a bell. "First thing in the morning," promised Mathes, "which isn't too far from now—we'll pull his yellow sheet. Trace him back to his mother's knee."

"And check him against Cruz," insisted Lattimer.

"If there's anything to check," said Mathes.

"You couldn't dig up his—Velic's—record right now?" asked Lattimer. "After all this, I sure am curious—"

"Later," said Mathes. "I'm busy now. Just got a call." Mathes explained he had a body on Sutton Place, a man with his genitals cut off. A prominent businessman but apparently gay. Maybe killed by his lover. Did Lattimer want to come? Might be a story.

Lattimer said thanks but no. What he really wanted was a Xerox of Velic's picture. Mathes shrugged an okay and gave the mug shot book to another cop. Mathes returned to his phone.

The cop brought back Velic's picture for Lattimer, and also agreed to take Maria home. Lattimer wished he could go home, too. He called his newspaper and told the night editor about the Sutton Place killing. Then he allowed himself a yawn. Barney James was probably in his own bed but, as Lattimer remembered, Barney's couch wasn't too bad. He headed for the door.

As Lattimer was leaving, Detective Carl Mathes covered the receiver and called to him. "Hey, you're sure you don't want to come? This guy's apartment is full of leather stuff. Whips, chains, the works. Hell of a story."

"Thanks," said Frank Lattimer. "But the story is Janko Velic."

MONDAY

Dobbs Ferry, New York

After the attack on Paul, Joan Scully had offered Barbara Justin the use of Joan's apartment for the night. "Or at least," Joan had said, "let me ride back to Dobbs Ferry with you." But Barbara had said she was all right. She had answered the police as best she could—"No," she said, "I have no idea why anyone would want to hurt him. No, no enemies"—and then she fled, to drive back alone, to find refuge in her own home.

She found some refuge, but little rest. Half a dozen times during the night she had gotten up and looked in on the sleeping forms of her children. They were so innocent, she thought, so trusting, so fragile. Life was so fragile. On Saturday, only a few inches closer and Steve would have had a burn-scarred face—instead of the funny face he had now, a face on which eyebrows would soon grow back. But would Steve's father get *his* life back? Barbara Justin had stroked Steve's hair and then returned to her own bed but, unlike Steve and Melissa and Laurie, she was not trusting enough—not anymore—to sleep easily. Now, at 7:30 Monday morning, she dragged herself through fixing breakfast for the children. Steve, unfortunately, was alert, worried and full of questions.

"How's Dad?" he asked. He read his mother's mood. "Is he worse?"

"Later, Steve. Later," she said. She saw no reason to tell the children about the attack on their father. She could envisage no way it could become news. Perhaps later, after Paul recovered . . . if he recovered . . .

"Come on, out you go," she said, and shoved them all out of the house. The girls went to their summer play program. Steve went off to the Bedloes'. Alone, Barbara Justin stared at the kitchen phone. Her mother would be up now. Barbara hadn't talked to her since Friday night. She hadn't wanted to bother her mother in the small hours of the night, but certainly, she felt, she could call now.

She did.

"Barbara!" said Elizabeth Everett Yates, cheerful but concerned. "How nice to hear from you. And how is Paul? And how are you?"

Barbara Justin had intended to tell her mother matter-of-factly. She thought she had gotten all her crying done yesterday at supper. But as she started to talk, Barbara again burst into tears. Her hand clutched the receiver like a life preserver and she sobbed and sobbed. And her mother again offered to come to Dobbs Ferry and stay with her, but Barbara again tried to be strong and said, "No, no, not yet," and sobbed some more and ground the receiver into her tired, haggard, tear-slicked face.

New York City

At eight in the morning, Dr. Jonathan Kitteridge, the chief of neurosurgery, returned. He was tall, formal and imposing. Trailed by Dewing and Falcone and a half-dozen interns and medical students who were following him on morning rounds, he swept into intensive care like a duke surveying his duchy.

"What's this?" he asked, indicating the New York City policeman guarding the ward.

"As I started to explain," said Dewing, "an attempt was made on Dr. Justin's life last night."

"Really? By whom?"

"The police don't know. But they think he was a professional."

"A professional?" Kitteridge was wryly interested, as if learning for the first time that the killing art—like the healing art—had its professionals.

"Yes, sir," said Falcone. "He gave Nurse Abrams a ... well, it looks like a karate chop. She's home now. And they think he—the man—could try again for Dr. Justin."

"Why?" asked Kitteridge.

"Nobody knows, sir." Falcone was not about to suggest the reporter's crazy idea to the august chief of neurosurgery. "Anyway," Falcone said, "that's why the cop is here."

The group went past the policeman and clustered at Justin's bed. The intensive care nurses joined them. "Well," said Kitteridge to Dewing, "bring me up to date."

Dewing coughed. "Dr. Falcone," he said, "has been with Dr. Justin all weekend. I'll let him present the case."

"Yes," said Falcone. He tried to be all business. "It was a difficult weekend. The neurological status is unchanged. Its course has been complicated by the pneumonia that the patient developed earlier last night—pneumonia with high fever and deteriorating blood pressure."

With Justin's temperature stabilized at 100.5 degrees, they had taken him off the cooling blanket at 2 A.M. But Falcone was less confident about holding Justin's blood pressure at 100.

"Have you learned anything more from your tests?" asked Kitteridge.

"Thus far, everything is negative," said Falcone. "Negative arteriogram, negative skull films, negative tap, negative toxicology." But Falcone wondered about the drug which, the reporter claimed, Justin's attacker had been trying to administer. It was too bad they'd failed to recover any of it from the floor.

"Was he working with anything in the lab?" continued Kitteridge.

"Ordinary reagents," said Falcone. "None we can implicate." But did it mean anything, he wondered, that the attempt last night had been made with a drug?

"So," said Kitteridge. His impressive eyebrows came together. "As I see it, we have a man in deep coma, with brain not adequately controlling respiratory or circulatory systems." He shot Falcone a piercing look. "What's your differential diagnosis, Doctor?"

Dr. Joseph Falcone hesitated. "I would suggest either a massive stroke," he said, "or diffuse encephalitis." What else could he suggest? he wondered. Let somebody else advance the reporter's crazy idea that Justin was *not* in a coma.

Kitteridge considered this. Then he turned to the interns and med students. As he often did when one was present, he picked on a girl student. "Dr. Happe, what would you do next?"

Dr. Happe was a tall, earnest brunette. "Has he had an EEG or brain scan?" she asked Falcone.

"Very good," conceded Kitteridge. "Has he, Doctor?"

"Scheduled for today," said Falcone.

"What if those are normal?" persisted Kitteridge to Dr. Happe.

"The only thing left," said Happe, confidently, "would be a brain biopsy."

Kitteridge held up his right index finger. "A major step," he said, "but a necessary last thing to do." He addressed the whole group, in a summing-up tone: "This is a good case for students to think about, and I urge you to read more about the differential diagnosis of coma. Particularly read the monograph by Plumb and Posner." Several students wrote the names down. "And now," said Kitteridge, "to X-ray."

And the chief of neurosurgery led his entourage out the door.

Justin heard them leave, as he had heard everything else. Coma, he thought bitterly. I wish I were in a coma and didn't have to listen to that. He sensed that Kitteridge regarded him the way he, Justin, regarded his hamsters. "A good case," indeed!

And the words "brain biopsy" again sent chills through his feverish body.

New York City

There was a ringing. A ringing. A ringing. Frank Lattimer sent a sleepy hand searching for the alarm clock. No, that's not right, he thought. I didn't set the alarm. Did I? His hand hit something plastic—the clock—and groped around it. Right. The alarm was off. The ringing continued. It now sounded awfully like a phone. But nobody knows I'm here, he protested. Only Joan. And she knows I got to bed late. She wouldn't call so early. And it *is* early, isn't it? It feels like I just hit the pillow (and how nice, he thought, to have found Barney's bed empty last night). Lattimer opened one eye. The clock face was turned away, but, by the light, it sure looked early. He found the phone. He picked up the receiver and spoke into what he hoped was the mouthpiece and not the earpiece.

"Barney James isn't here," he slurred.

"That's fine, Lattimer. I want you."

"Who's this?" he asked.

"You mean you don't know your master's voice? Maybe you should find another one."

"Oh, hell, Knappy," said Lattimer. "Go away." Just to hold the phone in his hand was more than his battered muscles could take. Now the karate aches were really settling in. "Go away," he repeated.

"I've been calling all your known haunts for the past half hour," said Oliver Knapp, "and I'm not about to go away. You called here on Saturday and asked for information on Oakes-Metcalf, did you not?"

"I may have been so indiscreet."

"Not at all," said the newspaper's assistant city editor, mixing equal parts jocularity and asperity. "We appreciate your calling once a month to tell us how you're earning your paycheck."

"My mistake."

"Indeed. Because, if you're onto something, we'd like to know it also."

"Onto something? Hell, Knappy, I haven't had time yet to read the material Ganz sent. It's sitting at home, unopened."

"That's not what I mean," said Knapp. "I mean something more *news*worthy than Ganz's files."

"Newsworthy? All of a sudden? At—at—what time is it anyway? Six? Seven?"

"Eight-oh-eight. And it's not all of a sudden. At ten last night, Prentice's people called and—"

"Whoa. That's Prentice as in . . .?"

"As in Prentice for President. They're switching his campaign kickoff today from Washington to New York. To an outdoor announcement in front of—look, do you remember his Cancer Control Act?"

"At eight-fifteen in the morning? No."

"Well, look it up. Because his announcement is in front of the Oakes-Metcalf Institute."

"Huh?"

"And he's sharing the platform with the head of the Institute and some researcher named . . . wait . . . here it is." Knapp read, "Dr. Hugh J. Underwood."

"Jesus," said Lattimer, wide awake.

"Jesus as in Christ?" asked Knapp. "I gather that means you *do* know something. Now what is it? Who is this Underwood? What's going on? Come on, Lattimer, pretend you work here—TELL ME!"

"I don't know anything," said Lattimer.

"The hell," said Knapp.

"If I know anything, I'll call you later."

"Later will be too late. The damn thing is at one o'clock. And they're playing tight-mouthed until then. But we've got five hours. Can we break it? Do you have something we can go with? Come on, GIVE."

"According to the Geneva Convention," said Lattimer, "I only have to give you my name, rank, serial—"

Knapp saved Lattimer the trouble of doing what Lattimer was about to do himself: Knapp hung up.

Lattimer immediately dialed Joan's number.

"Hello," she said.

"Hi," he said, quickly. "Look, Underwood's going to make some kind of announce—"

"Wait," she said. "Last night. How did—?"

"Fine," he rushed. "Fine. I found our man. But—"

"That's all?" she asked. "Suddenly it doesn't matter?"

"It matters. It matters. But listen. . . . "

Lattimer quickly recounted Knapp's phone call. Joan Scully said she had no idea what was going on. "But as soon as I get in, I'll corner Hugh and ask him. And then call you."

"No you won't," said Lattimer. "I'll call you. At 10:30?"

"Fine. But why don't I call you?"

"Because I won't be here."

"Why not?"

"As long as I'm up, I might as well go buy some flowers."

"Huh?"

"Explain later," he said. "I'm rushing. Bye." He hung up, swung his feet out of bed and started to move.

"Aaagh," he yelled. He fell to the floor, clutching his left hamstring. He stood up and started limping to the bathroom. I forgot, damn it, he thought. Today I'm rushing slowly.

Lander, Colorado

Haydn's Surprise Symphony filled the bathroom with warmth and brightness. Trimming his beard in front of the mirror, Dr. Christopher Ives tried to be happy. He was up early after a restless night. He wasn't sure which was worse: helping sentence Paul Justin to death yesterday at dinnertime—or learning a few hours later that Murdoch's man in New York had failed to carry out the death sentence. "But what will we do?" Ives had cried to Murdoch. "We wait," Murdoch had said. "The hospital will be swarming with cops now. We wait a couple of days until they relax, then get another man in." Ives had nodded, confused. The whole thing made him sick. He just wanted it over with, so he wouldn't have to think about it.

And after a bad night, he was pretty much succeeding in not thinking about it. He had showered and so felt less soiled. Looking in the mirror now, he didn't see the face of a person who *looked* bad. He was awash in sunlight and fresh morning air, and music from the one Denver station that sometimes played classical. As the andante movement came to its "surprise", Christopher Ives even tried humming it, "Ta-ta-ta-ta-ta-TUM."

The concerto ended. The seven o'clock news came on. The announcer talked about wheat prices and the threatened strike of city firemen and the crash of a light plane near Leadville. "Now," said the announcer, "turning to the national news. The presidential season begins in earnest today in New York City, where Governor Arthur Prentice of Indiana will announce his candidacy . . . "

Ives had been only half listening. But, at the next words—"in a speech and rally outside the famed Oakes-Metcalf Institute"— Ives's fingers convulsed on the scissors. He sliced off more hair than he meant to.

He spun his head to the radio. "Speculation is," continued the announcer, "Prentice will link his candidacy to the eradication of the disease. And, in Pittsburgh, U.S. Steel announced a price hike of . . . "

But Ives didn't hear the rest. All right, he told himself, don't overreact. It doesn't mean anything. Doesn't mean anything. But then why—objected the part of his mind that was upset—why in front of Oakes-Metcalf? Why not Sloan-Kettering, which was even more famous? Or why not the National Cancer Institute in Washington? Or someplace back home in Indiana? God knows, Prentice must have made sure that some hospital or university *there* got funds from his Cancer Control Act.

Why, demanded Ives, why at Justin's place?

In a sick panic, he got dressed. The news ended, the classical music—Vivaldi now—continued. But Ives was right back in the awful feeling of last night. He left his room and knocked on Murdoch's door. The ex-FBI man opened it. First thing in the morning, with an old bathrobe wrapped half around his hulking body, Murdoch looked even droopier, more cadaverous than ever. He stared bleary-eyed at Ives, silently rebuking Ives for waking him up.

Ives ignored the rebuke. He told Murdoch the news. Murdoch shrugged it off. "Coincidence," said Murdoch.

"But the file," insisted Ives. "Justin's file—that Cruz couldn't find. You don't suppose Prentice—"

"Jeez-us," said Murdoch. "You really are in a bad way. Look at you." He pointed. "You're shaking."

Ives looked at his hands. They were trembling. "All right, Ed," he agreed, "all right. So I'm scared. So maybe I should be. What if we're not the only ones with the cure? What if they catch your man in New York? What if they come here after us? What—"

"SHUT UP!" thundered Murdoch. He sighed. "Jesus," he said, more softly. "I don't know how to answer you. In the first place, my man is out of New York. He caught a plane out last night and he'll be here by noon. In the second place—"

"Here?" asked Ives.

"Yeah. With all our pigeons arriving tomorrow, we're going to need better security. He'll be in charge of it."

"A thug? A hired killer? Here?"

"Who do you think all our people here *already*—who do you think *they* are? Social workers? Where do you think I found all these guys we put these nice white lab coats on? Huh?"

Ives backed away, holding up his hands. "All right. All right. I don't want to know."

Murdoch smiled. "Yeah," he said, satisfied. *"Don't* know. You stay in your room, Doc, and read your technical journals. Don't listen to any upsetting news on the radio. Don't look at anybody walking the halls. Just collect your share of a billion plus."

Ives turned away so he wouldn't have to see Murdoch's ugly, mocking face. Okay, he told himself. I'll stay in my room today. But he knew he was too nervous to read. He knew he'd have to listen to the radio.

"A carnation," said Frank Lattimer. "A carnation for my buttonhole. If I had a buttonhole."

"Red or white?" asked the salesgirl, amused.

"You decide," he said.

Lattimer wasn't wearing a jacket—just the shirt and slacks he'd put on yesterday afternoon for the picnic supper. And they were a bit wrinkled after going through a fight and then a night at police headquarters. But Lattimer also wore his most charming smile. So the girl responded.

"Red," she said, reaching for a carnation.

Lattimer pointed at his face. "To match my bloodshot eyes?" he joked.

The girl laughed. She handed him the flower. He stuck it in his shirt pocket and handed her the money.

"Is there anything else?" she asked.

"Uh, yes," said Lattimer, "as a matter of fact. You see, I'm Frank Lattimer ... the reporter ... I called you yesterday about what happened on the subway...."

The girl stiffened.

"You are Teresa Vitiello, aren't you?" asked Lattimer. He was sure he recognized her voice from his phone call.

"Yes," she admitted.

"Well, I'm really sorry to bother you but—"

"I told you—I didn't see anything." Vitiello had backed up against the glass case of flowers.

"Yes," said Lattimer, pleasantly, "but you did say you were closest to ... to the man ... and I have a photograph which I wonder if you ... "

"A photograph?" She was curious.

"Yes."

She changed her mind. "No," she said.

Lattimer grinned. "Don't you think they're bloodshot?" he asked.

"What?"

"My eyes."

Vitiello looked more closely. "Yes. I guess so. Why?"

"I got them staying up all night finding this photograph," said Lattimer. "I think it's a photograph of someone you may have seen in the subway. Could you please look and tell me? Otherwise I'll have to stay up all night tonight checking more photographs. And tomorrow no amount of flowers will make up for how I look."

The girl smiled. "You're too much," she said, softening a bit.

"Yes," said Lattimer. He dug a photograph out of his pants pocket and laid it on top of the counter, facing Vitiello. The girl bent down toward it carefully, as if it might bite.

"No," she said. "I never saw him." She smiled easily. "See," she said, "you were wrong." Now she was relaxed.

"I guess so," said Lattimer. He dug out another photograph and laid it on top of the first.

The girl bit her lip.

Lattimer waited.

The girl picked up the police photograph of Janko Velic. Lattimer had cropped off the numbers across Velic's chest, so it now simply looked like a bad four-shots-for-fifty-cents photo. Lattimer waited.

"It was dark," she said. "And crowded. But I think—I think, yes."

Lattimer waited.

"He was standing next to me. And there was a man ... another man ... in front of us. And then the train came ... and the man in front of me ... sort of ... dived." The girl shook her head, trying to shake away the memory. "And I think I screamed and the man next to me—" She tapped the photograph. "He was gone." She trembled.

Lattimer touched the girl's hand, gently and briefly. He gathered up the photograph of Janko Velic. And the photograph of Barney James's father, which he'd found in Barney's bureau. Then he purchased one perfect rose and gave it to Teresa Vitiello.

He left the Gem Flower Shop. From the phone booth on the corner, he called Detective Carl Mathes.

"I have some interesting news for you," began Lattimer.

"Just what I was going to say," said Mathes.

"Oh?"

"No, it's your dime," said Mathes. "You first."

"A witness to Cruz's death just identified Janko Velic as being directly behind Cruz on the subway platform."

"Goddamn," said Mathes.

"You bet," said Lattimer.

"How?"

Lattimer explained he'd gotten Vitiello's name and had just shown her a photo. Mathes chewed out Lattimer for butting into police business. Mathes said that now maybe he shouldn't tell Lattimer what he, Mathes, had discovered.

"Aw, sure you will," said Lattimer.

"Well," said Mathes, grudgingly, "we got two things, actually. First of all, Velic. An interesting yellow sheet. Several murder arrests, no convictions. And I've checked around—this Velic seems to be a hired killer. But very careful, doesn't get caught."

"That's one," said Lattimer. "What's two?"

"Two," said Mathes. "Two is we just got the report from the FBI you were screaming for. Cruz's fingerprints belong to somebody else."

"Somebody named Morales? Somebody named Santiago?"

"Nope. All aliases. Our boy's real name is—was—Cristobal Rivera. And he's got a record even longer than Velic."

"For what?"

"You want it, you got it," said Mathes. "Numbers, drugs, strong-arm, the works."

"Any previous connection between him and Velic?" asked Lattimer.

"None. Rivera was strictly small time. Velic's a pro."

"But," persisted Lattimer, "somebody must know both of them. Know them well enough to hire both of them."

"Aw, come off it, Lattimer. You and your cockamamy theory that—"

"So who *would* know them both?"

"Could be a *lot* of people," said Mathes. "Checking it will take time."

"And I assume you are checking?" asked Lattimer calmly.

"I can assure the gentleman of the press that we are."

"Starting with?"

"Starting with their arrest records," said Mathes. "As you said, it's all we have in front of us right now. Once we eliminate the obvious—"

"—you can tackle the difficult," said Lattimer. "Like any good reporter would," he added.

"I won't deign to answer that," said Mathes.

"I'll keep in touch," said Lattimer. And he hung up and hailed a passing cab. "Public library," he said. "Forty-second Street." It was 9:05. He hoped that the library had survived the city's budget crunch and was open this early.

New York City

Every morning, the virology section of the Oakes-Metcalf Institute was supposed to spend the first hour checking and feeding its supply of cells. But this morning, nobody was doing that. Instead, the section was convulsed as the researchers shared the incredible facts and rumors they had learned since they left work on Friday: that, Friday evening, Roberto Cruz had been killed by a subway train; that, last night, someone had tried to kill Paul Justin; and that, this noon, Senator Arthur Prentice and Dr. Hugh Underwood would make some kind of announcement in front of the Institute.

Wojik, Crawford, Holmes and Beauchamp told each other what they knew. Joan Scully said nothing; she didn't know where to begin. And she was waiting for Underwood. She and Lattimer hadn't discussed it on the phone, but she had a horrible premonition of exactly what Underwood was up to. And the enormity of it left her speechless. She secluded herself in the sterile room. She fussed with the petri dishes.

At 9:30—a half hour behind his usual punctual start—Hugh Underwood came into the section. With him was Warren Brown. The researchers were doubly surprised: the head of the Institute rarely came down from his top floor office. And their section head, normally so calm, looked very ill at ease. He even seemed to drag his bad leg more than usual. Joan Scully compared him to how she had last seen him, on the beach on Fire Island on Saturday night. She wondered if he had made it to his home in time to see his wife balling the two young men. But she guessed Underwood wasn't half as shaken by what had happened this weekend as by what he was about to do.

Her guess was correct.

Warren Brown started it off. In warm, syrupy words he reviewed the "great accomplishments" of the section. The "wise leadership" of Hugh Underwood and the "noteworthy contributions" of Paul Justin, who had now, "lamentably, been stricken while so young." To Joan, it sounded like Brown was rehearsing for a larger audience. Brown brushed over the "rumor" (he called it) of "a crazy man breaking into Paul's ward last night" and didn't even mention Roberto Cruz. Apparently, thought Joan, lab assistants were like the pipettes they washed—cheap and replaceable.

Then Brown started to get to the point. He discussed Paul's "determined research of the 'C' particle theory, under Hugh's wise tutelage." At this, Stefan Wojik shot a look at Underwood. The section head wouldn't meet his eyes. Brown talked about "Hugh's commendable modesty" in not wanting to trumpet his and Paul's progress. And then Brown switched to economics. They all knew, he said, about the squeeze on the Institute, about the threatened cutback of federal money. "We are not certain," said Brown, "that we will be able to maintain the staff of this section at the level we would like to."

Crawford, Holmes and Beauchamp looked worried.

"But, happily," said Brown, "events have worked together to bring us a solution." He cited the fact that Underwood and Justin's "C" particle research had been carried on under a grant from the Cancer Control Act—

"What?" demanded Wojik. "That is not—"

But Brown ignored him and sailed smoothly on. " . . . Cancer

Control Act made possible by the foresight of Senator Arthur Prentice, and now that their research has indeed identified the 'C' particle, I am certain that—"

"Identified?" burbled Crawford.

"Hugh!" stormed Wojik. "Is any of this true? You never believed in the 'C' particle. You never—"

Underwood looked up from the floor, which until now, Joan observed, he must have found intensely fascinating.

"We did the research together, Stefan," he said, in a small voice. "After hours. Outside regular work. He consulted me."

"That can't be," began Wojik. "Paul kept his own notes. He put them"—Wojik pointed to the file cabinet—"under lock and key in there. Where is *your* proof?"

"I kept a separate copy," said Underwood. "And now that Paul is . . . is sick . . . I must carry on alone."

"You *didn't* work with him," Wojik insisted.

"I did," said Underwood.

"You—!" Wojik's voice was rising higher, his Czech accent growing even thicker. The other researchers stared at him. The tension in the lab was at a breaking point.

Warren Brown softly stepped between the two men. He laid a hand on Wojik's shoulder. "Dr. Wojik," he said, "I understand your desire for fairness to Paul. But, now, you must also be fair to your section head. Can you offer any *proof* that he did not direct Paul's work?"

Ah, thought Joan. Brown was too clever by half. He had confronted Wojik—and all of them—with a researcher's most difficult problem: trying to prove a negative.

Wojik shrugged off Brown's hand. "It's a lie," he said. He looked around the room, at all his colleagues. "And we all know it." He looked for agreement.

But Holmes and Beauchamp were too junior to go against Brown and Underwood. And Crawford was too political. And Joan—when Wojik's eyes met hers, she knew this was not the time or place to take a stand. When Frank has dug to the bottom of this and has the proof, *then* we'll throw it in their faces. But not prematurely, not now.

She looked sadly at Wojik—and looked away.

"Then I resign," said Wojik simply.

Brown nodded, as if he had expected it. "All right," he said, "and will you—"

"Don't worry," snapped Wojik. "I'm not going to destroy myself or this Institute—which I value more than *you* apparently do—by making a public"—he waved his arm—"public spectacle over this. Not *now*, anyway," he warned.

"Very well," said Brown. He turned to the rest of them, as if

Wojik no longer existed. "Now I'd like to discuss what will happen this noontime. To begin with—"

But Crawford couldn't wait. He crowded in on Underwood. "The 'C' particle, Hugh? You really found it? You did?"

"Yes," said Underwood, modestly. "And—"

Crawford seized his hand and pumped it. "My God, man. That's great! That's fantastic! I knew you'd do it!" He stopped—and flung out his arms. "And the programming? To shut it off? How far away?"

"A year, perhaps," said Underwood. "Perhaps less."

"Jee-sus!" cried Crawford. He grabbed Underwood's hand again. "Sir," he said, "this is a great moment. This is a privilege. This is—"

And Holmes and Beauchamp moved in so they too could share in the moment. Warren Brown beamed at the scene. Joan looked at Stefan Wojik. He was off in a corner, already clearing out his desk. Joan pushed past the knot of happy, congratulatory researchers. In the clean, antiseptic lab, she felt suddenly soiled.

I've got to get some fresh air, she thought, going out the door.

On her way down the hall, she stopped off in the animal room to look at Wilbur. The hamster labeled "Justin AX532-06" was sleeping peacefully in his cage. He still looked in good shape. In better shape than I'm in, thought Joan Scully.

New York City

It was amazing, thought Frank Lattimer, the things you could find in the New York Public Library. Once, doing a story on a local developer who was trying to build a high-rise in the face of violent opposition from neighborhood groups, Lattimer had stumbled on—in a dusty cardboard file box, on a bottom shelf, in a little alcove—the developer's unpublished master's thesis (written twenty-five years before, when the developer was still idealistic), detailing and attacking the same loopholes in the zoning code he was now hoping to slip through. Which, when Lattimer published it, helped scuttle the project. Ever since then, Lattimer had had a great fondness for the library. And although the material he was examining this morning in the reading room had been a lot easier to find, he hoped it would be as valuable.

So far, it had given him two names. The thick *Guide to U.S. Foundations and Eleemosynary Institutions* told him that the Endicott Foundation—which Underwood had said had funded the virology section—was 100 percent funded by the Dacey Pharmaceutical Company of Kansas City, Missouri. And Dacey's current annual report told him that Dacey's director of research—who, Lattimer figured, would pass on such grants—was one Christopher Wren Ives, Ph.D.

The current annual report also reminded Lattimer of something he knew: Dacey was the company about to go under because of that vaccine it had made that gave kids polio. Interesting, thought Lattimer, but does it mean anything? It did explain why there were no pictures of company officers in the current annual report—they didn't dare show their faces. To find a picture of Christopher Ives, Lattimer had to go back to a report before the polio scandal. There was Ives, looking up from a microscope. Intelligent, roly-poly, a self-satisfied smile peeking out from under his beard.

Okay, thought Lattimer. He Xeroxed the photograph of Ives. He returned the materials to the desk and walked out of the high, sunlit reading room, nearly empty first thing in the morning. It was 10:10. He went downstairs and started making phone calls.

The first was to Tom Munro, at IBM in Armonk.

"Yeah, I just got it developed," said Munro. "The Biology Department says it's three pictures—successive enlargements—of a muscle cell of a Syrian hamster."

"IBM has a biology department?" asked Lattimer. "Why?"

"We've got everything," said Munro. "They tell me they're trying to build a computer memory out of amino acids."

"Frankenstein," said Lattimer. "But the main thing is—is that cell normal?"

"Normal? Oh, sure. If your hamster hadn't been sacrificed, he'd be scampering around now."

"Thanks, Tom."

"Anytime."

His next call was to Dacey Pharmaceutical in Kansas City.

"Dr. Ives's office," said a secretary.

"Dr. Ives, please," asked Lattimer.

"He's not in, sir."

"Oh. Will he be in later?"

"Who may I say is calling?"

Lattimer identified himself and his newspaper. He explained he was checking out a lead that said Dacey was developing a breakthrough cardiac drug. When the secretary spoke again, he sensed she had tightened up. On the one hand, Dacey had already had enough newspaper coverage, thank you. On the other hand, she had probably been told to be nice to the press.

"Well, sir," she said, "he's on vacation."

"Oh," said Lattimer, "when will he be back?"

"I don't know, sir."

"Did he say where he was going?"

"No, sir, he didn't."

"Oh," said Lattimer, trying to keep it light. "Isn't that unusual? I mean, wouldn't he tell you? And wouldn't he take a definite amount of time? One week? Two?"

"I'm sorry. He didn't say."

"Hmm. Well, when did he leave?"

"Last Monday." The secretary was becoming cool.

"You mean he was gone all last week?"

"No, he was in on Monday morning but then he left."

"Isn't that unusual?" asked Lattimer. "Most people would leave on a Friday."

"Sir," said the secretary, now definitely cold, "I simply don't know."

"Well," asked Lattimer casually, "how about his home number? Could I try him there?"

"I'm sorry, but I can't give you that. Would you care to speak to someone else in research? Perhaps Dr. Burroughs?"

Lattimer consulted his watch. It was 10:25. "No, thank you," he said. He hung up.

Immediately, he called Kansas City information and, to his surprise, learned that Christopher Ives's home phone number was listed. He dialed the number.

A woman answered and Lattimer again identified himself. He said he was doing a story on a new cardiac drug and was looking for Dr. Ives.

"Well, I wish I knew," said the woman, forcing a laugh. "He just said he was going away on business."

"You are . . . ?"

"Mrs. Ives."

The woman sounded sad and Lattimer sensed an opportunity. Without seeming to invade her privacy, he expressed sympathy that her husband was away and, apparently, hadn't called. "Is that correct, Mrs. Ives?" he ventured. "He hasn't called you?"

"I'm afraid so," she said. "The phone keeps ringing but it's only Katherine. She calls two, three times a day, collect."

"Katherine?"

"Our daughter. She's in between her freshman and sophomore years at Ann Arbor. So she's traveling all around the country this summer. On her own. Trying to push herself out of the nest. But, poor thing, she's so lonely, she keeps calling home for cheering up."

Lattimer had the image of the two lonely Ives women talking to each other.

"But Dr. Ives hasn't called?" repeated Lattimer. "Hasn't said where he is?"

"Not a word from him in a week," said Mrs. Ives. "Very unlike Christopher."

Lattimer expressed more sympathy and hung up. It was 10:30.

He called Oakes-Metcalf. The phone rang for a long time without an answer. Lattimer figured the preparations for Prentice's announcement had the switchboard busy. When the operator finally did answer, she told Lattimer all the lines to Virology were busy. Lattimer waited some more. Finally, he got Joan Scully.

"Frank, you won't believe this," she began—quickly, intensely and very angrily—"but Underwood has the goddamn nerve to claim credit for Paul's discovery."

"Then there *is* a discovery?" asked Lattimer.

She told him what Underwood and Brown had told the virology section. "The son of a bitch," swore Lattimer. "Did you call him on it?"

"Well, all of us know he didn't work with Paul—if that's what you mean."

"No, I mean call him on it: Tell him and the staff you know he and Cruz stole Paul's notes and then had Paul knocked out."

"But, Frank," said Joan, "we *don't* know he did that." She hesitated, groped to make sense of it. "Personally, I can't believe that Hugh would—"

"Maybe, maybe not," said Lattimer. "At the very least we know he's stealing Paul's work and for that I'm going to crucify him. Where is he?"

"Now? I don't know—he went out with Brown."

"Brown's office, then?"

"I don't know."

"Well, I'm going to find out. Can you get me transferred to Brown?"

"I'll try."

"Okay. I'll call you later." Frank Lattimer stayed on the phone as Joan Scully tried to raise the Institute switchboard.

Houston, Texas

The bedroom of the Presidential Suite of the Loring Memorial Hospital was quiet. After Nurse Crippen had given Ash his nine o'clock shot of morphine, Trumbull had come in and asked her to leave. Nor would Trumbull let Virginia Ash or Del Erskine watch. Unlike his faith healings on television, this was a matter between Trumbull and Matt Ash alone.

Trumbull sat silent by the side of the bed. Twenty minutes passed. Finally the old man in the bed spoke.

"What do you want, preacher?" he asked quietly. The pain in his gut was now a dull, faraway ache. He felt peaceful.

"Whatever you want," replied Trumbull.

"You want me to confess my sins?"

"Do you?" asked Trumbull.

"Well, Ah've *thought* about 'em," admitted Ash. "Thought about Betty Sue anyway. Ah believe that, sometime durin' las' night, Ah may even have apologized to her." He turned and smiled at Trumbull. "That what you want?"

"What do you want?"

"Shit," said Ash. "Ah want to get the hell out of this funeral parlor. Either die or get well. One or t'other. Not this. Lousy pain."

"Well, it's your choice."

"Simple as that, huh?"

"Simple as that."

"You really think ma bad, bad life has caused ma cancer?"

"Yes."

"Don't any good people get cancer?" Ash asked slyly. "Innocent l'il five-year-old chile with leukemia?"

"Sure. But you're not him."

"Shit. You don't give a fella a break."

"You don't give yourself a break."

"Hell, Ah 'pologized to Betty Sue. You wan' me to ask her forgiveness, too?" Ash demanded.

"She's dead. She can't forgive you."

"Well—what, then?"

"You know what."

"Ask God to forgive me?"

"Yes," said Trumbull.

Ash sighed. "Ah knew we'd come around to this."

Trumbull said nothing.

"Hell," said Ash. "Man in a white beard up in the clouds? Ah don't believe it."

Trumbull said nothing.

"Don't you understand?" asked Ash. "How *could* he be there an' let things happen? Let five-year-old chillun die of leukemia? Let ma mamma die of pneumonia? Let ma poppa run away?"

Trumbull leaned forward slightly. "We can't understand God, Matt. We can't know His purposes. We can only love Him. And turn to Him."

"Ah *did* turn to Him," insisted Ash. "When I lost ma mamma and poppa. And he gave me nothin'."

"He gave you an uncle who loved you."

"Aw, shit."

"Didn't he?"

"Yes—but—but it wasn't what Ah wanted. Ah wanted *them*."

"God doesn't always give us what we want. But He gives us something."

"Ha!" laughed Ash. "Then how do you know he'll give me a healthy body again? Huh? Huh? Got you there."

"I don't know that He'll take away your pain in *this* life," said Trumbull. "Although I *have* seen Him do it. Before my eyes. But I *do* know He'll take it away in the next."

"Huh?"

"If you die of this cancer, Matt," said Trumbull, "you'll die fairly soon. Only a few months of this pain. And *it* will be over. A few months. You can bear that. But *eternity*, Matt. Think about an eternity of this pain, or worse."

Ash looked blank.

"Eternity in hell," said Trumbull softly, "eternity burning in hell because you rejected God today."

Ash struggled. "There isn't any hell, any—" he tried to say.

"Do you know that for sure?" asked Trumbull sharply. "Do you know that so sure that you'd sink all your money into it, put all your—what is it?—half-billion dollars drilling *that* hole?"

Ash said nothing.

"Could be a dry hole," said Trumbull.

Ash swallowed.

"All right!" Ash yelled. "Ah ask His forgiveness."

Trumbull listened.

"Forgive me. All right? Forgive me!" Ash was shouting at the ceiling. "Ah'm sorry for all Ah did. Ah regret it. Ah don't want it. Ah'm sorry, do you hear me?" Ash shot a glance at Trumbull.

"I don't buy it," said Trumbull.

"What the hell do you *want*?" sobbed Ash.

"The truth," said Trumbull. "Not an act. 'For the Lord seeth not as man seeth; for man looketh on the outward appearance, but the Lord looketh on the heart.' And your heart doesn't believe."

"It *wants* to believe," shouted Ash.

"Why?" asked Trumbull softly.

Ash sputtered. "Why? Why—to be healed. My body. Or—or—if Ah can't have that, to go to heaven. Like you said."

"No dice," said Trumbull. "God doesn't make bargains. You can't say you believe in God for five minutes this morning and think He'll give you eternity in return. No. I said to you yesterday, I'm not here to sell you God or Christ. I'm here to sell you yourself."

"How?" demanded Ash.

"Ask His forgiveness and nothing else," said Trumbull. "Forgiveness for its own sake. Forgiveness for your sins. Forgiveness so you can have your own self back—the innocent child you once were. So you can be that child again, be reborn again—so you can be that child *now*—whether or not you still die of cancer, whether or not you lapse tomorrow and still go to hell."

Ash looked hard at his bedside visitor.

"For a man who promises to heal people, you drive a tough bargain, preacher."

"No tougher than the ones you've driven, oilman."

Ash turned his eyes again to the ceiling. His right hand groped for Trumbull's. Trumbull held it.

Matt Ash spoke again. This time the swearing, the objections, the shouting and the bargaining were gone. In their place was the simple voice of a child who had once believed, and still remembered how to say, "The Lord is ma shepherd; Ah shall not want. He maketh me to lie down in green pastures; he leadeth me beside the still waters. He restoreth ma soul; he leadeth me in the paths of righteousness . . . "

Trumbull heard him out. And as the Psalm continued, he heard remembered belief become present belief. And when Ash came to the end, Trumbull joined in, saying with him, " . . . dwell in the house of the Lord forever."

"Amen," said Matt Ash. "Lord," he said, in the same simple voice, "forgive me."

"Amen," said Richard Trumbull. He moved his head into Ash's field of vision. "Matt, do you take Jesus Christ, the son of God, as your Savior?"

"Ah do."

"Then, as Christ said, 'Rejoice with me; for I have found my sheep which was lost.' " Trumbull laid his left hand—Ash still gripped his right—on Ash's stomach, just above the protruding tube. "And as Christ healed the sick so I ask Him to act through me, unworthy instrument, and heal this man. Lord"—Trumbull raised his eyes— "we ask your forgiveness of your servant Matt Ash, for the sins of his soul which are visited on his body. And if it be your will, make his body whole again so he may live out his years in praise of you. Lord, we ask that this tube be removed and that Matt Ash be fed instead with the grace of God. For 'He shall feed his flock like a shepherd; He shall gather the lambs with his arm.' "

Trumbull paused. "In Christ's name," he said, "let it be done. Let him be healed."

Trumbull snatched his right hand out of Ash's grasp. He pressed both hands against Ash, one on either side of his stomach. "Healed!" cried Trumbull, in his rich, rolling baritone. "Healed!"

"Healed!" repeated Matt Ash.

"Healed!" cried Trumbull. His face gleamed with joy. He flung his hands in the air. "And you *will* be!"

"Yes!" cried Ash, trying to sit up. "Ah feel it! Ah feel it!"

"Praise God!" cried Trumbull. "Virginia!" he yelled, even louder. "Del! Mrs. Crippen! Come in and see what the Lord has wrought!"

The door flew open and Virginia rushed in. Sobbing, joyful, choking incoherent words, she flung herself on her husband. "Matt... Matt," she said. Nurse Crippen and Del Erskine followed her in. Crippen looked skeptical but pleased for the old man. Erskine was, as usual, professionally impressed with Trumbull.

"Ah believe!" Ash was crying. "Ah believe in God! And He has healed me! Praise God! Praise Him! Praise you, Reverend!"

"Yes," cried Virginia, spinning around and enveloping Trumbull in a huge, fleshy embrace. "Yes, Reverend, yes!"

Over her shoulder, Trumbull's eyes glared and pleaded with Erskine. Three days, his eyes were saying, three days without a drink. But now I've done it, so now you've got to let me have a drink.

And Erskine's eyes shot back: No. Not done yet. You've got to stay around and put the touch on her. So stay drunk on *Jesus*, Reverend. Drunk on J. C., not J & B.

New York City

Dr. Warren Brown's secretary swore on the phone that neither Brown nor Underwood was in Brown's office. "I really don't know where they are," she said. "I sure *wish* I did." To Lattimer's ear, she sounded honestly distraught. He imagined her receiving dozens of phone calls asking about the one o'clock announcement—from the media, from politicians, from Institute staff and trustees—and wishing Brown were there to help.

Lattimer called his newspaper. He got someone in the city room and, without identifying himself (he didn't have time for questions), Lattimer asked where Prentice was staying. The Waldorf, he was told. Lattimer called there. The Waldorf kept him hanging on the line five minutes. They switched him around for another ten. Finally he got Prentice's assistant press secretary. He also swore that Underwood wasn't there—nor did he know where he was. "Don't lie to me, Ben," warned Lattimer. "Lie to you, Frank?" said the man. "They don't *tell* me enough around here so I even *could* lie to you."

Lattimer called Underwood's apartment in Manhattan. He got busy signals for ten minutes before he got through. Mrs. Underwood answered. Yes, she said, she remembered him from Saturday night. (Lattimer grinned at the memory.) No, she had no idea where her husband was. Just that she was about to be picked up by Prentice's people and taken to the Institute, to be with her husband for the announcement. There was so much Lattimer wanted to ask her—mainly what had her husband told her about "his discovery"—but that seemed less important than getting hold of Dr. Underwood. "I have no *idea*," she wailed. "Ever since he went sailing with that man Wozinsky yesterday, it's just been *craziness*."

Wozinsky, thought Lattimer. He knew who Wozinsky was. He called Wozinsky's law firm on Park Avenue. Wozinsky's secretary said Mr. Wozinsky was busy and couldn't come to the phone. "Well," asked Lattimer, "could I speak with Dr. Underwood?" The secretary answered, "Mr. Wozinsky is busy *with* Dr. Underwood."

Ha! thought Lattimer. He hung up the pay phone in the public library—which, he figured, he'd been stuck to for the past hour and a quarter—and ran, leg still aching, for the street.

Forty-second Street shimmered with heat waves and with the exhaust from buses. The day was becoming another scorcher. Lattimer hailed a cab and urged it through the molasses-slow traffic, thickening now near noontime—urged it up to Park and Fifty-third. He got out at the glass and concrete tower and took the elevator to the thirty-sixth floor, to the offices of Palmer, DeWitt, Wozinsky and Houk.

He asked the receptionist to check with Wozinsky's secretary. "Yes," the receptionist told him, "Mr. Wozinsky, Dr. Brown and Dr. Underwood are still here. Who may I say is calling?"

"It doesn't matter," said Lattimer. "I'll wait for them out here."

The receptionist looked at him as if he might be one of New York City's crazies. And Lattimer knew he was being very unprofessional. But he didn't want them to know he was here. He wanted to confront them all with the truth—they had to pass him to get to the elevators—and hope that, taken off guard, Underwood would crack and confess. Lattimer realized it wasn't just the story that he wanted—there were other, perhaps better, ways of getting the story. No, he wanted some visible revenge for what Underwood had done to Paul Justin.

The clock above the receptionist's desk read noon. Lattimer realized that, back at his newspaper, Knapp would be growing increasingly angry at being unable to get a lead on the Prentice announcement an hour from now. Lattimer sympathized with his editor. And, at the moment, Lattimer wasn't doing anything except waiting. He might as well call. Palmer, DeWitt, Wozinsky and Houk had thoughtfully provided a phone in the reception area. Lattimer used it.

"Ganz?" said Lattimer. "Listen, get me Knapp. Tell him I *do* know something about Underwood."

Lattimer heard Ganz yell, "Oliver! On three!" Then Ganz said to Lattimer, "And the police want *you*. A detective Mathes called ten minutes ago. Says he's got something. Frank, is this the meat company thing?"

"Mathes has something new?" asked Lattimer, excited.

"Ah, Lattimer," said Oliver Knapp, coming on the line. "You do have something for your humble employer after all?"

"Later, Knappy," said Frank Lattimer. He hung up. He dialed Mathes's number.

"Okay, Carl," he said, trying to hold down his excitement. "What is it?"

"I can't tell you on the phone," said Mathes.

Lattimer said nothing, hoping Mathes would say more.

"Let's just say," added Mathes, "that I don't necessarily think it's cockamamy anymore. I suggest we meet. Now."

"An hour from now?" asked Lattimer.

"Fifteen minutes from now. No more. I'll be in the Deep Blue Oyster Bar." And Mathes hung up.

Frank Lattimer got to his feet. He dashed—limped—to the elevator. As he passed the receptionist, he noticed she was staring at him. Lattimer realized he still had a carnation sticking out of his shirt pocket. He took it out and, with a bow, handed it to the receptionist. Now she didn't wonder if he was crazy. Now she was convinced.

Houston, Texas

The last two times Ray Ryker had seen Harry Wissenbach—on the barbed-wire hunt and then last night at the River Oaks Club—their business discussions had been colored by the casualness of their surroundings. But this morning, at Wissenbach's bank, it was all business.

Wissenbach led Ryker down into the air-conditioned hush of the safe deposit vaults. He stood by as the safe deposit officer turned one key in Ryker's box and Ryker turned his own. The officer slid out the box and carried it to a cubicle. Ryker followed on his heels. He was impatient. He had set in motion the wheels that would shortly make him $18 million poorer. The sooner it was over, the sooner the pain would be over, too. Already this morning Ryker's broker had informed him he'd managed to sell all of Ryker's municipal bonds and common stock. "Even made an extra thousand or so on your IBM—caught it up an eighth," he'd boasted. "Swell," Ryker had said dryly. He was gaining pin money and losing a fortune. And since Ryker's accountants had also informed him this morning that they had no idea who had been digging into his finances, Ryker had no idea who was about to *gain* this fortune.

Ryker now took the bonds out of his safe deposit box and stuffed them in his small suitcase, along with the stock certificates he'd brought from his office. Wissenbach and the safe deposit officer hovered at a discreet distance, to give Ryker privacy. But even if they had been crowding over his shoulder, they would have seen only more papers—deeds, tax returns, insurance policies. There were no old photos, no old love letters. Ray Ryker led a sparse, unsentimental life.

He snapped the box shut. The officer slid it back into the vault. The two men turned their respective keys. Ryker plunged ahead to the elevator, followed by Wissenbach. Back up on the main banking floor, Ryker tossed the suitcase into the waiting arms of the private guard he had hired that morning. The guard set off for Ryker's broker with paper worth $14.8 million. Ryker went into Wissenbach's office to dispose of the other $3.2 million.

"Slocum Double-Plate Lock Link," said Wissenbach proudly, pointing to the newly mounted strand of barbed wire prominently displayed on the wall behind his big swivel chair. "An' the fella that almost stopped us from gettin' it."

Ryker didn't understand. He looked more closely. On the same piece of wood as the barbed wire, Wissenbach had also had the rattlesnake's tail mounted.

"Swell," said Ryker, dryly. He was in no mood for other people's pride. He snapped open his thin attaché case—which he'd also been carrying with him all morning—and put its contents on Wissenbach's desk in two piles.

"Three certified checks totalling $1.7 million," said Ryker, referring to one pile. (He'd collected the checks this morning—the proceeds of selling all of his OFI stock to the other partners.) "And my shares of Climatron," he added, referring to the other pile. "And a letter of agreement for the sale."

Wissenbach read the letter. He passed another certified check to Ryker. It was for $1.5 million, for Climatron. Ryker inspected it and passed it back.

"Ah guess we're all set," said Wissenbach.

"You'll deposit those four checks," said Ryker.

"Yup."

"And you'll be receiving another deposit from my broker by the end of the day."

Wissenbach looked up, cagily. "Really clearing out, huh, Ray? Really gonna put together enough for Texahoma?"

"Who said I was buying Texahoma?" said Ryker, coolly, and

started out the door. It was intended as a good exit line—to bring Wissenbach up short.

But Wissenbach topped it. "Well, then," joked the banker, "it isn't going to pay for havin' the Reverend Trumbull cure the old man, is it?"

"What?"

"Trumbull. The cancer healer. The guy Virginia called in."

"Called in where?"

"Over at the hospital," said Wissenbach. "He's been there since yesterday afternoon." Wissenbach eyed Ryker. "Hell, man, didn't you know?"

"Of course," snapped Ryker, a quick lie. Inside, he was raging. For all the money he spent, his people simply *didn't keep him informed*. And with no information, there was no control. And with no control . . . Ryker stormed out of Wissenbach's office.

New York City

"How are the Little Necks?" asked Mathes.

"Fine," said Lattimer. He had barely touched them. His stomach was still trying to recover from last night. "How are the cherrystones?"

"I've had better," said Mathes.

"Well . . . " said Lattimer.

"Well . . . " said Mathes.

The two men were in a booth in the back of the restaurant, a block from police headquarters.

"Well," said Lattimer, "why am I here? What couldn't you tell me on the phone? What couldn't wait an hour?"

Mathes pushed his clams away and spooned horseradish sauce onto oyster crackers. He ate one after another that way, downing beer in between. Finally, he said, "When I get back from lunch, I'm going to find my boss, Captain Barnwell, looking for me." Mathes ate more crackers with horseradish. "And Captain Barnwell is going to tell me, officially, that there will be no more sharing of information on this case with a certain member of the press."

"But why?" asked Lattimer. "And how's he going to make it stick? I think that when Whitcomb—"

"Whitcomb nothing," said Mathes. "It has come to the attention of the Department that a certain member of the press had been obtaining certain improper favors from the Department. And has then been usurping certain functions of the Department."

"Such as?"

"Such as handling the personal effects of a victim of a suspected crime."

"Oh," said Lattimer, "now you admit Cruz was murdered."

"And improperly obtaining information about the victim from the property clerk's office. And improperly entering the residence of the victim. And improperly obtaining names of witnesses to said crime—and then questioning them." Mathes paused in his eating and talking. "Shall I go on?" he asked.

"Not necessary," said Lattimer.

"So Whitcomb won't be able to help you anymore," said Mathes. "And *I* won't be able to help you anymore." He paused. "After I get back from lunch."

"But you haven't gotten back from lunch yet," pointed out Lattimer.

"Correct."

"You have not been officially instructed yet."

"Correct."

"So what are you going to tell me, Carl?" asked Frank Lattimer.

Mathes looked at his watch. "Almost one," he said. "I wonder what that announcement, that rally, uptown is going to be like. I hear thousands of people are going. Big crowd control problem. It's really short-handing the Department."

"What are you going to tell me, Carl?"

"I compared Cruz's—I mean Rivera's—arrest records with Velic's. Checked everything, including arresting officers. Found an interesting thing. May mean nothing, of course. The last person who arrested Cruz, four years ago in Miami, was an FBI man named Ed Murdoch."

"Yes."

"And seven years ago," continued Mathes, "on a murder charge, on Velic—the collar was also made by this Murdoch."

Frank Lattimer sipped the rest of his own beer. He set the glass down. "So what does that mean?" he asked.

Mathes spooned some more horseradish onto crackers. "Probably nothing. But you got me curious, Lattimer. So I called a couple of friends of mine at the Bureau here in the city. Asked them, did they know Murdoch?"

"And?"

"And one said yes, he did. Worked with him in the Knoxville office ten years ago. Said he wouldn't trust Murdoch any further than he could throw him. Said he suspected Murdoch of some dealings on the side."

"What dealings?"

"Wouldn't go any further. Just said he didn't trust him."

"Do you think," said Lattimer, "that this Murdoch would have hired both—"

"I think nothing."

"Uh-huh," said Lattimer. "And where is Murdoch now?"

"My friend didn't know."

"Too bad."

"So I checked the Bureau personnel department in Washington."

"Goddamn, Mathes," said Lattimer. "You *are* suspicious."

"It's catching. Anyway, they said Murdoch left the Bureau three years ago."

"For where?"

"They weren't sure. Somebody there thought they'd heard he'd joined the security department of some company somewhere, some big company in the Midwest."

"And?"

"And that's it," said Mathes. "Now you know what I know. And that's *all* you're going to know from me. 'Cause after Barnwell officially tells me—" Mathes broke off. "Hey, Lattimer, where you going? Can't you at least—"

Frank Lattimer was up and digging in his wallet. He pulled out a ten-dollar bill and laid it on the table. "Thanks, Carl," he said quickly. "The lunch is on me."

"Well . . . "

"Let me at least pay for the horseradish," said Lattimer and he was on his way out of the Deep Blue Oyster Bar.

New York City

Joan Scully walked alone through the halls of the Oakes-Metcalf Institute, lost in thought. It was a few minutes before one o'clock. Around her there was a mounting excitement. Staff members met each other in the halls, exchanged brief, intense bits of gossip about the rally about to begin outside. The rumor had spread that Dr. Hugh Underwood was going to announce—"Can you believe it?" they said—a cure. The staffers crammed to the windows for a bird's-eye view of the rally. The sound of the huge crowd below in the street—a heavy, eager buzz—penetrated the walls of the Institute. And the electronically amplified music of the rock band playing for the rally made a mockery of "Hospital Zone, Quiet."

But Joan walked away from it all. She was thinking of other, truer scenes: Frank scouring Roberto Cruz's garbage for a clue to whose cure it *really* was. The look on Barbara's face when she heard Paul had pneumonia. The shambles of Paul's bed after somebody—

who?—had tried to murder him. Thinking of this, the noise outside dimmed for Joan. She heard in her memory the labored *whoosh* of the respirator keeping Paul—barely—alive.

She looked around her. She was on the enclosed bridge over the street connecting the Institute to the Hospital. The bridge was crowded with spectators. It was the very best place to see the rally. Joan walked quickly on. She realized her feet had been taking her toward Justin. She wanted to get away from this trumped-up celebration. She wanted to see him.

At Paul Justin's bedside, Dr. Michael Dewing heard the growing sound of the crowd and the music and became even more impatient to leave and go see what was happening. It was obvious to him that there was nothing to learn here. Because he and Falcone were looking at page after page of an EEG that made no sense at all.

"I can't believe it," Falcone said again. He had been saying that for the last half hour, ever since the technician had turned on the machine and the pens had started making squiggly lines on the paper. "I can't believe it," he repeated. "Nothing but alpha waves. If anybody should have a flat line it should be this guy."

"Screwy," said Dewing. It was more than screwy, it was weird. They had been assuming Justin had no brain functions and now this—normal alpha waves. But neither man had any idea *how* it could be normal.

"Well," said Dewing, "that's it. We'll have to do that brain biopsy."

"We can't get him on the schedule today," said Falcone. "It'll have to be tomorrow afternoon."

"Okay," said Dewing, walking away, "do it."

Falcone was a little annoyed at Dewing for leaving. The EEG wasn't over yet. But as Falcone stayed to the end—another fifteen minutes—there was no change. Just those inexplicable alpha waves.

In the corridor leading to intensive care, Joan Scully passed Dewing. She started to ask him how Paul was, but then realized Dewing was intent on getting to the rally. As she poked her head into Paul's room, past the frowning cop guarding the doorway, she saw Falcone and the technician and the EEG console.

"Oh," she said, "I'm sorry. Am I intruding?"

"No," sighed Falcone. He motioned to the cop to let Joan in. "We're just wrapping up here."

The technician was removing the electrodes from Paul Justin's head.

"How is he?" asked Joan.

"The same," said Falcone. But that wasn't quite true. In order to hold Justin's blood pressure around 100, they recently had been forced to double the Levophed flow—from five drops per minute to ten.

"And what does that"—she gestured at the reams of paper in Falcone's hands—"tell you?"

"Nothing," he said.

But Joan Scully wanted to know more. "Is it a flat line?" she persisted.

Falcone was surprised by her knowledge. "No," he said, "as a matter of fact, it's normal as hell."

"Then he really could have blinked at us?" asked Joan.

"Oh, come on," said Falcone.

"It's possible," she persisted.

"Don't think so, Miss," said the technician as he wheeled the EEG unit out. "I didn't see any."

"Look," said Falcone, "if he is conscious, there's only one thing it could be. And I seriously doubt it." He waved his hand as if to dismiss the idea. "But we might as well check," he said.

"What?"

"Hysterical coma. Hysterical conversion reaction."

"Isn't that what Freud—?"

"Yes," said Falcone. "Big among his patients. The turn-of-the-century Austrian disease. A totally psychogenic paralysis."

"Paul isn't a turn-of-the-century hysterical Austrian," said Joan.

"At this point in this case," said Falcone, "I'll check for anything." He turned a dial on the respirator. "First, we give him one hundred percent oxygen. For fifteen minutes."

The two of them waited. Falcone sat down. Joan saw a deep fatigue on his face. She realized that he, like Frank, must have been up late last night because of Paul. And not just because his job demanded it. Joan saw in Falcone the same dedication her father had had as a doctor. She reached out and lightly touched the assistant resident on the sleeve of his rumpled white coat.

"Thanks for trying," she said softly.

Falcone nodded. Then fifteen minutes were up. He disconnected the respirator tube from Paul Justin.

"Now," said Falcone, "if he *does* have a hysterical coma, he should breathe. People can will themselves every other kind of paralysis—but they can't hold their breath indefinitely."

Falcone and Joan Scully waited. Joan looked at the wall clock. One minute passed. Two minutes.

"Doctor . . . " said Joan nervously.

Two and a half minutes.

"Doctor," she said, "without oxygen . . . "

"In fifteen minutes, he stored up plenty," said Falcone. "There's no risk."

Three minutes.

"Dr. Falcone," said Joan firmly.

But Falcone was already re-attaching the respirator tube. The machine resumed its task of making Paul Justin's chest rise and fall.

"Thanks for trying," Joan said again.

Falcone left. Joan Scully was alone with her colleague.

Paul Justin's face was pale and sweaty. His eyes were closed. His mouth sprouted the obscene respirator tube.

"Paul?" whispered Joan.

There was no response.

"Paul . . . can you move your eyelids?"

No response.

"Paul," she said. She felt heartsick. "Paul, they're trying to kill you. They're trying to steal your cure. Can you fight back? Tell us anything?" She knotted her fists. "Please?"

Paul Justin's eyelids remained as shut as if someone had placed pennies on them.

Joan straightened up. Maybe, she thought, maybe they never moved last night. Maybe Frank *wanted* them to move so much that he convinced us they did move. Maybe we imagined it all.

The high-pitched whine of electronic feedback from a public address system cut through her thoughts. It was immediately followed by a garbled, but booming, amplified voice.

The rally had begun.

New York City

Outside the restaurant, the first pay phone that Lattimer found swallowed his dime but gave him no dial tone. The second phone booth had a man in it. It looked as if the man was going to be there a-while. At the third pay phone, Lattimer was lucky. He called Dacey Pharmaceutical and asked for their security department.

"Security," said a man.

"Ed Murdoch, please," said Lattimer.

"He's not in."

So, thought Lattimer triumphantly, Murdoch *does* work there. Lattimer clenched his fist. This was it: Dacey. The Endicott Foundation. The research grant to Justin. And then Cruz. Velic. Murdoch. It all fit together. Lattimer tried to keep his voice casual. "Oh," he said, "will he be back after lunch?"

"Who's calling?" asked the man.

Lattimer identified himself and his newspaper.

"I'll check," said the man. "But I think he's out again this week."

Lattimer waited. Finally the man came back. "Still on vacation," he said.

On "vacation" with Ives, you mean, thought Lattimer. Damn it, he thought, I was *right*! "Do you know where he is?" asked Lattimer. "No."

"When he's expected back?"

"No, sorry. Listen, mister, what's this all about?"

"Just checking a story," said Lattimer. "Thank you."

He hung up and called United Airlines. No, they had no direct flights to Kansas City, they said. Try TWA. Lattimer dialed that number. TWA put him on hold: "All reservations personnel are busy."

Outside Lattimer's phone booth, a woman, weighed down with packages, waited impatiently.

Finally, TWA would talk to him. The next flight left La Guardia at 2:30, arriving in Kansas City at 4:16 local time. And yes, they had a seat left. But he must be there by 2 P.M. And it was now almost 1:30.

"I'm *calling* from La Guardia," lied Lattimer. "Hold a seat and I'll be there."

He hung up and called Oakes-Metcalf. But all he got was a busy signal. Prentice's rally—going on right now, he realized—must be tying up everything. Lattimer tried to think how to get a message to Joan. Ordinarily, he'd call his newspaper and have them call her. But he didn't want them to know where he was going. So he called Detective Prosser at the 19th precinct. Prosser said Lattimer had some nerve and Lattimer agreed. "Okay," said Prosser, "I'll call your redhead for you first chance I get."

"Thanks," said Lattimer. He dashed out of the phone booth, barely missing the woman.

New York City

All morning, the streets of Manhattan had been full of sound trucks blaring out the message: "... 1 P.M. today ... big rally ... free concert by the Silver Hammer ... important announcement by Senator Arthur Prentice ... Oakes-Metcalf Institute ... 1 P.M. today ... big rally ... " And all morning the sidewalks had been full of personable young people (where, wondered Prentice, had Lapidus found so many so fast?) passing out handbills with the same message. And when Prentice left the Waldorf-Astoria for a morning walk (like Harry Truman—he hoped the media would make the comparison), he saw it was also stenciled on all the crosswalks. My God, he thought, Lapidus must have had people up all night!

And if none of that worked, there was now Maxwell's Silver Hammer themselves, blasting concentric rings of 2500-watt amplified sound all over the Upper East Side, sound drawing a crowd like a magnet. The band was set up on one side of the platform that Lapidus's people had erected in front of the Institute. Prentice and his family—his wife, Lynn, his children, Robert, Jeffery and Nancy—sat on folding chairs on the platform. Alongside them were Hugh Underwood and his wife, Warren Brown and a scattering of other notables. With help from Jack Lynch, his top aide, Prentice tried to concentrate on penciling in a few last-minute changes in his speech. But the Silver Hammer was too loud. The band launched into the final chorus of their latest hit, "The Road Back." In the solid mass of hot, perspiring humanity jamming the whole street from York Avenue to the river, crowding up against the platform, the young people went wild. Maxwell tossed his head and mowed his electric guitar across the crowd like a machine gun. "And when I *hit* the *road* that *takes* me *back* to a *world* that *ought* to *be* ... " he sang. He threw his infectious grin at Prentice. Nancy cried, "Oh, Daddy, that could be a great campaign song for you. You know—you could make this country like it ought to be. Or is that too corny?" Lynch poked his head in. "Not too corny at all," he said. And Prentice, giving up on his speech, yelled at both of them: "But a *softer* version, huh?" And he grinned back at Maxwell. It *would* be a great campaign song, he thought. He bathed in the warmth of the music and the enthusiasm and the huge crowd pressing in on them. And he marveled at the magic of it all. How the magic words "cancer cure"—whispered in Maxwell's finely tuned ear—had convinced the young musician to support Arthur Prentice. And not just support him, not just donate the gate receipts of a concert. No, for the man Maxwell had treated so coolly only two days ago in L. A., for the man Maxwell now said was "for real, not just another politician, but for real" ... for Prentice, Maxwell would do more. He'd cancel a recording session to fly east for this campaign kickoff. And play his heart out. Prentice now bathed in the warmth of Maxwell's music and the anticipation of the huge crowd pressing in on them all. Prentice knew the crowd was here either for the Silver Hammer or out of curiosity. But after they hear me, thought Prentice, they'll be here for *me*. With the message I have today, I'll reach them, I'll move them more than any rock star ever did.

"Ought to be
Ought to be
Gonna be!"

Maxwell hit his final guitar riff. The last notes and the cheers ricocheted back and forth off the high facades of the Institute and the Hospital. Maxwell waited for them to die and then he said, "Thank you, folks, thank you. But today, the Silver Hammer is just the warm-up. 'Cause today the main act is my good friend, Senator Art Prentice. . . . "

Art? Prentice asked himself. Well, okay. Sounds pretty good, actually.

" . . . He's the man," continued Maxwell, "who's gonna help make this world like it ought to be. How? Well, we're not here"—Maxwell waved his arm at the huge Oakes-Metcalf complex—"here, where they treat The Big C, by accident. So, to find out what it's all about, I'd like to introduce the man who'll introduce the man who'll introduce *the man*." And he pointed at Prentice. "*Short* introductions, folks," he promised the crowd. "First of all, the State Senator from this district, Mr. Joel Shevach." And Maxwell clapped his hands close to the microphone.

Prentice had wanted the mayor or at least the local congressman. But this far before the election, neither was willing to do anything that even *looked* like an endorsement. So Prentice had to settle for Shevach. But Shevach did all right. He talked about how fortunate this district and this city were to have "this great Institute and hospital." And he kept it short. He introduced "the man who runs all this," Warren Brown.

Brown thanked Shevach. He thanked the Silver Hammer for playing and made a joke about thanking the police for not enforcing the "Quiet, Hospital" signs today. He said, "I don't know, we've tried every *other* way of treating cancer—maybe we should try rock music. But, seriously . . . " And Brown went on to talk about the difficulty of their task at the Institute and Hospital. About how they—and all cancer researchers across the country—had appreciated Senator Prentice's Cancer Control Act. About how he knew Prentice personally and what a humane, far-seeing man he was. And now, the man himself. Senator Arthur Prentice . . . and Brown backed away from the microphone, applauding, as Prentice walked toward it. And the crowd joined in with polite applause.

"Thank you," said Arthur Prentice. He cleared his throat. "Thank you." He gazed across the sea of upturned faces that filled the street between the hospital and the Institute. He saw more faces watching from the windows of the hospital and from the high, glassed-in bridge that connected the two buildings. The faces were curious but skeptical. What could a politician tell them? The reporters near the platform looked equally skeptical and bored. The most alert people were the half-dozen Secret Service agents that flanked

Prentice. He watched as, like him, they swept the crowd with their eyes. In a few minutes, Arthur Prentice would be an officially declared candidate for the presidency of the United States and, as such, officially protected. It was a heady thought for Prentice. He began his speech.

"Thank you," he said again. "It's a pleasure to be here in New York City. I knew I was in New York as soon as I got in the cab at JFK. Pulling away from the curb, my cab just missed another cab and the other passenger—another out-of-towner, I believe—yelled, 'Hey, you almost hit us.' And my cabby replied, 'In New York, "almost" don't count.' "

Prentice paused for the laughter. He got it. "Yes," he went on, "this is a tough town. A tough town that's too tough to call it quits. That's why I've consistently voted in the Senate for federal loans to help this town get through its fiscal troubles. Because I know you *will* make it."

Applause.

"And because this is a tough town, I know you're wondering what do I—a politician from Indiana—have to offer to you today. Why are you spending your lunch hour standing here when you could be girl-watching or"—a bow to women's lib—"man-watching on Fifth Avenue?"

Chuckles and scattered applause.

"Well, I'll answer that tough question. I'll answer by saying I *do* think I have something to offer you—something a little more special than just another man running for office. Because I'm not just talking about *me*—I'm talking about what I can do *along with* some of the people up here on this platform. And believe me, when you put a senator along with some doctors, the senator knows who's more important—and it's not him. It's like the story of the three men—the doctor, the architect and the politician—debating whose profession was founded first."

Prentice saw that, on many of the faces, the skepticism was softening. The realization was growing that this wasn't going to be a typical political speech.

"So, which *was* founded first?" asked Prentice. "The doctor said, 'Well, Eve was created from Adam's rib and that was a surgical procedure—so certainly there had to be a doctor around to do it.'

" 'No,' said the architect. 'Because before Adam and Eve were made, the *world* had to be created out of chaos—so certainly there had to be an architect around to do that.'

" 'But, ah,' said the politician, 'who created the *chaos*?' "

More laughter. Prentice knew he had his audience with him. Now—to the heart of it. "Remember," Lapidus had told him last night on the phone, "once you *have* the crowd, forget them. Let them be background—let them be applause. There'll only be five thousand of them. After the jokes, face the TV cameras and talk to the millions who'll see you on Cronkite tonight." So Prentice picked out the cameras on top of the networks' panel trucks parked across the street and looked them in the eye.

"But seriously," he said, standing a little straighter, speaking in lower and more measured tones, "I think in this case, I'm a politician who can help *end* some of the chaos. Certainly, for the last ten years, there has not been, in all modesty, I don't think, any public official in this country who has worked harder to fight one of the greatest creators of chaos in the life of the American family.... " He paused. "And I mean cancer."

The crowd stilled.

"Chaos because cancer strikes one out of every four Americans. So if you have at least four people in your family, the chances are that one of you will get it." Even deeper stillness. The noise of midtown, midday Manhattan seemed far away. "And although, thanks to the work of great institutions of research and healing such as this"— Prentice waved his hand to encompass Oakes-Metcalf—"over a million Americans who *had* cancer are alive, well and free of the disease, the hard fact is that, this year alone, four hundred thousand of us will die from this disease. And four hundred thousand more next year. And the next."

Chaos, thought Prentice. He had been tempted to extend it as a metaphor in the speech: The chaos of the disease itself—of cells gone wild. The chaos of funding prior to his Cancer Control Act. But Lynch had argued that Prentice should be restrained: Don't scare these people. And don't blame other people.

So Prentice turned from death to dollars. He explained that the cost of cancer each year was over $15 billion. And that federal outlays for cancer research had been only $100 million each year—less than the cost of one nuclear submarine. And how his Act had increased that amount by 50 percent. And targeted it to where it would do the most good. Targeted several research grants to this Institute. And one in particular to Dr. Hugh Underwood, chief of the virology section. "And will Dr. Underwood stand up, please—and tell us all what the results of that research are?"

The hush of the crowd was broken by an expectant murmur. Something was coming, something important.

Hugh Underwood stepped forward, uncertainly. Prentice ushered him to the microphone. Underwood nervously held some notes.

"Uh, yes," he said, too far from the mike.

Prentice caught Lynch's eye and Lynch smiled. Lynch had been pleased with Underwood. "Not just because he's black," Lynch had said, "although that's a hundred delegates right there. But because he's honestly humble. Not a scientist on the make. He *looks* like a man who's spent his life over a microscope."

Underwood's talk was true to character. He haltingly described his research—"with my colleague Dr. Paul Justin, who, I'm sorry to say, is ill and cannot be with us today." He thanked, in passing, the money and the Act that had made the research possible. And then he concluded: "So we have finally isolated this 'C' particle. This one cause of cancer. This one cause of all cancer."

In the crowd, people were turning to each other. Prentice could sense what they were saying: "Does this mean . . . ?" "Hey, if this guy is right . . . " Directly below the platform, a man with a TV minicam was working his way through the crowd, catching reaction shots. In Prentice's mind's eye, he saw Lapidus working these shots into TV commercials for next spring's primaries.

And then the clincher: "And we are confident," said Underwood, in his solemn, believable voice, "that within the year we will know how to correct this particle and thus cure cancer. For all time."

There was a wave of sound—applause, excited talk, scattered cheers—from the crowd. And Prentice, shaking Underwood's hand and putting an arm around him, rode that wave: "Thank you, Doctor," he said, simply. And then he faced the camera trucks again. "And on the heels of this great accomplishment—and on what small part I hope I have played in it—I hereby announce that I am a candidate for the office of President of the United States. If, together, the American people can accomplish *this*—this triumph over our most feared enemy, this chaos in our midst—then together, I am confident, there is *nothing* we cannot accomplish. So I say to you that . . . "

There was more. More points. More things he said he would do as President. His vision of America. But Arthur Prentice knew it was all incidental, all filler material. Already many of the reporters had dashed into the Institute, probably to fight for the phones, thought Prentice. Because *that* was the story: the cure for cancer. And his role in it.

Arthur Prentice was supremely happy. He finished his speech and waved his arms above his head. He accepted the crowd's full-throated cheers. Maxwell's Silver Hammer let loose with a hard-driving song.

Many Places

The news of Dr. Hugh Underwood's impending discovery swept like wildfire that afternoon. Frank Lattimer was above it, on the plane to Kansas City, but throughout America and the world his fellow reporters fanned out to record its impact. There was much to record.

In Underwood's hometown of Montgomery, Alabama, a city councilman started a drive to rename a street after him.

In Billings, Montana, a church bake-sale committee voted to donate half its funds to the Oakes-Metcalf Institute, to help Underwood's research.

In Cincinnati, Ohio, a man hurled a brick through the windows of the American Cancer Society, yelling that the cure was a hoax.

In San Diego, a leading cancer researcher agreed with him—but he stated it more decorously to the press.

In Cambridge, Massachusetts, and in Baltimore, Paris, and Tokyo, other cancer researchers hailed Underwood—cautiously.

In dozens of cities, cancer patients phoned Oakes-Metcalf demanding the cure *now*. And in Glasgow, Scotland, a woman spent her life savings to fly to New York to demand it in person.

In Johannesburg, South Africa, three jailed black nationalists started a hunger strike to dramatize the fact that their government permitted *no* black scientists.

And in Moscow, American correspondents noted and discussed the significance of the delay in getting an official Soviet reaction.

But the press missed some of the more interesting reactions. For instance, there was no reporter outside Lander, Colorado, in the Saddleback Sanitarium, in the room of Dr. Christopher Ives. . . .

Ives stared dumbfounded at the radio. Then he flung open the door and rushed down the corridor, past startled attendants, to Murdoch's office. He burst in. "Ed!" he cried. "Ed! The news! Prentice's announcement! He made it with Underwood! That's Justin's boss! Underwood says he and Justin worked on the cure! He claims he—"

Murdoch was up out of his chair. "SHUT UP!" he thundered. "NOT NOW!" He waved his arm to indicate the third man in the room.

Ives stopped. He hadn't noticed the other man. He was a thin, slight, unremarkable-looking person, possibly in his forties. His face was dark. His features were slightly Balkan. He sat, hands folded in his lap, silent and very composed.

"Janko," Murdoch said to him, "will you leave, please? I'll call you."

Janko Velic left the office. As soon as the door closed, Ives continued screaming. "Underwood claims he'll have the cure in a year! That means *he* must have Justin's notes. You see, Ed? You see? That means I was right. You said I was foolish to worry—but *I* was right." He took a breath. "God," he lamented, "it's all over now. What are we going to *do*?" He slumped into the chair the thin man had vacated. He held his head in his hands.

There was silence in the room. Then Murdoch's voice rumbled, low and calm. "Do? Why, we're going to keep on doing what we've *been* doing. When our pigeons stop to think about it, they'll realize they can't afford to wait a year. Because they'll be dead in a year." He paused. "And I think a phone call from me would be a nice reminder of that fact."

Ives looked up at Murdoch. He tried to dare to hope his partner was right.

"Now get your crying face out of here," said Murdoch. "I can't sound very positive on the phone if I have to look"—he hurled a box of Kleenex at Ives; it hit him on the cheek—"look at *that*."

Ives left. Murdoch started placing his calls. He first called the people whom he knew would be most nervous. So it was another hour before he reached Ray Ryker.

For Ryker, a cure for cancer a year from now had little claim on his attentions. He was a hell of a lot more worried about the crazy "faith healing" that he'd just learned about. He was in his office at Texahoma, on the phone to Dr. Castle, the head of Loring Memorial. He was telling Castle to "get that goddamned charlatan out of your hospital right now or I'll come over and do it myself."

"But I don't have any authority to do it," Castle protested. "Trumbull hasn't violated any visiting hours, disrupted hospital routine—nothing."

"Damn it, Castle," snapped Ryker. "Find *some* excuse or I'll do it for no excuse. How about practicing medicine without a license?"

"Huh?"

"Faith healing, you moron. How about that?"

"But—"

"Enough to get your precious accreditation as a hospital yanked. Like me to do that?"

"You couldn't possibly—"

"No? Maybe not. But I could make it very messy for you. Now get—"

At that moment Ryker's other phone rang. It was a number he'd given to only a few people. He answered it. "Yes?"

"Mr. Ryker," said the low, gravelly voice. "I'm calling about Mathew Ash."

"What?" asked Ryker. Then he recognized the voice. "Oh, shit," he snapped. "*You*? What the hell do you want? I've got my goddamn money ready for you. So what else? You want to let me talk to Goodhue? Is he ready to tell me to send it? Is he?"

"No . . . but I thought—"

"Well, if he's not ready, why are you calling? You want to put Goodhue on," asked Ryker with heavy sarcasm, "and we'll try the number and letter code again?"

The voice laughed.

"Well, is there any *other* news?"

"No . . . but—"

"Is the deal still on?"

"Yes," said the gravelly voice. It gave an admiring chuckle. "Mr. Ryker, it's a pleasure doing business with you."

"The feeling's not mutual," said Ray Ryker. And he hung up.

He turned to the other receiver. "Now, Castle . . . " he began, "about Reverend Trumbull. I *do* have an alternate proposal . . . "

At that moment, the man under discussion could not actually be thrown out of the hospital. Because he wasn't in it. The Reverend Richard Watson Trumbull was finishing lunch with Virginia Ash in the huge formal dining room of the Ash mansion just outside the city.

The white-jacketed black waiter left the room unobtrusively, leaving a double portion of chocolate mousse cake in front of Virginia. Trumbull just sipped his coffee.

"Reverend, you're sure you won't have some cake?" asked Virginia.

"Mm. Thank you, no, ma'am," said Trumbull.

Virginia was worried about the man. He had arrived late for their lunch, looking upset. And he had barely touched his food. Virginia, who was still full of enthusiasm from this morning's healing, gorged herself. She poked her fork at some cake crumbs that were threatening to fall out of her mouth. "Reverend," she finally asked, mouth full, "is something wrong?"

"Mm?" he said. "Oh, no." He fiddled with his cup and gazed out of the French doors to the vista of rolling farmland.

" 'Cause I'd think you'd be very satisfied," said Virginia. "You healed my husband. And now this wonderful news from New York about a cure for *every*one, in just a year. Lord be praised."

"Be praised," said Trumbull, automatically.

Virginia suddenly had a thought. " 'Course," she said, "if everyone's gonna be healed of cancer soon, you won't have to heal 'em." She looked at him questioningly. "Do you heal people of other afflictions? Somehow, I think of you as just a—what do you call it?—specialist."

"I'm afraid other people do, too," said Trumbull.

"Oh," said Virginia. She found her napkin, wiped the smeared chocolate off her lips. "But you'll still heal people," she said. "Have your TV show and all? Run your Center in Atlanta?"

"May be a problem," admitted Trumbull. "We depend on the

generosity of people who are . . . ah . . . afflicted. Perhaps when they are no longer . . . " He trailed off.

"Money?" asked Virginia, abruptly. "Money? My, is *that* all you're upset about?"

"A bit," said Trumbull.

"Well, good Lord," said Virginia Ash. She shifted her huge bulk in her chair and leaned forward to seize Trumbull's wrist. "Reverend," she said, "money's no problem at all. For what you've done for my Mathew, you can depend on me as long as I live. And afterward, after we're both gone—well, there's Mathew's will."

"His will?"

"He wrote one day before yesterday. I'm sure that, after what you did for him this morning, he'll be happy to tear it up and leave—" She considered a moment. "Oh, most everything, I guess . . . we have no children, you know. . . . "

"I know," said Trumbull, sympathetically.

"Yes. Well . . . " She brushed the napkin to her eye. "Would a couple of hundred million do?" she asked.

"Just fine," said the Reverend Richard Watson Trumbull.

"Well," said Virginia, "why don't I call Mr. Shurcliff? He's Matt's lawyer and I'm sure he can work something out. . . . "

But all the money in the world couldn't have put an end to the turmoil that was now engulfing Barbara Justin. All morning she had been trying to hide out from the world. She had not read the paper, watched TV or listened to the radio. She had talked with no neighbor. After clearing away breakfast, she had called Oakes-Metcalf, obtained the name of a cancer specialist in private practice and made an appointment to see him that afternoon. Then she had curled up on the couch and, finally, slept until 1 P.M. She had prepared a simple lunch and was eating it when, at 1:30, the phone rang.

"Mrs. Justin? Tim Henderson of *The New York Times*. I wonder if you could tell me your reaction to the news that your husband and Dr. Underwood have . . . "

It was the first she had heard. Her reaction was one of confusion. The "C" particle project? She thought Paul had put it aside. And working *with* Hugh Underwood? She thought Underwood had opposed the project. And a cure? A real cure, a year away? The idea flooded her with bitterness. In a year, would it be too late? Would her breasts be already lopped off? And Paul—what glory would there be for Paul? Would he be able to move, to shake a congratulating hand? Would he even be alive?

She tried to put her thoughts in order to give the newsman a rational, positive reply. But, as she hung up, she didn't think she had succeeded. And as soon as she hung up, the phone rang again.

"Mrs. Justin? Stephanie Hough of ABC-TV. Could you tell us . . ."

But Barbara couldn't tell them anything that sounded sensible, either. And the phone rang and rang and rang. . . . *"Washington Post*—What do you think of your husband's work being used by Senator Prentice to advance his own candidacy?" . . . "Associated Press—Is there any connection to a reported attempt on your husband's life last night?" . . . *"Daily News*—Like to get some human interest. Was your husband motivated by any history of cancer in your family? . . . "

"No!" she cried. "No! No!" And she hung up and the phone rang again. And then the front doorbell. She went to the door.

"Mrs. Justin? Joe DeGrazia of the Westchester *Globe.* I wonder if you—"

He was a pleasant-looking young man. She fled from him like a leper, running through the house. But going out the back, the phone still ringing, she swung the screen door into a photographer.

"Hey, lady," he objected. He grabbed for his camera.

"Sorry," she said. She put a frozen smile on her face as he snapped her picture.

The picture hardly showed her real feelings.

New York to Kansas City

Frank Lattimer was having a nightmare. And the nightmare had an extra-terrifying quality because part of his mind *knew* it was having a nightmare—and was forced to watch it. His mind watched as, one after another, different women were set down on his uncle's carpentry table, clamped down with a vise and then attacked (oh, Jesus, said his mind) with a giant steel file. The file moved back and forth across them, filing their bodies down. No blood flowed, there was no tearing of flesh. But each woman was, somehow, reduced. First a tall, bony woman with a sharp nose. Who's she? his mind asked. Oh, he realized—Ruth Swope, the secretary to the high school principal back in Wilkes-Barre. Then a woman Lattimer knew very well—his own wife (ex-wife, his mind reminded him), Mary Ann. Then several other women Lattimer had slept with these last few years, from one-night stands (which his mind was surprised he remembered) to old reliables like the actress. Then—and now the terror became intense—Joan Scully. The rough-edged file moved across her body and, as it did, his mind rebelled because he saw that, instead of breasts, her chest was flat, covered with curly black hair. And the hair on her head was black and her eyes weren't Joan's blue-green but black also, and she was Joan and not-Joan, and somehow this was the worst of all and . . .

Frank Lattimer awoke with his cheek in a pool of sweat on the tiny airline pillow. His forehead was pressed painfully hard against the airplane window. He shook his head to get out the nightmare and the cramp in his neck. Jesus, he thought. He rarely dreamed. Or at least, he rarely remembered his dreams. What the hell was all that?

He looked out the window. Small puffs of clouds over green and brown hills. He looked at his watch: 3:30. Western Pennsylvania, he figured. Maybe just past his hometown. He was glad to wake up, but he wished he could have gotten some *good* sleep. He was running short of it these last few days. Oh, well. Lattimer looked around the cabin for a stewardess, couldn't find one. He pressed the call button and one appeared, standard good-looking American blonde, open face, even and shiny teeth when she smiled. She smiled and said, "Yes, sir?"

"Listen," said Lattimer. "Do you have any of those macadamia nuts?" He had to put *something* into his stomach.

"Sorry," she grinned. "Wrong airline. That's on United. How about dry-roasted cashews?"

"And a drink."

"And a drink," she agreed. She was still smiling, as if she knew some secret. "What'll it be?"

"Sherry," he said. "Dry."

She looked surprised.

"I've got to stay awake in Kansas City," he explained.

When she came back, the man in the aisle seat had left to go to the men's room, so Lattimer could ask her: "What's the secret?"

"Secret?"

"You're still grinning at me."

"I am?"

"Sure," he said, taking the sherry and the cashews, "and it can't have been anything I said. I mean, I didn't get a chance to try *any* of my traveling salesmen's jokes."

"You're not a traveling salesman," she said.

"I could be," said Lattimer. "And you *could* be grinning over the joke I told about the stewardess and the one-eyed Texan."

"Oh, God," the stewardess said, flipping her shoulder-length blond hair that looked, thought Lattimer, naturally streaked. "You know *that* one?"

"Or you could be grinning because I told you the seat belt's stuck on my belt buckle and could you please reach your hands down here and—"

She laughed. "That one's been tried on me, too."

"But not by me," said Lattimer.

"No," she said, mock-gravely.

"So why?" he asked.

"Well, if you must . . . " she said.

"I insist."

The stewardess thought about it. "I never," she said, spelling it out, "have seen a man get onto an airplane looking more as if he were fighting a war. And then wake up looking more as if he'd lost it. I'd say you don't need a sherry. You need a double scotch."

"Yeah?" asked Lattimer. "Well, you should see the other guy."

"Yeah? How is he?"

"Much better off than me."

The stewardess laughed.

"Are you laughing at me?" Lattimer asked sternly.

Her hand flew to her mouth in mock dismay. "Oh, no, sir," she said. "That wouldn't be right. Not according to TWA regulations. We're not supposed to laugh at passengers."

"I should hope not," he agreed. "But what if I weren't a passenger?"

"Then I'd laugh."

"After we land in Kansas City I won't be a passenger," pointed out Lattimer.

"But you said you have to stay awake in Kansas City," she pointed out. "Business, Mr. Lattimer."

"My business will be over by, say, seven o'clock."

"I don't date traveling salesmen."

"But I'm not—"

"I know," she said. "You're a war casualty. So I accept."

"Fine," he said. "The American Restaurant?"

"Never heard of it. But I accept."

"And whose company will I have the pleasure of?"

"Jennifer Byrd."

"Any relation to the admiral?"

She looked pleased. "Yes, as a matter of fact. Very distant but related." She held out her hand. "I'll also accept a dollar fifty."

"For . . . ?"

She grinned. "That price? For the sherry."

Lattimer dug out the money and handed it to her. As she took it, the plane hit an air pocket and her hand hit the seat back.

"Damn," said Miss Byrd. She inspected her fingers. "Broke my nail. Have to file it down."

"Don't *say* that," said Lattimer.

She looked at him curiously.

New York City

Except for those doctors and nurses who were tending patients who would otherwise have died—and for those few curmudgeons who wouldn't have left their labs to witness the end of the world—Joan Scully supposed she was the only person in Oakes-Metcalf who hadn't watched at least part of the big rally. Instead, she hid out in the deserted cafeteria. She unhappily toyed with a container of yogurt. Dimly, she heard the cheers outside. She waited until they subsided. Shortly after 2 P.M., when she figured the show was over, she went back to the virology section.

But the show was far from over. When she got off the elevator on the eighth floor, it looked to her as if half the Institute had tried to fight their way into the section. But since they weren't used to fighting, they'd mainly lost out to the media, who were. Joan caught a glimpse of Lou Beauchamp trying to answer a TV camera stuck in his face, and she turned and started to walk away.

She ran directly into another mob sweeping down the hallway toward the section. At its edges were more Hospital and Institute personnel. Closer in were more media people grabbing shots and firing questions. Even closer in, clearing a path through the mob, was a circle of determined-looking young men in suits and ties. Secret Service, guessed Joan Scully. And in the middle of the circle were Hugh Underwood and Warren Brown and a smiling man who Joan Scully guessed was Senator Prentice.

This mob bore down on her. She tried to flee the other way, but saw Hugh Underwood point to her, and a half-dozen media people peeled off to surround her. She was swept by the mob into the already jammed section.

Flashbulbs blinded her. Wires and cables tripped her. She was backed up against the centrifuge. Intense strangers, wielding notepads and microphones, hurled questions at her:

"What do you think of your boss's discovery of the 'C' particle?"

"Will you be working with him to find the cure?"

"How long do you think it will take?"

"Are you grateful to Senator Prentice?"

"Do you think he'll be President?"

"Do you think he'd make a good President?"

"What do you think of Underwood personally?"

"Have you followed his work?"

"What work do *you* do?"

"Why did you go into cancer research?"

"Is there a history of cancer in your family?"

"What . . . ?"

Joan answered as best she could, and, rather than lie, she answered as little as she could. She imagined how the TV cameras were recording her confusion. She supposed the print reporters would misquote half of what she said—if that mattered. She looked to her colleagues for help. But Crawford and Holmes and Beauchamp were as besieged as she. (She felt Stefan Wojik had been so smart to quit and go home this morning.) And Underwood was also holding forth, taking Prentice and his entourage on a tour of the equipment-crowded and people-crowded section.

"Now, here, Senator," Underwood was saying—as a mass of TV cameras followed, like a school of huge, dark fish—"here is where we first isolated the . . . "

Joan Scully felt sick to her stomach. Unlike this morning, when Underwood had had the decency to look uncomfortable claiming credit for Paul's work, he now looked very comfortable indeed. And that empty politician, Prentice—playing along. Joan felt it was like an Alphonse-Gaston act: "The credit is all yours." "No, the credit is all yours." And the media eating it up, playing it up.

"Could we see Justin now?" said one of the TV people, tugging at Warren Brown's sleeve. "If we could see him now, I can just make the six o'clock news."

"Yeah," demanded another reporter. "And what about the tour of the hospital, Doctor? You said Prentice and Underwood were going to visit some sick kids?"

Joan looked for someplace to run to. She couldn't stand it. If this was what Frank's "profession" was like . . . bloodsuckers, manipulators . . . do anything for a story, do anything to *make* a story. Damn them, damn them all.

New York City

Dr. Picard was old, slight, dapper and very European. Dr. James Cassidy was middle-aged, large and hearty. Even the eyeglasses he now wore didn't disguise the fact that he had probably devoted as much time at college to football as to pre-med. His office, one block from Oakes-Metcalf, sported bright prints of the American Civil War and nineteenth century baseball players. It was a far cry from Picard's rich, dark consulting rooms and Barbara Justin was not reassured. She wanted Picard's quiet sympathy. But Cassidy's approach to disease was a vigorous, intelligent attack.

"Sorry to hear about your husband's illness," he said, almost matter-of-factly. "We're all very impressed that he may have been onto a cure. Now"—with no change of emphasis—"about your lump. Can you tell me how long you've had it?"

"Two weeks."

"And what did your doctor in Boston think?"

Barbara told Cassidy that Picard had not been sure. "But," she added quickly, "he said that if it is cancer, I probably won't have to lose the breast."

Cassidy suppressed annoyance. What, he wondered, was a G.P. doing venturing an opinion like that?

"Well," said Cassidy, "let's find out some more."

As Picard had done, he took a brief medical history. As Picard had done, he had her change into a gown. Then, as with Picard, Barbara lay on an examination table—while Cassidy felt her breasts and under her arms. But unlike Picard, Cassidy made no reassuring comments.

Barbara next expected Cassidy to continue Picard's routine and give her a mammogram. But instead, Cassidy took out an empty hypodermic syringe.

"What's that for?" she asked, alarmed.

"I'd like to get a specimen," said Cassidy. "It won't hurt much." He held her left breast in one large hand. He located the lump. He carefully slid the fine needle into the lump.

It hurt Barbara a lot.

Cassidy withdrew the needle and Barbara stopped gritting her teeth. She looked at the syringe. It still looked empty.

"What did you get?" she asked.

"Some cells," said Cassidy. And a little tissue juice, he thought. But what he had hoped to get was fluid. If the lump were only a cyst, the needle would have drawn fluid and the lump would go away.

"What will you do with the cells?" she asked.

"The lab will make a smear," said Cassidy. "All right," he concluded, "you can get dressed."

Barbara retied her gown and sat on the edge of the table. "You're not going to take a mammogram?" she asked.

Cassidy suppressed more annoyance. The trouble with breast cancer was that every woman who came to see him about it seemed to have read the most recent and popular stuff on it—from articles in *Cosmopolitan* and *Ms.* to whatever first-person account of mastectomy was now inching up the best-seller list. With these women, Cassidy spent much of his time trying to undo misinformation. Barbara, of course, hadn't dared read anything. But Cassidy didn't know that.

"A mammogram isn't necessary," said Cassidy, a bit brusquely. "As a matter of fact, no matter what the smear shows, we want to take that lump out."

"Oh," said Barbara. She was relieved at the idea of no more lump. And she was very, very worried: Would it hurt? Did Cassidy mean *just* the lump, or more of her breast? Did . . . ?

"Yes," said Cassidy, "and I'd like to do it right away." He looked at some papers on his desk. "Ah," he said, "we're in luck. I can get you on the operating schedule tomorrow morning."

"Tomorrow?" gulped Barbara. This was all going too fast.

"Yes," said Cassidy. He could see the strain that Barbara was under. So normally, Cassidy—who was not an unfeeling man—would have postponed operating on her until the crisis with her husband had passed. Until he either recovered or died. But earlier this afternoon, Cassidy had checked with Dewing and Falcone. They had told him that Justin's condition was stable. For all they knew, the man could stay in his coma for days or weeks more. And Cassidy knew that the lump couldn't wait weeks. If it was malignant, it could metastasize even further by then.

"Tomorrow, then?" said Cassidy, looking for agreement.

"What—what will you do?" Barbara was afraid to find out.

"We'll remove the lump and get it analyzed immediately to see if it's malignant. If it is, well, I'm sure you've read about the controversy about what to do next."

"Ye-es," said Barbara tentatively. She had avoided reading about it, but she couldn't avoid having heard about it. She was aware that there was a trend against radical surgery. And she clung to Picard's having said that her breast could be saved.

"Well," continued Cassidy, "if it is cancer, we don't want to run the risk of leaving any cancerous cells behind. Cancerous cells that are *out*side of the lump. So what we should do is remove the breast and the lymph nodes."

"No!" cried Barbara. "Picard said—"

"Mrs. Justin," said Cassidy, firmly. "You've come to me as a surgeon. I'm giving you my opinion as a surgeon. I'm not talking about a radical mastectomy—that involves cutting out chest muscle and leaves the patient with a weak arm. I'm talking about a *modified* radical that will permit you a return to all your normal activities."

Activities, thought Barbara. As if I were a tennis pro mainly worried about keeping a strong serve. What about *me*, how I look, how I'll feel about myself?

"Uh," she said, "I can't . . . not right now . . . "

"Mrs. Justin," said Cassidy. "It would be a lot easier for you if we do it all at once. The analysis of the lump takes only ten minutes while you're still on the operating table. So most patients give me permission ahead of time to continue and perform the mastectomy, if necessary, then and there."

So I would go into the operation tomorrow, thought Barbara, be made unconscious, not knowing whether, when I woke up, I would have a breast or not. No, thank you.

"No," said Barbara.

Cassidy had run into this before also. So he gave up. "All right," he said. "We could do the mastectomy later in the week." Cassidy kept talking about the mastectomy because he felt Mrs. Justin had better face the possibility of it. He didn't like the feel of her lump.

"All right," Barbara agreed, relieved. "But *this* operation ... for just the lump ... will it hurt afterward? ... Will my breast look ... how?"

"You'll be a little sore," said Cassidy. "And have a small scar you'll hardly notice. It's minor surgery. You'll only be under anesthesia a half hour."

"And you'll tell me the results when?"

"I'll wait till you're fully awake. A few hours later. And you can go home tomorrow or Wednesday."

"Well ... " Barbara stood up. "I guess I'd better go home now and get ready."

"There's really nothing to *get* ready, Mrs. Justin. I need you checked in by this evening anyway. So why don't you check in now?"

"But my things ... my ... "

"All you need is a toothbrush," said Cassidy, kindly. "And I think we can supply you with one."

Barbara knew her last delaying tactic was undone. She stood up. She tried not to slouch. She tried to be brave. Paul! she cried inside. Paul! "All right," she said. "Where do I go?"

Kansas City, Missouri

The Dacey Pharmaceutical Company was set in a manicured industrial park along the Missouri River in what used to be tobacco fields. The building was modern, massive and low, presenting a blank face of concrete to the road. A monolithic stone sculpture sat in a square reflecting pool at the entrance. The effect was not that of a company going bankrupt. The effect was also not that of a company that would easily yield up any secret. But the truth was that Dacey *was* going bankrupt. And, at a quarter to five, as Frank Lattimer walked in, he was hopeful that appearances were likewise deceiving—that Dacey would tell him what he needed to know.

Lattimer had rushed to catch the plane because it would get him here before the end of the business day. And that was a good time. Because now people would have their minds on going home. And so somebody might let something slip, something he'd keep a tight grip on at any other time. Plus there was always the chance of buying somebody a drink, loosening him up that way (in which case Miss Byrd would have to wait). Frank Lattimer was perfectly prepared to spend all day tomorrow here, roaming the building, picking up information that way. But he hoped for a break tonight.

In the reception area, he signed in and received a visitor's I.D. badge which he was told to wear on his suit. Then a secretary came to escort him to Ives's secretary's office.

Inside, the building felt as oppressive as outside. The receptionist and Lattimer's escort said little. As for the people they passed in the corridors . . . to Lattimer's eye they didn't look happy the day was over; they looked relieved. And the corridors went on like a maze that some Dacey scientist might send a rat through. The fact that the corridors and work areas were all color coded in soft pastels didn't soothe Lattimer; he was too aware of the attempt at psychological engineering behind it.

Still, Lattimer figured there had to be a flaw somewhere. And he was betting it lay in Ives's domain. Murdoch, as head of security, would run a tight operation. If any of his people knew where he was or what he was doing, they probably wouldn't tell. But Ives . . . Lattimer remembered the soft face in the annual report. Ives's people were his best chance.

Lattimer's escort turned him over to Ives's secretary, Sandra Rainey. Miss Rainey was young, black, beautiful, pleasant and totally unhelpful.

"I'm sorry you came all the way out here, Mr. Lattimer, because, as I said on the phone, I really don't know *where* Dr. Ives is."

They were standing outside Ives's large office, whose windows gave out onto the lawn rolling down to the river. The few other people around were getting ready to leave. Lattimer was surrounded by quiet and order: clean desktops, banks of white filing cabinets, tasteful graphics above them, rich brown carpet underfoot. There was no loose end to grab.

But wait, thought Lattimer. Do I detect a bit of complaint in Miss Rainey's voice? Okay, go with it.

"Gee," he said, taking a chair next to her and leaning back, relaxed, "that must be tough on you, too. I bet all kinds of people are asking you where he is. I know *I* was pretty hard on you this morning."

"Oh, that's okay," said Rainey. "You weren't bad." Unconsciously, she picked up Lattimer's cue and also leaned back in her chair. "But I mean, with these legal hassles and him being director and being sued ... I've got lawyers, other directors, even Mr. Dacey himself—*every*body's looking for Dr. Ives. All last week and today."

"Pretty inconsiderate of him not to leave word."

"Yeah," said Rainey, taking out a cigarette. "But he's under a lot of pressure. Just had to get away."

"I can sure understand about the pressure," said Lattimer, reaching over to light her cigarette, "but it's not fair that it gets passed on to you."

"Thanks," said Rainey, drawing in on the cigarette. She blew out some smoke. "But he doesn't pass it on." She gazed at the smoke spiraling upward. She smiled. "Well, he *does* get sort of uptight by the end of the week."

"We all do," agreed Lattimer, not having any idea where this was going, but figuring he was getting Rainey to open up. Maybe later she'd tell him something of substance.

Later came right away.

"Yeah," said Rainey, "but every Friday morning, after he sees Lindenmeyer, he comes in bright and cheerful. Wednesday morning, too, come to think of it."

"Lindenmeyer?" asked Lattimer.

Three desks away, another secretary waved good-bye. " 'Night, Sandra. Call Bob later for me?"

" 'Night, Alice," said Rainey. "I will." She and Lattimer were now alone.

"Lindenmeyer?" he repeated.

Rainey suddenly rummaged in her purse. "Now, where did I put Bob's number ... ?" She looked through scraps of paper. "Oh, yeah," she said to Lattimer, distracted. "Lindenmeyer. His psychiatrist." She snapped her purse shut and turned to Lattimer. "Oh," she said, "I shouldn't have said that, should I?" She dropped cigarette ashes on her skirt.

"Said what?"

"About Dr. Ives's seeing a psychiatrist."

"That's okay," Lattimer reassured her, "lots of people do. It's a sign of health."

Rainey brightened up. "Yeah, I guess so." She brushed the ashes off.

"By the way ... " said Lattimer with great casualness. (Although Lattimer felt anything *but* casual. For he knew this was it: A man may not tell his wife where he's going on vacation. He may not tell his secretary. But he sure as hell tells his psychiatrist.) "Where's Lindenmeyer? In town?"

"No," said Rainey, "out at the Menninger Clinic. Dr. Ives is real dedicated. Drives there every Tuesday and Thursday afternoon."

"Menninger Clinic? That's Topeka?"

"Right."

"Ah," said Lattimer. He kept the conversation going for another fifteen minutes, expressing sympathy for the legal problems of Ives and of Dacey Pharmaceutical. He said he was really interested in finding out more about the new cardiac drug and could he come back tomorrow and talk with Dr. Burroughs and others in the research department? Rainey said he was welcome to try. He walked her out of the building to the parking lot and said good night. He figured that by now she'd half-forgotten she'd told him about Lindenmeyer.

As soon as Rainey had driven away, Lattimer went to the phone booth in the parking lot and called the Menninger Clinic. The switchboard said that Dr. Lindenmeyer was out but would call in later. Lattimer left a number where Lindenmeyer could reach him. He said it was urgent. The switchboard operator was used to urgent calls to psychiatrists. She promised Lindenmeyer would return Lattimer's call.

Frank Lattimer hung up. He looked at the concrete fortress that was Dacey Pharmaceutical. He laughed at it. Some fortress.

New York City

Actually, Barbara Justin was able to find three more delays before she checked into the hospital.

The first delay was necessary: She called Mother Yates. The two women discussed the crazy announcement Prentice and Underwood had made and how the media had seized it. And Barbara told her mother about her operation scheduled for tomorrow. Could her mother come and stay with the kids while she was in the hospital? "Of course, Barbara," said Mother Yates. "I'll catch the six o'clock shuttle. And I'll stay as long as you need me."

The second delay proved futile: Feeling guilty about running away from Dobbs Ferry today, possibly leaving her children to the media's tender clutches, Barbara called home. But neither Steve, Melissa nor Laurie was there. She could give them no comfort; she could get none from them.

And the third delay also felt futile: Barbara went upstairs and looked in on Paul. He looked the same as he had late last night. And Dewing told her there was no change. No change in temperature or blood pressure. No change in the coma. Dewing said they would have to do a brain biopsy on Paul tomorrow afternoon, and handed her the form to approve it. Barbara signed mutely. She felt she was signing her husband's death sentence.

Then Barbara went to the admitting office. She gave the woman behind the desk her name, address and Blue Cross number. When asked whom to notify in case of an emergency, she automatically started to say "Paul Jus—" She stopped herself. "Elizabeth Yates," she said.

A nurse escorted Barbara to her room, on the floor below Paul's. It was semiprivate. The other patient, Mrs. Ambrose, introduced herself. "Here for my third time, honey," she said. Barbara didn't ask what kind of cancer Mrs. Ambrose had or what the doctors did to her each time she came in.

The nurse had Barbara change into a hospital gown and then took a brief medical history. Barbara was annoyed at having to give the same answers she'd given Cassidy only two hours ago. The nurse took Barbara's pulse, blood pressure and temperature. She took a blood sample, gave Barbara a glass jar and asked for a urine sample. In bored tones, the nurse showed Barbara how the hospital bed worked and how to ring for someone. She snapped a name tag around Barbara's wrist and left.

Barbara lay under the sheet and stared at the wall. She sensed the hospital's attempt to strip her of any identity except that of "patient." She felt cut off from humanity. And too close to humanity: On the other side of the dividing curtain, Mrs. Ambrose had her TV set tuned to some mindless game show. There was no escaping the screams of joy of the contestants. Dinner arrived. Eating gave Barbara something to do. And the food wasn't bad. But she discovered she had no appetite. The Swiss steak stayed half-eaten on her plate.

Barbara wondered how she was going to get through the evening. The hospital wanted her to be "patient"—a fitting word, thought Barbara. Briefly, she envied Paul his unconsciousness. She bit her tongue at the unworthy thought.

New York City

In the middle of the afternoon, after the newspaper and TV people had left the virology section, the second wave hit: the magazine correspondents with more leisure to dig, the science and medical reporters who had more knowledge with which to dig. From three to four to five and later, they sat around the section and spun out their questions: Does Underwood's discovery correspond with Heubner's description of a "C" particle? How did Underwood go about looking for it? Once he found a suspicious acid base, how did he go about synthesizing an RNA molecule to include it? And now how would he develop the programming to turn it off? How, for instance, would he . . . ? Crawford, Holmes and Beauchamp—and even Joan Scully—tried their best to answer. Researchers from other sections—from assistants to chiefs—crowded around and offered their own opinions. They vied with the reporters, with each other and with Joan and her colleagues. Everybody wanted to support or qualify or debunk. Willy-nilly, Joan found herself forced into defending or attacking—and all the while she knew it was a lie. A lie, a lie, damn it! she wanted to scream. Finally, she couldn't take it anymore. Picking her way through the crowd and through papers and even some equipment that the mob had knocked to the floor, she got out of the section.

She went to the ladies' room and made up her face. She shook her head at the mirror. I guess I'll go home now, she thought. Frank'll probably call and we can get together and have a laugh—although maybe a slightly bitter one—over all this. A troublesome thought struck her: Unless he's too busy chasing his story to rest? She couldn't keep up with him through another night like last night.

Balanced between hope and irritation, Joan Scully walked out of the ladies' room. She ran right into David Crawford.

"Oh, there," he said, "I hoped I'd catch you. You just got a call from a cop named Prosser. He said he was trying to call all afternoon but our lines were busy. He left a message from a Frank Lattimer?" Crawford made the last sentence into a question, as if to ask: Just how important is this Lattimer to you? And what does he have over me?

Oh, hell, thought Joan Scully. Frank is *back* at the police station.

"Anyway," continued Crawford, "this Prosser said that Lattimer said, quote, 'Have last deadline to make. Gone to Kansas City. Will call you tonight. Signed, Simple Ace Reporter.' End quote." Crawford smiled at Joan. "Cute, huh?" he asked.

Cute, no, thought Joan Scully. Damn his deadlines. Damn his Kansas City. This time it's not funny. Kansas City? she wondered. Sure? Why not? Why not the moon? And I should stay home and wait for his call like a good little girl? The nerve.

The disgust must have shown on her face because Crawford's face turned shrewd and cheerful. "Hey," he said, "hell of a day, huh? I don't know about you but I could use a drink. Want to join me at Desdemona's?"

Joan Scully looked at handsome, eager, aggressive David Crawford. She didn't like him any better, but at the moment she didn't actively *dis*like him. And he had two pluses: He knew—a little—of what she'd been through today. And he was not in Kansas City.

"You're on," she said.

Desdemona's was a dark and comfortable restaurant and bar.

Joan sat with David in a quiet corner and matched him scotch for scotch, no water or soda. She didn't say much. She let David go on about how it was a neat play by Brown and the Institute to let Hugh Underwood take credit for whatever Justin had discovered. About how everybody in the section could share in Underwood's present success. About how to gauge—in six to nine months—if Underwood really would find the cure and, if it looked like he wouldn't, how to get *away* from Underwood.

When Joan listened to what David was actually saying, she got turned off. When she let herself just listen to his aggression—and be influenced by her third scotch—she got turned on. After an hour and a half, by the beginning of the fourth scotch, she was ready to go to bed with him. In fact, she was about to suggest they leave. But then, through the liquor, Joan heard David say one thing more. David had been talking about Dr. Hazeltine, the professor who was directing David's Ph.D. About how, in the wake of Underwood's claim, Hazeltine's career would be eclipsed. "Poor bastard," David was saying. "And of course, this weekend when I talked to him, he didn't have the slightest inkling. In fact, he was all puffed up about this secret consultation he was going to do for the Kupitz family. One of them's got cancer, I guess. Anyway, Hazeltine wasn't supposed to tell me about it, he said, but it was so funny, such easy money, he just had to. Ten grand just to fly off somewhere to check something out for Kupitz. Hell—ten grand. That's nothing compared to what old Hughie's going to get. I mean, all the grants to look for the cure. And if he finds the cure, all that Nobel Prize money."

"Kupitz," said Joan. "That rings a bell. Didn't I read something about Kupitz recently? Who are they?"

"Hell," said David Crawford, "the Kupitzes are only slightly poorer than the Rockefellers. All of it in the hands of one brother and sister, I think. Up in Connecticut somewhere. I think Greenwich, Hazeltine said."

"Yes," said Joan slowly. Now she knew she remembered the name from an article she'd read recently. Where was it? *Time*? *Newsweek*? Something about how the rich stay rich? "So what's Hazeltine checking?" she asked.

"Beats me."

"I mean, if he were flying somewhere—you know—to check with another specialist, that still wouldn't be worth anywhere near ten thousand dollars. And it wouldn't need to be a secret."

"Beats me," said David Crawford. He looked at Joan quizzically. Joan knew he was trying to figure out why, out of all he'd said, this was the only thing she'd really responded to. "Maybe," suggested David, "this Kupitz is just, uh, tight with his personal life and loose with his money." David chuckled at his play on words.

"No," said Joan. The article came back clearly now. She remembered it cited the Kupitzes as being very tight with their money. Very quickly, Joan was going cold stone sober. It was as if she had drunk nothing. Because now she also remembered her conversation with Frank yesterday, after they proved to themselves that Roberto had stolen Justin's notes. She remembered Frank saying what someone could do with a secret, stolen cure for cancer. "Find the richest cancer victims in the world," Frank had said. "They'd pay a fortune for it." Maybe, thought Joan, *this* is where Justin's notes have ended up!

She looked around Desdemona's for a pay phone, spotted one, said, "Excuse me" to a startled David Crawford and left their table. She dropped a dime in the phone and called Connecticut information. She knew that, ninety-nine chances out of a hundred, the number was unlisted.

"I have an M. Kupitz," said the operator. "On Dingletown Road."

"You do?"

"Yes, would you like the number?"

Joan wrote down the number. It must be another Kupitz, she figured. But she called anyway.

"Kupitz residence," said an old man's voice.

"Uh, do I have the right Kupitz?" asked Joan.

"You have the only Kupitz in Greenwich."

"Uh, well, could I speak with Mr. Kupitz?"

"Who may I say is calling?"

"Uh, Joan Scully."

"And what is this in reference to?"

"Uh ... uh, I'm a colleague of Dr. Hazeltine," she lied. "Dr. Joan Scully." Well, she told herself, I *will* have my doctorate soon enough.

"Yes, Doctor," said the man. "Will you wait a moment?"

Joan Scully hung onto the receiver. She looked at her watch. It was a quarter to eight. Around her, Desdemona's singles meeting time was going into full swing. Men and women were five deep at the bar, trading witticisms, glimpses of chest hair and cleavage and, hopefully, phone numbers. Waiters and busboys maneuvered perilously through the throng with trays of drinks and dishes. More people stacked up at the door, trying to get a seat—or even standing room. The din was terrific. Joan smiled to herself. This phone was usually used to check up on romantic and business affairs, not cures for cancer.

"Yes?" said a man's voice on the phone. "Hello?"

"Oh," said Joan. "Yes? Are you Mr. Kupitz?"

"Yes," said the light, pleasant voice. "How can I help you?"

Joan was unnerved. "*The* Mr. Kupitz?" she asked. "The family that has ... uh ... employed Dr. Hazeltine?"

"Yes?"

"Well, my name is Joan Scully. I'm a colleague of Dr. Hazeltine and ... " She stopped.

"Yes?" the man encouraged her.

"Well ... " Joan didn't know how to proceed. She tried to think how Frank would do it. Come on, she told herself, lie like he would. "Well," she said, "while Dr. Hazeltine is out of town, he's asked me to keep in touch with you. While he ... checks out things for you. But frankly, he didn't tell me too much. So I wonder if you ... ?" She paused. Then she blurted, "What *is* Dr. Hazeltine checking?" Hell, thought Joan, it sounds so lame. There was nothing else to do but make a guess, confront him with it: "Is he checking out a cure for cancer?" she asked. "Has someone offered to sell you one?"

God, she thought. Too blunt. I've blown it.

She hadn't. "Oh, yes," said Kupitz matter-of-factly, almost cheerfully. "That's what's happening, all right. I know Dr. Hazeltine thinks this cure is all nonsense but Rebecca and I agree that we ought to at least—" He stopped. Joan Scully strained to hear what was happening. "Oh, my," said Kupitz, "I really can't talk about it now. A pleasure, Miss Scully. Good-bye."

He hung up.

Slightly dazed, Joan stood with the receiver in her hand. Then she hung it up. She made her way through the boisterous crowd and sat down next to David. He asked her, What was that phone call all about? What's going on? But she didn't answer. So he changed the subject and went on about the Institute and his career. About how maybe with the new money flowing in to Underwood he could get promoted from assistant to associate. And then he could get a better apartment, although the one he had now wasn't bad—and Joan knew he was trying to get her to come back to it now. But she was oblivious to him. She was thinking intensely, wondering what to do about Kupitz.

Finally, she excused herself again, went to the phone and called Hertz. When she returned to the table this time, she told David, nicely, that she had to leave. She had other plans.

Kansas City, Missouri

The evening with Jennifer Byrd started well.

When he got back to the center of the city, Lattimer managed to find a men's clothing store that was still open. So he presented himself at the American Restaurant in new slacks, shirt, sports jacket and silk tie. And Miss Byrd, he decided, didn't look bad herself. This afternoon, she had been quite nice and efficient in her TWA uniform—but that was hardly the effect of the black dress she now wore, high at the neck but leaving her creamy shoulders and arms bare. There was a gloss on her lips and shadows over her large eyes that weren't airline-issue either. And three golden bracelets on her left arm rang lightly, musically, against each other when she laughed, which was also light music. No, Frank Lattimer decided, the effect was more what one would call stunning.

The dinner was her equal. Passing up the Maryland turtle steak and the Montana elk, they shared one order of applejack chicken (with chestnuts, apples and heavy cream) and one order of Plymouth clam pie (with mushrooms and shallots). Lattimer felt his body's various appetites returning. Miss Byrd and he traded forkfuls of food, sipped the good California wines and talked of happy, inconsequential things. Jennifer Byrd said it looked like Lattimer had won his private war, whatever it had been. "Peace is declared," she was saying. "The boys are home."

At that moment, the waiter reappeared. "Telephone call for you, Mr. Lattimer," he said quietly.

Jennifer Byrd looked puzzled. "I'm sorry," said Lattimer, "I had to tell someone I was here." He excused himself. He followed the waiter to the phone, next to the kitchen.

"Hello," he said, "this is Frank Lattimer."

"This is Dr. Walt Lindenmeyer," said a hearty, flat, Midwestern voice. "My answering service said it was important. Something to do with Chris Ives. . . .Who are you and what's the story?"

"I'm a friend of Ives's," said Lattimer, "and I'm really worried about him." Lattimer looked around. In contrast to the elegant, quiet dining room, the kitchen was a hubbub. It was hard to hear and be heard.

"Why worried?" asked the psychiatrist.

"He called"—Lattimer had to raise his voice over the banging of a pot—"he called me in New York today. He said he's desperate. He said he wants to commit suicide."

"Yes?" prompted Lindenmeyer.

"So I flew out here—to see him right away. But he's not home. I wondered if you knew where he was."

"You're a very good friend to do that, Mr. Lattimer," said Lindenmeyer. "But I don't remember Chris mentioning you."

"Old friend. From ten years ago. Haven't seen each other since. But maybe—I guess he felt he could turn to me. So where is he, Doctor? I know if I could see him, I could help."

"Mmm," said Lindenmeyer. There was a pause. "No," he said. "I don't know where Chris is. Although he has—"

Lindenmeyer's voice was drowned out by the sous-chef yelling at one of the waiters.

"What?" asked Lattimer.

"—said he has called me. My answering service told me."

"He called you!" said Lattimer. "But he didn't say from where?"

"No, not according to what they told me."

"Did he say *why* he called?"

"No. Apparently not. Although now that you tell me Chris is talking suicide, naturally I'll play back the tape and see if I can learn anything. And try to find him. So I thank you, Mr. Lattimer. You've been very helpful."

It was clear Lindenmeyer was about to hang up. "Wait!" Lattimer yelled, over the kitchen noise. "Tape? What tape?"

"Oh," said Lindenmeyer. "My answering service also tapes all calls I get. I don't quite trust them to report back to me exactly everything my patients say. So it's all on tape," he chuckled. "Sometimes they say the damnedest things without meaning to."

"Could *I* hear the tape, Doctor?" asked Lattimer.

"I'm afraid not," said Lindenmeyer. Lattimer could hear the surprise behind the professional coolness. "That's confidential."

"But," persisted Lattimer, "as a friend, perhaps I could tell—"

"Thank you very much," said Lindenmeyer, all the heartiness gone, only the flatness remaining.

"Doctor!" said Lattimer, knowing that he sounded crazy, as crazy as he imagined some of Lindenmeyer's patients might sound. "It's really important to me. For reasons that are even more important than Chris's life."

"More important than his life?" asked Lindenmeyer.

"Could I come out and explain it to you?" asked Lattimer. "And then, if it makes sense to you, let me listen to the tape?"

"No," said Lindenmeyer. "Not the tape. But if you come out tomorrow, I'm sure we can discuss it."

Lattimer considered it. A nice drive through the Kansas wheatfields tomorrow, the sun glowing golden on the wheat . . . He could leave around noon. Probably stay in bed late with Jennifer. She had said her flight out wasn't until afternoon. So, a leisurely breakfast. After a leisurely night. She was waiting for him at the table now. The chicken and the clam pie would still be warm. It was all very attractive. Except that tomorrow didn't seem soon enough. Things were happening too fast. The attack on Justin last night, Underwood and Prentice's announcement today . . .

"How about tonight?" asked Lattimer.

"Tonight?" Lindenmeyer's voice was full of wonderment.

"How far away are you?"

"Mr. Lattimer, Topeka is seventy-five miles away from K.C."

"I'll be there in an hour and a half. Less."

"But—"

"I'll take just fifteen minutes of your time."

"But you—"

There was more noise from the kitchen, somebody yelling about salmon and then dishes clattering.

"Your address. Please?"

"173 South—"

"Please, sir," said the headwaiter to Lattimer "we must have this phone back. There is a pay phone—"

"Shh," said Lattimer. "What?" he asked Lindenmeyer.

Unwillingly, the psychiatrist finished giving his address. Lattimer thanked him and walked back into the dining room.

Jennifer Byrd looked up and pretended a pout with her beautiful mouth. "Rats," she said. "Back so soon. I'd hoped I could finish the rest of the chicken."

"You can," said Lattimer. He sat down and touched her hand. "I'm really sorry," he said. "But I've got to run. My war."

"Frank," she said. She looked hurt but not angry.

He took out his wallet and handed her sixty dollars. "This ought to cover it," he said. "And for dessert, try the maple mousse. It's made with rum sauce. Maybe I'll see you another time in the friendly skies."

She smiled. "You've still got the wrong airline."

He rose to leave.

"It really is business?" she asked.

He nodded.

"You'll be back—when?" she asked.

"I don't know. Not until real late."

"Come by," she said.

"It might be—"

"Come by," she said. "The Prom-Sheraton. Room 412. Can you remember that?"

"I think I can manage," said Frank Lattimer.

Houston, Texas/Lander, Colorado

After the lawyers left his hospital suite, Matt Ash was alone with Nurse Jambois. He lay peacefully looking at the ceiling.

"Cool," he said, remembering. "Cool an' damp. In the middle of that desert ... so green. The water slides down that cliff maybe a hun'red feet into the pool. Slides down through columbine, wild rye, maidenhair." He turned to Jambois. "Pretty word, huh, 'maidenhair,' pretty maiden?"

Jambois smiled.

"An' all around the pool . . . willow, oak, cottonwood . . . shadin' the pool. So green. Cool green. An' you can hear the tree frog an' the cliff frog. An' once Ah saw there, through the trees, a golden eagle there. An' bats." He looked at Jambois again. "Did you know bats can be beautiful?"

"No, Mr. Ash."

"Well, the spotted bat is. An' Ah saw it there, too. Near that pool. An' the cliff frog. Did you know the cliff frog makes a noise only when it's damp 'nough for him?"

"No," she said, warmly, interested.

"Well, it's true. But Ah heard him cry there. In that pool in the middle of the desert. Heard him cry."

Matt Ash closed his eyes, remembering. He remembered being a young man exploring West Texas, walking through the desolate uplands north of Redford—and finding Chorro Canyon and the nameless stream that tumbled down the rockface into the hidden pool in the lush green forest. He remembered returning there several times and then not anymore, not for a long time.

"It's still there, you know," he said to Jambois. "You can still go back. Like the Reverend said, like you can still go back to Jesus. Still there." He smiled. "Think Ah'll go back," he said softly.

Nurse Jambois regarded her resting patient. His rugged, weathered face, in repose, took on almost the dignity of a sculpture. He was a man transported, for the moment at least, beyond any concerns that required Mashing.

Jambois looked at her watch. It was 9:15. And apparently, she thought, he was also beyond feeling the pain of his cancer. Jambois was young, but she had been a nurse long enough to know what the mind could do for the body in a terminal case—at least for a while. She was pleased to be able to skip the 9 P.M. shot of morphine.

But in the sanitarium high on Saddleback Mountain in the Colorado Rockies, the mind inside Christopher Ives's younger and basically healthy body was demanding drugs. And not mere 5-milligram Valium. No, he craved stronger stuff—maybe even Thorazine—to really knock himself out. Anything to dampen the anxiety that rose steadily higher inside him, up from his empty stomach, till it threatened to choke him, like a man suffocating in his own vomit. All day long, Ives had wanted to call Lindenmeyer. It was Monday—the psychiatrist had been in his office. But now that Ives *could* have reached him, he had been afraid to. What could he, Ives, say to him? What could he dare confess to now, now that he had gone so far, now that it would all come to a conclusion tomorrow? He simply didn't dare call Lindenmeyer. And he felt he couldn't keep down food. So Ives, who had always had easy access to drugs at Dacey, now reached into his desk drawer and came up with the Thorazine. Then he stopped himself. No, that was for psychotics, and he wasn't *there* yet. Instead, Ives made do with a 10-milligram Valium. He hoped—but doubted—that it would quiet his fear.

Greenwich, Connecticut

Once Joan Scully left the Connecticut Turnpike and headed north, through downtown Greenwich and into the back country, she became lost several times. The country lanes were dark and winding and changed names constantly. The homes and estates were mostly set back off the road, hidden by woods and stone walls. There were no street numbers to follow, only mailboxes and small discreet signs— "Foxcroft," "High Hill"—on private gates. And there were no places to ask directions, no gas stations or stores. It was a world cut off. But finally, she found it. "Kupitz." She turned onto the gravel road, past the gate house and then a half mile more, past a stable and a guest cottage, to the main building. It looked as if it was originally a Revolutionary-era farmhouse, added onto many times since, but still beautifully proportioned, quiet and expensive.

There were a few lights on. Joan Scully rang the front bell.

A distinguished older man with the deferential air of a servant opened the door.

"Yes?"

"Uh ... I'm Joan Scully. I ... I called earlier. I talked to Mr. Kupitz. Is he here?"

"Yes, ma'am. Will you wait a moment?"

Standing alone in the large hall, surrounded by what she suspected was an authentic Chippendale sideboard and Hudson River School canvases and, underfoot, an Aubusson carpet, Joan Scully suddenly wondered what on earth had possessed her to—

"Ah, Miss Scully. How good of you to come."

The middle-aged man coming toward her, smiling, had a book under one arm and eyeglasses pushed up past his high forehead into his unruly salt-and-pepper hair. As he took her hands—"I'm Michael Kupitz," he said—the book fell to the floor. Both flustered, they both knelt to pick it up. *The Realm of the Seljuk Turks* by O. W. McArdle. "My specialty," explained Kupitz. "The First Crusade. I'm writing a biography of Stephen of Blois, but McArdle is very little help on background—he gets so many details wrong. Won't you come in?"

He led Joan into the library and gestured to two Queen Anne chairs facing the marble fireplace. "Do sit down. Would you like a drink? I only take sherry myself but I'm sure Hargrove can find anything you want." Kupitz was bubbling cheerfully.

"Uh . . . sherry," said Joan Scully.

"Fine," said Kupitz, pressing a small bell next to his chair. "You know, when you asked on the phone about Hazeltine, about what errand he might be running for me, I'm afraid . . . well, what could I say? I mean, yes, of course I'm dying of cancer and the doctor is trying to track down some sort of cure for me but it's very awkward discussing *details* on the phone. I mean, Rebecca came in and I had to hang up. She thinks I talk too much. But since you care so much that you drove all the way out here—" The old servant appeared. "Ah, Hargrove, some sherry and two glasses. And"—Kupitz turned back to Joan—"now that I can *see* you and you look so obviously sincere . . . well . . . why should it be a secret? The fact of the matter is that Hazeltine is going to check out this interesting offer I received just a few days ago. You see, these chaps say they have a drug or something that can fix up my bone marrow, make it good as new. And do it right now—not have to wait a year like this claim I heard this chap made this afternoon. Because I don't *have* a year—more like a few months, really. Anyway, I don't actually *believe* it'll be 'good as new'! But if it could give me a year or two more, I could at least finish Stephen—"

"Stephen?" asked Joan. She was too stunned by Kupitz's whole monologue to think straight. She had come anticipating the most difficult business of prying information—and now this smiling man was simply laying it all out for her. Offhandedly.

"Stephen of Blois," explained Kupitz. "Of course, thirty-odd million is a lot for that, for one good biography. But what *else* am I going to do with the money? Travel? Entertain? Entertain whom? The only people I really know are some scholars in the Crusades and frankly, from the way they sound in their letters, so jealous of sharing any information, I doubt they'd like to share some sherry. In fact, Miss Scully, you're the first person to come calling on me . . . oh, certainly a long time. Although I keep our phone listed, just in case. Well, of course I would like to retrace Stephen's march through Syria, but that's impossible for a Jew. But that's really the only place I've an itch to go." He paused. "Well, it *might* be interesting to travel to see Belsen again. Although, if Hazeltine says I should accept this offer, I will *have* to travel—tomorrow as a matter of fact, and to where I have no idea. Isn't that a marvelous idea? A mysterious, imminent journey? Yes, Miss Scully?"

Joan was holding one hand to her head. Her head was reeling.

She was trying to understand. One question at a time, she thought. Take it slow.

"Thirty million," she began. "Is that dollars? Is that the cost of . . . of . . . ?"

"Of the cure," said Michael Kupitz. "That's a lot of paper plates and paper towels but Great-Uncle Daniel made sure we could afford it. Or the bank can."

"Paper . . . ?"

"The family fortune," Kupitz explained. "We sold to Kimberly-Clark forty years ago. Now the bank clips coupons, I'm told."

"Oh . . . and the people who called. They are . . . ?"

"No idea. No idea at all."

"And you're going . . . ?"

"Who knows where."

"But tomorrow?" asked Joan, for confirmation.

"Yes."

"To do . . . ?"

"To—to get the drug, I guess," said Kupitz. "If Hazeltine says so. You see, he's already there. Wherever it is. Checking it out."

"Oh," said Joan. It made no sense. It made terribly clear, terribly awful sense. "And Belsen? Did you say 'Belsen'?"

Michael Kupitz rolled up the sleeve of his old cardigan sweater, then rolled up his shirt sleeve. He showed her the tattoo.

"I was a child, of course," he said. "Mother took me to Budapest that summer. A long story. Anyway, we couldn't get out. Uncle Daniel's money didn't count over there." Kupitz let the sleeves fall back down. "Maybe the money will buy something now," he said, shyly.

Joan Scully wished the sherry would come. She wished something stronger would come. She looked at the dear, innocent, scholarly man in the Queen Anne chair. How could she begin to get through to him? "Mr. Kupitz," she began, slowly, "if the cure *is* a cure then I'm very happy for you. But haven't you thought what it could mean . . . to other people? Don't you think you should tell—"

"He's going to tell no one," said the woman's voice. "And neither are you."

Joan Scully turned around quickly. The middle-aged woman, standing with her arms crossed, glared back. Joan saw the resemblance immediately. The same high forehead, the same intelligent face . . .

"Uh . . . Miss Scully," said Michael Kupitz uneasily, "this is my sister, Rebecca. This is . . . "

But Joan also saw that where, on Michael's face, the family features were soft, on Rebecca's they were hard, determined.

"... Miss Joan Scully," concluded Michael.

"And *who* is Miss Scully?" asked Rebecca.

"Uh ... " began Joan. "A friend ... of a friend of Dr. Hazeltine. I ... I work at Oakes-Metcalf. He ... the friend told me Dr. Hazeltine was doing something for you. I wanted to find out what." It all sounded so lame to Joan. And the woman's flat statement about telling no one worried Joan.

"And now you have," said the woman, flatly. "Have found out."

"Uh ... I guess so."

"And you thought you'd stop it? Stop Michael from possibly being saved? Let him die?"

"No! No ... I ... "

"That's what would happen," said Rebecca Kupitz, "if you told anyone. The police, the press, your own Institute would come down on us like demons. Michael would never get his shot." She glared at her brother, she shook her head sadly. "Why," she asked, exasperated and affectionate, "why did you talk to her?"

Michael Kupitz was clutching McArdle's book. "I didn't think?" he suggested cheerfully.

"No," said Rebecca, sadly. "You didn't. Once again, I have to think for you." She turned back to Joan Scully. "So you see, my dear, you are going to tell no one."

"I could promise," said Joan.

"Promise," said Rebecca, ironically, dismissing the word. "Hargrove!" she called.

The butler emerged from the hall into the room. He held a pistol in his hand, pointed at Joan. Hargrove was old but his hand and gaze were steady. Joan was terrified. Her hand flew to her throat.

"You're ... you're not going to ... " she gasped.

"Good Lord, no. We're not going to kill you," snapped Rebecca Kupitz. "Just lock you upstairs for a few days until we find out if this cure is for real. And, if it is for real, until Michael receives it. Then," she shrugged, "you're free. And don't worry. It's the best guest room and Mattie—that's Mrs. Hargrove—is an excellent cook. You'll dine well. You'll have time to read." She allowed herself the trace of a smile. "Michael has an excellent library of books on the Crusades." She turned to the servant. "Hargrove," she said, indicating he should escort Joan.

Hargrove advanced apologetically—but steadily—with his gun. Joan Scully stood up. "I'm really sorry," said Michael to Joan. He sounded like a little boy who'd been caught eating too many cookies and wanted to be reassured he wasn't all bad.

"It's okay," said Joan to Michael. I could grab Hargrove's wrist, she thought. Or simply run past him—he might not dare shoot. After all, this *was* back country Greenwich, where servants in big old farmhouses on rolling estates didn't shoot guests in the back.

But he might.

"Okay," said Joan to Hargrove. "I'll go. But could you bring up that sherry, too? I could use it now."

Topeka, Kansas

The few psychiatrists Lattimer had met in New York had not overly impressed him. One, at a party, had refused to laugh at jokes because, Lattimer sensed, the man had felt he couldn't drop his professional demeanor in the presence of several ex-patients. Another psychiatrist, with the reputation of working wonders in sorting out other people's lives, came to Lattimer's attention when, in the midst of his fourth divorce, he shot his wife's lover. But Dr. Walt Lindenmeyer seemed different. He came to the door of his split-level ranch house in the plain but prosperous Topeka neighborhood wearing old corduroy pants and a work shirt. He had several ball-point pens stuck in his shirt pocket and a copy of *People* magazine under his arm. His middle-aged face was strong and open, with clear blue eyes behind rimless spectacles. He looked as if he might run a hardware store or be the athletic director of a local college.

"Sorry I'm late," said Lattimer.

"No, it's all right," said Lindenmeyer. "Come on in." He ushered Lattimer into the living room and introduced him briefly to his two teen-age sons, who were watching television and munching pretzels, and to his wife, who was making a stained-glass window. He fished a couple of Cokes out of the refrigerator and took Lattimer back to his study. He waved Lattimer to an armchair. Lattimer regarded the diplomas on the knotty pine paneling, the bulging bookcases, the comfortable old couch.

"I'm impressed you drove all the way out here," said Lindenmeyer, looking at him levelly, "for Chris. But I checked with his wife and she doesn't know where he is—"

"I called her, too," said Lattimer.

"—and I got hold of the tapes from my answering service—"

Lattimer leaned forward.

"—but I'm afraid," continued the psychiatrist, "that there's nothing on them that hints where he is. So that's about it."

"Oh," said Lattimer.

"So you don't even have to tell me," said Lindenmeyer, "what this reason is that's even more important than Chris's life. Or why, when you called his wife this morning, you said not that you were his friend but a reporter doing a story on drugs."

"Oh," said Lattimer, embarrassed.

"I called Mrs. Ives this evening," explained Lindenmeyer, "and she told me about you."

"Well, you see, what I'm really after—" began Lattimer.

"I'm really less interested in you," said Lindenmeyer, "than I am in Chris. I take it he *didn't* call you threatening suicide?"

"No," said Lattimer, "he didn't." Lattimer felt about one inch high.

"Good," said Lindenmeyer. "I was worried." He took a sip of Coke. "Well," he said, "I guess if you want Chris you'll just have to wait till he comes back." The clear blue eyes stared clear through Lattimer. "Although why you'd want to hound a man about that terrible polio vaccine mess that wasn't even his fault, that stopped being news two years ago, is beyond me."

Lattimer rolled his own drink between his hands. "It's not the polio vaccine," he said. And he proceeded to tell Walt Lindenmeyer the whole story.

Throughout, Lindenmeyer's expression never changed. He listened attentively. When Lattimer finished, he was aware of a huge silence in the study.

Lindenmeyer rubbed an eyebrow. "Damn little evidence to base your conclusions on, I'd say," he said. He sounded to Lattimer like a Kansas farmer matter-of-factly doubting an Easterner's claim about a new chemical fertilizer.

Lattimer gestured at the couch. "You base conclusions on a lot less, Doctor. Dreams, adolescent memories."

Lindenmeyer smiled. "Have you ever been in analysis, Mr. Lattimer?" he asked.

"No."

Lindenmeyer shrugged. It wasn't a superior shrug. Just that of the Kansas farmer. "Anyway," said Lindenmeyer, "it doesn't matter. Even if I believed your story, believed that Chris is up to something no good, I still can't do anything for you."

"Let me listen to the tapes," Lattimer persisted.

Lindenmeyer sighed. "Sure," he said, "why not? There's nothing on them."

He picked up two tapes from the top of his desk. He threaded one onto a tape recorder. "This is Saturday's," he said. He ran the tape on fast forward, watching the tape counter as he did. He found the right place and pressed the "play" button.

Lattimer heard the professionally friendly voice of a woman say:

"Good afternoon, Dr. Lindenmeyer's office."

And then a man's voice, low, tense and hurried: "Uh, is he there, please?"

"No, I'm sorry. The doctor will be back on Monday. Who's calling, please?"

"Chris Ives. Look, is there any way I can get hold of him? Could you give me his home number?"

"No, I'm sorry. Not unless this is an emergency. Is this an emergency?"

"No." A sigh.

"Well, if you give me *your* number, I'll have the doctor—"

"No!" The man's voice exploded.

"—have him call you?"

"No. No, thank you. Goodbye."

There was the *click* of a phone being hung up.

Lindenmeyer stopped the tape and rewound it. "As you can hear," he said, "there's nothing."

Lattimer thoughtfully ran a thumbnail between his two front teeth. "I guess," he said. "But did Ives ever call you before and not get you and ask you to call him back?"

Lindenmeyer was puzzled. "I suppose so," he said. "Why?"

"So where would you call him?" asked Lattimer.

"At his office or his home."

"So why *wouldn't* he want you to call him wherever he is *now*?" asked Lattimer.

"I don't know," said Lindenmeyer. "And it certainly doesn't suggest where he is."

"Mmm," said Lattimer. He sank back in the armchair and gazed at the ceiling. "Could you play back Sunday's call?"

Lindenmeyer did. The same woman answered. The same man talked. Listening, Lattimer juxtaposed the self-satisfied face he had seen in the Dacey annual report with this scared voice.

In a near whisper, the man's voice begged: "But I've got to talk to him."

"Well," said the woman, "if you could give me your number, I'm sure the doctor—"

"I can't *do* that!" the man's voice cried. And the man hung up.

Lindenmeyer stopped the tape. Lattimer pointed a finger at him. "It's not that Ives doesn't want you to call him," said Lattimer. "It's that he doesn't want you to call him at *that* number. Why? And what number could it be?"

Lindenmeyer shrugged.

"Is he having an affair?" asked Lattimer. "Is he shacked up somewhere?"

"You know I can't answer that," said the psychiatrist.

"Well, when did he say he'd be back? When's his next session?"

"We left it open."

"He didn't say where he was going? Or for how long?"

"A vacation, he said."

"And he didn't call you *today*?" demanded Lattimer. "After he wanted so much to get you this weekend, he didn't even try today?"

"No," said Lindenmeyer. "But sometimes crises solve themselves."

"Yeah," sighed Lattimer. "Sure." He stood up. "Well, Doctor, thank you very much. I don't suppose if he *does* call tomorrow—or soon—that you would ask him where he is and then maybe let me . . ." Lattimer's voice ran down. "No," he said, "I don't suppose you would tell me."

"I'm afraid not," said Lindenmeyer. He stood and shook hands with Lattimer. It was a firm handshake, but it was also clearly dismissing Lattimer.

"Well, let *me* tell *you* one thing, Doctor," said Lattimer. "From what I know of people, I bet that it's not dreams that have got your patient worried—it's reality. It's what he's messed up in."

"Maybe," said Lindenmeyer, noncommittally.

"Dreams," snorted Lattimer. He was frustrated. He was frayed from the long trip to Kansas City and then here to Topeka and the idea of the long trip back. And all for nothing. He was bugged at this psychiatrist who—although he seemed on the surface to be different from the others Lattimer had met—still had nothing valuable to impart. "I'll tell you a dream," said Lattimer. "And you tell me what there is to it."

"Well . . . " said Lindenmeyer.

"Real quick," promised Lattimer. And he quickly told Lindenmeyer the dream he'd had on the plane this afternoon. When he finished, he demanded, "Well?"

"Well," asked Lindenmeyer, "what do you think?"

"I don't know," said Lattimer.

"What do you associate with a file?"

"A file? It doesn't make any sense. The only files I deal with are file drawers."

"So that's your association."

"That's what it means?" asked Lattimer. "I'm really dreaming about file *drawers*? That's what it means that the women are being filed down? My mind makes a cheap pun like that?"

"You tell me."

"And why is the last woman—Joan—why does she have no breasts and black hair?"

"I don't know," said Lindenmeyer. "Whom do you know who looks like that?"

"Certainly no woman," said Lattimer.

"Well," shrugged Lindenmeyer. "And now," he said, "I think you'd better go. It's already very late."

Lindenmeyer walked Lattimer back through the house. His sons had gone to bed, his wife was watching the news. Lindenmeyer picked up a pretzel that had gotten mashed underfoot. On the front stoop, under a globe lamp, the two men said good night. Lattimer thanked Lindenmeyer. Moths dive-bombed the lamp. Around them was the hum of crickets and soft wind in the trees and the smell of the prairie far off. Walt Lindenmeyer cocked his plain, square, Midwestern face at Lattimer.

"Just ask yourself one other thing, Mr. Lattimer: Where are *you* in the dream? We always put ourselves in our dreams, too."

"I'd rather know where Ives is," said Frank Lattimer.

New York City

The greatest tribute that Senator Arthur Prentice received this day came shortly after ten o'clock in the men's room of the private dining room of Antonio's restaurant on Kissena Boulevard in Forest Hills, Queens.

There had been earlier welcomes. After the announcement at Oakes-Metcalf, Prentice and a half-dozen staffers and the Secret Service men had gone on a tour that included the Three-I League: Little Italy, where his staff had made sure some boccie players would stop and invite the senator to bowl a few. Then the Lower East Side, where the staff made sure the senator would be given knishes to nosh and where, his mouth full, he talked of America's commitment to Israel. And then Bay Ridge in Brooklyn, where his staff had been sure the senator would be asked by the monsignor of St. Aloysius to draw the winning number that would send two parishioners on a vacation in Ireland. And everywhere, in addition to the prearranged welcomes, there had been spontaneous welcomes from people who had heard Prentice promise the cure for cancer and who, skeptical New Yorkers that they were, still believed enough to smile and say, "Good luck" and, "Hey, if you really do it . . . "

But this tribute in the men's room wasn't planned at all. Prentice's staff had arranged for the senator to be the guest of honor at a private dinner for the Queens borough president. And leaving the dinner, just stopping in the men's room, on his way to La Guardia to catch a plane home for Indiana, Prentice suddenly found himself locked in by a thirteen-year-old groupie who wanted to give him a blow job.

"What?" he asked. He didn't mean "what." She was very forthright about what she wanted to do. He meant "why"—but he was too overwhelmed to speak straight.

"Because you're famous now," she said. "And my thing is to do the famous first, before other girls can."

"The famous?"

"Sure. Like I did Bobby Dugan right after his swim." (Dugan was the young Canadian who had swum Lake Ontario on the Fourth of July). "And I did Herb Koleszar the day they arrested him." (Koleszar, an ex-mental patient, had machine-gunned twenty-three people in a Phoenix shopping center in May.)

"Koleszar?" stammered Prentice. "Where?"

"In jail," said the groupie, calmly. She had short blond hair and hardly any breasts or hips. She wore hardly any makeup on her innocent face. Prentice thought she could have stepped out of a Norman Rockwell painting.

"So you're going to do all the presidential candidates?" asked Prentice. "The day each of them declares?"

The groupie was insulted. "Are you kidding?" she asked. "Do politicians? Hey—I want to do you because you helped discover the cure for cancer."

Prentice shook his head in wonderment. In his twenty years in public life, he had never received such a compliment. He would have to tell Jack Lynch about this. Prentice wanted to reach out and touch the girl like a daughter—indeed she was younger than his daughter—but he was afraid the gesture would be misunderstood.

"Thanks," he finally said, warmly, "but no."

"No?"

"Sorry. And I've really got to catch a plane now."

"No?" She was crushed.

He smiled and tried to push past her to the door.

"Hey," she said. She stopped him and then started to unbutton her blouse. Prentice was alarmed. The young girl held out a breast for him. "Hey," she said, "if you don't want to let me do you, could you at least . . . take a look."

"Look?" asked Prentice. Look at what? he wondered. He saw her breast plainly enough.

"Look and see . . . " She hesitated. "I'm afraid . . . this lump." She pointed. "Is it . . . ?"

Prentice looked closer and made a show of examining it. His forefinger prodded it professionally. "No," he declared, authoritatively, "it's not cancer."

"Oh," she said, tears in her eyes. "Thank you. Thank you, mister."

And Arthur Prentice left to rejoin his entourage and catch his plane. But as he walked out of the men's room of Antonio's restaurant, he was already airborne. He was famous, he was Albert Schweitzer—hell, he was God.

The two men who had shared the platform outside Oakes-Metcalf were also enjoying feelings of Godliness.

For Hugh Underwood, it was a feeling of floating and great calm, supported by a cloud of marijuana in his head. Underwood was not a cigarette smoker so, as he had explained to his wife many times, he'd never had success with grass before. He simply didn't know how to get the smoke down into his lungs. But she had accused him—rightly, he knew—of being too much of a "tight-ass middle-class nigger" (her words) to really try. But tonight, for the first time, it had worked. The day had shaken something free in Underwood. The interviews with the press and television, the congratulations of his colleagues, and then watching himself later on television, on both the local and national evening news ... the feeling of power had loosened him up and turned him on. And with Ceilia by his side all day, beaming at him, he had wanted to turn that power on with her. It was not until nine o'clock that they were alone back in their Manhattan apartment. Ceilia took out some grass—"top Colombian," she had said—and rolled a joint. And he smoked it effortlessly with her. And another. And soon they were making love. And he didn't come quickly as he usually did but instead lasted and lasted and Ceil came several times and called him "my super-nigger" and time was elastic and he felt he could suspend himself above her and pump into her powerfully forever....

For Warren Brown, it was a feeling of God-like order. As an administrator, Brown thought of God as the great administrator. And, after a meeting with his staff at the Institute that went on into the night—a meeting at which they organized how, over the next weeks and months, to take advantage of Underwood's discovery and the publicity—Brown was as pleased as he imagined God was on the seventh day of Creation. Brown's desperation of last week, desperation over HEW fund cutbacks, was long gone. In its place was the confidence that the Institute would prosper. The meeting ended with mutual congratulations. With one of his aides, Brown went to the rooftop restaurant of a nearby hotel. They sipped drinks and looked at the lights of Manhattan. Brown knew the young man was a homosexual and that he was attracted to Brown. When the young man dropped the hint, Brown turned it gently aside. He instructed his aide to regard the city—the powerful glow from the great skyscrapers, streaks of light on the parallel and perpendicular streets making a gridiron of order to the horizon. That's what turned on Warren Brown.

New York City

After dinner, one of the nurses took Barbara Justin down the hall for an X-ray. No, the nurse answered Barbara, it wasn't a mammogram. Just a standard X-ray for anyone being admitted to the hospital. When Barbara returned to her room, she discovered that she had missed her mother. The nurse on duty said Elizabeth Yates had stopped by on the way from the airport to Dobbs Ferry. Barbara was disappointed not to have seen her. I could use some comfort, she thought, some support. Her mother had left a gift, a book—fifty years of *New Yorker* cartoons. Barbara started leafing through it. But then a resident arrived to give her a physical exam. Eyes, nose, mouth, heart, lungs, abdomen, breasts. Barbara was feeling increasingly *handled*—not a person, only a body. The resident took her medical history, her third of the day. When he left, Barbara didn't have the energy to go back to the book. She lay, discouraged, listening to Mrs. Ambrose's TV set, now running cops-and-robbers shows. The evening dragged on. A nurse appeared to hand Barbara a sleeping pill and warn her not to eat or drink anything after midnight. Barbara swallowed the pill eagerly. Sleep would be a blessing. As she lay there, waiting for it to take effect, she idly opened the book of cartoons again. This time, she noticed her mother's inscription on the first page: "Life is the game that must be played/So live and laugh, nor be dismayed." It sounded to Barbara like a quote, she didn't know from where. Barbara smiled. That was her mother all right. Meeting disasters with a cup of hot tea and an optimistic piece of poetry remembered from college. Hot tea, thought Barbara. She rang for the nurse. If it wasn't yet midnight, she'd take a cup. And pretend she was sharing it with her mother.

One floor above, Paul Justin wished he could ring for a nurse. The top of his nose was itching fiercely and he couldn't scratch it. Amazing, he thought, how such a simple thing as relieving an itch, that we do practically unconsciously a dozen times a day, could be so important when we *can't* do it. But even if he could ring, he doubted a nurse would have come quickly. Because now he could hear both nurses, out at their desk, busy arguing with yet another representative of the media (or were there several this time?) who had managed to sneak through the police cordon guarding intensive care. He wanted to interview, he said, Dr. Paul Justin.

"Get out of here!" shouted one of the nurses. "Out!"

"But I just want—"

"Don't you understand, you idiot?" she shouted. "He's in a coma! He *can't* talk!"

"Well, then, let me ask *you* a few—"

"Out! Get out!"

And then Justin heard Falcone appear with someone else (a cop?) and get rid of the media people.

Justin didn't know whether to cry or laugh at the absurdity of it. Assuming he could do either. Ever since Underwood and Prentice's news conference this noon, the media had been trying to get in to see him. If not for a statement, then at least for something. A glimpse. A photograph. Some film of him *not* talking. But they'd had to settle for Dewing and Falcone and the cops all telling them, "No, we don't know when he'll regain consciousness. No, we don't know who attacked him last night. No, there's no connection between that and his work with Dr. Underwood."

Oh, thought Paul Justin, if I *could* talk, what I would tell you! I would tell you what a liar my boss is. I would tell you the cure is mine. I would tell you . . .

I would tell you my nose itches like hell.

Dobbs Ferry, New York

Elizabeth Everett Yates had had a hard time getting her grandchildren to go to sleep. This morning, from their friends, the children had learned what their mother had not dared tell them—that last night somebody had tried to kill their father. This afternoon, they had learned that their father had helped Dr. Underwood make some big cancer discovery. And this evening, Elizabeth Yates had to tell them that their mother was in the hospital, too.

All the news was too unnerving to the children. And the constant ringing of the telephone—the media besieging with still more questions—made it worse. Finally, around ten o'clock, when it was obvious no one could get to sleep, Mother Yates took the phone off the hook and challenged all her grandchildren to a game of Monopoly. Within an hour, she was beating them all—all except Laurie, who had nodded off on the living room rug. Soon afterward, the cat walked through and scattered the pieces. Steve and Melissa grabbed throwpillows off the couch and hurled them at the animal.

They couldn't reconstruct the game. And by now, they were calmed enough to go to bed. Mother Yates tucked in Laurie. She sat for a few minutes with Melissa on the edge of Melissa's bed. Together they looked out the window into the night sky. Melissa wished on a star for her mommy and daddy to be well and she told her grandmother how her daddy was telling her all about stars and constellations. Then Mother Yates said good night to Steve. Steve was irritated at something. He said he didn't think it was right for Senator Prentice to claim credit for his dad's work. "I still think Prentice is lousy—he's not half as good as Reed."

Elizabeth Yates ruffled Steve's hair. She reflected on how the cat and Senator Prentice had become targets for the children's anger—a way for them to vent feelings they could not express directly.

Elizabeth Yates drowned her own feelings in a cup of hot tea with milk. And went to bed.

Kansas City, Missouri

"And now here?" she asked.

"Uh-huh."

"And like this?"

"Oh, Jesus."

"And then we do this . . . "

"For how long?" he gasped.

Making love to Jennifer Byrd was nothing like making love to Joan Scully. The first time with Joan, on Friday night, had been hard, fast and direct: on the floor of her apartment, wham, slam, bam. The second time, on the beach on Saturday night, had been tender and lingering, with touchings and explorings that were almost shy. But this, with Jennifer, was . . . there was only one word for it: expert.

They did one position and another and then, just when Lattimer felt he was finished, exhausted, she led him into something else, and when she subsided, he led. Back and forth, over and under, and when it was finally done, *he* was done, flat out, emptied. And yet filled—filled with pleasure and with the knowledge that sex had never taken him so far.

Jennifer lay content. She turned over on her side, facing Lattimer, and fell asleep with a smile on her lips. Lattimer lay on his back looking at the ceiling. He thought he would fall asleep, but he did not. Something was nibbling his mind. He looked at his watch. It was almost two o'clock. Almost three in New York. He thought about Joan, asleep in her apartment. Suddenly—and the feeling surprised him—he wished very much he were with her. He also suddenly understood what his dream meant.

For years, he realized, for his whole adult life, he had been filing people away. He had had relationships with women, presumably on equal terms. But with each, the point came where he could or would not give more of himself or accept more from the woman. And so he had finished enjoying each and then ... filed each away. So they became simply ... data. This one liked Marx Brothers movies. That one liked the beach. This one wore jeans. That one swore like a trooper. Et cetera. Data that had no more impact than any data he might dig up for a story.

But while he had done that, a part of him hadn't liked it. And that part was now protesting. Protesting especially—he remembered the greatest terror in the dream—that he might do this to Joan also. And protesting at something else as well. What had Lindenmeyer said? "Where are *you* in the dream? We always put ourselves in our dreams." Lattimer understood now: the transfiguration of Joan, breastless and with black hair. That was *himself*. For just as he filed other people away, so he had filed himself away, reduced his own feelings to mere facts, refused to go with his feelings.

Well, damn it, thought Frank Lattimer, very much awake in room 412 of the Sheraton Hotel in Kansas City, I don't like that action one bit. He looked at Jennifer Byrd. Looking at her told him something. It told him Jennifer was the *last* relationship he was going to file away. Because it told him he was in love with Joan Scully and when he went back to New York tomorrow he was going to tell her so and, for once in his life, stick with it all the way. Make a commitment. And make it work.

But go back to New York defeated? With this story at a dead end? There was something else nibbling at Frank Lattimer's mind. It was Ives's voice on the tapes. Not just frightened. But also rushed and hushed. Why? Lattimer pounded a fist into the mattress. Of course. Ives sounded as if he were afraid of being *overheard*! So *that* was the reason he hadn't wanted Lindenmeyer to call him back: Somebody else might learn he had called Lindenmeyer to begin with. And what did *that* tell Lattimer: It told him there was one long shot that might reveal where Ives was. Because if Ives was afraid of having his call discovered by somebody he was with, then he might also have pro-tected himself against having the call show up on the monthly phone bill, on the listing of long distance numbers called. In short, Ives might have charged the call to another number. And the safest number to charge it to would be Ives's home phone. And that's why, before flying back to New York tomorrow morning, Frank Lattimer knew he was going to make some phone calls and twist some arms—to get the records of Missouri Bell.

He figured his newly realized love for Joan Scully could stand being delayed by those few calls.

TUESDAY

New York City

Eight o'clock. Morning rounds. On the fifth floor of the Oakes-Metcalf Hospital, Paul Justin lay awake, listening, as Kitteridge, Dewing, Falcone and the interns and medical students rehashed his case. Temperature steady around 100. Blood pressure holding around 100—held by Levophed that was now up to fifteen drops per minute. Kitteridge expressed surprise at the normal EEG. He agreed to the need for the brain biopsy.

"Scheduled for four o'clock today," said Dewing.

Hearing that, Paul Justin clutched up inside. But the next words out of Dewing's mouth were even worse:

"It was simple to get his wife's permission," added the neurology resident. "She's right downstairs. In for a breast biopsy today. Probable mastectomy."

Kitteridge gave a sympathetic snort. "When it rains, it pours, eh?" he said. And he and his entourage moved on to the next case.

Oh, Jesus, thought Paul Justin. Oh, Jesus. Breast cancer. So that's why Barbara was so distant. So that's why . . . oh, Jesus. If only I had been able to reach her on the phone on Thursday, tell her of my discovery, maybe *she* would have told *me* . . . so maybe she would have held off on this . . . this . . . Paul Justin's mind balked at the thought: this operation, mastectomy. His wife's lovely breast lopped off, the slick purple scar where once had been . . . oh, Jesus. Hold off on it, he ordered Barbara, trying to will his thoughts down through the concrete that separated them and into her room, into her mind. He visualized her lying awake as he was, waiting for the day's scalpel. Alone. Fearful. Oh, Jesus, hold off a day, a week, a month, however long it takes until I can move again and get out of here and give you my cure. Oh, Barbara.

His closed eyes welled up with tears.

On the fourth floor of the Oakes-Metcalf Hospital, Barbara Justin woke up. For one sleepy moment, she thought she was at home in her own king-sized bed with Paul. Then she heard the "Today" show on Mrs. Ambrose's TV. Barbara looked at the impersonal hospital walls. She swallowed. Her throat was dry. She felt the heat of the city pressing on the outside of those walls. Her throat was dry because she was thirsty and she knew she was not allowed to drink. And it was dry because she was very afraid.

Greenwich, Connecticut

If Mrs. Hargrove was really as good a cook as Rebecca Kupitz said she was, you couldn't prove it by breakfast. Breakfast for Joan Scully was a bowl of Rice Krispies and a pot of coffee brought in by Mr. Hargrove. Joan glumly poured milk into the cereal and listened to the snap, crackle and pop—weak sounds, the cereal was old—while Hargrove started to go out the door, ready to relock it.

"Couldn't I at least get some eggs?" asked Joan.

"I'm sorry," said Hargrove, sincerely. "But Mrs. Hargrove is busy helping the master and missus pack. They just received a call and must be at Kennedy airport by ten o'clock."

"Call?"

"Dr. Hazeltine. He said the cure's legitimate. And the people who own the cure have told the master and missus to come get it now."

"They called?" asked Joan. "They're going now? Hey, look"—she set the cereal down quickly, spilling some of it—"I've got to talk to them first. Please." She rose. "Let me go down with you."

Fearing a trick, Hargrove quickly went out the door. "I'll ask them to come up," he said, locking it.

Joan Scully waited. She knew what she had to do. It was bad enough being locked up in this room. She had been restless—to get back to the Institute, to see what would happen next with Underwood, to talk to Frank. But it was worse knowing that now she was being left behind here while the Kupitzes went blithely off to get—to get a cancer cure? The very thing she had been trying so *hard* to track down?

Hargrove came back with Rebecca Kupitz. "Let me go with you," Joan Scully begged. "I've got to go with you."

Rebecca regarded her. "You'll try to run away and tell somebody."

"No," said Joan, trying to make the truth clear. "It's more important to me that I see, actually see, what this is all about. But," she hastened to add, "I won't just be a spectator. I can actually *help* you."

"How?"

"Look," said Joan Scully. "What if Hazeltine is wrong? What if it's not a cure? You could be out thirty million."

"It's too late for half of that thirty million," said Rebecca Kupitz, smiling ruefully. "I just now ordered it transferred to their Swiss bank account."

"Then let me help protect the other fifteen million," insisted Joan. "Look, this is my field, too. I'll come and double-check Hazeltine for you. Make sure that he's right."

That was probably a lie. In the short time she would have, wherever she was going, she'd be unable to check whether Michael Kupitz was being injected with—for all she knew—a sugar solution or a poison.

Rebecca Kupitz seemed undecided.

"Look," said Joan. She had a sudden insight. "It's costing you ten thousand for Hazeltine. I'll only charge you one thousand."

Rebecca Kupitz laughed. "So it's not a favor?" she chuckled. "So it's a business proposition? Okay, now you're talking my language. A thousand it is. Ask Mrs. Hargrove for an extra toothbrush."

Houston, Texas

As he did every Tuesday morning, Ray Ryker was doing isometrics: doorway press, lateral raise (also in the doorway), knee pull (using a broomstick), interior knee press, exterior knee press, abdominal contraction and heel press, dead lift, underleg curl (with the broomstick again), doorway toe raise.... He was in the middle of the doorway toe raise, pushing his palms hard against the top of the doorway and pushing his calves hard so his heels stayed up, when the phone rang.

Ryker let it ring. "Nine thousand ... ten thousand," he finished counting. He relaxed. He went to the phone—his unlisted number.

"Hello?"

"Hello, Mr. Ryker," said Dr. Goodhue. "It's ... "

Without any real hope, Ryker pressed the button on the other phone to start the trace again.

" ... me, Goodhue."

"And me," added the gravelly voice.

"Okay," said Ryker. "I've got the money for you. What have you got for me?"

"Well," said Goodhue, excitedly, "I wouldn't have believed it—in fact, I didn't believe it—but the leukemia counts are down, the tissue samples are—"

"Cut it short, Goodhue," said the gravelly voice. "What you're trying to tell your boss is, the cure is for real."

"Is it?" demanded Ryker. "Is it, Dr. Goodhue?"

"Well, of course, I can't be certain, I mean I should have weeks on this, not days, and some—but only a small minority—of the other experts here don't agree, but I think . . . "

Ryker tried to be pleased that Goodhue was prattling on. It gave the phone man more time to trace the call. Except he, Ryker, couldn't stand the prattling.

" . . . it *is* a cure," concluded Goodhue.

"Will it cure Ash?" demanded Ryker.

"Well, I can't *guarantee* . . . " said Goodhue, a trace of whine beginning to creep in his voice.

"Damn it, Goodhue—" began the gravelly voice.

"No, that's okay," said Ryker. "Goodhue would hedge if you asked him his name. I'll pay the first nine million."

"Fine," said the gravelly voice. "Pay it now. And pay attention now. You got a pencil?" The voice paused. "Or you got a way to record me that doesn't show up?"

Ryker chuckled. They were two professionals—he and the man with the cure—with professional respect for each other.

Ryker picked up a pencil. "Shoot," he said.

"Cable account number 6023-1, Crédit Lyonnais, 38, Rue de la Paix, Zurich, Switzerland."

"Got it," said Ryker. A numbered Swiss account. His respect increased. "But when does Ash get the cure?"

"As soon as I get confirmation of the deposit. About eight to ten hours from now. So get Ash on your plane now."

"To where?"

"Chicago. You'll be met at Butler Aviation at 12:45."

Chicago again, thought Ryker. Where they pulled that electronic search trick with Goodhue. Well, this time we won't lose them. This time . . . "Met by whom?" asked Ryker. "And how? I got a sick man here. He's hard to move. What do you—?"

"Ah, Ryker," said the gravelly voice, "you know better than to ask. Just be there. And be prepared to pay the second installment this afternoon. 'Kay?"

"Okay," said Ryker.

And the line went dead.

Ryker waited. His other phone rang. It was the local switching office of the phone company. It was Fred Hisiger again.

"Uh, sorry," said Hisiger, "but I traced it back to the Delta Tandem and—"

"Never mind," said Ryker. He knew that this time he himself had helped to blow the trace. I should have pretended to get the account number wrong, he thought. Or the arrival time. Get Mr. Gravel Voice to repeat it. Take up more time. Shit, he thought. Am I slipping?

He hung up on Hisiger. He called Wissenbach to order the money transferred. He called the ambulance company, to get them ready. He called Texahoma transportation, to make sure the company jet was ready. He called Texahoma security, to make sure the electronics he had ordered were ready. He called Dr. Castle at Loring Memorial. And lastly, he called Arnie Sandahl and Liz Davis.

"I'm giving you two goof-offs one more chance," he began. "Back in Chicago . . . "

The phone traces had failed. The attempt to follow Goodhue had failed. The geographic code on Goodhue had failed. Well, this time, thought Ryker, we won't fail.

" . . . right?" he insisted to Sandahl.

"Right," said Sandahl, with forced confidence.

Ryker grunted. He hung up and went back to isometrics. The last exercise: toe pull. Ryker put on work gloves and sat down. He looped clothesline under his feet and lifted his legs off the floor. He inhaled. He extended both legs hard against the clothesline while pulling hard with his arms. "One thousand . . . two thousand . . . "

Nobody was going to beat Ray Ryker. Nobody could be as strong, as tough, as controlled.

Kansas City, Missouri

"Whit," insisted Frank Lattimer, "you've just got to use your influence."

"Damn it, Frank," said Lieutenant Pete Whitcomb, "you've already turned this department upside down. Now the word is out, officially, and you know it: We can't do any more for you."

"But this is the last thing I need. The phone company's records for Ives's home phone."

"Oh, Frank, come off it. It's such a long shot."

Frank Lattimer felt incredibly frustrated. Until this phone call, he had not laid out to anyone except Joan Scully all that he knew or suspected. The laughter with which Whitcomb and Mathes had greeted his suggestion on Sunday night that the cure for cancer was at the heart of all this . . . the laughter made Lattimer hold back telling the police much more. But now he had almost every single piece of the puzzle. Now he could lay them all out for Whitcomb, show him how they fit to make a picture. Now Whitcomb should see the picture—and believe it. Except, Whitcomb didn't.

"No, it's *not* a long shot," said Lattimer. "Look what we got. We know Ives channeled money into the virology section to keep Justin working on the 'C' particle."

"Just because this Endicott Foundation granted money," said Whitcomb, "doesn't mean—"

"Shut up and listen. We know Cruz stole Justin's work and—"

"You don't know that either. All you know is he had a key—so he *could* have stolen it."

"Damn it, Whit, will you *listen*? We know Justin did find the cure—"

"*You* say he told you that. With his *eyelids*, yet. Come on, Frank, you heard what Underwood said yesterday. All they've done so far is isolate that . . . that particle."

"—and that Velic tried to kill Justin, so whoever did steal Justin's work would be the sole owners."

"That's your guess."

"And we know that Velic went to Cruz's place in Harlem. Maria saw him. And we know that when Cruz was killed, Velic was a foot away. Teresa Vitiello saw him. So the connection is there. And we know that one of the few people who've had anything to do with both Velic and Cruz, who could have hired *both*, is Murdoch. And we know Murdoch now works with Ives at Dacey. And they're both missing now, for Christ's sake."

"And you think, because of the way his *voice* sounded, that Ives charged a call to his home phone?" demanded Whitcomb. "And that'll tell you where he is? Frank, you're grasping at straws."

"I tell you—it's worth a look," said Lattimer. "I've got everything else. All I don't know is where to *find* Ives and Murdoch."

"Aw . . . " There was a moment's silence from Whitcomb's end of the wire. "Yeah, but where does Underwood figure in? *He* can't be working with Ives and Murdoch."

"Of course not. They've got to be viewing him as a big problem. Look, if you had the cure for cancer and you were about to sell it to a bunch of rich people and then somebody else said they were going to come up with the cure for *free*, wouldn't you try to make your sale *fast*—before your clients changed their minds?"

"This is the goddamnedest bunch of conjecture—"

"So that's why," Lattimer cut in, "I need those phone records *now*."

There was another pause. Then Whitcomb sighed. "Okay," he said. "I'll get the court order. You'll have those records this week."

"This week isn't soon enough. I want the records today."

"There's no way I can—"

"Today, damn it. Use your influence."

"Damn it yourself, Lattimer. My influence doesn't count for anything up against the U.S. Constitution. Have you heard of that document? Says something about no unlawful searches and seizures? Jesus Christ, I thought the press was the goddamn guardian of the Constitution against the rampaging police."

"Whit—" began Lattimer.

"Court order tomorrow. If I can. Records soon after. That's *it*. Now good-bye—before I change my mind."

And he hung up.

It was Lattimer's turn to sigh. He looked at the still-slumbering Jennifer Byrd. He looked at the front pages of the Kansas City newspapers—full of Underwood's claims. It hurt to read them. Lattimer opened his black book and dialed another number in New York.

New York City

To prepare Barbara Justin for her operation, the nurse asked her to remove any objects from her body. Barbara handed over her engagement and wedding rings. The symbolism of it didn't escape her: If she lost a breast, she wondered, what kind of sex life, what kind of marriage, would she have?

But the nurse didn't give Barbara much time to think about that. For the nurse now gave her a shot which made her sleepy. And two attendants came in and helped her slide off her bed and onto a gurney. And now they were wheeling her out of her room and down the corridor. Her view of the world encompassed only the acoustical ceiling tile and the lights. They stopped and waited for an elevator. They entered. They descended. Like a descent into hell, Barbara thought vaguely. Or perhaps that was too strong, she thought. We're just going to a way-station today, to purgatory. Hell would come if she needed the second operation, the mastectomy. Her mouth felt dry. The nurse said that was from the shot. Barbara knew it was also from fear.

They rolled her out of the elevator and down another corridor and into another room. It registered on Barbara: operating room. They helped her slide, sleepily, onto the operating table. She caught a glimpse of gray walls and nurses in gray. The nurses were unpacking instruments. Dr. Cassidy came into view over her head. "Hello," he smiled, "how are you feeling?" "Fine," lied Barbara. "Fine," agreed Cassidy. He withdrew. Barbara sensed another man setting up a

machine by her side. "Good morning," said the man, "I'm your anesthesiologist, Dr. Wolmuth. I'm going to give you a shot now, which
will put you to sleep.... "

She felt the needle slide into her arm. She felt her head go
groggy. She welcomed unconsciousness. Unconsciousness would take
her out of this alien place. She felt a mask go over her face. She had a
sudden shudder of suffocation and tried to will the irrational thought
out of her head and then lost any willpower and then slipped away....

One of the nurses untied Barbara's hospital gown and uncovered
her down to her waist. The intern dipped two squares of gauze into an
iodine solution and, one square in either hand, began scrubbing her
chest vigorously. Meanwhile, just outside the operating room, Dr.
Cassidy scrubbed his hands. He put on a gown and gloves. The intern
finished prepping. Cassidy entered and placed sterile towels around
the iodine-colored area.

"Skin knife," said Cassidy. The nurse placed it in his hand.

Cassidy located the lump and started making an incision over it.
As he cut down to it, he could now really feel it. A benign lump would
be soft. This one was not. He went down a half inch, through the fatty,
yellow tissue to the lump itself. Then he veered around the lump,
being careful not to cut into it. Tiny blood vessels severed and
spurted. The intern clamped off the bleeding. A full inch down. The
deeper Cassidy went, the harder the lump felt.

"Has the look of cancer," he remarked to his assistants. "Lady
wouldn't believe me."

Cassidy now had a cut two inches long and an inch and a half
deep. He could feel that the lump was about the size of a large thim-
ble. Around it, he had carefully cut out a clump about the size of a
Ping-Pong ball. He freed the ball from the last strand of tissue. He got
a clamp on the ball and pulled it out.

"Get the pathologist," he said. "And number eight gut."

With the tan-colored gut, Cassidy started sewing together the
bottom of the wound. Four neat stitches. The pathologist appeared.

"What's the story?" he asked Cassidy.

"Get me a frozen," said Cassidy.

The pathologist went away with the lump in a metal dish. Now
using black silk thread, Cassidy quickly sewed up the top of the
wound. The anesthesiologist cut off the gas and let Barbara breathe
pure oxygen. The intern taped sterile gauze over the sutures. Barbara
began to move around a little. She began to emerge out of what felt
like a night-long dream.

But, in reality, it had all been very fast. The operation had taken
only thirty minutes. And in only five minutes more, the pathologist

came back in with the verdict. An undistinguishable murmur of voices floated into the end of Barbara's dream.

Kansas City, Missouri

The sign on the door said, "Stephen Pfaff, Inc., Electronic Security." Inside, Stephen Pfaff told Lattimer he really shouldn't be doing this.

"I'm straight now," he insisted. "I make my living showing companies how to guard *against* electronic crime. Hey—and it's a good living." He waved his arm to take in his domain. Pfaff had a spacious suite high up in a new Kansas City office building. On either side of Pfaff's own corner office, where he and Lattimer now sat, there were a half-dozen associates and secretaries, all working in quiet surroundings that bespoke money, solidarity, confidentiality.

"Harry Margolis," Lattimer reminded him. "Harry said you owe him a favor."

"Yeah," said Pfaff. "Harry testified for me three years ago back in Brooklyn. 'Expert witness,' Harry. Said what I was accused of doing was, technically speaking, impossible. Helped me get a suspended sentence."

"Was it?" asked Lattimer. "Impossible?"

Pfaff looked at him sharply. Pfaff had the clean, intelligent, horn-rimmed glasses, white-buttoned-down-shirt look of a computer scientist, college professor . . . which he had been. Pfaff shifted a paperweight on his desk. "That hardly matters," he answered. He played with the paperweight. He set it down next to the small computer terminal on his desk. He made up his mind.

"Okay," said Pfaff, "I told Harry I'd do this for you, so I'll do it. What's the number?"

Lattimer told him Ives's home phone number. Pfaff wrote it down.

"And you want?" asked Pfaff.

"The record of all calls originating elsewhere but charged to this number."

"What time period?"

"Most recent. Particularly a call on Saturday and again on Sunday to this number in Topeka." Lattimer gave Pfaff the number of Lindenmeyer's office.

"Okay," said Pfaff. "Be patient."

He went over to a file cabinet and took out a thick, unlabeled ring-bound book. "I shouldn't even have this," explained Pfaff. "It's just tough to throw stuff away, you know what I mean?"

Lattimer smiled encouragingly. Pfaff closed the door to his office. He sat down at his desk and flipped through the book. He stopped and turned to Lattimer.

"This really is for a news story?" he asked. "It's not going to hurt anyone?"

"Mr. Pfaff," said Lattimer. "It's going to help a lot of people."

"Sure," said Pfaff, unhappily. He turned to the keyboard of the computer terminal and, referring back and forth to the book, started making entries via the keys.

"The dumb phone company," Pfaff explained, as he pressed keys. "I ran a seminar for them a year ago, told them an outsider could access their computer right off the phone lines. They didn't believe me. Said they have safeguards. Well, they do"—he pressed one more key—"and they don't." He pressed one more key. "Sure, they're pretty well protected against monetary theft. I mean, if you asked me to invent a phone bill overcharge for you and then force their computer to print up a check repaying you oh, say, a couple of thousand . . . well, I could do it, I guess. But it'd be tough. But this—just getting a record—it's child's play." He tapped the ring-bound book. "I can pick it right off existing programming."

Pfaff pressed one last key. He waited. Lattimer waited. The quiet, expensive office was even quieter.

Then the terminal's printer began to chatter. The printing keys flew on a moving sheet of printout paper. Lattimer rose and joined Pfaff in looking at it.

"Oh, hell," said Pfaff.

"What?" asked Lattimer. The top of the printout listed Ives's name, address and home phone number. Beneath that, it said, "Last 30 days. Calls charged to." Beneath that were three columns headed "Date," "Origin" and "Destination." But Lattimer saw what was wrong. Instead of filling in all the columns, the printing keys were skipping wildly. They were printing some dates without origin numbers or destination numbers, some origin numbers without dates or destination numbers, and some destination numbers without dates or origin numbers. In a crazy-quilt pattern. Even the dates—at least those being printed—were out of order.

And so many calls. Who could be making them all? wondered Lattimer. Then he saw that all the destination numbers being printed were the same number: Ives's home number. Collect calls. Lattimer looked to see where they came from: Over a dozen different area codes. Now who . . . ?

The keys stopped. They had printed incomplete information for over eighty calls. Stephen Pfaff tore the printout from the terminal.

"Okay," he said, half to himself, "if at first you don't succeed . . . " He consulted his ring-bound book again.

Who, wondered Lattimer, was making all those collect calls from all over? Oh, of course. The Ives's insecure daughter. Traveling the country this summer, calling home several times a day to tell Mom and Dad (when Dad was there) what she was doing. Well, what she was doing, thought Lattimer, was muddying the waters. The few calls that Dr. Ives may have charged to his home phone were being obscured by her many calls.

What can I do? Frank Lattimer asked himself. Well, Mrs. Ives had said that Dr. Ives hadn't called home—and Lattimer believed her. So, if none of the collect calls were from him, Lattimer could eliminate them. Lattimer took a pencil and drew a line through every origin number that had Ives's home phone as its destination number. That left Lattimer with over fifty origin numbers that had no destination number next to them.

Next, he drew a line through every origin number that showed either no date or a date other than this last Saturday or Sunday. That left Lattimer with fourteen possible origin numbers. Probably most of them represented calls made by Ives's daughter. But Lattimer wagered that Ives himself had made at least one of them.

Which one?

"Okay," said Pfaff, looking up from his book. "It appears as if the phone company has protected itself better than I thought. But I think there's a way around them. Let's try again." And he again began pressing entry keys.

And what if we don't do any better this time? thought Lattimer. "You know," he said to Pfaff, "if this doesn't work, I'll settle for the addresses for those fourteen numbers. Okay?"

But before Pfaff could answer, the printing keys began flying: "Warning. You are attempting an unauthorized data access. Be advised that pursuant to Article 27, Section 131B of the . . . "

"Oh, hell!" cried Pfaff. "Oh, Jesus! Now they'll . . . oh, my God . . . how will I explain it?! Oh—" He turned to Lattimer. "Please, get out of here. I never saw you. Harry never sent you."

"But the addresses," said Lattimer.

"Nothing. No more. Out."

Lattimer took the printout with the fourteen numbers. He could call them all, on his own, and ask for Dr. Ives. But he could get lies for answers. He needed the addresses. The addresses wouldn't lie.

"Out, damn it." Pfaff was pushing Lattimer out of his private office. Secretaries were turning around to stare.

Lattimer tried to think. He looked at his list. It was like Poe's purloined letter. Maybe the one number was here, staring at him from amid all the others. But how to spot it? Letter, he thought, as Pfaff firmly escorted him to the outer door. Letter. Letter. Envelope.

Hold on! The envelope in Cruz's garbage. The Denver postmark.

"Excuse me," said Lattimer to the worried, distracted Stephen Pfaff, "but what's the area code for Denver?"

"Uh ... Denver," said Pfaff. "Uh, all of Colorado is 303. Why?"

Lattimer ran a finger down the list of fourteen numbers. There it was. A 303 number. The only 303 number. 303-991-4848.

Lattimer seized Pfaff's shoulder. "Find me the address for this one. Just this one."

Pfaff objected. Lattimer urged. It was no contest. One minute later they were back in Pfaff's private office and the printing keys on the computer terminal were coughing up the information:

"Saddleback Sanitarium, Saddleback Mountain Road, Lander, Colorado."

Lattimer tore off the printout. "A sanitarium," he said gleefully. Of course, he said to himself. Ives's daughter wouldn't be calling from there, but Ives would. A sanitarium was a perfect headquarters for him.

Lattimer shook Pfaff's hand. "Thanks," said Lattimer, "thanks a lot. And I hope I haven't got you into trouble."

"A sanitarium," said Pfaff. Lattimer could see what the man was thinking. He was thinking what the secretary in Wozinsky's law firm had thought: that maybe Lattimer belonged in a sanitarium.

"Well, don't worry," said Frank Lattimer. "That's exactly where I'm going."

Houston, Texas

"Saving Grace, Incorporated?" read Ryker. "What the hell is Saving Grace, Incorporated?"

"It's the name of Reverend Trumbull's crusade," said Virginia Ash.

"Healin' crusade," put in Matt Ash.

"Oh," said Ryker. "Sure."

"So he can carry on his good work," said Ash, from his bed. "Heal other people like he healed me."

"Forty-nine point five percent of your assets will buy a lot of healing," said Ryker, dryly.

"Matt and I thought we should give a lot *more* to the Reverend Trumbull," said Virginia. "But Trumbull said *I* should have an equal share."

"Real nice of him," said Ryker. He read the rest of the new will. Yes, another 49.5 percent went to Virginia Ash. And one percent to Homer P. Finley.

"Homer's going to be mighty unhappy though," said Ryker. "You knocked him down from around a half billion to a mere five million."

"Aw," said Matt Ash, "Ah was jes' angry on Saturday when Ah made out that will to Homer. Ah jes' wanted to get back at people." He smiled beatifically. "But Ah ain't angry no more. Ah been saved—ma body an' ma soul. Ah foun' the Great Healer. Ah foun' *God*."

"Swell," said Ryker. He looked at the new will once more. Unlike Saturday's do-it-yourself will, this one had been drawn up last night by Shurcliff, Ditullio and Emmons, Ash's blue-chip law firm. Which would make it more difficult for someone to contest, if someone got a notion that Trumbull was playing Svengali and unduly influencing Matt Ash. But hell, thought Ryker, who would contest it? Virginia? She was thrilled Trumbull was so generous as to "let" her have an equal share.

Ryker sighed. He tossed the will at his boss. This time it landed, tentlike, on top of his clasped hands. Ryker didn't care anymore. He was past worrying about whom he'd have to try to buy Texahoma from once the old man died. He was determined to buy it from him while he was still alive—and to keep him alive however long that took.

And to keep him alive, Ryker was taking him out of this hospital. Now.

"Well, folks," said Ryker brightly, "enough of this silly stuff about money." With a sudden exertion of will, he had completely changed his demeanor. Ray Ryker was now smiling and walking toward Virginia Ash, hands extended, palms open. He had on his best aw-shucks, Jimmy Carter, Sunday-go-to-meeting charm. It was an act that still worked on those few unwary businessmen Ryker dealt with. It began to work on Virginia Ash now.

"What is it?" she asked.

"Good news," said Ray Ryker. "The real reason I came here to-day." He put an arm around her ample girth and addressed her and her husband. For a moment, Nurse Crippen, watching from the corner of the room, saw Ryker and Virginia as a very odd couple indeed: the small lean man embracing a woman nearly half again as big as himself.

"What reason is that?" asked Matt Ash.

"To take you home," said Ryker dramatically. He brandished an official piece of paper before them. "You're so well, so healed by the great Reverend Trumbull, that Dr. Castle has discharged you!"

"Oh, Matt!" cried Virginia, happily. "Oh, Ray!" She squeezed Ryker with elephantine joy.

From the bed, Matt Ash beamed. "Ah think that's jes' fine, Ray."

"Right!" said Ryker. "And I say, 'Why wait a moment longer?' So right here and now, as a big surprise present—"

Ryker turned and called to the door: "Okay, gentlemen, come in."

Ryker turned back to the Ashes with the air of a magician orchestrating a child's birthday party. The door opened and, with a theatrical sweep of his hand, Ryker waved in two white-clad men carrying a stretcher.

"The ambulance," announced Ryker, "is waiting outside to take you home."

Virginia clapped her hands with glee.

The two attendants, assisted by Nurse Crippen, worked quickly. They disconnected the tube leading to Matt Ash's stomach. They moved Ash onto the stretcher. They transferred the I.V. bottle to a pole attached to the stretcher. And they carried Ash out the door, Ryker following.

Virginia tried to trot along with them. Ray Ryker turned back to her, full of solicitude. "Mrs. Ash," he said, "no need to rush. I'm just going to see he gets in the ambulance okay. Then I'll be back. Pick you up? Drive you home? I've got a surprise waiting at your house, too."

Virginia stopped. She panted a thanks to Ryker. Ryker gave her a last, winning smile and followed the stretcher around the corner.

In the elevator, one of the attendants gave Ash a sedative. Ryker touched Ash's shoulder encouragingly. The elevator doors opened and the small group proceeded toward the back door, where the ambulance was waiting.

But, at the nurses' desk that guarded the door, they were confronted by the Reverend Richard Watson Trumbull.

Trumbull looked angry enough to kill. Ryker tried to get the drop on him. He boomed a quick, hearty, "Hello, Reverend. Thanks to you, Matt's real better. We're taking him—"

"Home?" objected Trumbull. "What kind of bull crap is that?" He positioned himself to block the way to the door.

"Home?" asked Ryker, wonderingly. "Who said 'home'?"

"Mrs. Ash," said Trumbull.

Oh, thought Ryker. He couldn't believe it had been coincidence to run into the preacher here. Trumbull must have talked to Virginia only seconds after they carried Matt out. Ryker was impressed that Trumbull had made it down here before them. A back stairway?

Trumbull was crafty as hell. And not a drop of sweat on his handsome face, although he was dressed in—ridiculous for Houston in July—suit, tie and vest.

"Well, she got it wrong," said Ryker. "She wants him home so bad, she must have heard it that way. What it is, see, is we're transferring him to another hospital."

"What hospital?"

"Westminster," said Ryker quickly, naming an exclusive private hospital.

"I don't believe you," said Trumbull. "I think you're trying to take him away somewhere, away from my good healing powers." Trumbull had now raised his voice for all the doctors and nurses to hear. He loved a public performance. "You're a jealous man, Ray Ryker, jealous that God's will has succeeded where your crass money has failed. You're—"

"And you're full of shit," said Ryker softly, firmly. He nodded at the stretcher-bearers. "Let's go," he said.

The attendants started forward. Trumbull put up a hand to stop them. The lead attendant started to shoulder past him. Trumbull grabbed the side of the stretcher. He and the attendant started wrestling for it. The stretcher tipped. Matt Ash started sliding out.

"*What the hell?*" yelled Ray Ryker. Ignoring Ash's falling body, he flung himself toward Trumbull. His eyes were blazing, his teeth gleamed in his open mouth. Frightened, Trumbull took a step back.

Quickly, into the gap between the two men, went Crippen. She was a nurse and she hated violence. And she was a big, stocky woman. "No!" she said. And quickly the two attendants caught Matt Ash before he hit the floor. For a moment, all were frozen in a tableau: Ryker about to swing at Trumbull, unsure if he should go through Crippen. And the attendants unsure whether they should restrain Ryker or rush Ash to the ambulance or simply bolt from this whole mad scene. And, around them, a dozen startled, immobilized doctors and nurses.

"No," said Nurse Crippen, in a voice full of steel. "Reverend," she ordered, "lay off. Mr. Ryker—get out of here."

"Don't talk to me—" began Ryker, between clenched teeth.

"Out," she repeated.

Ryker shook his head hard, like a dog shaking a postman's pants leg on which he has a firm grip. Ryker directed the attendants out toward the door. Belatedly, a nurse rose from the desk to ask what was going on. "Where are you taking ... ?" Ryker, in cold, undisguised anger, threw at her the piece of paper he had waved before Virginia Ash. The nurse read it. It was a legitimate discharge paper signed by

Dr. Castle. Ryker's eyes met the nurse's, daring her to say anything. The nurse lowered her eyes. Ryker nodded grimly. The attendants carried Ash out.

Ryker smiled to himself as he followed them. He knew Castle had been only too happy to accept Ryker's proposal: "Discharge Ash to me and I won't make a stink over Trumbull's presence." But behind them, from the hospital, came a last wail and curse:

"May God damn you, Raymond Ryker!"

Then the Reverend Trumbull tried to compose himself. He ducked into the nearest doorway, dug into the bulging pocket of his beautifully tailored suit and brought out the pint of vodka. He took several huge swallows.

New York City

In the recovery room, the nurse kept on asking Barbara for her name and room number, over and over again. Finally it penetrated Barbara.

"Barbara Justin," she answered sleepily. "402."

She was now vaguely aware of being surrounded by other people lying on carts, also recovering from operations. The scene bothered her, reminded her somehow of a morgue, although she had never seen a morgue. She hoped the nurse would take her out. Satisfied that Barbara was awake enough to give her name and room number, the nurse did wheel her away.

Back in her room, in bed, Barbara dozed for an hour. Then the soap opera on Mrs. Ambrose's TV set woke her up for good. This time Barbara was grateful for the noise. It had interrupted a bad dream, the kind that often comes at the border of sleep and waking. This one, gratefully, she couldn't remember. She sat up in bed. As she did, her breast hurt. She touched it quickly, through the nightgown. For a moment, she'd had a sudden fear that Cassidy had betrayed her, had removed the breast. But there it was, under her hand, apparently the same size as before, but covered with a dressing and tender.

The lump, she thought. Was it—she had trouble facing the word—cancerous? She reached to ring for the nurse, to ask her. But her hand faltered. She couldn't face asking. She knew she'd find out soon enough. She reached instead for the book of *New Yorker* cartoons and turned the pages, smiling, chuckling, trying to lose herself.

An hour more and Dr. Cassidy came in.

He looked bluff and hearty as usual. Did that . . . ? she dared hope. But then his first words . . .

"How are you feeling, Barbara?"

... told her the truth. The words were cheerful, but with a hint of reserve, a hint of telling her ...

"Fine," she answered.

... to be ready for something.

"Fine. Well, the operation went smoothly. That lump's all out. But I'm afraid ... "

Yes, she knew.

" ... it's cancer. The biopsy shows it."

"Oh." Her voice was very small.

"Yes," he said. "I'm sorry," he added. "So I think we'd better schedule that next operation soon."

"Soon," she repeated numbly.

"I have an opening on Friday. How does that sound?"

"I ... "

"Can I schedule you for Friday?"

"I don't know."

"Well ... " Cassidy spread his hands. "If it were my wife or my daughter, I would urge them to." He paused. "Please decide soon," he said kindly.

"A ... modified ... radical ... mas ... ?" She let the last word hang in the air, uncompleted.

"Yes."

"I ... yes. I'll decide soon," promised Barbara. She closed her eyes and laid her head back on the pillow. She willed all this to also be a bad dream.

"Fine," said Cassidy's voice, in the darkness. "Well, you can go home today when you feel up to it. Or you can stay overnight. I know you have a lot on your mind."

When I open my eyes, thought Barbara, he will be gone and the bad dream will be over. She heard him cough lightly, heard his footsteps withdraw. She opened her eyes. He was gone.

The bad dream wasn't over.

Kansas City, Missouri

The next flight to Denver left Kansas City at noon but the Continental Airlines reservations clerk said it was full. "Wait-list me," said Lattimer, and he took a cab to the airport.

In the cab, he considered what had happened to last night's resolve to return to New York by now. He knew very well what had happened. What always happened. Getting the story took precedence. Well, he thought, I'll see Joan tomorrow. And I can certainly talk to her now.

So, at the airport, his first call was to New York City.

"Virology," said David Crawford.

"Is Joan Scully there?" asked Lattimer.

"No. Who's this?"

Lattimer identified himself.

"Jesus," said Crawford. "You again. No—and I don't know where she is, either. She ditched me last night in a big rush. If you can't keep track of her, I sure can't."

And Crawford hung up.

In a big rush? wondered Lattimer. To where?

He checked in with Continental and was told there were no cancellations. He shut himself back in a phone booth and made a second call, to Lander, Colorado. 303-991-4848.

"Forty-eight, forty-eight," answered a man, very briskly.

Lattimer smiled to himself. It was a good thing he'd gotten the name and address of this place from Pfaff, because it was obvious that the very brisk man was volunteering nothing.

"Yes," said Lattimer, "this is Stanley Cooper of Cooper Laboratory Supply in Chicago. We have a problem with that shipment you ordered . . . I need to speak to Dr. Ives about it."

"Ives?" said the man. "Ives? There's no Ives here. Who'd you say you were?"

"Cooper Laboratory Supply."

"Give me your number and we'll have somebody call you back."

"Fine," said Lattimer. He invented a number in the 312 area code and hung up. Well, scratch that, he thought. It had been a long shot, but he felt if he could have gotten Ives on the phone and rattled him, maybe he could have rattled something out of him. But: nothing.

So Lattimer's third call was to New York City.

"Lieutenant Whitcomb," said Whitcomb.

"I'd like to thank you for your help," deadpanned Lattimer. "I found out where Ives and Murdoch are."

"Okay," sighed Whitcomb. "I'll bite: Where?"

"Saddleback Sanitarium, Lander, Colorado."

"So?"

"So doesn't that strike you as odd?"

There was a pause.

"I mean," said Lattimer, "can you think of any *legitimate* reason for their being there. In a sanitarium?"

"I'm thinking," said Whitcomb.

"I'm thinking somebody—in some official capacity, maybe the Colorado State Police?—ought to check it out."

Whitcomb grunted, noncommittally.

"Because," continued Lattimer, "I'm going to check it out *un*officially. Sort of usurp police functions. And you know how us amateurs tend to botch things up."

Whitcomb gave the same grunt.

"I knew I could count on you, Whit," said Frank Lattimer. And he returned to the Continental counter where he was told that, yes, now there was a cancellation on the noon flight.

Before catching it, Lattimer even had time to go to the airport gift shop and order a big, but not gaudy, bottle of Jennifer Byrd's perfume, to be delivered to her at TWA with a good-bye note.

Chicago, Illinois

In one of their more ambitious undertakings, the U.S. Army Corps of Engineers reversed the flow of the Chicago River, deepened it and then joined it by a series of locks to the Des Plaines, so freighters could navigate from the Mississippi to Lake Michigan. Where the Chicago River winds through the Loop, there are drawbridges to accommodate these freighters. And now, going south on the Outer Drive, approaching a drawbridge, was a panel truck containing Ray Ryker.

Ryker didn't know where he was. He, Matt Ash and the nurse he'd hired just for this trip—a Miss Elsberry—were locked in the back, without a window. That made Ryker tense. He concentrated on the road noises, trying to figure out where the driver was taking them. Well, wherever, thought Ryker, this time my people won't lose track.

Back when they had landed at O'Hare, back when the three of them had been shepherded into the truck, Ryker had been confident that Arnie Sandahl and Liz Davis had seen them go—and had followed closely. And Ryker was still confident. For even if Sandahl and Davis somehow lost visual contact with them—if somebody pulled a trick like the "state trooper" had pulled on Goodhue—there was an electronic back-up. Inflight from Houston to Chicago, Ryker had had Nurse Elsberry peel back the tape that held the tubes tight against Ash's stomach. Beneath the tape, Ryker had then placed a small but powerful radio beeper. The beeper would be picked up by a monitor in the car Sandahl and Davis were using. So the truck might go through all kinds of evasive maneuvers, but to no avail. Sandahl and Davis could still track it anywhere within a ten-mile radius.

But Ryker's confidence was misplaced. From the moment that Liz Davis switched on the monitor back at O'Hare, it had been dead. "But it worked perfectly yesterday," she protested. "The truck—it must be the fucking truck," said Sandahl. "They must have figured

Mr. Ryker would play cute. They must've lined the truck with solid lead or something." So Sandahl had tucked his Plymouth only three cars behind the panel truck and all the way south and east from O'Hare, didn't let it get any further ahead. He sweated and cursed in the traffic. Liz Davis held her head and said she needed a drink. They tried not to think about what the truck might do to shake them.

"Oh, shit," said Liz Davis.

As the panel truck now crossed the drawbridge, the warning lights went on for the Drive. The drawbridge bells began to ring. The traffic slowed. "Arnie!" cried Liz Davis. "Go!" And Sandahl tried to cut his car around the BMW directly ahead of him. A Chevy in the next lane promptly hit them. Sandahl leaned on his horn and accelerated between the BMW and the Chevy, tearing metal on both sides. The drawbridge gates began to descend across the Drive.

"Shit. Shit. Shit," said Liz Davis. The BMW, the Chevy and a half dozen other cars—and their own—came to a halt in front of the bridge. The owners of the BMW and the Chevy were opening their doors.

The drawbridge gates were now fully down. "Son of a bitch!" yelled Sandahl, looking wildly up and down the Chicago River. "And there isn't even a boat coming."

"They got to the drawbridge operator, too?" asked Davis, incredulous.

"Must've," said Sandahl.

The BMW owner was stalking toward them. Liz Davis helplessly flicked the dials on the dead radio monitor. "Work, goddamn you, work!" she pleaded. The BMW owner was now yelling and pounding on the window of the Plymouth, trying to get at Sandahl. And the drawbridge started rising before them, blocking out the sky.

On the north bank of the Chicago River, Sandahl gazed at the towering bridge. "Mr. Ryker," he observed to Davis, "is not going to like this."

But on the south bank of the Chicago River, Ray Ryker, who had heard the bells ring and guessed their meaning, sped away believing he was still in control of things.

New York City

In the space of three working days, the virology section of the Oakes-Metcalf Institute had lost most of its staff. On Friday, it had lost Justin and Cruz—violently. On Monday, Wojik had resigned. Today, Joan Scully hadn't come in—and nobody knew where she was.

And today, to all intents and purposes, it had also lost Hugh Underwood.

Underwood had spent the morning taping an appearance for the "Today" show. He had had a long, leisurely lunch with some of the Institute's trustees and wealthy friends at the private midtown club of one of the trustees. And after lunch he went to the hospital to see Justin.

Unlike his last visit to Justin, on Saturday morning, this one was not casual. It had been planned by Warren Brown and forced down the throat of the chief of neurosurgery. "The media have a right to see Paul Justin," Brown had argued. "He's legitimate news." Kitteridge replied that there was nothing to see: "The man's in a coma. He has pneumonia. I won't have a pack of bloodhounds on top of him." It was an uneven fight; Brown had the authority. "All right," Kitteridge had conceded, "3:30 to 3:45. Fifteen minutes and they're out. And not coming back."

So at 3:30 Hugh Underwood and the media descended on intensive care. The media would record The Simple Human Drama of the Great Scientist Visiting the Bedside of His Stricken Colleague. Underwood had mixed feelings about it. He liked Paul, he was worried for him, he hoped for his recovery. Yet if he did recover—which seemed, Underwood was told, increasingly unlikely—what would he say about Underwood's partial theft of his discovery? Or am I really stealing it? wondered Underwood. He was so caught up in the rush of events, he was beginning to believe the praise that people were heaping on him. The lunch had particularly impressed Underwood; he knew he was one of the few blacks ever invited to that private club. And he had been treated as if he belonged—as if he, too, were a man who could manage great events. So Underwood now decided that this stage-managed scene with the media wasn't particularly exploitive after all. His outlook was colored by two martinis before lunch, drinks he rarely had.

The two martinis worked well on camera for Underwood. They slowed down his already slow, patient pace. They made him choose his words with even greater care. Each word hung heavy with solemnity: "What—Dr. Dewing—is the—prognosis—for Paul?" The TV cameras rolled as Underwood "conferred" with Dewing at the nurses' station. They caught the look of concern and efficiency on the faces of the nurses. Then they followed Underwood in to Justin's bed. They recorded the drip of the Levophed, the *ping* of the EKG tracings and then Underwood's voice as he said, "Paul—I wish—I only wish—you could hear me. We're—going on—Paul. I'm carrying on—our work." Underwood briefly clasped Justin's shoulder. He turned and walked away, his limp giving him added dignity. His face was a mask of dignity, his eyes were near tears. The cameras zoomed in for a close-up of Underwood's face. Cut to a close-up of Justin's face, eyes closed, a tube in his mouth.

Christ, thought one of the cameramen, it's the goddamnedest invasion of privacy I've ever had the privilege to shoot. Worth a fucking Emmy.

True to his word, Dewing had them all out at 3:45. At 3:50 came the real—and unsimple—human drama.

Nurse Lopez came in to check that the media hadn't disturbed any equipment. She found that the equipment was fine. But Paul Justin was not. He looked deathly cold, and waxen, as if he had suddenly been shoved in a freezer. Lopez felt for his pulse. There was hardly any.

"Dr. Dewing," she called.

Dewing and Falcone came back.

"Weak," she said.

Dewing seized Justin's wrist and felt for himself—and could feel only a flicker. He then tried to take a reading from the cuff—and got none. But Justin's heart was beating a normal seventy-five times a minute. So Falcone saw that the problem was what he had feared most: The combination of pneumonia and coma had pushed Justin into septic shock.

"Turn up the Levophed," ordered Dewing.

The Levophed had been going in at fifteen drops per minute. Now Lopez turned it to twenty. Justin's pulse was still weak and fluttery.

"Higher," said Dewing. "And one gram of hydrocortisone." The cortisone, which would require a few hours to take effect, would also help stabilize the blood pressure. *If* it took effect.

Lopez gave the cortisone I.V. She increased the Levophed to twenty-five drops per minute, to thirty, to forty.

"Higher," said Dewing.

Fifty drops per minute, sixty. Some color returned to Justin's face. A stronger pulse returned. Dewing was able to read a blood pressure at 95—down a bit from where they had been holding Justin. Even as Dewing read it, it began to slip. Down to 90. To 85.

"Higher."

Lopez increased the Levophed to seventy drops per minute.

"And double the concentration."

The Levophed had been going in at 2 amps per 500 cc's. Lopez pushed it to 4 amps.

Dewing measured a blood pressure of 90. "Holding him," he said at last. "But only barely."

Falcone was relieved—and worried. They had reached the limit of Levophed; any more would cause kidney damage. So now they could only hope that the cortisone would work. They would have to wait—and hope that, meanwhile, Justin's blood pressure dropped no further

Nearly three-quarters of an hour had gone by since the sudden pressure drop. During that time, neither Dewing, Falcone nor Lopez had been much conscious of the outside world. But now that the crisis was temporarily over, now that the retreat had been temporarily stabilized, the world rushed back. Nurse Hughes, who had taken Abrams's place on the 3 P.M. to 11 P.M. shift, stuck her head in the doorway with an announcement.

"The TV people are demanding to get back in," said Hughes.

"What?" thundered Dewing. "Who told them?!"

Nurse Hughes gestured at Mrs. Nowlis's bed. "Mr. Nowlis," she said. "On his way out. He was here for visiting hours, while—while this happened."

"No," thundered Dewing. "Keep them out!"

"I am," said Hughes. "And the police are helping. But they're camped out in the corridor."

"Ghouls," said Dewing. "The only person allowed in from now on is Mrs. Justin. Call her."

"Now?" asked Hughes.

"Now," said Dewing. "Don't scare her. But tell her she'd better come up and see her husband again. Because"—Dewing looked at Falcone and the two nurses—"I don't know how much longer we're going to be able to keep him."

Lander, Colorado

Per instructions, the Kupitzes and Joan Scully flew from New York to St. Louis. There they were given only minutes to catch a plane to Denver. There they were quickly herded into a limousine which deposited them at a rent-a-car office in the suburbs, where they were given a car and more instructions: Drive west on U.S. 285, through Kenosha Pass at 10,000 feet and then onto a narrow side road winding north into the mountains.

They were worn out from the trip. They were worn out from making all the connections that left them only minutes to spare. "I know why they've done it," said Rebecca Kupitz, who was driving. "So we can't have anybody follow us and see where we're going. So we can't try to get our money back."

"But we see where we're going," said Michael Kupitz.

"I'm sure they've thought of that, too," said Rebecca.

Joan Scully said nothing. She was too busy marveling at the magnificent scenery. And besides, she knew, guiltily, she had nothing at stake. She wasn't dying of cancer. She hadn't lost fifteen million dollars nor was she about to lose fifteen million more. After three frustrating days in hot, cramped New York City, chasing down clues that led nowhere, and then a night in a locked room, she was thrilled to be out in this high country with faraway peaks and valleys, with the smell of pine in the cool, clean air, closing in on whatever the truth really was.

The road was twisting tighter now. "If we *did* have somebody following us," said Rebecca Kupitz, "they sure couldn't see us now." And then coming around the next curve, she had to slam on the brakes because there was a tractor-trailer truck stopped in the road, its back to them.

A man walked over from the trailer truck and looked into the car. He compared their faces with two photographs in his hand. "Hey," he said, pointing at Joan Scully, "who's she?"

"Who are you?" demanded Rebecca Kupitz.

The man grinned. "It doesn't matter," he said. He waved at another man standing behind the truck. The other man quickly opened the rear doors of the truck, hopped inside and let down a ramp. The first man instructed Rebecca Kupitz to drive up to the base of the ramp. The two men quickly unreeled a cable from the inside of the truck and attached it to the car's front axle. They started a motor and the cable began pulling the car up the ramp. Less than two minutes after the Kupitzes and Joan Scully had been stopped on the road, they were inside the trailer truck with the doors locked behind them— moving up the road to parts unknown.

"Very neat," said Rebecca Kupitz.

"Very lousy," said Joan Scully, looking at the dirty metal walls.

Lander, Colorado

Lander, Colorado, was an old mining town that had gone to seed and was now coming back. In the early '70s, ex-hippies from Haight-Ashbury, the East Village and points in between bought some stores and houses, fixed them up and settled in. A few years later, upper-middle-class professionals from Denver, turned off by the high prices of Aspen and Vail, started building weekend homes. They had to drive almost an hour to find good skiing but, years ago, someone had started making ski trails on nearby Saddleback Mountain and now there was talk of reclearing those trails. In the meantime, the three groups—the original townspeople, the ex-hippies and the weekenders from Denver—lived in uneasy harmony with each other and worried about being Aspenized all over again. Thus the large, bearded man with one earring who ran Lander's general store had mixed emotions about the sanitarium being reopened.

"Hey, man," he told Lattimer, "I guess it's a good thing. Turning it into a fat farm, you know. Get people in touch with their bodies, right? And when patients actually start coming, it's gotta help my business. But so far, hey, just a lot of traffic going back and forth and nobody stopping."

"You ever see anybody who runs it?" asked Lattimer. "Anybody who works there?"

"Hardly. I think they got a big staff—but they seem to stick to themselves. Funny, huh?"

Lattimer showed the proprietor the picture of Christopher Ives which he'd Xeroxed off the Dacey annual report.

"No, man. Sorry. Doesn't ring a bell."

"Okay," said Lattimer. "Thanks. How do I get up there?"

The bearded man gave him directions to Saddleback Mountain Road. "Just follow the traffic," he added, "you can't miss it. Hell of a lot of traffic going up there today. Like the Long Island Expressway."

"Well," said Lattimer, "is there a way to avoid that? You know, another way up?"

The proprietor thoughtfully pulled the ear lobe that didn't have an earring. "Why do you want to know?" he asked bluntly. "You want to *sneak* in? Why?"

"Well," said Lattimer. He sized up his man. "I've been hired by the venture capital group that's backing the sanitarium. My employers have heard that the sanitarium has been buying up and shipping in some reducing drugs—some experimental stuff that's officially labeled narcotic. Now my people want to check that out and, if it's true, get that stuff the hell out of there. Otherwise, the rumors are going to start attracting federal narcotics agents. And if they come up here"—Lattimer spread his hands—"well, nobody in town'll be able to buy so much as a stick of grass."

"Bad news," agreed the ex-hippie. "Okay, tell you what. About a mile up the road, there's a dirt road, goes off to the left, used to lead to some cabins nobody lives in anymore, goes around the back side of the mountain. It stops a couple of hundred yards below the sanitarium. You'll have to hike from there."

"Good enough," said Lattimer. He turned to leave.

"Hey," said the proprietor. "If you're going hiking, you don't want to be wearing those city shoes." He pointed to his shelves. "Got some good Pivettas. Only fifty-two dollars."

Lattimer smiled at the bearded businessman. And twenty minutes later he had parked his rented car at the end of the dirt road and was crunching through the underbrush in his new pair of boots. Above him and to the right, on the south face of the mountain, the white walls of the sanitarium gleamed in the afternoon sun. Above him and to the left, on the north face, a thin, patchy, white snow field extended from the peak—just above the sanitarium—down to about his level. Lattimer worked his way up the steep slope toward the building, his leg aching. If the mountain won't come to Mohammed . . . thought Frank Lattimer, trying to overcome pain with philosophy.

The underbrush was starting to give out now. Lattimer tried to use what was left to hide himself from view from the sanitarium's windows. And then, edging closer, he noticed: All the windows in this wing were covered by an opaque plastic. Odd, he thought. The plastic blocked a fabulous view. More boldly, he walked up to the base of the building. There was no door. He started working his way around the building and, as he did, he came in sight of the main road. He heard traffic coming up.

He threw himself down in the grass and watched. A tractor-trailer emblazoned "Pomeranz Transport" labored around the curve. It headed for a large garage attached to the sanitarium and disappeared inside. The garage doors closed. Lattimer still had seen no one, but if he kept moving in this direction he'd come in view of some windows that weren't covered. He retraced his steps and then went further. There was a door. He tried it. It was locked and there was no keyhole to pick. Just a smooth, unyielding handle.

Well, thought Lattimer, time to test Murdoch's security systems. Lattimer had a hunch that, up here, the most that Murdoch feared were local teen-age vandals. And they didn't usually carry credit cards. But Lattimer did. He slipped his American Express card in the crack between the door and jamb, right below the lock. He jerked the card up smoothly and the door swung open. "Don't leave home without it," said Lattimer. He stepped inside the sanitarium. Trespassing again, he thought. Joan would not be pleased.

Lattimer went in with only the barest plan: stay inconspicuous (if the sanitarium staff wore white, maybe he could find a white coat to wear), observe what he could, *maybe* (if it wasn't too risky) corner Ives alone and try to shake him. And then get out. But where to start? Frank Lattimer found himself confronted by stairs going up and going down and by two intersecting hallways. He went to his right. The hallway was deserted but brightly lit. There was nowhere to hide, so Lattimer adopted a casual, confident walk, hoping it would disarm anybody he met.

Around the next corner, he heard several sets of footsteps approaching.

Lander, Colorado

"Frank!" exclaimed Joan Scully.

She couldn't help herself. She and Michael and Rebecca Kupitz were being escorted through the sanitarium by a pleasant young man in a white lab coat. The young man had smoothly apologized for all the problems of getting here, including what he called "that unfortunate ride in the truck." He had assured them they could shortly confer with Dr. Hazeltine and see the proof which had convinced Hazeltine. And he'd told them that as soon as confirmation was received on the transfer of the first half of the funds, Michael Kupitz would receive his shot. "And now," the young man was saying, "if you'll just wait down here . . . "

Joan Scully hadn't been sure what to think. The young man was so courteous and reassuring, it felt as though he was trying to put something over. And yet, she asked herself, if it was for real, if there was a cure, how would it be any different? Either way, she was fascinated—and offended.

And then startled. Turning a corner, they ran into Frank Lattimer.

He was sauntering along, hands stuffed in the back pockets of his pants, looking as if he owned the place. Joan cried his name. Immediately, she bit her lip. Frank blinked once, stepped out of their way and kept walking. But their young escort stopped cold.

"Hey," he said to Joan, "you know that guy?"

"N-no," she stammered. "He just looks like—reminds me—"

But the escort wasn't listening. He had pivoted. "Hey, fella, who are—?" Frank broke into a run and turned another corner. The escort sprinted after him, braked hard at a wall phone and yanked the receiver. "Security!" Joan heard him bark. "Security! Intruder on first floor, west wing, heading toward service area."

Running—or rather, trying to run on one bad leg—Lattimer had also heard the man's call. He cursed his luck. How the hell had Joan gotten here also? And he dove through the first door he could find. It was a storeroom. Light bulbs, paint, cleansers, tools. Lattimer quickly considered and discarded the idea of grabbing something. There were too many people here—Ives and Murdoch's people—for him to fight his way out swinging a hammer. No, he'd just have to run and dodge his way out.

So when Lattimer opened and ran out the door on the other side of the storeroom and came face to face with Janko Velic, he was barehanded. Which was too bad. Or perhaps just as well. Because although the man with Velic had a gun drawn, Lattimer would have probably smashed Velic's face with the hammer anyway and risked catching a bullet.

As it was, Lattimer simply stopped, and said, "Hi, Janko. Wearing doctors' whites again, eh? I think it takes a little more than that, though, to pass your residency. I think they still have a character requirement."

Velic didn't understand, but he did understand he was being baited. He made a move toward Lattimer.

"Come *on*," said Velic's partner, putting a hand on the sleeve of Velic's lab coat. "Not in the halls. Remember what Jones said. We've got guests all around. No disturbances."

Velic stopped, reluctantly.

"Jones?" asked Lattimer. "Would that be Jones a.k.a. Ed Murdoch?"

Velic looked startled. He recovered. He and his partner led Lattimer away.

Joan Scully was also being led away. After making his phone call, the polite young escort led the Kupitzes to their suite of rooms and locked them in—"for your protection," he said. Then he led Joan back through the sanitarium. She was scared. Not for herself—the Kupitzes had explained she was a friend of theirs and a colleague of Hazeltine's—but for Frank. How could he explain what he was doing here? What would they do to him? Her anger at him yesterday for going off to Kansas City now seemed so wrong. Her willingness to go to bed with Crawford now seemed like a betrayal. And now she *had* betrayed him by calling out his name. Oh, Frank, she said to herself. I love you.

"Oh, Frank," she said, as the escort ushered her into the big room with the screen and the armchairs. Because Frank was sitting in one of the chairs. She rushed toward him. But he held up one hand in warning and put a finger to his lips.

"But, Frank, I—" She stopped herself. She wanted to go to his arms, to hold him, to be held. But he stood up casually and offered a hand to be shook. He said, in a cocktail party voice, "Why, Miss Scully, good to see you again. Although in strange circumstances, right?"

Dumbfounded, her eyes pleading with his, she limply shook his hand. "When was it we saw each other?" he went on. "Last Friday, in your lab? You must have wondered about all those questions I pestered you with, right?" He nodded for her to agree.

"Right," she said, without conviction. What kind of play was this? she wondered. For what audience?

"Well, I've found out the damnedest things since then," continued Frank Lattimer. "I know that, as I suspected, Justin *did* find the cure for cancer. And it was stolen by Cruz, who was working for two guys at a pharmaceutical company. Now I've learned that *their* names are—"

"All right, mister," came the gravelly voice over the loudspeaker. "That's about enough. You have any more to say, you can say it to us privately. We'll question the lady privately, too."

Joan Scully and Frank Lattimer exchanged glances. The door to the room was unlocked and the smiling young escort came in. Behind him stood Velic and his partner.

Lattimer turned to the TV camera. "The lady doesn't know anything," he said. "I don't know how she got here any more than you do." At least that last statement is true, thought Lattimer. God, I wish she *weren't* here, he thought. He wanted to hold her, to tell her how much he now realized he loved her. He wasn't afraid of what they'd do to him—he had a ploy ready for Murdoch—but he was very afraid of what they might do to Joan. "So let her go," Lattimer concluded.

"Take her outside," rumbled the gravelly voice.

"Don't worry," Joan started to tell Frank. "I'm sure Michael Kupitz will—"

"Out!" yelled the voice. The escort hustled her out the door and relocked it.

Lattimer was alone again.

"Okay," said the gravelly voice, calm again, "a nice performance. You stopped Miss Scully from saying what she knows. Now, would you like to tell us what *you* know? Or would you like Mr. Velic to have another chance at you? I think he's eager."

Frank Lattimer sank back into one of the large, comfortable armchairs. He folded his hands in his lap and smiled expansively at the TV camera.

"Happy to," he said. And he quickly told Ives and Murdoch everything he knew, omitting only two things: He omitted the names of the people—from Maria to Dr. Lindenmeyer—who had helped him piece the story together (he was afraid of reprisals). And he omitted the fact that the Colorado state police would be arriving (he hoped) any minute.

He also invented one detail: "And that, plus all the corroborating evidence, is typed up and held in sealed envelopes in New York City. One envelope with my lawyer. The other with a literary agent. If I'm not physically back in their offices by 5 P.M. tomorrow—not a phone call, mind you, but *me*—they open those envelopes."

There was silence in the screening room.

Finally Murdoch—Lattimer knew the rumbling voice was his—spoke. "You're bluffing," he said.

Lattimer smiled. "Maybe," he replied. "But you can't take the chance I'm not. You can't have Velic kill me."

There was silence again.

"No," came Murdoch's voice again. "We won't kill you. Today. But we'll make you fairly uncomfortable while you wait."

Lander, Colorado

Joan Scully had been confident that, once she was separated from the Kupitzes, Michael Kupitz would kick up a fuss. She was right. So when the polite young man took her out of the screening room it was not—as Lattimer had feared—to grill her further. Instead, he escorted her back to the Kupitzes' "suite" and locked her in with them.

"I was on the phone," explained Michael Kupitz, pointing at the receiver on the coffee table. He laughed. "The operator answered and said, 'Room service' and I told her the only service I wanted was to get you back here. Unharmed. Otherwise, I told her, they could keep their cure for cancer and I'd keep the other half of the purchase price and go back to Greenwich this minute, thank you."

Joan Scully laughed and hugged the timid middle-aged man.

"But," asked Rebecca Kupitz sharply, "who was that man—Frank? Why did he run?"

"Well," said Joan excitedly, "he was the man who... " She stopped. She looked around the room. Hidden microphones here, too? she wondered. "... who is only a reporter," she finished. "Just a reporter who was pestering me. Hey," she said, changing the subject. "I'm starving. Do you think room service would send up a sandwich? And when do we get to see Dr. Hazeltine? And the proof?" Joan was trying to keep herself busy so she wouldn't dwell on what might be happening to Frank Lattimer.

What was happening to Frank Lattimer was that he was being tied up. Velic and the other security man had led him from the screening room down a main corridor and then down a narrow, seemingly less used corridor that ran deeper into the building. Here, unlike the rest of the sanitarium, the walls had not been freshly painted and there were fewer lights in the ceiling. The corridor dead-ended at a wall. On either side was a door, each door with a covering over a peephole to let those outside look in. Velic unlocked one of the doors and thrust Lattimer inside.

It was a small, bare, windowless room with a minuscule bathroom alcove. There was nothing on the walls. There was nothing on the floor, except a bed in the corner. Velic and the other man pushed Lattimer to it.

"Empty your pockets," ordered the other man. Lattimer did. "Now lie down," the man ordered. Out of a pocket of his lab coat, Velic took a spool of thin but strong-looking wire. Lattimer, half-sprawled on the bed, understood.

"Hey," protested Lattimer. "You don't have to tie me down to it. I'm not going anywhere."

"When someone opens the door," explained the other man, "you could try to jump them." He shoved the gun into Lattimer's spine, forcing him flat. "I've heard you're crazy."

"All right," said Lattimer. "All right. But hell—don't tie me *flush* to this thing." He had no idea how he could escape, but he figured he had to buy himself some leeway. "At least," he argued, "give me enough slack—enough wire—so I can make it to the toilet."

"You're afraid?" asked Velic, delighted. It was the first time Lattimer had heard him speak. His voice was soft and ugly. "You're so afraid, you're going to pee in your pants?" He was snipping the wire with a wire cutter.

Velic chuckled. His smile was as thin as the wire in his hands. "Sure," he said. "We'll let you go pee-pee." He shook the metal frame of the bed. It didn't budge. Lattimer realized it was bolted to the floor. Velic cut more wire. Swiftly, expertly, he tied Lattimer's hands behind his back. He tied his arms to his sides. Then he cut a longer length of wire. He tied one end of it to Lattimer's wrists and the other to the bed frame. It gave Lattimer enough wire to make it to the bathroom alcove but not to the door.

Lattimer tried to shift his hands slightly. The wire dug in. "Hey," he protested. "That hurts."

"Consider yourself lucky," said the other man. "The last guy they had in here—back when this was a loony bin—was probably in a straitjacket." He and Velic laughed.

They left the room and locked the door behind them.

New York City

Because Barbara Justin had just come out of an operation, the hospital felt she shouldn't walk yet. So a nurse pushed her in a wheelchair to intensive care. There Barbara was wheeled through a gauntlet of reporters. Yesterday, besieged at home by them, she had been terrified. Today, she was numbed by events. She went through the reporters in a daze, not hearing their questions. And inside, she had barely any questions for Dr. Dewing: "How is Paul?" "Not well, I'm afraid." "You said his blood pressure is dropping?" "Yes." "Can you do anything?" Dr. Dewing looked uneasy.

Barbara understood. She asked to be left next to the nurses' station. She didn't want to go in and see Paul. She looked at the policeman guarding the door to the ward. She looked away. Dr. Falcone stopped by and said something comforting to her. She didn't hear. She was thinking—as clearly as she could, which wasn't very clearly— about her operation three days from now. Because of what was happening to Paul, should she postpone it? She didn't know. Somehow, she didn't care. Get it over with, she thought.

Get it *all* over with, she thought, not hearing Falcone. She asked the nurse to wheel her to a phone, so she could call her mother and tell her what was happening.

Standing over Paul Justin, Falcone felt helpless, too. When he and Dewing had called Barbara at 4:45, Justin's blood pressure had been 90. Now, at 5:45, it was 80. And still dropping. The cortisone was apparently failing to take effect. And there was nothing more they could do.

Lander, Colorado

After they locked the door on him, Lattimer started hopping around to the furthest limit of the wire that attached him to the bed. And it took him only five minutes of close inspection to prove that his room—his cell, really—had been designed for violent mental cases. For not only was the bed bolted to the floor; there was *nothing* that an occupant could throw or break. Or, in this case, use to cut his bonds. The light bulbs were all recessed behind steel mesh and there were no light switches or electrical outlets. The knobs had been removed from the radiators and, in the tiny bathroom, there was no shower head or drain plugs. The toilet tank was sealed and there wasn't even a toilet paper holder. All that did move were the faucets and the toilet flush lever. Lattimer turned his back to them and tried, awkwardly, to unscrew them. He failed. In short, there wasn't a single loose screw or metal edge he could use on the wires.

Lattimer hopped back to the bed. He lay down on the thin mattress—on his back and on his bound hands—and stared at the ceiling. He wasn't giving up, but it did look pretty bad. He tried to imagine the last person to lie here, back when this was a private insane asylum. If the person hadn't been crazy when he went into this room, Lattimer figured, he sure was by the time he got out. I wonder, thought Lattimer, what that person thought of, lying here? An interesting question.

Lying on his hands and wrists hurt. So Lattimer turned to the wall. And got the answer to his question.

Close to the corner, partially hidden by the pillow, there was tiny writing on the wall. Lattimer peered closer. It was a cramped script, done in a thick pencil point and thus very blurred. But Lattimer could make it out.

It said: "they want to kill me but i won't let them kill me if they try to kill me i'll kill myself first."

Yeah, thought Lattimer, how? Strangle yourself with your bare hands? There's nothing else in here.

Then, below the first message, Lattimer saw there was another. But the metal bed frame blocked him from reading it. How had the person even managed to write there? wondered Lattimer. Then Lattimer realized that perhaps the bed hadn't originally been bolted down. Lattimer struggled to make out the beginning of the message. Then, slithering like a snake, he went under the bed to decipher the end of it. He emerged shaking his head.

For the second message said: "they think i'm worth just two bits but if they come for me i'll give myself a shave and a haircut two bits the last shave of my life."

Last shave of my life, thought Lattimer. Did that mean a razor? Had the last, crazy occupant of this room hidden a razor somewhere in here? And if he had, could it somehow, possibly be here *still*? Lattimer doubted it. But he had nothing else to do with his time. He started looking.

The place to hide a razor blade was in the mattress. And this mattress seemed old enough to have been here forever. So Lattimer started inspecting the sides of the mattress, inch by inch, looking for a slit. He did the two sides that faced out into the room. Then, lying on his stomach on the floor, he used his legs to pull the mattress off the bed. He inspected the other two sides of the mattress.

Fifteen minutes later, he was sure there was no slit. So either the mattress had been changed or the blade had been removed some other way. Because Lattimer couldn't imagine anywhere else in the room where it could be. If there had ever even *been* a blade.

Hell, thought Lattimer. He lay down on the bed again. He caught another view of the handwriting on the wall (yeah, he thought grimly, the handwriting *is* on the wall) and it troubled him. With his head, he nudged the pillow to cover it completely. Moving the pillow, he uncovered a portion of the bed frame. And on the frame, scratched in the metal, was another message.

"They think i'm insane but i'm not insane they are insane."

The content of the message didn't matter. What mattered was the way it was scratched. With a thin metal point. The point of what could only have been a razor blade.

Lattimer sat up again. All right, he thought. So the crazy man *did* have a razor blade. So it's worth looking for some more.

But where? If not in the mattress, then somewhere else close to the bed. Close enough so the man could scratch this message and then quickly hide the razor blade.

Close to the bed, huh? Lattimer again slithered under the bed. Lying on his back, he tried prying up the flooring with his fingers. But it didn't budge. And there was no molding. So where?

In the bed? he wondered. He inspected the metal frame. With his chin, he tapped its tubular legs. It would be a terrible blow if the crazy man had unscrewed a cap at the base of a leg and hidden the razor blade inside—then it was *still* inside, only Lattimer couldn't get it because now the legs were bolted down! But, no, thought Lattimer, it had to be in a more quickly accessible hiding place.

So he inspected the top of the frame. And there, neatly wedged in the crack where one piece of metal overlapped the other, was a sliver of a different kind of metal. Lattimer turned his back to it and tugged at it with his fingernails. It was rusted tight. It wouldn't budge. Lattimer tried harder. He couldn't see what he was doing, but he felt he was developing a better sense of touch. Then he felt his fingernail break. He cursed softly. He tried again.

The razor blade came out.

He held it gingerly between the thumb and forefinger of his right hand. He strained his fingers until, just barely, he felt the blade touch some of the wires. Working, in effect, in the dark, he started, awkwardly, painfully, to draw the blade across the wires. Lattimer thanked the long-gone crazy man for his precious, crazy gift. He only hoped it would cut.

Lander, Colorado

For the first time in many years, Ray Ryker didn't feel he was in control of things. He was inside somebody else's scheme, inside somebody else's walls. First, inside the panel truck from O'Hare to Midway. Then, inside the plane to Denver. Then, inside another truck—again shut up in the back, with no view—up the mountains to this building. And now, inside this building, inside this room, waiting. His fists balled hard in his pants pockets, he paced the room. Goodhue was let in, to explain the proof he had seen, but Ryker wouldn't listen.

"Goddamn it!" he yelled. "Don't you see? It doesn't matter. I've paid nine million already. I can't get it back even if you say you've changed your mind."

"I haven't changed my—" began Goodhue.

"Then shut up. Ash'll get the shot. And I'll pay the other nine million into their fucking Swiss bank and we'll get *out* of here!" Out of here, he thought, so he could get hold of Sandahl and Davis. So they could tell him where they'd followed him to, tell him what this building was. So he could find out who owned it. So he could track the bastards down and get his eighteen million *back*.

Goodhue had never seen the small man so intense, so ferocious. Sweat beaded on Ryker's face. He ground his teeth. His eyes were slits. Goodhue felt that any moment Ryker might actually kick the wall. He watched him pace to a wall, stop, turn, pace to another wall, stop, turn. . . . Goodhue remembered his first impression of the man: a high-strung animal, barely restraining itself. Well, now the animal was restrained externally. And couldn't stand it.

Goodhue was frightened again. In the last few days, he had gotten to feel almost comfortable in the sanitarium, at home with lab equipment and the six other doctors. But now, seeing Ryker again . . . Goodhue's nose twitched. He backed away from this dangerous man.

"Out of here," Ryker was cursing. "Out of here."

Goodhue glanced at Nurse Elsberry. She also had pulled away, shrunk back into a chair. Only Matt Ash was spared. He lay, still unconscious, still heavily sedated, on the gurney in the middle of the room. He was the unmoving, unknowing centerpiece of their concerns. The centerpiece—but his mind, dreaming, was far away. He dreamed he was standing on a hillside near a great marble temple. The Reverend Trumbull was standing near the temple, waving at him to come up, come up and be healed. And then in his dream he was confused and angry at himself for doubting. Virginia was next to him on the hillside and she, too, urged him to climb up. He felt a rush of love for her. And this, too, confused Ash. Hesitantly, he set out, up the rocky slope, toward a new, whole body and a new, whole soul.

There was a polite knock on the door. The key turned in the lock. An attendant came in, smiling.

Lander, Colorado

Down the corridor and up one floor, the phone in Murdoch's office rang. Murdoch picked it up and listened. "All right," he said. "Fine." He hung up.

He turned to Ives. "That was Switzerland. Ryker paid us."

Ives smiled. The day was going well. That was $612 million in so far. By tomorrow he and Murdoch would have well over a billion. And then they could get out of here and on their respective ways. Rich and free, thought Ives. One day away. His smile broadened into a grin. He stroked his beard.

Murdoch picked up the phone. He alerted the treatment room and told an attendant to go get Ash. As soon as he set the phone down, it rang again. Crédit Lyonnais was now confirming that Kupitz's money had also been deposited. Murdoch called the treatment room and told an attendant to go get Kupitz. As he was setting the phone down again, an attendant burst into the room.

"Tried to get you on the phone . . . " exclaimed the attendant. He was upset. His words were falling over each other. " . . . gotta tell you . . . there are two state police downstairs . . . they say they want to talk to you."

Murdoch wheeled on the man. "Who else knows?" he shot.

"I . . . I don't know. Several guys. I . . . " The attendant looked worried.

"Get out of here!" snapped Murdoch. "And keep your mouth shut."

The man fled. The door slammed. As it did, Murdoch jumped to the window wall, which faced the front of the building. He flattened himself against the wall and inched, pistol drawn, to the edge of the window.

"Ed!" cried Ives. "For Christ's sake! They just want to talk to us!"

"You believe that?" rumbled Murdoch disdainfully. "I know how it works. Once they get us downstairs, they arrest us."

"But how—how do they know?"

"Shut up," said Murdoch. He peered out the window. "Two of them," he said, half to himself. "Two in their nice, neat gray uniforms. Nice toy soldiers. Standing at ease at our front door. Waiting for us."

"So what are we going to do?" cried Ives.

"No one in the car," said Murdoch, oblivious to Ives. "No one next to the radio. Dumb toy soldiers," he added with satisfaction.

"Ed! You got me into this. Tell me—"

"You got yourself into this," said Murdoch. And he aimed and sighted the pistol.

"No!" cried Ives. He lunged for Murdoch. "Don't!"

Ives hit Murdoch's arm. The arm smashed the window. Glass flew. Murdoch's hand and wrist streamed blood, but he still gripped the pistol. "You stupid son of a bitch!" he screamed. Ives, at the window, saw the two state policemen react to the noise. They dashed behind their car and aimed their pistols over the hood.

Then Ives felt a terrific blow on the side of his head. Murdoch had clubbed him with the pistol. Ives toppled to the floor.

"You fucking coward!" swore Murdoch. He set the gun down and tore off a strip of bloody shirt to make a tourniquet. Ives looked up at him dully. Murdoch was breathing heavily, fighting shock. As he wrapped the tourniquet, he chanted, "Okay for us to kill people in New York, Doctor, huh? But not on your precious front lawn, huh? Not so you have to see it, huh? You'd rather go to prison, huh? Well, not me. 'Cause there's still a way out. We got chips and I'm gonna play them." Murdoch pulled a larger gun out of his desk drawer. He tied the last awkward knot on the tourniquet and made for the door.

"Ed!" cried Ives. "Wait. Take me, too."

Murdoch turned. "All right, Doctor," he said scornfully. "I didn't get you into this—but I'll get you out."

"But how?" asked Ives, staggering to his feet. "What . . . chips?" His eyes wouldn't focus. He hung back. "How?" he repeated.

But it began to dawn on Ives that he didn't want to know. Whatever the answer, it would mean more violence. Because he saw Murdoch was trigger-happy. Wanting to shoot the police . . . wanting, five days ago, to shoot the monkey. Both times Ives had stopped him. But Ives couldn't stop him forever. Murdoch would get them both killed—Ives knew it for sure.

"Last chance," said Murdoch.

Ives shook his head. Through the dizziness in his head, he realized something: the monkey.

Murdoch was gone. Ives was alone. He sank down on the floor next to the desk.

The monkey, thought Ives. While all the other monkeys had tried to scamper down the slope, the one monkey had climbed up over the mountain to freedom. Up over the mountain. To the north face. Where the snow still lay on the old ski trail.

Dr. Christopher Ives tried to get up again. He wanted to go in the opposite direction from Murdoch, toward the nearest back door out of the sanitarium. But his body wouldn't cooperate.

Lander, Colorado

Joan Scully had spent most of the last hour with Dr. Hazeltine, locked up in one of the sanitarium's small lab cubicles. There they pored over the data Hazeltine had been accumulating in the past two days, including a small sample of the supposed cure itself. Joan's hands trembled when she held the bottle. This, she thought, it's all been for this. Because she believed now that Paul Justin *had* found the cure and that Ives *had* stolen it, she tried to play devil's advocate with Hazeltine. But his tissue samples, his leukemic counts, the contents of this little bottle ... as far as Joan could tell, with what scant time and equipment they had to check with, it all checked out. In fact, she had just told Hazeltine she concurred when the smiling young escort reappeared, reclaimed the bottle and said they were ready to give Kupitz his shot.

Joan and Hazeltine followed the escort back to the Kupitzes. Michael Kupitz looked up from reading *The Realm of the Seljuk Turks*. He didn't seem overly excited when Joan said she agreed he should accept the shot and pay another $15 million. He simply said, "Well, fine. Let's do it." But Rebecca Kupitz winced. Perhaps, Joan realized, she let me come along because she hoped I'd label the cure a fraud.

The four of them followed the young escort back through the maze of corridors of the sanitarium. They passed a few other staff members in the hall. Two staff members looked nervous. One was whispering intensely to another. Joan's group came to a huge pair of double doors marked "Treatment Room." Their escort made a show of ushering them in. Inside, in the gleaming, futuristic anteroom, Joan was annoyed. Why hadn't they simply given Michael his shot back in his suite? Why in this glorified place instead? Well, she answered herself, I guess when you're separating a man from $30 million, you want to impress him. The woman behind the huge white Formica desk—a tall, stunning blonde, also in a white lab coat—stood up and said, "If you'll be seated, Mr. Kupitz ...? You're next."

They all sat. The phone on the woman's desk buzzed discreetly. She picked it up and listened. Her face grew instantly troubled. "Police?" she said into the phone. "Here?"

"What?!" asked Rebecca Kupitz. She was on her feet. So was Joan and the escort and Hazeltine and Michael Kupitz. Everyone was shouting and asking questions of the receptionist and each other. Rebecca Kupitz's voice cut harshly through them all. "Damn it," she roared, "the police are *your* problem and you goddamn well deserve it. But *we* paid our money and my brother gets his shot." And she rushed for the door leading to the inner room and threw it open.

Lander, Colorado

Janko Velic was going to the cafeteria for a cup of coffee when an attendant ran by and said there were state police at the door. Velic briefly considered calling Murdoch to see what his employer wanted him to do. But Velic decided no. Money bought his loyalty but it didn't buy his loyalty where his own skin was at stake. So Velic quickly returned to his small room. He collected his cherished knives and those few other items that might identify him and stuffed them all into an airline flight bag. All except one knife. That one he slipped in the pocket of his lab coat. It was his favorite—a small blade from twelfth-century Persia, reputed to have been used by one of the Assassins themselves. During the last week, when Velic worked for Murdoch, he had used the weapons that Murdoch told him to: Velic had killed Roberto Cruz with a push; he had tried to kill Paul Justin with a drug. But now that Velic was killing for himself, he would kill his favorite way. On his way out of the sanitarium, he would visit the only witness to his attempted murder of Justin. He would slit Frank Lattimer's throat.

Velic looked through the peephole into Lattimer's room. The reporter was lying on his back. Velic could see the wire around his arms and legs and the wire attaching him to the bed. Velic unlocked the door and stepped into the room. Lattimer turned his head.

"Hey," began the reporter, "when am I going to—"

Velic closed the door and moved closer. His hand was in his pocket, on the knife.

"Don't worry," said Velic, smoothly. But Lattimer must have sensed something, for he started screaming, "No! No! Don't!" and began to thrash. Now Velic reached for Lattimer's hair, intending to pull the reporter head-first off the bed while his other hand brought his knife around the neck, across the throat of the trussed-up, helpless witness.

For the witness, it had been an anxious wait. With the insane man's old razor blade, Lattimer had managed to cut at the wires around his wrists. But it had been slow and painful. Many times Lattimer had driven the blade not into wire but into his own flesh. And, as his hands had grown slick with blood, many times he had dropped the blade. Each time, as he had searched blindly for the blade and found it again and attacked the wires again, Lattimer had stared straight ahead at the door, fearful that someone would come in and catch him. Time flew. He hacked furiously. Finish the job *now*, he told himself. Quickly. Before the door opens. And then the last wire had dropped from his wrist. His hands free, Lattimer had quickly cut his arms and feet free. Then he had rewrapped the wire loosely around his arms and feet and clasped his hands behind his back, around the razor blade. He had lain on the now bloody mattress and waited.

Lattimer hoped the loosely wrapped wire would fool whoever came in. He hoped the wire would actually work in his favor. After all, if they hadn't bound him they might walk in with a gun, stand across the room and simply shoot him. But since they had bound him they might come close and be off guard. But as he lay, waiting, time had now passed too slowly. Come in *now*, damn it, swore Lattimer, before I bleed to death.

Finally, the door opened. Lattimer turned to Velic. He feigned fright. He thrashed as a bound man would. He hoped it would hurry Velic into coming close, distract Velic so that Velic wouldn't notice that the wires no longer bound him, make the killer come close enough so that he, Lattimer, could . . .

Velic's hand reached for Lattimer's hair. Lattimer hurled himself into Velic. He clubbed his left arm into Velic's jaw. His right hand, gripping the razor, slashed at Velic's face. Velic grunted in surprise. Velic's knife continued its arc and sliced Lattimer's right shoulder. Lattimer screamed. He butted his head into Velic's chest and both men tumbled onto the floor.

The razor blade was gone. Lattimer drove his empty hands at Velic's throat. He saw, out of the corner of his eye, Velic's knife again descending on him.

Lattimer rolled on the floor, pulling Velic with him. The knife point hit the floor but Velic still gripped the handle. Lattimer grabbed for Velic's wrist. He seized it but, with all the blood, his grip was slippery. Any second, Velic would break free and plunge the knife into him. Goddamn it! Lattimer's mind screamed. This goddamn snipe hunt is not going to end like *this*! But there was nothing he could do. His hand was slipping. With his other hand he fought off Velic's attempt to claw his eyes out. Any second now . . .

Lattimer looked around desperately. All he could see was Velic and the wire they had dragged with them, wire that led from Lattimer's legs to the bed, but now was half-tangled all around them. A loop of it lay only six inches from Lattimer's hand.

"No!" screamed Lattimer and suddenly let go of Velic's wrist.

That surprise bought Lattimer a half second. And a half second was long enough to grab the loop of wire and slip it over Velic's head. Velic plunged the knife. With both hands, Lattimer tightened the wire.

Velic gasped. He dropped the knife. He screamed and gurgled. Lattimer watched Velic's dark eyes pop, his tongue pop, his dark face turn pitch black. Velic's hands grabbed for the wire. Lattimer was scared. He wanted to relax on the wire, stop the garroting, but he didn't dare to until Velic went unconscious. So he pulled harder. The wire dug into his hands. This is for Justin, Lattimer told himself. For what you tried to do to Justin.

The wire dug into Velic's throat. Velic tried to pry it away. He couldn't. He made a strange, strangled noise, perhaps a word in his native Croatian, perhaps simply an animal cry. Then his eyes rolled into his head. His body went limp.

Frank Lattimer had killed him.

Lattimer lay panting, bleeding, on the hard, stone floor. Your own fucking wire, he told the corpse. Your own.

Lander, Colorado

Ray Ryker was watching the attendant depress the plunger on the syringe, pumping the serum into Matt Ash's thin arm, when the door flew open and the tall woman burst in.

"My brother gets his shot now!" she yelled. And behind her, Ryker saw more people—three men and two women—pour into the treatment room. The attendant with the syringe looked up, startled. Ryker didn't know what was happening, but he knew one thing that *had* to happen. He grabbed the attendant's shoulder. His eyes blazed fiercely at him.

"Keep going, man," he commanded. "Finish it. Give him all of it."

The attendant hesitated. The room was in an uproar. Several of the attendants were trying to subdue the tall woman. Ryker put his own thumb on top of the attendant's thumb on the plunger and started to force it down.

"Not so fast!" the attendant protested.

"Ryker!" cried Goodhue, his rabbit face twitching in fear. "You could kill him!"

"Whaaat?" Matt Ash asked, the noise overcoming his sedation. He tried to raise his head from the gurney.

And at that moment the other door to the room flew open and the big, hulking, droopy-faced man came in with the huge pistol in his bleeding hand.

Joan Scully stood dumbfounded. What was all this? For the third time in three days, she was having a gun pointed at her. But this was not Lewis Schwerin defending his dry cleaners. Nor was it Hargrove the butler defending his master. This was, Joan knew immediately, a killer. But while her mind speedily ran through these impressions, her body froze. And so did everybody else's. The statuesque blonde and the polite young escort stood rock-still, pinning Rebecca Kupitz's arms behind her back. Another attendant stopped in the act of grabbing for the short, intense man who was himself grappling for the attendant with the syringe. Michael Kupitz was staring at the clear liquid in the syringe that, he knew, could be his salvation. And Hazeltine was staring at the other man in the room and saying, "Goodhue? Arthur Goodhue? You, too? What—?"

And the man with the gun said, superfluously, "Don't anybody move," in a deep rumbling voice, which Joan instantly recognized. Covering them with his gun—which looked even more hideously threatening to Joan with blood dripping all around it—the man quickly opened the small refrigerator. He reached in and took out a metal box. Instinctively, Joan knew what it was. The cure, she thought. Enough bottles in there to—to what? To bargain with the police? To set up business somewhere else? She stared at the man's patchy features. She had never hated anyone so much in her life. Go, she thought. Go! Take your lousy cure and get out of here!

Get out of here, Arthur Goodhue silently pleaded. Get out before the gun goes off. Goodhue was convinced he was going to be killed. I knew I never should have come, he told himself. I *knew* I never . . .

And Matt Ash was wondering if he was dreaming again or hearing all this on a TV show. . . .

And Ray Ryker kept pressing his thumb on the attendant's thumb on the plunger. . . .

And then there was noise out in the corridor and somebody shouted, "In there!" and the state police burst in through the anteroom.

They were only two state troopers. They were trying to cover and sort out a room full of a dozen people. They didn't have time. The man with the gun fired one shot and everyone dove, screaming, for the floor. Everyone except Matt Ash, who lay on his back on the gurney, above them all, with a syringe in his arm, wondering all the more.

As Goodhue dove for the floor, he saw one trooper looking frantically for the assailant. Then Goodhue concentrated on staring at the linoleum.

As Ryker hit the floor, he saw the gunman start to head for the door he'd come in from. The gunman realized he was too far away and grabbed for the person nearest him.

"Hold it!" the police were yelling. "Don't try it!" And Joan Scully cautiously looked up from the floor to see the gunman holding Michael Kupitz, holding Kupitz as a shield between himself and the police. The man's left arm—the arm whose hand clutched the metal box—was around Kupitz's throat. And his right hand held his pistol against Kupitz's temple.

Lander, Colorado

As Janko Velic was carefully opening the door to Lattimer's room and Rebecca Kupitz was throwing open the door to the treatment room, Dr. Christopher Ives was again trying to get to his feet. This time, he succeeded. He made it out to the hall. From somewhere toward the entrance of the sanitarium he heard shouts. Several attendants rushed past him. You run, too, Ives told himself. Run! Reeling down the hall, barely able to keep from colliding with the walls, knowing he should be lying down, knowing he probably had a concussion, Ives ran.

Lattimer also picked himself off the floor. He stripped the lab coat off Velic and put it on, then put Velic's knife in a pocket. During the struggle with Velic, Lattimer had heard only his own and Velic's grunts and screams. Now, as Lattimer went to the door, he was conscious there had been other noises. And as he slowly opened the door and looked down the narrow, deserted corridor, he saw, at its junction with the main corridor, a scene of chaos. People of all sorts— attendants, men in business suits, a few well-dressed women, even a child—milled and dashed about and shouted and questioned and jostled and screamed at each other:

"... state police ... "

"... I want my shot ... "

"... get out of here ... "

"... over six million dollars, goddamn it ... "

"... where's my aunt, my aunt? ... "

"... illegal. If they find out ... "

And then their yelling was punctuated by a gunshot.

The people scattered every which way. Lattimer ran toward the main corridor and grabbed the first person he could—a young attendant. With his bloody hands, Lattimer shook the man's collar and, from only an inch away, yelled into the man's face. His young face turned as white as his lab coat. Yes, imagined Lattimer. I must be some sight.

"Where's Joan Scully?" bellowed Lattimer.

"Who? What? I don't—"

"The woman who ... " It was no use, Lattimer realized. He couldn't explain who she was. "The police," he began again. There were more gunshots from deep in the sanitarium. Lattimer pressed on: "Are the police here?"

"People *said* so. Coming this way."

"Did they get Murdoch? Or Ives? Who's *shooting*?"

"Who? I don't know. Nobody knows—" the attendant gasped. "*You* tell me. What's happening? What?"

Exasperated, Lattimer felt like choking this man also. "Chubby man with a black beard," snapped Lattimer. "Smokes a pipe. Looks like a professor. *Runs* this fucking place. Now where *is* he?" Lattimer tightened his grip. The attendant's neck and shirt front were covered with Lattimer's blood. His eyes rolled wide with fear.

"Don't *know!*" he wailed.

"I saw him," said another, smaller voice.

Lattimer wheeled. Leaning against a wall, as if shell-shocked, was a frail girl in her late teens. She stared into space. "I saw him run that way"—she pointed, without looking—"out the back." Her arm collapsed to her side. "I was going to get my shot," she explained in a monotone. "I was going to get it this afternoon, they promised." Her eyes locked on Lattimer. "Do you think I'll still get it?" she asked.

"I don't know," said Lattimer softly. And he ran in the direction she had pointed, his hamstring and shoulder hurting like blazes.

New York City

At 6:30, Paul Justin's blood pressure was barely over 70. At 7:30, it was 65 and his urine output had stopped. For the last hour, Dewing had made himself scarce. Falcone was angry. Some doctors couldn't stand being around while a patient died and Falcone saw that apparently Dewing was one of them. But Falcone stayed. Partly he stayed because he figured he owed something to Justin and his wife. And partly he stayed because, unlike Dewing, he hadn't given up yet.

Still, Falcone wondered if it was an empty gesture. Like Dewing, he realized there was nothing he could actually *do* for Justin. So to give himself the illusion of activity, he tried to talk to Barbara: "Would you like some dinner sent up from the cafeteria?" "No." "Is there anyone else you'd like to be here? A friend or a relative I could call?"

Barbara considered. No, she didn't need her mother here. And she didn't want the kids here. She preferred that they remember their father as laughing and playing with them, full of life. Not lying pale and helpless and unconscious, attached to machines and bottles. That was also why she didn't want to go in and see him again.

She turned her wheelchair away from the room where he lay. "No," she said numbly to the doctor (later, she thought, later I'll break down and cry). "No, thank you." She wheeled herself to the nurses' desk.

At the desk, Nurse Hughes wished Barbara hadn't come her way. Ever since the film of Underwood at Justin's bedside had been shown on the local news at six o'clock and then the national news at seven, Hughes had been fielding calls from nuts. They called with all sorts of news of their own: They told her Justin wasn't sick, merely faking it to get publicity for his cancer cure. They told her Justin was being punished for tampering with nature. They told her they knew what was causing Justin's sickness—and they had the cure for it. After receiving a half-dozen such pieces of news, Nurse Hughes had asked the switchboard to screen all calls to intensive care. But some nuts still got through. And Hughes was afraid they might upset Barbara Justin.

"Thank you, sir," Hughes said firmly to yet another caller, and hung up.

Lander, Colorado

For Joan Scully, it was the last straw. Michael Kupitz had survived Belsen, where he had watched his mother die. Now he was dying of cancer and the drug that could save him was being snatched away. And *now*, now instead of at least dying at home, in bed, in dignity, surrounded by his beloved books, he stood a fair chance of having his brains blown out in this madhouse by this monster.... Joan wanted to spring to her feet and kill the droopy-faced man barehanded.

Except she knew the slightest move might get Michael Kupitz killed instead.

"Nobody move," announced Ed Murdoch. "Me and Mr. Kupitz— we're going for a walk." And he started edging for the door, a hammerlock and a .45 Magnum on Kupitz's head.

The two Colorado state troopers followed Murdoch with their guns. Rebecca Kupitz watched in horror. Ray Ryker watched detached. Arthur Goodhue didn't dare watch.

"Shoot him!" Michael Kupitz choked out the words. "I'm dying anyway. I'm—"

Murdoch was now partly framed in the open door. His eyes swept the room. Joan realized that in another second they would meet hers. It would be too obvious to shout, "Behind you!" He'd never fall for that. But maybe a more subtle version of the same ... ?

Just before Murdoch's eyes reached her, Joan stared wide-eyed over his shoulder, and then tried to stifle her look of relief.

It worked. Murdoch spun his head to the doorway. For an instant, his gun hand dropped away from Kupitz's head. Now shoot! Joan pleaded to the police. And before her thought was even complete, there was another shot in the room. Murdoch screamed and started to fall. His arm holding the metal case jerked and the case flew open. Bottles flew into the room. Murdoch fired again and the polite young escort made a terrible gasp. The troopers fired again. Murdoch hit the floor. Those few glass bottles that weren't already smashed were now smashed by his heavy body.

Lander, Colorado

Out the back door of the sanitarium, the land slanted steeply upward. There were no trees here, just a rock face to which clung a few low bushes and patches of snow. It was easy for Lattimer, emerging into the afternoon sunlight, to spot high above him on the rock face the moving figure of a man.

Frank Lattimer hesitated. The man was already several hundred feet distant, near the summit. In another minute he would disappear over the summit. And the only way up after him would be on all fours. Lattimer would have to drag himself up the rocks with his injured hands. I should go back, Lattimer told himself. Find Joan. Get Murdoch, if the police haven't. But in that confusion, how? Here the challenge was simple and direct: up the mountain. And if he didn't do it, nobody would. Ives could get away. After nearly a week of tracking his man through phone calls and file cabinets and computers and libraries, Lattimer finally had his man in the open. He had to get him. Personally.

Frank Lattimer attacked the mountain.

As he reached for each handhold, his shoulder burned. As he secured each handhold in the cold snow, his hands stung. As he brought his leg up to each foothold, his pulled hamstring ached. He dug his new hiking boots into the mountain. He didn't look up to see where Ives was. He didn't dare look down to see how precarious his own position was. He only looked at the next rock in front of him. And the next. And the—

His bloody hand slipped on the snow and moss. He lost his grip. With only a few fingertips of the other hand he dangled a hundred feet in the air. He gasped. All the injuries that his body had suffered this week assaulted him at once. He felt too battered to hang on. He hung on. He regained his grip. He drove up again . . . up and just over the summit.

At the top of the mountain, Dr. Christopher Ives was also gasping. He lay on his side, gulping and twitching like a fish out of water. He was proud he had made the climb. He could not understand *how* he had made it. Perhaps only terror had made it possible—the terror of going to jail. But where could he go now? Where had the monkey gone? Ives raised his head. He couldn't see the monkey. He assumed the monkey was dead somewhere on the mountain. But the monkey had tried. He would keep trying, too. Ives got to his knees, gripped the rock for support and looked down the north side of Saddleback Mountain.

The north side was a gentler slope than the side he had just climbed. Indeed, a hundred yards down, Ives could make out a tiny shack and the last of a row of towers that had once supported a tow line. He realized he was looking at an abandoned ski slope. Too bad I don't have skis, he thought. For this north side of the mountain was covered with snow—not patches, but a broad snow field extending from the summit where he crouched, down the old ski slope and into a small valley through which ran a dirt road. On skis I could make it to that valley in five minutes, Ives gauged. If I had skis. If my head weren't swimming. As it is it'll take me an hour. Ives started trudging awkwardly, down through the foot-deep snow.

Lattimer reached the summit as Ives reached the shack. Lattimer saw the man go inside. Rest there, Lattimer mentally commanded Ives. Rest there until I can get you. Lattimer would lead Ives at knife point down into the valley, to the road. There, he figured he could flag a ride. Lattimer also figured Ives *would* rest in the shack. After all, Ives could not possibly imagine that he was being followed, that anyone was crazy enough to climb the mountain after him. Lattimer plunged down toward the shack, leaving a trail of blood behind him in the snow.

But, halfway to the shack, Lattimer saw Ives emerge. Carrying a pair of skis.

Lattimer's heart sank. He started to his right, to put the shack between Ives and himself. If he could circle the shack and reach Ives before the man put on the skis . . .

Lattimer came around the side of the shack, only twenty feet from Ives and on level ground. But at that instant Ives drove his ski poles into the snow and propelled himself forward. Lattimer ran and yelled at Ives. The bearded man's head spun in surprise. He started to fall. Then, with an enormous effort, he threw his body back over his skis and sped off down the mountain.

For a moment Lattimer watched him go. Back and forth he wove across the old slope, barely but skillfully avoiding the rocks that jutted in his path. Lattimer realized he couldn't count on Ives to fall. So Lattimer rushed into the shack. If there had been one pair of skis and boots in there, there might be another.

There were. Lying in a corner was a pair of battered, old wooden skis and poles. And boots with rusted buckles. Lattimer grabbed them and ran back outside. He saw, partway down the mountain, that Ives was temporarily delayed—poling across the slope, trying to get to deeper snow. Lattimer figured maybe he still had time. He jammed his feet into the too-small boots and wrestled with the buckles. He set the skis on the snow, pointed them down the mountain, and slammed his left boot into the binding. As Lattimer bent to secure the binding, he saw Ives reach the deep snow and take off again. Supporting himself on the poles, Lattimer started to put his right boot into the ski. The right pole snapped in half. Lattimer fell and hit the free ski. The ski took off down the mountain.

Skiing again, doing a christie around an old log, Ives heard the shout high above him. But its meaning was lost in the wind of his movement. Too much had happened in the past several minutes: Finding the skis. The appearance of the stranger. Ives's fear that the stranger might pursue him on skis (Damn! He should have broken the other pair!). Ives tried to block all this from his mind and concentrate on his skiing. He was thrilled how easily the skiing had come back and how quickly it cleared his head. It calmed him more than any Valium. But watch it there. Patch of ice. Turn. Okay. Straight down again. Good. Got it. Flying. Free. Christopher Ives exulted in the newfound physical grace within his body.

And up on the summit, Frank Lattimer watched with mixed feelings as the runaway ski took a final leap at Ives and Ives instinctively turned to look and the ski missed him by inches but Ives, off-balance, tripped and smashed backward into a boulder.

Lander, Colorado

The chaos in the treatment room hadn't ended with the gunshots. The state police were barking questions at everyone and then calling their headquarters for more reinforcements. "It's bigger," Joan Scully heard one say, "than anybody said." And even bigger than that, thought Joan. She found the Kupitzes sobbing joyfully with their arms around each other and she gave them both a hug. She picked her way past where Murdoch lay (the police were also calling for an ambulance) and came upon the polite young escort. His whole chest was blown away. Joan asked the receptionist for her lab coat and then covered his body with it. The receptionist and the two surviving male attendants were busy telling one of the cops that they knew nothing about all this. Joan cut in to ask about Frank, but they said they had no idea where he was. She pushed past Hazeltine and Goodhue, who were exchanging what little they knew, and tried to interrupt the trooper who was on the phone. She tried to explain about Frank. The trooper didn't understand.

"All right!" said Joan, exasperated. "Then I'll find him myself."

She headed for the door to the anteroom.

"Hey!" the trooper shouted. "Nobody leaves!"

Joan turned. She pointed at the back door, through which Murdoch had tried to flee. "Nobody?" she asked. "Then why is that man leaving?"

It was true. Ray Ryker was trying to slip out the back door. Once he was satisfied that old man Ash had received his shot, he saw no reason to stick around and be asked embarrassing questions. Who knew? Once these idiots in uniform found out what this sanitarium was all about, they might arrest him for buying the cure—which, he suspected, was stolen property. Best to leave quickly, get back to Houston and surround himself with good lawyers.

But now that redheaded woman had spotted him. "Hold it," the state policeman was yelling at him. "Come back here, Shorty."

Shorty! Nobody, nobody had called him that for years, not since he could remember. Not since that horrible night on the playground when his big stepbrother . . .

Ray Ryker's control, held so carefully all these years, snapped.

"'Shorty!'" he yelled. "You son of a bitch!" he screamed, going for the trooper. "Nobody calls me that! Nobody! Nobody!" Forgetting all his carefully honed boxing moves, Ryker went for the trooper with wild, flailing, crazed arms and legs, kicking, punching.

In his red-blind rage, Ryker was as easy to handle as a bull, driven mad by picadors, is handled by the matador. Arthur Goodhue watched with great satisfaction as the state trooper grabbed one of Ryker's arms, twisted it behind his back, grabbed the other arm and then handcuffed both together. "Mister," said the trooper, "you are under arrest for assaulting an officer." And he reached in his breast pocket, brought out a Miranda card and started reading Ryker his rights.

While the trooper was busy with Ryker, Joan Scully slipped out the same door that Ryker had been heading for. She found herself in a corridor full of milling people. Frank Lattimer was nowhere in sight. Joan Scully went through the first available doorway. It was an office and it had a phone.

Briefly, Joan considered what to do. If she couldn't get hold of Frank, whom could she reach? She dialed an outside line and then dialed the Justin home in Dobbs Ferry, New York.

A woman answered.

"Barbara?" asked Joan Scully.

"No. This is her mother."

"Where is Barbara? This is a friend of hers."

"I'm afraid she's in New York, at the hospital."

"Can you get a message to her?"

"I'll try."

"Well ..." Joan tried to figure how to put the sense of all this into a short message. "Well, to begin with, tell her Paul did find the cure." Joan looked out the office window to the lawn where a state policeman was chasing three men in white lab coats. Their coats were flapping behind them in the wind. "And that's just to begin with," said Joan Scully.

She managed to talk for another minute before the line went dead.

New York City

At 8:30 Eastern Daylight Time, Paul Justin's blood pressure dropped below 60. Dewing was back and Falcone corralled him. They stood over their patient.

"If his pressure doesn't go back up within an hour," said Dewing, "there'll be brain damage. An hour and we'll have to give up."

Falcone didn't like hearing it—but it was only what he had told himself. Actually, Falcone told himself, we've *already* given up. The cortisone hadn't worked and they couldn't increase the Levophed flow. So the combination of pneumonia and coma was destroying Justin's blood vessels, making them go as limp and spread as wide as ... as wet noodles.

Falcone tried to shake the distasteful comparison out of his head. He went toward the nurses' station, to see Barbara Justin again, to say *some*thing to her. But he saw that Nurse Hughes was beckoning to Barbara.

The phone at the nurses' station had rung again. It was a woman claiming to be Barbara Justin's mother.

"Excuse me," said Nurse Hughes to Barbara, "but what's your mother's maiden name?"

"My mother's?"

"Yes."

"Everett. Why?"

"She's calling you," said Hughes, handing Barbara the receiver.

Barbara listened. Mother Yates relayed what Joan Scully had just told her. Through her numbness, Barbara tried to figure out what it meant to her. So Paul had not just isolated the "C" particle but had also found the cure? Well, that was nice. It should make her feel proud. But from what her mother said that Joan said, most or all of the serum was spilled on a floor somewhere in Colorado. So it didn't sound as if there was something she could *take* for her cancer—instead of having the operation this Friday. Well, of course, she could wait until she found out more. She supposed that was another good reason to postpone the operation.

But with her newfound courage—and with an equal amount of blank resignation—Barbara still wanted to get it over with.

And no matter how excited Mother Yates sounded, both women knew her phone call was no help to Paul.

Lander, Colorado

When Lattimer made it down the slope to Ives he found the man lying spread-eagled in the snow, face down. Lattimer's first thought was that Ives was unconscious. But then he saw him moving his head from side to side, trying to get it out of the snow, trying to breathe. Lattimer couldn't understand why Ives didn't simply roll over. He bent down next to him and scooped the snow away from his mouth.

"... dead," the moan escaped from Ives's mouth. "All dead ... can't feel anything ... can't move ... "

Lattimer understood quickly. "Your arms?" he asked.

"Nothing."

"Your legs?"

Ives silently shook his head, his mouth agape.

Lattimer realized that Ives had hit his spinal cord and was at least temporarily paralyzed. The skis and poles lay in a broken heap.

"I'll get help," said Lattimer, and he started to stand up.

"No ... " gasped Ives. "Don't ... leave me. ... Who are you?"

Ives's eyes were caked with snow. Lattimer brushed them off so he could see more clearly.

"Oh," Ives sighed. "The reporter ... you called the police?"

Lattimer nodded.

"They freed you?"

"I freed myself," said Lattimer. "I killed Velic."

"Thank you," said Ives. "He deserved it. And Murdoch?"

"I don't know."

"It doesn't matter," said Ives. "Nothing matters." He closed his eyes. "The monkey went over the mountain," he said. "And fell down."

"What?" asked Lattimer. "Look, you need help. I'll go get a doctor."

From deep inside the snow-coated beard came a faint chuckle.

For a moment, the chubby man reminded Lattimer of Santa Claus.

"And go release your story, of course," chuckled Ives.

"Of course," admitted Lattimer.

"But it's not complete," pointed out Ives. "You don't know how I found out about Justin, to begin with. How Murdoch found out which millionaires . . . had cancer. How . . . " He trailed off. "No," he said, "you only know half."

Lattimer realized Ives was right. "And I don't know what drug you gave Justin," said Lattimer. "Or if there's an antidote." He seized Ives by the shoulders and glared at him. "*Is* there an antidote, goddamn it? Is there?"

"I'll explain," sighed Ives. "I'll tell you all."

"Why?" asked Lattimer suspiciously. Why was the man so willing to incriminate himself?

"Because," blurted Ives, now sobbing. "I've got to tell *some*body! Because I can't keep carrying it around!" He drove his head down into the snow.

Lattimer reached out and gently touched Ives's hair. The calls to Lindenmeyer, thought Lattimer. The messages—the confessions that Ives hadn't dared leave with Lindenmeyer's answering service.

"You're right," said Lattimer softly. "You can tell me." Santa Claus, thought Lattimer, *does* have a present for me.

Ives raised his face from the snow. His face was wet with tears and snow.

"It began four years ago," began Ives, "at a medical conference in San Francisco. . . . "

Ives's voice was weak but steady. Lattimer bent down in the snow to listen. He wished he had his pen and notebook, but he doubted his fingers could write anyway. So he tried to remember, to remember every detail. He kept his ear to Ives's mouth and his eyes to the road in the valley, watching for a car.

" . . . so Cruz gave him a shot of anectine," Ives was saying.

"Anectine?" asked Lattimer. Ives had been talking for fifteen minutes now. And Lattimer knew that whatever time he'd lost—an hour perhaps—by coming after Ives instead of immediately filing his story was being more than made up for by the facts Ives was giving him. But now he really *had* to get to a phone and call New York.

" . . . a poison," said Ives, "like curare. Tell Justin's doctors. They'll know what to do. . . . "

"He'll recover?"

"I think so . . . if you tell them soon."

"I will," said Lattimer. "Now let me go and find a phone!" It was obvious no car was going to come. And how many miles to town? And how—with his injured leg and shoulder (how much blood had he lost, anyway?)—was he going to make it? Lattimer stood up. He felt dizzy. The world tilted. Hell, he thought, we're *both* going to die here.

"... and then Murdoch had Velic kill Cruz ..." Ives was saying.

But Frank Lattimer didn't stay to hear the rest. Because, on the road below them, he saw a pick-up truck.

Running down the mountain was almost as bad as climbing up it. With each stride, the snow-covered ground jumped up to meet Lattimer, slamming his legs into his torso. And as he gained speed, he had to fight to keep his legs from running out from under him, fight against going head-over-heels into the snow. He ran off-balance on an injured leg while flapping an arm on an injured shoulder and yelling for the goddamn truck to "Stop! Stop! Help!"

By the time Lattimer reached the road, the truck had passed. But Lattimer couldn't stop. And as he flew across the road, he felt something tear in his bad leg—and he sprawled screaming on the gravel.

Lying there, he heard the truck brake. He stared at the sky and heard the truck come back. Somebody got out and helped him to his feet. It was a young, strong, smooth-faced kid. A farm boy.

"Hey, mister," said the boy, "what—?"

"Man up there," gasped Lattimer, pointing up the mountain, "needs help."

"Hey, mister, *you* need—"

"He needs a doctor. But we can't move him. Back injury. And I've got to get to a phone. So take me—"

Another man came out of the truck—the boy's father. The three men talked. Lattimer made them understand. The boy agreed to climb up the slope to Ives, to wait with him. The father agreed to drive Lattimer to the nearest phone, which was in Lander. To call for a doctor. Lattimer didn't explain the other calls he had to make. That would have made it too complicated.

Twenty minutes later, the pick-up truck dropped Lattimer off at the Lander general store. Lattimer hobbled inside.

"Hey, man," said the bearded proprietor with the one earring. "What happened to you?" He rushed to catch Lattimer before he fell.

"You got a phone?" demanded Lattimer.

"Sure." He pointed. "But—? Hey, they did that to you—worked you over—just because of those reducing drugs?"

"Something like that. You got dimes? Give me dimes." Lattimer held out his palm and shook it impatiently.

The proprietor dropped coins in it. "Here. But—?"

"No time," said Lattimer. He hobbled over and closed himself in the phone booth. His favorite place, Joan had said. He started dialing.

Every ten minutes by the clock on the wall, Falcone took Justin's pulse. At nine o'clock, he had trouble getting one at 50. At 9:10, he couldn't find one at all.

"No pulse!" cried Falcone.

Falcone and Dewing looked at the EKG monitor. Until now, it had been displaying a normal heartbeat of 70 to 80. But now it was "pinging" wildly, irregularly, racing up to 140—as the heart desperately tried to pump more blood. But in this case, the pump was connected to pipes that were too big. The blood was pooling, was going nowhere, was failing to reach Justin's organs.

Dewing felt Justin's hands and feet. They were cold and clammy. And his skin was turning bluish-gray.

"Looks cyanotic," said Dewing.

Justin's whole body was ceasing to function. He was dying of septic shock.

"That's it," shrugged Dewing.

"No!" yelled Falcone. "He's not going that easy!" He jumped up on the bed and knelt at Justin's side. He started vigorously pressing on Justin's chest. Press, rest. Press, rest. Press, rest. Sweating, grunting, Falcone kept up the cardiac massage for one minute, for two minutes, for three . . .

Drifting off to a final blackness, Paul Justin felt muffled blows to his chest. . . .

Outside, by the nurses' station, Barbara Justin heard Falcone's cry and sensed this was the end. She stood up, out of the wheelchair, wondering if she should, after all, go in . . . see Paul . . . ? Suddenly, she felt very alone. She wished she'd asked her mother to be here.

The phone at the nurses' station rang.

"Intensive care," said Nurse Hughes.

It was Lattimer. "Get me Dr. Falcone," he said.

"The doctor is busy right now."

"Damn it, this is Frank Lattimer. I know what's wrong with Justin. Falcone should know."

Hughes was very dubious. Lattimer's name meant nothing to her. To her, it sounded like another nut was calling.

"Give me your phone number," she said. "The doctor will call you back."

"But Falcone knows me," insisted Lattimer. "He'll want to know what I've found out."

"He'll call you back."

"Well, is Dewing there?"

"He's busy, too. They'll *call* you."

Lattimer was mad. "Look," he said, "I'm Frank Lattimer. I'm a friend of Paul's. I'm the guy that saved his life on Sunday night when that goon attacked him and Nurse Abrams. Now I tell you I've found out what's wrong with him! Will you get a doctor for me?!"

Hughes was less sure that the caller was a nut. But she could also see—through the open doorway—that Dewing and Falcone were, to put it mildly, really very busy. And besides, how could the caller have possibly found anything?

"Why don't you tell *me* what you've found," Nurse Hughes suggested into the phone.

Lattimer sighed. He debated hanging up and calling back in half an hour when maybe Falcone and Dewing wouldn't be so busy. He could use that half hour to phone the Lander Hospital and get help for Ives. And phone the story into his newspaper.

He didn't hang up. "Anectine . . . " he began.

Meanwhile, Falcone was continuing the massage. His arms were getting tired. He looked at Nurse Lopez who was holding Justin's wrist. She shook her head. Still no pulse.

"An amp of calcium," said Falcone. That might stimulate Justin's heart to pump more regularly. Dewing nodded agreement—but both men knew it wasn't much of a chance. The problem wasn't in the heart; it was in the blood vessels. The blood vessels were ceasing to function. Death was five to ten minutes away.

"Anectine," Frank Lattimer said to Nurse Hughes. "Justin was given a shot of anectine on Friday. One hundred eighty milligrams of anectine in oil. *That's* what paralyzed him. You got that?"

"I've got that," said Hughes. She looked again through the doorway. If the doctors pulled Justin through this crisis, she'd tell them. "Thank you, Mr. Lattimer," she said. She started to hang up.

"Lattimer?" said Barbara Justin, curious. The name had penetrated through her haze. She could use a friend to talk to. "Is that Frank Lattimer?" she asked Nurse Hughes. "Could I talk to him?"

"I guess so," said Nurse Hughes. She handed Barbara the phone.

Nurse Lopez gave Justin the shot of calcium. Justin's heart continued beating wildly. Falcone continued giving the external heart massage.

"Oh, Frank!" cried Barbara into the phone. "He's dying! Right now, he's dying. His blood pressure dropped this afternoon and they haven't gotten it back and . . . I think . . . " From the nurses' station, Barbara could now see the frenzied scene around her husband's bed. She saw Falcone frantically pressing on Paul's chest. "Oh, Paul! Frank . . . I think . . . "

"He's dying?" asked Lattimer.

"I—"

"And the nurse is just sitting there?"

"Sitting?"

"I told her what they did to Paul. The anectine!"

"Anec—?"

"Barbara," said Frank Lattimer, fighting to stay calm and controlled, "Barbara. *You*. Right now. Go tell the doctors: Paul was given anectine. Anectine. Say it."

"Anectine," she said.

"Cruz gave him a shot of anectine on Friday morning," said Lattimer. "Anectine. That's a poison. Anectine in a solution of oil. That's what did this to him."

"Anectine in oil," she managed to say.

"Go tell them," he ordered.

Barbara broke from the phone and tripped over her wheelchair. She recovered and ran toward Paul, talking wildly and waving her arms. The big cop at the door to the room grabbed her. She wrestled with him. Dewing and Falcone turned to look in amazement.

Sobbing, crying, struggling, Barbara cried out the message Lattimer had given her.

"Anectine," muttered Dewing.

"Sure!" cried Falcone. That explained a lot: Justin's erection, his eyes "accidentally" opening and then blinking, his normal EEG . . . My God! thought Falcone—Scully and that reporter are right. We don't have a coma, we don't have a brain-related accident, we've got a *poisoning*. And I should have suspected it, thought Falcone. When the man tried to put the drug in Justin's I.V. on Sunday night, I should have suspected what that meant. It meant this whole thing *began* with a drug back on Friday . . . And my God!—if Justin's not comatose . . . ? Here we've been assuming he's been unconscious and instead his brain has been fine and . . . oh, Jesus, could he have been *conscious* all this time, aware of what we've been doing, been saying?

"Well," said Dewing, "it's good to know. But it's academic. There's no antidote."

Barbara Justin was sobbing.

"No pulse," said Nurse Lopez.

"Wait," said Falcone. He snapped his fingers. "Neostigmine."

"What?" asked Dewing.

"In long-term conditions of anectine poisoning—and four days is long—you get results with neostigmine." Falcone yelled to Nurse Hughes: "One cc. Stat!"

Barbara buried herself in the cop's burly arms. Nurse Hughes grabbed at the medicine cabinet at the nurses' station. Falcone stood impatiently waiting. Hughes rushed over with a vial and a syringe. Falcone drew liquid from the vial into the syringe and inserted the syringe into the I.V. tubing that fed into Paul Justin's arm. He pressed the plunger. The liquid disappeared into the tubing.

They all waited.

Just a little muscle tone, pleaded Falcone. If the neostigmine could undo the poisoning, undo the paralysis and give Justin's blood vessels just a little bit of tone, help them constrict just a little bit so the blood could flow . . .

Falcone looked at the clock. He watched the sweep of its second hand. It seemed to drag. Fifteen seconds. Thirty seconds. Forty-five seconds. One minute.

"I've got a pulse," said Lopez.

"Give him another cc!" cried Falcone, ecstatic. He bent to take Justin's blood pressure himself. By God! he thought, we *are* going to save you.

And they did. Fifteen minutes later, when Paul Justin's blood pressure was in the sixties and rising and the doctors were grinning and Barbara Justin was holding her husband's hand as if she would never let it go, Nurse Hughes returned to her station. She found the receiver still off the hook. She picked it up, hoping Mr. Lattimer might still be there, so she could apologize and thank him. But she only got a buzzing noise.

"Thank you, anyway," she said softly, to the buzz.

New York City

It had been a busy day for news. In Africa, there was a border clash between Uganda and Kenya. In Italy, a German industrialist had been seized by left-wing terrorists. In Washington, Congress had passed parts of a new welfare program. In New York City, the mayor had attacked Con Ed for overcharging. And everywhere, people were still reacting to Underwood's dramatic announcement of yesterday.

In the offices of his newspaper, assistant city editor Oliver Knapp helplessly watched the front page being remade for the third time. He noted that the mayor's attack—his department's only contribution—had only a small foothold here.

Then the AP teletype chattered with news of a nursing home fire in Florida—fourteen dead. So, on the fourth remake, the mayor got axed. Knapp complained there ought to be *something* of his on page one.

"Sorry, Knappy," said the managing editor. "But what the hell ever happened to your man's promised thing on the meat scandal? Or whatever he was trying to dig up at Oakes-Metcalf?"

"Damned if I know," said Knapp. He refused to admit that Frank

Lattimer had plain disappeared for the last day and a half. Knapp promised himself that when Lattimer did appear, he'd fire him.

"Call for you, Knappy," said Ganz.

Knapp took it.

"Knappy," said Frank Lattimer, "I think I've got a story for you."

Fifteen minutes later, the front page was remade for the fifth and last time. By Oliver Knapp.

Lander, Colorado

Before today, Larry Blair of the Colorado State Police had never handled a case more complicated than a hit-and-run or fired bullets at anything more than targets on the range behind his barracks. If his superior, Captain Dienstag, had known what he was sending Blair and his partner, Bob Powell, into, he never would have sent them. But Blair had done surprisingly well. It had been Blair—not Powell, who was more experienced—who'd brought Murdoch down. And it had been Blair who, when all these millionaires and cancer specialists said they were here for a cancer cure, cut off the sanitarium's switchboard and had warned Powell not to broadcast the news over the police radio. Jesus, thought Dienstag, what if the media got a crazy thing like *that* before we could really check it out! While the dozen other officers Dienstag had brought restored order to the sanitarium, Dienstag and Blair tried to check out what else they knew.

They already knew a lot. And they would find out more. But they sensed there was some information they would never get, some connections they would never make.

"The Lander Hospital says Murdoch will live," repeated Blair.

"And," said Dienstag, "they've also got this guy Ives—his partner."

"Why? Why the hospital?"

"Smashed up on skis somehow. In the spine. Doc says he's going to be a quadraplegic."

(Ives would view it as a fitting punishment: He would go through life as paralyzed as he had once made Paul Justin paralyzed.)

"Huh!" said Blair. "How about the rest of the staff? We're holding a couple of dozen here."

"And I figure about thirty more ran out and down the mountain. But it's a long way to nowhere on foot. We'll have most by morning."

"But from what these millionaires and cancer specialists say, Murdoch had people working for him all around the country."

"Well," sighed Dienstag. "That's not our problem."

"But the millionaires are. What do we do with them?"

"Keep holding the ones that are well. Get the sick ones—like that old guy, Ash—out of here."

(Ash would go back to Houston cured of cancer. Ryker, now hand-cuffed and fuming in a police car, knew he'd never get his $18 million back from the Swiss bank, and knew Ash would never thank him for buying him a new lease on life. He also knew he could look forward to nothing more in Houston than more years of fighting Ash and Virginia—and now Trumbull!—for control of Texahoma.)

"What about the ones who keep yelling for their cancer shot?" asked Blair.

"Tell them the truth," said Dienstag. "Their bottles are all broken."

(Michael Kupitz was not among those yelling. He was simply happy to be alive. If later, after this mess was sorted out, someone would give him a shot, well, he'd be grateful.)

"And what about the cancer specialists?"

"Hold them, too. *Every*body here has either broken some law or is a witness."

"That woman Scully says she's got to get out and find this guy Lattimer."

"Lattimer?" asked Dienstag. "Who the hell is Lattimer?"

"I don't know. But she keeps talking about Lattimer and Justin and Underwood and—"

"Underwood? The black guy in New York with the *real* cancer cure?"

"Yeah. She says Velic locked up Lattimer, and—"

"Velic? The guy we found strangled?"

"I think they call it garroted," said Blair. "Anyway, I don't quite understand it but she claims that . . . "

And at that moment, under their window, Frank Lattimer screeched his Jeep to a halt in front of the sanitarium. He had bor-rowed the Jeep from the bearded storekeeper back in Lander. In it, he had bulled his way through the police barricades on the road leading to the sanitarium. He certainly wasn't going to let himself be stopped now by the young state trooper who was trying to bar the front door. Whizzing along on crutches—also borrowed from the storekeeper—Lattimer bore down on the trooper.

"Out of my way, goddamn it!" roared Lattimer. Propelling him-self on one crutch, swinging the other crutch like a club, Lattimer pushed past the man and into the entrance foyer.

"Joan!" he yelled. "Joan Scully!"

She heard and came running. They hugged each other sound-lessly for a long time. There was a lot each could have asked and told the other. But all Joan said, finally, was, "Well, Ace, did you make the deadline? Because we're cut off here."

"Oh, yes," said Frank Lattimer, smiling a bit. "The news is going out now."

Purdy's Falls, Indiana, and New York City

The last torchlight parade in Purdy's Falls had been in 1840, for the presidential campaign of William Henry Harrison ("Tippecanoe and Tyler too"). So, to cap the hometown welcoming and presidential re-announcement of Senator Arthur Prentice, Prentice's aides had organized a torchlight parade tonight. It made a neat bracket, said Jack Lynch: From the frontiers of modern medical research to nineteenth-century frontier America.

And Prentice was enjoying every minute of it. It was a great end to a great day. Early in the morning, as labor leaders looked on, he had greeted workers at the gates of U.S. Steel in Gary. In mid-morning, as ecologists looked on, he had walked the Dunes State Park. At noontime, as sports fans looked on, he had gone to the "Brick-yard" to pose with the winner of this year's Indianapolis 500. Two P.M. found him across town addressing the state legislature. And then the rest of the afternoon was a motorcade with his family, friends and well-wishers through the Indiana countryside, ending here in his hometown with a giant church-style supper on the field behind the Grange Hall and now this parade. From one stop to the next, Prentice had been thrilled—especially because, at each stop, someone in the crowd had asked him about the cancer cure. And when the 500 winner had said, "Senator, I'd like to thank you ahead of time for curing me, 'cause I'd like to tell you and America that, for a month now, *I've* had The Big C," Prentice knew that it would be on every TV evening news program in the country. Prentice felt pride to receive such welcomes and to be able to give such benefit to this land he loved. He stood now on the rickety bandstand in the dusty village green of the little town he was born and grew up in, surrounded by his former neighbors, listening to the high school band and the cheers. It was ten o'clock. The rally was almost over. As its last rendition, the high school band played a tinny, amateur version of "The Road Back." Prentice put his arms around his wife and his three children. He had it all. This afternoon, in the car, he'd even told his family he'd given up smoking.

Lynch tapped him on the shoulder. "Senator," he said, drawing Prentice aside, "there's something you should know about."

Lynch told Prentice about confused early reports coming out of

Denver. It would be on radio and TV within the hour; some reporter named Lattimer promised the complete story in the morning paper. What, asked Lynch, are we going to do?

Arthur Prentice looked out over the crowd of torch-lit faces. He imagined how quickly their red, happy glow would—when they learned Prentice had based his campaign on a lie—turn to red anger. And I thought I was so smart, thought Prentice. I thought I had it all figured. "Do?" he said to Lynch. "Why, until we learn more, we'll enjoy the evening. I'm sure it's nothing." But in his bones, Arthur Prentice knew it was the end. I wonder, he thought, if I could have won without using this cancer cure business? And I wonder what kind of President I would have made. Maybe even a good one. And I wonder whether I'll even be able to be a senator anymore? He doubted it. He foresaw the scorn that would shortly be heaped on him. And that made him look back—back to only three nights ago in the house in Malibu, to the moment when the phone call from Wozinsky came through. If only the phone had never rung, thought Prentice. If only I'd had to contend with nothing more serious than a roomful of bored rich people—rather than have to deal with this disaster. Well, he thought . . . enough of it. Arthur Prentice waved back at the cheerful crowd and tried to enjoy the last hour of the last evening of his last campaign.

An hour later and seven hundred miles away, the surrounding faces were glowing not from torchlight but from liquor and a sense of power. Flushed with her husband's success, Ceilia Underwood had invited a few friends over for a celebration party in their Upper East Side apartment. But most of their friends were so thrilled to come, they couldn't resist telling some of *their* friends, who even told some of *theirs* . . . and so the Underwoods' apartment was crowded with a dozen people they knew and a hundred gate crashers, everyone feeling pleased and powerful to rub elbows with the man who was being celebrated across the nation.

At first, the Underwoods had been taken aback by the crowd. Then Ceilia was thrilled. She sent out for more liquor, more food. Hugh understood her thinking: This wasn't like those parties on Fire Island where she felt she had to suck up to people. Here, they'd suck up to her. She put her arm through his and stood regally in one corner of the room. All the guests fought to get at them. They praised Hugh, they praised her for supporting his career. . . . She gazed up at Hugh devotedly. He smiled back. Truth to tell, he still felt uneasy with this attention, from others and from her. He thought he knew who he was: A black man who slowly, carefully, one foot after another—and one foot that limped—had built a life in a white man's world. A life where he had thought he could pass undetected. And now? Now he had appropriated another man's work, now he had allowed others to claim that that work would *transform* the world. And now he was in the eye of the hurricane.

Across the room, Hugh Underwood saw the front door open again and his neighbor from across the hall, Mrs. Stanley Pollock, come in. She looked upset. Had she come to complain about the noise? She fought through the crowd to Underwood. He tried to make room for her, to quiet people down so they could all hear what she was trying to say. Something about something on the news? "What, Mrs. Pollock? What is it?"

Mrs. Pollock told them.

In the confusion that followed—his guests looking shocked, looking at him, asking him and each other, "Is it true?" and then looking away in embarrassment, moving away from him as if he were a leper, the whole party dissolving—two voices pierced Hugh Underwood. One voice was Ceilia's, whispering fiercely at him, loud enough for others to hear: "You son of a bitch. You crawly nothing. You really fucked yourself this time, didn't you? Well, you're not going to fuck *me*, too." She grabbed the arm of the nearest man, Tom Cole, one of their best friends. "Come on, Tom," she said. "Take me out of here."

And the other voice was in Hugh Underwood's head, his mother's voice from long ago, telling him about the white man she worked for, the man whose floors and toilets she cleaned: "He been stealin' from his company, Hugh. He done been found out an' gonna be fired. 'Cause he don't do honest work like I do. An' like you gonna do. 'Cause you ... " (fiercely, proudly) " ... you gonna be a *doctor!*"

A half hour later, Warren Brown was landing at Kennedy Airport, on the last flight from Washington. He had had an excellent day. In the wake of yesterday's announcement, the HEW officials hadn't merely junked their threatened cutback in funds—they had fallen all over themselves showering *new* funds on Oakes-Metcalf. They had treated Warren Brown as a hero and had tried to share his glory. After all, hadn't they administered the Cancer Control Act funds that had led to Underwood's discovery? Brown, good diplomat that he was, was quick to agree.

Except that now, walking through the terminal to get a cab, Brown passed a teen-ager with a portable radio and heard the news.

Oh, Jesus, he thought. What would happen now? He thought furiously. He decided that *his* career was safe. He would say he simply took Underwood's word that the discovery was Underwood's. And if Prentice went down in flames—well, that was Prentice's fault for basing his campaign kickoff on Underwood's claim. After all, he, Brown, certainly hadn't arranged yesterday's rally in front of the Institute. And, as for the Institute ... well, Justin's serum wasn't going to be given to everyone tomorrow. The FDA (which was part of HEW) would demand it be tested rigorously. That would keep the Institute busy another year or so. And after that, well, they could probably switch over to tackling heart disease. That killed more people than cancer anyway.

So by the time he made it to the front of the taxi line, Warren Brown felt okay. He sank into the back of the Checker knowing that, although the next few days and weeks might be tough, he was going to survive. Like the HEW officials who outlasted all senators and congressmen, an institute chief could outlast all researchers. Administrators always survive.

As the cab turned west onto the Long Island Expressway and headed for Manhattan, the big rainstorm—which had threatened all week but never quite happened—struck. Inside the storm, Warren Brown rode safe and dry.

WEDNESDAY

New York City

They were all gathered in Paul Justin's new private room in the Oakes-Metcalf Hospital: Paul and Barbara, and Steve, Melissa and Laurie, and Mother Yates and Joan Scully.

It was a few minutes before the 10 A.M. news conference was scheduled to start. Outside the room, down the corridor, they could hear the buzz as the crowd gathered. Soon, a dozen members of the media (hundreds had asked; only a dozen could fit in) would be admitted with cameras and lights and microphones and notepads. The guard opened the door and Warren Brown stuck his head in.

"Ten minutes?" he asked.

"Fine," said Paul Justin.

Brown looked around the room. "I thought Lattimer was going to be here," he said.

"So did I," said Joan Scully.

"Well ... " said Brown. He left. Paul Justin and Joan Scully caught each other's eyes and exchanged wan smiles, anticipating the onslaught to come. Both of them were tired; both had been through a long night.

Paul Justin was still weak and tired from the illness that had nearly killed him. Shortly after the neostigmine had been administered to him at 9 P.M., his blood pressure had returned to normal and stayed there. Soon after that, he had been able to breathe on his own; the hated respirator tube had been removed. By midnight, the penicillin and the hydrocortisone had finally taken effect: he had turned the corner on the pneumonia and was out of septic shock. Paul Justin could move and could talk. The doctors and nurses withdrew. And so, for an hour in the middle of the night, he and Barbara had exchanged private thoughts.

Barbara had told Paul about her breast cancer, about her fears for herself and for him. And how, having gone through all that, she felt she never again would fear simple daily problems so much. Because now she knew she could cope. And how, having experienced how precious her body was to her, she wanted to have sex with him. In turn, Paul had told Barbara of his fears while lying conscious but helpless for five days. And how he had missed her and how he had felt when he learned she had cancer. He had told her there would now be a storm of controversy over his serum—people demanding to have it at once versus the FDA demanding several years of tests. But one thing, said Paul, he was sure of: The serum *worked*. And as soon as they let him out of this hospital bed, by the end of this week at the latest, he was going to his lab and prepare a dose for her. So she could cancel her operation. Then Barbara had said she hoped the Nobel Prize Committee didn't learn of this breach of professional ethics. And they had both laughed softly. And eventually, around 3 A.M.— after consenting to a 10 A.M. news conference that, it seemed, the whole world was demanding—Paul Justin fell asleep.

Joan Scully had not gotten much more sleep. After Frank Lattimer had returned to Saddleback Sanitarium, he had paused only briefly for medical attention—stitches for the knife wound in his shoulder, bandages for his cut hands and, for his hamstring (not just pulled this time, but torn), advice from Dr. Hazeltine to "stay the hell off it." But of course, Frank didn't stay off it. For the next hour and a half he had zipped around the sanitarium on crutches, getting the rest of the story from the state police, the oncologists, the millionaires and those members of the staff who were willing to talk. And since Frank's hands couldn't hold a pencil, he'd dragged Joan around with him and made her take notes. By then—nine o'clock Mountain Time—the earlier story that Frank had filed was breaking on TV and radio. So Frank had persuaded the police to let him call the rest of it in to his newspaper. Then he and Joan Scully had driven to Denver and made the last flight to New York.

It had been a strange, long flight—for the Frank Lattimer that Joan found herself with was a man she had only caught glimpses of before. Frank, she felt, would have had every right to exult in what he had just gone through—the triumph he had just achieved and the honors, including probably a Pulitzer Prize, that he would now receive. But instead, Frank had been quiet, almost reflective. He had stretched out his injured leg across an empty seat and leaned back against Joan. Then he had reminisced about his mother and father, about how they loved each other. And about how, despite the hard times in Cardiff (and hard times had been the *only* times he had previously told Joan about), they had made a great family. Frank said he wanted the same thing; he wanted commitment. Joan said she did, too. And somewhere—30,000 feet above the darkened middle of the continent—Frank had placed a bandaged hand on hers.

They had landed in New York in the rain at 2 A.M., taken a cab to

Joan's apartment, crawled into bed and immediately fallen asleep. When they were awakened this morning at 8:30—by Warren Brown calling to tell them about the news conference—the day had been cool and fresh and she had wanted Frank. There was time to make love. But he had kissed her gently, left the bed, and shaved and dressed quickly. He told her he had something to do and would meet her at the news conference. Joan didn't know quite what to make of it and it struck her too much like Frank rushing out of bed on Saturday morning. She only hoped Frank was rushing somewhere for a good reason—and on crutches, yet. All she could think of was that last night, on the plane, she and Frank had reminded themselves that they owed some people something: Joan had said she would go up to the house on East 106th Street with the medical supplies she had promised Maria. And Frank had said he would go to police headquarters and make sure that Whitcomb, Mathes, Prosser and Humenuik got official praise—instead of blame—for stretching the rules to help him find the truth.

Well, thought Joan, sitting in Paul Justin's hospital room a few minutes before 10 A.M., I sure hope that's where Frank is. I hope he hasn't reverted to tracking down still another *detail* of that truth. Because it would mean a lot to have him here now. She wanted to share this moment with Frank.

Paul Justin read her mind. "He'll come," he said, from his bed.

She smiled.

Paul Justin wanted to see Frank Lattimer, too. For, as Barbara had told him last night, Lattimer had saved his life. And while Paul was still trying to absorb all the other things he had been told about people he'd known so well—Cruz dead, Underwood disgraced, Wojik first gone and now considering returning—he mostly wanted to reach out to the stranger with whom he had shared only a conversation on a stalled train. (My God, had that been only six days ago? It felt like a century.) He wanted to reach out and thank him. He, too, wanted to share this moment with Frank.

But, of course, it was good enough to share it with his family. Paul Justin listened to Melissa talk about the zodiac—she wanted to know if this meant that Cancer wouldn't be there anymore. He listened to Laurie talk about how excited and nervous she was that they were all about to go on TV. And he listened to Steve talk about how, with Prentice disgraced, his man, Reed, had a good shot at the presidential nomination.

Steve also wanted to know why his rocket fuel experiment had gone wrong. So Paul started explaining how the melting mixture of potassium nitrate and sugar must have coated the candy thermometer and insulated it, so it read a safe 205 degrees when the real temperature was well over the 230-degree danger mark. And Steve was listening intently, glad to have his father back. And Joan was concerned because she didn't have Frank back, and full of envy for Paul and Barbara, who were holding hands and smiling like young lovers while Mother Yates looked on, beaming.

And Paul was saying, " . . . so you'll get your eyebrows back soon, champ," when the door opened again and Frank Lattimer came in.

Lattimer carried a clear plastic box with plastic tubes attached leading to smaller boxes. And through the tubes, in and out of the boxes and around on the free-spinning Ferris wheel inside the big box, scampered a hamster.

"For you," Lattimer said to the three Justin children.

He set the boxes down and the children cried with glee and surrounded their new pet.

"Wilbur?" asked Joan.

"I liberated him from his cage," said Lattimer. "And bought him a home." Lattimer swung on his crutches over to Justin's bedside. "The kids told me you didn't want them to have a hamster as a pet—before this. But now that you have the serum, now that you won't have to experiment on . . . " He trailed off. "I hope," he said, "that it's okay?"

Justin half-rose from his bed and embraced Frank Lattimer. "It's okay," he said, his voice thick.

And Joan rose also and hugged Frank. She and Frank and Barbara and Paul were interlocked.

Melissa looked up from the hamster. "But what sign is Wilbur born under?" she asked.

"Cancer," joked Frank Lattimer.

"Mr. Lattimer," she objected, "you shouldn't joke about a yucky thing like that."

The door opened once more and Warren Brown entered. "Ten o'clock," he said. "I'm letting them in."

But first Paul Justin had an answer for his older daughter.

"No, honey," said Paul Justin, reaching over to include Melissa in the grown-ups' embrace. "No, now it's okay. From now on, Cancer is only a constellation."